Memories of A Hunter's Moon

by

M. Flagg

The Champion Chronicles

Cover Art by *Lisa Dawn MacDonald*

The Wild Rose Press, Inc.
PO Box 708
Adams Basin, NY 14410-0708
Visit us at www.thewildrosepress.com

Publishing History
First Edition, 2025
Trade Paperback ISBN 978-1-5092-6092-8
Digital ISBN 978-1-5092-6093-5

The Champion Chronicles
Published in the United States of America

Dedication

To my loving family and friends who encourage me to tell my stories, my appreciation and thanks. To all the readers who enjoy paranormal tales, many blessings.

Chapter 1

A Tale of Two Realms

Draven picked up his pace in the blood-red mist at the end of the Third Realm, and no, this vampire wasn't overjoyed to be summoned, ordered like a meaningless minion to appear before the War Council. Perturbed by the impromptu "request," he ran through the realm's lifeless outer-edge, then past sparce growing fields tilled by human blood slaves, only slowing when in the distance, the council building stood like a gauche, obsidian obelisk sixty-six feet high and as wide as a city block.

With confidence, his arrogant strides took the final quarter-mile, his proper posture perfect while centering the black silk tie. He smoothed his long black hair, always gathered at the nape of his neck with a thick leather strip. His black-on-black attire, custom-made or *haute couture,* hung with panache on a lean, six-foot-three-inch frame, enhancing both broad shoulders and trim torso. Not that the seven sires would care, even though he dressed to impress. No. They were intelligent like rattlesnakes and just as deadly, with long sharp fangs and egos that need stroking, elite rulers of the vampire realm who expected unwavering loyalty.

This dimension had existed for millenniums, known to vampires, witches and warlocks as well. It remained a barren sanctuary for blood-drinkers who grew weary of being hunted in the human world by Guardians of Souls. This city, however, had been specifically modernized by the Second Realm's three immortal sorcerers some sixteen years ago when thousands of portals closed.

The sorcerers of the Second Realm had gifted the inhabitant's daylight different from the human world. The conjure allowed just enough brilliance for animals to thrive, to farm food for human blood slaves so that hand-picked, wealthy vampires as well as the seven sires could feed. The rest of this realm's vampire population were ordered, in fact, to feed off each other. This didn't mean that all the undead inhabitants didn't fixate on off-the-menu fresh, rich, human blood.

Draven's eyes shifted left and right. The dwellings he passed sported shuttered windows against the weak autumn sun. Although the past sixteen years were like a grain in the hourglass of time to the undead, all Third Realm vampires accepted the new-normal free of those lethal mystical warriors. They created their own version of "life," running businesses and shops with products sent through from the human world. Only he, the Gatekeeper of the portal was allowed the privilege of travelling between the three realms. And as sure as his heart didn't beat, Draven sensed their envy.

At the bottom step of the council building he stared straight ahead while passing vampire guards, not brooking a single question and not at all interested. He often wondered what criteria had been met to be a guard in this realm. Or if, in fact, they were just for show. How prepared they were to tackle and subdue rebel vampires remained to be seen.

In the lobby, he locked down all personal thoughts.

He didn't like this realm. Yet he'd been contacted by an unknown dark seer and summoned. Although fed up with the seven sires, Draven tolerated them. The three immortal sorcerers in the Second Realm who created this surreal world had given only him the magical mantra to open one portal to the human world. And *that* incantation he'd take with him into Hell.

Call it a morsel of morality. Call it personal greed. Call it whatever… the seven sires would never syphon the incantation out of his astute mind. Nor would they be let through the portal to terrorize humans again.

As for the human world's other continents' Gatekeepers? They could do whatever the hell they liked. Draven didn't care. As long as he had the status of this continent's Gatekeeper, he believed the United States and Canada were off-limits and safe. That fact alone confirmed his mere morsel of morality, as if it had been built into his very DNA, the same as his prestigious musical abilities. Both had survived his turning in 1847. That anomaly, a "vampiric flaw," had allowed him to assist his brother in blood just weeks ago. They saved an innocent from a fate worse than undeath. But the War Council would never be informed. It would remain a secret—along with another he had kept hidden for decades.

Draven entered the windowless, sacrosanct inner chamber of black marble walls and floors. After the all-necessary deep bow, he took his seat at the carved oval table to join the seven sires. At the head sat Herodotus, the oldest sire—treated like a king, if one considered vampires a race of undead beings purposely created by God to trim the human population—which they weren't. *No. Not a race. Simply a collective of the unimaginable unnatural,* he thought, and he didn't view himself one of them.

No greeting came. No friendly chit-chat. Simply seven silent sires who, quite possibly, desired the end of his existence, thinking him the only obstacle between them and the endless crave to drink and drain in the human world.

When nasty old Herodotus finally made eye-contact, Draven redoubled his efforts to keep his mind an empty white board with not one black marker in sight. Stroking his neatly-trimmed beard like some wise, benevolent monarch, Herodotus said, "You have not fulfilled our request, vampire. Did you not understand our need?"

The question further infuriated him. "Not at all, Sire. I have not located a suitable dwelling for you."

Herodotus's hands swept wide at the head of the table. "For us, you meant to say."

Tricky bastard, really. "I stand corrected, Sire."

The facial expression appeared full of disgust, perhaps even deadly. "You have found not one private mansion? Not one lavish estate on your entire continent suits our needs? Need I state how impatient we grow."

Draven eyed the six who never spoke. In fact, he didn't even know their names. Didn't care, either. Yet seven sets of eyes bore holes through him like bullets through a paper target. "The markets are volatile. Interest rates rise each day. It may not be the right time."

"You cannot locate one parcel of land for us?"

The tone, forceful and irate, had him rethink a reply. *And there's the out, as if handed to me by magic.* "I shall turn my attention to land acquisition, Sire, with my deepest appreciation for your suggestion," he replied in as much of a humble tone as he could personally endure.

"Am I to believe that the idea of land acquisition never crossed your mind, Gatekeeper? Do you think me a fool?"

A very quick and quite astonished, "No, Sire, never," came from his lips.

In the blink of an eye, silver short-swords with ornate, jeweled hilts were pulled from their sheaths and placed on the table by each sire. *It only takes one across my neck to turn me into an afterthought.* Without breaking eye-contact, he acknowledged the threat with a grave nod. "I shall begin the search immediately upon my return, Sire."

"You will put all investments into aggressive placements, since money is always a primary factor."

"Of course, Sire."

"And then you will find suitable mansions and building properties for my consideration. Each one in different corners of the continent. You have two weeks. Make no mistake, vampire. You will deliver. Or I will deal with you in a way you will never forget."

When Herodotus stood, the sire's many-inches-less-than-six-foot stature wasn't impressive, but had Draven been human, he'd probably piss himself over such a stone-cold threat. He stood as well, bowed deep with a hand over his heart. After they exited, Draven left the council chamber in a hurry. *Nasty old Herodotus, known for cruelty. Warned by my very own sire to stay clear of him.* Striding past the guards he showed nothing but arrogance.

The main street appeared desolate. In more ways than one, this was a lifeless realm. The Second Realm with its witches and warlocks might be dubious at times, but it had variety and purpose. The human world remained his preference, always on the precipice of excitement and innovation; always humming with activity.

Midway into the growing fields, he breathed in the scent of living things. Horses and cows, sprouting greens and nourishment for human blood slaves. Even seasonal flowers. He broke into a run across the barren plains before being pulled into the rusty mist by the hum of vibration at the farthest edge of the realm. Opening the portal, he entered the blood-red swirl before stepping into the vault room adjacent to his office in a vast underground space. He punched in the four-digit code and opened the vault door.

The well-lit office, under the buildings he owned, was perfectly designed, both masculine and modern. A six-foot wide big screen was mounted on the wall over an expensive brown leather couch. Glancing up at the security feed, multiple angles of video streamed from his after-hours club called *Destiny*. Instead of going to his desk, he sank into one of two leather armchairs. The sight of those silver short-swords on the wooden table meant he'd been forewarned. He had walked the earth as a vampire for nearly one-hundred-eighty years. For the most part, his existence had been graced with good fortune. *But as everything has a beginning, everything also has an end.*

A sour scowl began. This repeated request from Herodotus created an uncomfortable dilemma. *What an odd place to be for a vampire. Make a moral decision to neutralize the sires, or act on the bastard's request and allow all seven back into the human world.* But... building their version of a palace on virgin land could take years. It would buy humanity some time. But… The moral high ground always had consequences. What he had done at the beginning of October could be considered treasonous. What he had done decades ago had been ingenious, even though it left him nothing but an empty vessel.

He had loved her. Since their first kiss, she had been his alone. In 1939, when the dogs of war bared their blood-stained teeth in France, her refuge against the inevitable destruction became an immediate priority. As if he could access his very soul, he took the moral high ground and left her standing on the icy black sand of a seaport in a neutral country. It had been a torturous decision. "The Hunter's Moon lit the sky, a brilliant glowing orb of orange, *ma chere*," he whispered as his eyes closed. "Five decades never apart, with each night as if it were our first time together." *Over eighty years without you, ma chere. Will this deep regret never cease?*

Chapter 2

Then
1887 Florence, Italy

"Tis an important night, Henri. Should you continue to be this cross, I shall have to find you a plump, ripe maiden in the piazza to drain after you fuck her." Rather loudly, Michael, whom he called his brother in blood, sighed and sank to a stone bench in the garden behind his current prissy lover's palatial home.

To Henri's dismay and less than interested in what Michael had to say, Henri paced along the walled garden path. Dressed impeccably, as was his style, he took in the beauty of the night sky. "I am not in the mood. Truly, I do not care for your Veronique, nor her lavish estate. And I detest being surrounded by so many egotistical sires, as well."

"Yet this midnight soiree is for you, to celebrate forty years as an immortal. Our sire will not tolerate ungratefulness, Henri. He may send you home to Hell if this snit continues."

"It is not a snit. And I do not care if Cyril approves my mood or not. Your Veronique is a wicked bitch. This place wreaks of excess in every way."

"Ah. Thus speaks the artist in you. Bohemians always puzzle me. So dramatic. So sullen all the time, as if the world revolves around your feelings. I daresay

8

Cyril will beat it out of you while I take Veronique many times throughout the day. Did I ever tell you about the tunnels below this magnificent structure? Tis like a clever maze, until one is far enough away to scent the sweetest neck to bite. I would take you down to walk them, but your new suit would be soiled. Thus, the inhabitants of Florence are safe. For the moment, at least."

The snippy Brit brought out the French in him, huffing, "*Arret! Ferme ta bouche!* Perhaps you have had too much champagne."

Michael threw back his head with another long sigh. "Not enough, is more like it. Let us get on with this celebration so Veronique and I can make good use of her boudoir. She is such a ravishing beauty."

Henri stopped pacing and glared down at him. "And a vicious killer, perhaps more so than you."

"We do have that in common, don't we. Along with the desire for sensual sessions full of erotic pleasure. Ah, my Veronique. Just the thought has me rising. I may have to find a whore or two."

"Either that or grab yourself and work it off by your own hand," he growled, more irate.

Both of them stood side by side when Cyril and another sire entered the garden. The unknown sire's short black hair and trimmed goatee matched his beady black eyes, giving one the impression of something sinister. Henri could just imagine Michael's erection dwindling in their presence.

"May I present my sons, Herodotus," Cyril stated in a proud voice.

Henri bowed, proclaimed a respectful, "Sire," as he straightened his back. Michael simply inclined his head—with an arrogant smirk and a visible tent to his trousers.

The sneer on the sire's face spoke volumes, as if he were high above Cyril in status. Yet all three of them towered over Herodotus, all three broad shouldered as well.

Then the sire's beady black eyes lingered below Michael's waist. "Were you mine, I would put an end to such an inappropriate show of sexual ego in a most painful way. I am quite baffled, Cyril. It is said that you demand proper social norms in your progeny. Apparently, this is not so." Eyeing their sire, Herodotus added, "Let us commence with our festivities. Walk with me, Henri."

Henri walked at his side while Cyril and Michael stayed behind. As they approached the open doors to the ballroom, Cyril's hissed admonishment and brisk slap to Michael's cheek for his bad manners made Henri smirk. Obviously, Herodotus was important, and as one says, the first impression lingers above all else.

In the ballroom, Veronique stood in a gown of black and gold, a vision of voluptuous beauty, which was, in fact, only skin deep. Henri often wondered how long Michael's current obsession with the female vampire would last. "We gather tonight to celebrate the youngest amongst us," Veronique stated in a breathy voice. Henri inclined his head and gave a fluid bow. "Forty years in undeath is no small feat. Guardians of Souls hunt us like vermin. Yet we still exist. Georgian seers sense us. Yet we still exist. Herodotus," she said with a flourish of her delicate hand.

The sire stepped forward to address the gathering. "Rarely do I leave the Roman countryside, but tonight, for Cyril's progeny, I graciously attend in Florence. Ah! I have brought a present." He snapped his fingers.

Two of the sire's vampire minions brought in a stunning woman. Tall and elegant in her step, she came to Herodotus as if in a trance, alive yet subdued, no scent of fear and dressed in flowing white silk and detailed lace. A long blonde braid flowed off her left shoulder and ended at her elbow.

Henri thought her beautiful. Had his heart beat, it would quicken. He whispered to Michael, now at his side, "What is this?"

"We are to witness a turning," his brother in blood whispered back.

"This is uncalled for. I will not have it."

"You will not stop it."

Henri tried again. "This is insanity!"

"This is his way," Cyril growled with a hand brutally clamped on his forearm, yet he didn't dare wince. "Do not call attention to yourself again, Henri," Cyril replied gruff and low.

The beast-within surfaced in Herodotus, with feral-yellow eyes, his fangs long and sharp. One hand held the back of the woman's neck. He pulled her close and bit into her jugular vein. Although disgusted by the sight and sound, Henri didn't dare turn aside. When death was a heartbeat away, the minions laid her across their arms. Herodotus ripped into his own wrist. As blood dripped into her mouth, he announced, "Suckle, my new child of the night." And she latched on, deeply drawing blood from his vein before becoming still. As she was taken from the ballroom, Herodotus licked his lips before stating like a king, "Let the festivities begin."

Henri stood straight-shouldered and stoic as the

orchestra performed Liszt's *Mephisto Waltz*, which was really an orchestral tone poem. Witnessing the turning slithered up his gut. Stepping out into the garden he raced across it to a far wall full of fragrant night blooms. His palms slapped the bricks as blood raced up his throat and spewed out his mouth. After a careful swipe of his lips, he reentered the ballroom obsessed with finding her.

The macabre scene revolted him as dancing continued with women in the arms of vampires, perhaps drugged or bonded blood slave. Michael waltzed Veronique across the dance floor as if their steps had been rehearsed. But his brother in blood did all things well and dancing was no exception. Graceful. Fluid. Sensual.

Upper echelon vampires appeared perfectly schooled in human male etiquette, well in control of their bloodlust. Many sires, including Cyril, had women's wrists in hand, sipping blood in between conversation. *How many will die tonight*, Henri wondered. With no one noticing, he made his way to the other side of the ballroom to slip through a door.

Where is she? Is she guarded? Will she awaken as I had forty years ago with enhanced senses and a hungry beast-within to sate? What an abomination! A *woman* had been turned—something Cyril cautioned against.

Going down stone steps, Henri took the only hall lined with oil lamps. The door to the left was closed, and he felt compelled to push it open and walk through. In a coffin lined with red satin, she looked beautiful in the initial sleep of undeath. Not petite. Taller than most. A narrow face with a narrow nose, yet full lips that he thought very kissable. A flawless example of Nordic heritage. *Who will teach you to feed? Herodotus or a lesser vampire?* Recalling his own disastrous first feed, he wondered if she'd be beaten if hesitant to kill? Something close to madness swelled within. Something possessive—because such perfection deserved perfection in return.

He had met only a few female vampires during the last four decades. Many were aggressive, cunning vixens who pushed caution away for sexual pleasure. And Guardians of Souls, those ferocious mystical warriors, were everywhere, waiting to stake them.

"You are curious," he heard and spun around to see Herodotus.

Afraid of being torn limb from limb, Henri bowed very low with his eyes cast down. "I apologize for my intrusion, Sire, now at your mercy."

"You are a strange one, vampire. There is passion in you and something I cannot discern in your curiosity." Herodotus moved closer. "Why are you in this room?"

"I do not know, Sire."

"You are intrigued by the turning ritual."

Too terrified to think, he answered, "Yes, Sire."

"Ah… you desire what your disrespectful brother has with Veronique, our host. To possess a female vampire. Do not deny the jealousy I sense."

"No, Sire." *Yet another hidden truth spoken out loud.* Michael could, in fact, charm any woman, alive or undead.

Herodotus stroked his new child of the night's cold, pale cheek still locked to Henri's eyes. "You do not sire. Neither does that other impudent son of Cyril. Your passion lies in the arts, not in grooming minions. I see it as clear as the night's sky. Ah… .The pianoforte. You are a master of the instrument, forever lost in minor melodies."

"Yes, Sire," he whispered.

Being read by this powerful vampire panicked him. Swiftly, Henri pushed the moral threads in him down as deep as possible. That one flaw alone might still get him torn limb from limb.

"Some of us are unique, Henri, as if our destinies, even in undeath, instruct us to keep a step apart. I have sired an army of minions, masculine and obedient. Yet tonight I have sired a woman. Do you find that odd?"

"No, Sire. You may have a need."

Herodotus snorted as if amused. "My harem services me well. No. She was a whim and ever so easy to glamour. A lonely, childless widow not yet thirty, smothered in grief with nothing left to live for. She yearned to experience one last sunset over the Arno, a dream of her late husband's. I found her ready to jump off the Ponte Vecchio. Quite pitiful." Herodotus circled him in slow steps as if lost in thought. "She is yours."

His head snapped up to meet those beady black eyes. "Sire?"

"Enjoy her while she lasts. Assuage every sexual desire the way your arrogant brother in blood does with Veronique, our princess. Use her. Fuck her to revive the passion inside you."

"Sire, I—"

Herodotus held up a hand. "No. I insist. Be sure to feed before you return at sunset because it will be your vein she takes when she awakens as one of us. Teach her to obey. Mold her for your pleasure and she will never leave your side."

Henri bowed low as Herodotus left the room. Then he followed a different corridor through twists and turns until he stood under the full moon. Michael would be busy with Veronique. Cyril wouldn't care where he went. So he walked to the Ponte Vecchio and strolled across. Tonight's victim would be healthy, in the prime of his life. *Perhaps a Florentine who keeps a dark secret. A murderer or a pedophile...*

The vivid recall of that fateful night in 1887 washed over Draven like a wave strong enough to drag a man out to sea and drown. He shook his head and opened his eyes. "Then I returned to wait, to protect you from all others. At sunset, I made you mine," he whispered, and then swallowed his guilt.

They had been inseparable for half a century. He loved her the first time he saw her. And he knew he'd never see her again.

Chapter 3

Now

Even after eighty-four years of loneliness in this isolated seaport, Luna recalled the first glimpse of her Henri as if it were last night. *1887. Florence.* Tonight, under the Hunter's Moon, memories of him, always bittersweet, knifed through her. Walking down the private road from her home, high in the volcanic hills above Husavik, one memory defined the only one she would ever love—throughout eternity. Approaching the icy shore of the sea, the first moments of undeath in his arms and under his protection began. "Do you remember our first kiss, my love," she whispered lost in emotions...

"What is this? Where am I" she whispered, more curious than panicked. She had no heartbeat yet moved as if still alive. Light from an oil lamp hung on the wall was dim, yet she could see perfectly well. Her throat dried as her tongue rimmed behind her lips, strangely aware of sharp upper canines. Sitting up with a straight back, she stared at the white lace and silk of a dress against red satin sides of a coffin—able to see every thread. The smell of earth, the dye of the cloth ran up her nose with a small sniff.

Then a different scent forced a turn of her head. He looked tall, with black hair pulled back and tied at the nape of his neck that accentuated a widow's peak. His features were handsome, angular with a straight nose and thin lips on an unreadable face. The warm-cocoa color of his eyes held intrigue. Dressed meticulously in high fashion with both arms at his sides, he stood—simply staring at her.

"You are not afraid," he whispered in a tender baritone while holding out a hand, which she took, so very mesmerized by the liquid charm of a French accent. He placed her hand on his broad shoulder as an arm slid behind her knees. She knew instinctively to hold tight, and when lifted off the red silk, she inhaled again, the musky scent pleasant. Then her eyes locked to the vein in his neck, and her canines tingled. His palm pressed to the back of her head, pulling her closer as if he were inviting her to… "Drink from me, *ma chere*. You must feed the beast-within," he added in a most erotic way.

Latched on, her fangs slid into his jugular. Each swallow of bitterly sour blood slithered through her, but it quenched a new type of thirst. She moaned as he gathered her dress, lifting it higher and higher. When his hand brushed her core, her legs loosened to welcome… *him*. The sound of buttons coming undone and pressed wool moving assaulted her ears. She drew deeper on his jugular. This time, when her dress lifted, she wrapped a leg around his waist. Gripping her bottom, he entered her, his erection thick and long, so satisfying that her canines slipped from his skin with a gasp.

"Lick the wound. Do it now," he said, his command hers alone to follow. "*Oui, ma chere, oui*," he whispered as if pleased. "Do you like the feel of me inside you?"

"Yes, oh yes," she whispered.

As he plunged deeper and faster, her head fell back and both hands gripped his arms. "Come for me," he ordered.

Her orgasm blossomed within like never before. She cried out, clutching his biceps through the heavy wool jacket. His erotic moan sounded close to a growl as his hands slid down her thighs. When he pulled out, her hand shot between them to grip his hard cock. His hiss was just as erotic. And it thrilled her.

Sinking to her knees, she studied him. He tugged her shoulders, but she shook him off, refused to rise, licking the length of him instead. She licked again and again before taking him in her mouth. He tried to step back, but she gripped his hips tight, taking what she wanted, what she craved. When he reeled, she sucked harder. Her long canines tingled while grazing such tender skin. He growled low in his throat, this time prying her loose and pulling her up. Then he captured her mouth and his tongue teased her fangs. She moaned, swaying in a slow grind.

"Welcome to your new existence, *ma chere*. I will teach you all you need to know." The slow grind continued until he hiked up her dress again. Her right leg hooked his waist and this time, he guided his thick erection into her. "Tilt your head," he whispered, and she did.

He pushed the long braid off a shoulder as a new kind of excitement built within her. After a slow lick to her neck, he sank his fangs into her vein. White-hot heat pooled between her legs. She cried out on the first deep draw, orgasmed again, and when his fangs left her neck, she felt boneless. The lick to seal her skin was sensual— in so many ways.

He withdrew, fixed himself with one hand while embracing her with his other. Her dress drifted down her legs and he pulled back to study her face as if to memorize it. When the heady sensation of erotic bliss lessened, she wallowed in every handsome feature. This time, their lips met again in a kiss that bound them together as if it were their destiny. Without knowing his name or him knowing hers, she sensed she was his. *Forever…*

The recall faded as Luna focused on the cold, angry water beneath the Hunter's Moon. That first night in Henri's arms had promised eternal love, but what he did a half-century later brought blood tears to her eyes. She walked out to the farthest point on the wharf overlooking the fierce, freezing Skjalfandi Bay. This time of year, longer nights blanketed the sea in hues of blue and black. Brutal arctic wind whipped strands of hair around the loose hood covering her head. Wrapped in a full-length fur coat, her body radiated no heat. Hugging herself for warmth was simply a human reaction.

Then she recalled a different memory of her Henri. Luna's neck craned back to stare at the bright-orange orb in the early November sky, a rarity that occurs every four years. Standing here had become a yearly ritual, like a religious feast. That night in 1939, the human husband and wife who would tend to her needs had already begun their trek up to the property secretly purchased by him. *I stood, lost and alone, watching you leave me.* Just like tonight, blood tears had streaked Luna's pale cheeks.

Henri's boat had slipped out of the bay to meet the cargo ship sailing under the French flag. Back then, there had been no wharf and every row of the oars as it left the shoreline filled her with emptiness. Yet even after the cargo ship sailed far out of sight, she had remained rooted to the icy black sand, lashed by the icy wind, hoping the rowboat would reappear so that Henri could leap ashore, draw her into a lover's embrace, and swear how he could not, would not, continue to exist without her. It didn't happen.

Had she been human, she would have eventually died from a broken heart. Had she been more resolute, she would have staked herself years ago, right on this very spot. But she wasn't resolute. She wasn't human. After so many decades together, after so many decades apart, she stood here every Hunter's Moon, wrapped in silence with blood-tears clouding her sight.

They had both sensed that somehow, by some unnatural fluke, she'd been made different. She had stayed at Henri's side under his unwavering protection. She belonged to the tall, handsome vampire who appeared quiet, aloof by nature. Yet when he touched a piano with such sculpted hands and impressive talent, what stirred in her felt ageless, human.

The same questions ripped through her psyche and cut like a razor blade. "Where are you tonight, my love," she whispered to the whipping wind. "Do you still exist? If so, then why did you never return for me?"

The emptiness of this place had kept her safe from a terrifying sire, from countless vampires, from a world war exploding throughout Europe. Just as she had decades ago, Luna turned her back on the icy sea. She didn't have to stand here stung by the wind to recall that particular night. It would replay in dreams until the end of her existence.

When will I except the fact that I will never see you again?

Leaving the wharf, Luna crossed the street to begin the trek up the volcanic mountain to her hidden home.

Glancing left, someone kept waving her way. Recognition brought a small smile to her eyes. Freya owned a gift shop and clothing boutique that remained busy year-round. All of Luna's hand-knit sweaters had been purchased there, her hooded fur coat as well. She sensed Freya's acceptance over the past twenty years, sensed both of them unique but in very different ways. Luna's grin brightened as Freya approached. "I haven't seen you for weeks."

Bundled up and still shivering, Freya replied, "I've just returned from an extended visit with my brother and his family in New York City, you know, my annual trip home." The gifted woman's eyes narrowed. "Luna, my friend, are you all right?"

"Perhaps it is just the night. Ugh, memories," she replied, always thinking it a relief that Freya could read her mood, that knowing what she was didn't terrify the woman.

"I've got a nice bottle of sweet red wine. Would you care to join me at home for a glass?"

She shrugged, shook her head. "I would not be good company tonight."

"Company is exactly what you need. Join me, Luna. I'm a very good listener and I sense you need a good listener tonight."

It couldn't hurt even if it wouldn't help. She nodded and fell in step beside her friend. Freya's shop was just off the main street of Husavik. In northern Iceland.

Chapter 4

Mysteries

Two weeks had passed since the visit with her friend. Why had she told Freya about the night she arrived on the shores of Iceland? What had gotten into her, replaying the memory of Henri, something so very personal? Yet on that night when Luna spoke about him, she had seen Henri as clearly as if he were standing right in front of her, just like that long ago night of the Hunter's Moon. On this bitter mid-November evening, Luna warmed her hands by the fireplace once again haunted by memories. Yet her home, spacious, sturdy and secure, had everything she needed for a simple existence in solitude.

As the decades passed, Luna's thirst had become minimal. It took little animal blood to sustain the necessary need. She had hunted at sunset with bow and arrow, always a precise shot, no doubt a life-skill that carried over into undeath. Whether taught by a relative or a husband, she enjoyed this type of hunting. It made no sound, just like her. Plus, it was considered civilized, acceptable. Rarely did she target the strong, healthy animal, but tonight it had been a stranded black sheep high up the volcanic hill. She took her sustenance and then brought it through death quickly, without unnecessary pain.

Rune, the grandson of the two humans who Henri sent with her, would butcher the animal. As always, she'd give the meat to him and Freya, especially during long dark months. Skins or hides were put to good use as well as every part of the animal. Like other seaport residents, Luna revered the earth, all creatures great and small and what they offered. She didn't hide from other people. They simply left each other alone.

Pleased with the roaring fire in the living room hearth, she sank to the sofa, studied the flames. Scenting Rune, she turned her head when he placed a large envelope in her hand.

"What's this," she asked.

"I found it on the doorstep this afternoon, madame."

When he left, she whispered to herself, "How odd." Slipping a finger under the thick flap that held Freya's scent, she pulled out three sheets of drawing paper with Freya's business card clipped in the corner, but no note of explanation. Staring at the top one, not thinking to look at the next page, she let out a sigh.

Memories had spilled out as if my glass of wine had turned on its side. Useless emotions surfaced as if I had no self-control. She rarely engaged in conversation. And when she did, it was always brief and soft. Not, however, on that night at Freya's. Definitely not.

Pulling off the first sheet, her jaw dropped. "How can this be," she whispered. *Did Freya walk my mind?* Indeed, both sketches were Henri. One stepped right out of her memories of him! The other, however, looked strange. *Are they both him?*

She couldn't be sure. The warm-brown of his eyes, a straight nose, and angular features were exactly as she remembered. The widow's peak so prevalent as well. In one sketch, his long hair was loose, just like the night he left her here. In the other, it appeared to be tied back, the way he wore it when out in public. Unexpectedly, in that sketch, Freya had him dressed in an old-fashioned, light-brown billowy shirt with some sort of cape draped over his broad shoulders.

"Rune," she called out, and when he entered, stated, "Please make contact with Freya tomorrow morning at her shop. Ask if she's free after sunset. I'd like to visit with her. Oh, and say I'll bring the wine. Purchase a fruity red for me to take."

"Yes, madame," he replied.

"Thank you," she responded as he left the room. It was no secret that Freya had the skills of a good witch. But these sketches? *Dear Henri.* Had her thoughts of him been so overtly strong, or was Freya more powerful than she realized?

****

Full of irritation and knowing he had to act, Draven sat at his desk, across from a business contact known for her discretion when dealing with him. In return for her loyalty, he sent many clients her way. Obviously, owning *Destiny*, such a prestigious after-hours club in Manhattan, meant overhearing conversations about buying or selling real estate in and around the city. His hearing as a vampire allowed him to eavesdrop, often giving this business contact the first and best shot at a new real estate deal, his version of insider trading and just as untraceable.

As usual, Mallory Godwin looked stylish in a navy-blue business suit and neat white blouse with many open buttons, suggesting full, supple breasts. Her short gray hair, not her natural color, coifed wispy and full, framed an attractive, tanned face, not a natural tan. Between the scent of expensive perfume, exotic creams under light makeup, and the odor of hair dye, his astute vampire sense of smell had him drawing breath from his mouth to speak. But he found her short skirt and navy-blue stilettos quite pleasant. With electronic tablet in hand, Mallory wore a smile that belonged in the bedroom.

"You must find me parcels of land capable of building a palatial space fit for a king. Each in different areas of the United States and one in the Canadian wilderness."

She didn't flinch or question his inquiry. "How large?"

"Massive. Need I repeat myself, Mallory?" He gave a slight frown, which added the scent of her arousal to the mix.

"This might take time if we're talking Canada as well as the states."

"Time is what I don't have. Send them to me by six a.m." He paused. If he were in the mood, he'd have given the woman a charming grin. "I also want properties already built upon across the continent, again, fit for a king. The pricier the better."

"That's a tall order, Draven."

Leaning forward, he decided to give that charming grin. "Perhaps this is too much for you and your connections."

"I didn't say that," she countered with a flutter of her fake eyelashes. "If you want the best, it takes time."

"Which I do not have," he replied. Of course, he had procrastinated, waited the full two weeks to call her. Mallory leaned forward, giving him a nice glimpse of perfumed cleavage. "None of these properties should be near a city or a densely populated area. In other words, the more remote the better."

Her shoulders straightened as she stopped typing, closed the devise, and stood. He sensed her tight, toned body radiate heat—and fear. "Tomorrow morning," she stated as she slid the tablet into her designer handbag, the perfect size as well as the perfect shade to match her expensive suit.

With a tilt of his head, he added, "Before six a.m. and you can expect a bonus."

Her eyes met his. "Then before six it is."

"Perfect," he said as he stood. "Someone will see you out." A trusted minion led her down the nightclub's wide hall with many mirrored unisex bathrooms.

Draven closed the door to his office. Leaning against it, he shut his eyes. Knowing Mallory, she'd come through even if it meant no sleep. He'd have properties in hand to present to the Vampire War Council, and then he'd quickly go through a boring explanation of each, establishing its many downfalls.

How long can I keep these rabid wolves subdued? Another month? Another year? Herodotus's threat infuriated him. Grabbing his long, black woolen coat, he pulled on new leather gloves. He walked into the club. Ignoring the throng of well-dressed clientele, he hurried up the stairs and through the bejeweled hallway to the outside of the trendy after-hours spot.

The bouncer, a trusted minion, held open the door. "Your car, my lord?"

"Not tonight, Donovan," he replied, turning down the block that led to the Hudson River. Sex with a favorite courtesan usually relieved tension. But a vile kill? That worked, too. He ran his tongue over his fangs and then tightened his jaw.

This kind of thirst had Draven on edge. There'd be no invigorating cat-and-mouse game tonight; no stimulating run to snag a gang member. He wanted simple. Craved the scent of fear and shock before biting a neck. As bloodlust took over, his sense of morality tucked itself much deeper inside and farther away.

Shadowing the highway along the river, the streets were still busy, full of sounds that assaulted his ears. Humans on their way home after a long day at work. Car horns and engines calibrating. Conversations, laughter, and arguments. The sound of people simply walking made him cringe.

He had to drink deep and long. There were no other options tonight. Crossing the highway at vampire speed, he raced down the embankment until he stood at the river's edge. Scenting the malodorous air, he set the beast-within free. The first one he caught would have to do. Barely in control, he acquiesced to the primal need.

Chapter 5

Her Henri

The next evening, dressed in blue jeans and a warm forest-green turtleneck sweater under her long fur coat, Luna walked to the edge of the sea. Tethered fishing boats rocked in the icy water. It wasn't the time of year for tourists, although a few had ventured this far north hoping to view the northern lights. She found their anticipation fascinating, keeping her distance but bundled up just like them.

Freya's shop was located a block off the wharf, on a side street as deserted as the seaport. Although full of authentic items, hand-carved, hand-made, organic, or tooled in this region of Iceland, the apartment behind the counter with the cash register and the display case was her destination.

Instead of pressing the security system's electronic doorbell, Luna waited for her friend to sense her presence, and admired Freya's colorful sketches of the wildlife next to ornate carvings of whales, puffins and seals, the jewelry with bits of volcanic rock in the window. Iceland had raw beauty. Simultaneously pristine and rugged.

When the quaint wooden door opened, Luna stepped through. Holding out the bottle of red wine, she captured the woman's soft-blue eyes. "Hello, good witch."

Freya's face lit up with a warm smile. "Welcome, my eternal friend." Leading her through the store and behind the counter, they went through the next door into her cozy home. The living space had old-world charm with wallpapered walls, classic furniture made of sturdy wood, and thick rugs covering its floors.

Standing in the living room, Luna waited while Freya went to the kitchen area, coming back with two wine glasses and a tray of cheese and sliced black bread. When Freya sat on the sofa, Luna sank into an armchair close to the fireplace, enjoying the warmth of the flames on her cheek. She slipped out of her coat and gloves, resting the latter in her lap.

As Freya removed the cork and filled both glasses, Luna studied her confident calmness. In her mid-forties, the round, robust woman's heart didn't race knowing she sat across from a vampire who had walked the earth since 1887.

After a sip of wine, Freya said, "You've received my drawings."

Luna sipped her wine as well before whispering, "Tell me. Please."

"I hope you don't consider it too nosy, but I see what I see and I sense what I sense." Freya paused as if to choose her words. "Rarely do I walk a person's mind, and although I know what you are, walking your mind is just as easy. I respect your privacy. But what you told me weeks ago, about the love you lost, came out so descriptive, Luna, so very vivid, that I could see Henri in your mind. Please forgive me if I've over-stepped."

Luna looked at the roaring fire. Why had it been so important to share her story? Why did she feel so exposed, even after eight decades? "You captured him perfectly. Down to the look on his face as he left me. What I do not understand is the second sketch. It is unlike Henri to dress that way, so rustic, oddly old-fashioned."

Freya sat forward and did a little wiggle. "I have a tale for you."

"I have the time," Luna answered. "Please. Leave out no detail."

"When you spoke of Henri that night, after you left, well, I felt compelled to sketch him as you saw him. Standing in the rowboat, the look of loss in his eyes, such handsome, singular features, the way his long black hair whipped his face and the set of his mouth, turned down and full of emotion."

"It is imbedded in my memory and always shall be. But the other sketch—"

Freya held up a hand. "No. It didn't come from your mind. This is why I sent them both." After another sip of wine, she put her glass down. "You know I close the shop for the month of October."

Luna nodded. "Yes. To visit family in New York City."

"I also use that time to search city boutiques for items rarely found anywhere in Iceland. But my trip is mostly about family and friends."

"Do you miss your life in the states?"

"Not really," she replied with a shrug. They both sipped their wine. "Husavik is my home. It's beauty. It's solitude. The city's too cacophonous for my psyche. I often wonder how my brother can stand it, how those of us who have the gift can survive being bombarded with feelings, thoughts, crime and sadness." Freya shivered with a groan in her throat.

"Yet you return there every year."

"Yes. And for the most part, I leave satisfied that everyone's healthy, living their lives with as much joy as me. This time, however, it felt different."

"How so?"

"There was tension. Worry. Fear about an unexpected event that centered around an innocent man lost in a dark magic spell." She paused to take another sip of wine. "My brother is a warlock. Tristan isn't as powerful as me, but his skills are noteworthy. There are covens and healing circles in the city. Many of them. Tristan belongs to a healing circle run by a very powerful good witch. It was during the first crescent moon in early October that a call went out to them."

"What kind of call," Luna asked, not seeing what this had to do with Henri.

"It's like a silent call. A feeling that a good witch gets when someone is in dire need. Apparently, a breach occurred between dimensions."

She leaned forward. "I don't understand. What dimensions? Are you saying there are other worlds that exist?"

Freya's head tilted a bit. "Of course there are other dimensions. Didn't you know this?"

"Honestly, I have to answer no."

"But you've lived well over a century, Luna."

"I had no use of that knowledge. Nor did any of those I... Henri didn't, either. And if he did, he didn't talk about such things." She took a longer draw of her wine. *Why hadn't he?*

"Let me assure you, other dimensions exist. We know of two realms in conjunction with ours." Freya paused. "Well, a huge paranormal event happened some sixteen years ago. It involved an ensouled vampire who obliterated three very powerful sorcerers."

"Ensouled vampire? I've never heard of such a thing," Luna said, shaking her head.

"He is… was… an anomaly. One of a kind. What he did altered our world. Milliona of portals shut down, leaving only one operational portal on each continent. But just before they all closed, thousands of vampires as well as witches and warlock left our human world."

Luna's shoulders drifted back. She finished the wine in her glass and set it down. "Where did the vampires go?" Freya picked up the bottle to refill her glass, but Luna put a hand over it and whispered, "No. Thank you."

Freya set the bottle down and cleared her throat. "In order to avoid the Guardians who hunt them, vampires and powerful sires now reside in the Third Realm. I understand that it was somewhat modernized but sealed off with magic by three immortal sorcerers to keep them out of the human world."

"I've known there are three sorcerers thought to be immortal on each continent, but—"

"Well, these three are different—with unimaginable power. The Third Realm is now uniquely conjured so it can sustain life, with hundreds, maybe thousands of human blood slaves for the wealthy, elite vampires to feed from."

A growing knot in her stomach made her more anxious. With another shake of her head, Luna replied, "And what does this have to do with Henri? Freya, be specific."

"Before I get specific, Luna, is what I sense correct? That you've had no contact with any other vampires since Henri brought you here?"

"No. I have never sensed others like me in Husavik.

Of course not," she replied as that knot in her gut tightened. "Henri brought me here because of its remoteness. There were many vampires in Europe. I didn't care to be with any of them. Henri and I only had each other for almost fifty years before the Second World War. I... We—"

"You loved each other exclusively and didn't care to associate with too many others who were undead," Freya whispered.

She gave a slow nod, lost in memories of Henri's protectiveness. *They* were different than the others. *They* loved with a passion, fed only when necessary and had no use for the sadistic antics of their sires.

"I see it, Luna. You kept your bond secret." Freya paused. "No. There are still vampires in the human world. Not nearly as many as there were sixteen years ago. They are still hunted by Guardians. But back to what I sent you."

"Is Henri in the Third Realm? Is that what you are trying to say?"

"No. Not at all. The second sketch I sent you is not a vampire named Henri. He is a very powerful vampire who still lives in our world. His name is Draven."

"Draven? I've never heard that name before."

Freya put her glass down and sat forward. "I looked it up. The name is said to have Anglo-Saxon roots. It means hunter, but some say it means protector. But again, I digress. In early October, right after the first crescent moon, Tristan's healing circle helped protect two mystical warriors who travelled to the Second Realm where witches and warlocks reside. They were accompanied by this vampire. Many times, when witches speak to one another, we link thoughts. When I linked to Mary Kendrick, the leader of the healing circle, I saw Draven as well as two mystical warriors with him, in my mind's eye. Then you told me about Henri. And when I sketched him, I sensed an uncanny resemblance. I felt compelled to sketch Draven, like I did when I sketched Henri. Is it possible..." Freya's voice trailed off.

"Is what possible, Freya?" Full of confusion, she gripped the arms of the chair.

"Is the vampire Draven, in fact, your Henri? Because that's what I sense. You're wondering the same thing. You question why he didn't come back for you."

"We loved each other, Freya. Fifty years, never apart! Why would he not come back for me? Why leave me here alone, in an endless existence? Without him. Without love."

Freya's eyebrows rose. "I don't have an answer, Luna."

Her brow knit. "Can you connect to your brother's mind again to see him?"

"No. It was the paranormal event that put the vampire's image in my head. This has nothing to do with my brother."

"If this Draven is still in the city, can your brother find him?"

"I suppose I could ask." Freya refilled her glass. "More wine?"

"No," Luna replied as she stood. "Please speak to your brother. Ask if he knows who this Draven is. Can you do that?"

"I'll go a step farther. If he can locate the vampire, I'll have him take a picture and send it to my phone. If you see a picture instead of a sketch, will you be able to tell if it's Henri?"

Pulling on her gloves and very bothered, she replied, "I don't know. Can you sketch the two mystical warriors you saw with him, in your mind's eye? I mean, why associate with those who are sworn to destroy us?"

"I sense there had been a crucial reason for them to associate with each other. But yes, of course I will sketch them. Is there anything else I can do, Luna? You look, um, I don't know—"

"A bit lost? Yes. I am. I'd like to ask another favor. All these things you talk about… Can you write it out for me to read and understand? And may I ask questions about changes in the world?" She stood, pulling on her coat. "Perhaps it was prudent for Henri to hide me here, away from the others. Perhaps not."

Following Freya, Luna walked through the store to the door. Freya said, "Everyone needs protection from time to time. You are a very different creature of the night, Luna. There is more humanity in you than in some people I know. The world has become a very cruel place since the Second World War. And believe it or not, it has recently grown even crueler. Henri must have loved you very much to hide you here. Yes. It's true. You've been cut off from the modern world. Have you missed much? I suppose so, in terms of inventions. But Guardians haven't hunted you down with a stake in hand. No vampires come searching for you. In many ways you're better off. Look. I'll write out as much as I can. And I'll sketch the mystical warriors who were with this Draven. Then we'll talk again."

As the door locked behind her, Luna pulled up her hood. Wind rushed up the street from the bay bringing with it an arctic mist. Very unsettled, she headed up to her home in the volcanic hills. Part of her wanted the second sketch to be Henri. Part of her didn't.

You did not return. You purposely left me alone in love. How could she ever forgive him?

Instead of taking a direct path home, she veered off to the left and broke into a run. Seclusion was one thing. Loneliness, thrust upon her and not of her choosing, was another. Whether the world had become crueler or not, she didn't care. During her time with Henri, decisions had been ripped out of her hands and placed in his. She had let him do this. Foolishly. After what she learned tonight, she was done with it.

Chapter 6

Services Rendered

Mallory Godwin made good on her promise. An hour before six on the dot, Draven studied a thick file on his desk. He motioned her to sit as he read. A minion came through the door to his home and placed a tray with two cups of coffee on his desk, but he left through the door that led back to the club.

"Help yourself," he said, but the woman looked positively shaken. "It is just black coffee. Do you require milk or sugar?" She shook her head and tentatively lifted the expensive cup rimmed with gold. "Tell me about the properties as I read."

Mallory cleared her throat, set down the cup, and opened a small laptop. "The Nevada property is the largest, a thousand acres of desert in the middle of No-Mans-Land but close enough for day, uh, I mean night trips to Las Vegas by limo. I'd suggest solar energy for this one, but water lines will have to be put in place. Internet access may be spotty."

"Pricey with many zeros after the number," he said with a wry grin. *Although, hunting humans in Vegas would be easy.* Herodotus would have a grand old time with show girls and despondent gamblers. The sires would also be out of his hair, nowhere near other populated cities. Thus, a good possibility. *Far enough*

away but a night-flight to access the portal is doable.
"Next," he said.

"The Canadian property is far north and very remote. The land is rugged and would need to be prepped during warm months. Water access and solar panels for electricity might take a long time to install. You're looking at a multi-year project. Of course, unlike Nevada, the weather is harsh most of the year. But the price is good."

"Yes I see, and much less expensive." The hardest selling point was a multi-year build. But Herodotus mentioned Canada for consideration. Unlike Montreal or Quebec, it would definitely keep the sire out of sight and out of mind. *God forbid I'm called to meet the sires up there in a frozen paradise.* Not a trip he'd willingly take. Air travel would also be an issue. But the timing: multiple years to make it inhabitable. He opened the next folder. "And Florida?"

Mallory leaned forward. "Again pricey."

"Very," he replied.

"Another thousand-acre property with wetlands and, uh, wildlife."

"Ah, yes. The dreaded alligators and venomous snakes."

Mallory nodded. "But all the necessary utilities are accessible, which saves you money. It has three bids on it. None have met the asking price and the owner is filthy rich. He'll wait for the right offer. Construction would be easy if you can find a reliable contractor. I've heard stories of people waiting days for air-conditioner repairmen to show." She leaned in, adding, "Access to a major airport is good. You can also put in your own landing strip since it's considered rural land for growing crops. Orlando has so many tourist attractions, just like Vegas, but I suppose a very different class of clientele. More family-oriented."

God truly forbid, he thought. *Although children are never turned, Herodotus may make one too many orphans of the young tourists who visit all those theme parks.* The alligator population would surely dwindle. No harm in that. *He might enjoy the hot climate, give him a false sense of security.* The sun, like in Nevada, would make vengeful vampire deaths very easy, and night flights were plentiful to the New York area.

"And the fourth?"

"This one's in Vermont with a very strange history. It's been on the market for years with no takers. Five hundred acres with an old, rutted access road. It had some kind of castle on it before an unexplained, truly horrendous fire back in two-thousand-five. It was owned by a recluse, apparently brought over brick by brick by a mysterious baron named Cyril… uh, something… from Slovakia. There are high stone walls and it even had a riding stable…"

As her voice droned on, expounding all the good qualities about this property, Draven leaned back in his chair. Unpleasant memories took hold. *Our sire's estate, before Zoltan got it in his twisted brain to nail Cyril in a pine box for transport back to Europe. Then both of them met final death at the hands of my brother in blood and his very capable human son.* He could smell the inside of the mansion, see the fineries their sire had had on display. *Well-kept stables with magnificent Friesians and many minions, most of them vampires, to keep everything in pristine working order… all turned to rubble and ash.* Realizing that Mallory had stopped talking, now staring his way, he leaned forward and said, "Another possibility."

"And the least expensive. Now for properties with existing mansions."

Ready to scream, he stood with a charming grin. "My dear, you have done a most magnificent job. Perhaps we can meet again in a few days to go through those."

"Oh. Of course," she said while closing her laptop. "I'm glad you're pleased."

"As I always am with your time and attention to detail. Full payment will be wired to your account along with the bonus. And again, I do apologize that we will have to meet again."

"It's always my pleasure."

"As it is mine. Let me walk you out." Taking her arm, he led her down the hallway and to the top of the staircase, which led to the street. Donovan, his bouncer, opened the door to the club and Mallory stepped out into the street.

Instead of going back to the office, Draven walked around the empty club. At the half-moon of a bar, he pulled out his cell phone and sent a text. Forty-five seconds later, liking the response a thin grin began.

The silence. The accoutrements that would turn the club into a lively, exciting night for his wealthy clientele were all clean and neat. Glasses sparkled behind the well-stocked bar, the dance floor buffed and ready. Tonight his employees, handpicked human minions, would serve any and all as if they were royalty. Doors opened at midnight, and now, with that ridiculous business of finding properties for Herodotus complete, he could indulge in other pleasures.

Entering his office, he left the door ajar, closed the files and placed them in the top drawer of his large wooden desk with a thick glass top. Pressing a button on the landline, he heard a reverent, "Yes, my lord."

"I am expecting company, Donovan. You will not need to escort her down."

Instead of sitting on the leather couch across the room, he paced the floor with slow, deliberate steps. With his suit jacket unbuttoned, he loosened his tie and opened the top button of his crisp black shirt. A minion entered with a bottle of top-quality scotch from the bar. Once the two-fingers were poured, he took the glass and downed it. When she reached for the glass in his hand, he stated, "I will serve myself."

"Yes, my lord," she replied with a curtsey.

"Give me your wrist," he ordered. Gripping the young woman's arm, Draven sank into her vein for a deep drink. Her blood swirled around his mouth before a smooth swallow. Sealing the wound with a slow lick, he dropped the minion's hand. "Go home now. Take tonight off." He wouldn't chance the possibility of her not performing up to par in his club.

He poured another drink, downing it in one swallow. It would take much more than this to have an effect on him. But the chaser, after a hard draw of healthy blood, not only served to cleanse his palette. It tempered his mood.

He sat on the edge of the desk with his legs slightly apart and his arms laced across his chest. The click of high heels approaching meant he'd have hours for pleasure. All she'd smell? Scotch and his expensive cologne. She already knew what he was. In fact, he had requested her specifically. There would be no need for charming foreplay or any misgivings about a romantic rendezvous. This was sex. Plain and simple.

The courtesan closed the door. "Lock it," Draven ordered, and then she came over with a sensual sway of her hips. The short black dress clung like a second skin. She tilted her head, offered her neck. A dispassionate lick confirmed no drugs or disease, and he allowed a pleasant grin.

Her hair was as black as his suit, neatly parted down the center, as smooth and shiny as satin. One look said what he wanted. She already knew how he preferred it. Sinking to her knees, she nuzzled his crotch and teased him through his trousers before she freed his erection, licked up the length to the sensitive tip of him. He shrugged off his jacket, let it fall behind him onto the desk. He unbuttoned the cuffs, untied his tie and let it drop as well. Then he let his shirt drop as her tongue teased even more.

His suit trousers slid down. Warm hands ran up his thighs and grabbed his ass. The back of his thighs met the desk as she removed his shoes and peeled off his socks. His fingers combed through her long hair as she worked him, sucking and sliding. Heavy and erect, when she took his balls in hand, knowing what gave him a thrill, he let out a groan and enjoyed an experienced touch. He fingered the thin straps of her dress, the silent command for her to stand. As the slinky fabric pooled at her feet, he scented her wetness through the scant black lace covering what he wanted. Call it a fetish or whatever new term was used, he liked to watch the reveal of a luscious bottom, the anticipation yet another thrill.

Holding her waist, he guided her to one of the armchairs across the office. She leaned back while he fondled a breast, his other hand diving under the lace. The soft whimper pleased him. In fact, every sound she uttered heightened his sexual desire. She turned and bent over the back of the armchair. He palmed her bottom. When her hands gripped the soft leather arms, he inched the delicate lace down to expose a little more skin.

"Shall I take you now," he whispered in a seductive tone. The buck and whimper had him inching the lace down again until she began to pant with a little wiggle, "Please, my lord."

A hand lingered on her bottom to throw in a little naughty fantasy. When the lace shimmied down and off, she leaned a knee on the back of the chair. He thrust into her and pulled out slow to palm her bottom again. He could keep this up for hours, but not this morning. Spreading her thighs, he thrust deep and hard.

Every high-pitched "oh yes, my lord," added to the pleasure of skin on skin as he fucked her. He liked a sex partner with stamina. Running a finger up her spine to the nape of her neck, he pulled out. Still erect, he stepped back and waited for her to come to him.

She knew not to touch his face, such an act of intimacy off limits. Nor would he caress her or take her in his arms. This wasn't love. Just lust. As her eyes focused on his hard cock, he raised an eyebrow. Like all of Cyril's progeny, he was well endowed. And he knew how to use it.

The courtesan's wriggles and whimpers continued as her hand slid lower to touch herself. She licked her lips in a wicked way. Ready for round two, he gave a nod. She sat on the desk and spread her legs. Licking his lips before he tasted her, it went without saying that she'd be generously paid when he was fully satisfied.

Chapter 7

Questions

Replaying the conversation with Freya, Luna paced in front of the fireplace in her living room. How had she allowed herself to be so closed off from the world? So much so that she didn't know anything about a mysterious event that took place years ago. Although she had hunted and fed tonight, the irritation brewing within had not lessened.

Angry at herself. Angry at Henri. Angry at her very existence.

Up until the sketches arrived, she simply accepted the *status quo,* as if in both life and undeath, there had never been a reason to be cross or suspicious. There had never been a reason to express outrage of any magnitude. Her only life-memory remained a sense of anguish, as if caught in a sudden overload of grief. Henri said she had been despondent on the night of turning. Why travel to Florence, only to stroll arm in arm with death? She sensed her heritage Nordic, not Italian. Had her deceased husband been the love of her life? He had said that Herodotus had sired her on a whim. *How does one do such a thing on a whim?*

She looked around the living room. *For decades, my home has meant safety.* Now, she felt strangled. In many ways, isolation in Husavik suited her calm nature. Not anymore. *I live in the past with no knowledge of the present. The road of recall holds no meaning now.*

"Rune," she called, and waited for him to reply.

"Yes, madame," he said.

How to say it? Where to begin? The son of her former servants was paid well and loyal to a fault. If her math was correct he'd be in his forties. Good Nordic stock bound by honor to protect her from harm during the day, to do her bidding without questions. She gazed into his blue eyes, wondering what he felt when he looked at a vampire.

"Have you sacrificed to take care of something like me," she said, a bit embarrassed about never asking before, and now, somewhat fearful of his response.

"Never, madame."

"Please tell the truth. That is all I seek."

With a shake of his head, he replied, "Never. It's been my privilege, as it was my father's and his father's before him. It is what I chose to do."

"You never thought to leave Husavik? To explore the world?"

"But I have, madame. In my twenties, when I attended university."

"How did I not know?" Had she become so complacent that asking about this never even crossed her mind? "And you chose to come back to Husavik?"

He shrugged a shoulder. "My father gave me a choice. Just as his father had given him."

"And you accepted it?"

"Why should I not? We've been well paid, madame. Monsieur Henri gave my grandfather enough gold to sustain a village, which was invested in securities after World War Two. Monsieur left specific instructions about our wages."

Again. So many questions. "Do you have a… a wife, a family?"

"I am divorced, but I have sole custody of my ten-year-old son. I employ a nanny who is with him when I'm here. What upsets you, madame? Why all these questions tonight?"

She gave an awkward grin. "I should have known these things. And it's my fault for never asking. Freya said the world has changed in the past eighty years. She is writing it all down."

He gave a slight laugh, at ease with her, which was fine. "That's an enormous task you ask. It would be easier to go on the web."

"The web?"

"The Internet. It's an electronic tool."

"And where would I find this Internet?"

He nodded once. "If you come with me, I'll show you my laptop."

"Laptop," she said as she stood.

"It's easy enough to use."

She followed through the kitchen and into the office, a place she never visited. It was her way of keeping human life and her vampire existence separate. The paneled room off to the side had a bed and dresser in the corner, a large wooden desk with bookshelves behind it. As he sat at the desk, she came around with tentative steps. The device looked the size of a small suitcase, bright and full of colored pictures. Her eyes went wide, then wider still.

"May I pull up a chair for you?" Luna moved back, still staring at this thing called a laptop. When he set the chair down, she sank into it. "I'm sure you've seen computers in the shops of Husavik."

"Yes, I have. I believe I saw one in Freya's home. But it never interested me." Now, curious and embarrassed, she grew even more angry with herself.

"This is called a mouse," he said with his hand on a small device. "It's easy to navigate. I type Husavik into this space here," he said, "and then hit enter."

"Oh my," she said leaning in. "It is the seaport and its history! The pictures are magnificent! How did you do that?" He chuckled again as she began to read.

"Here," he said, bringing up a different screen. "This is my cottage just off your estate, Madame."

She studied the aerial view. "What a wonderful tool! Can you see my home?"

"I'd rather not type your address in. There are many ways for others to access the web browser. Illegal ways. Plus, the laptop keeps a history of what I search, what I query."

"I must have one. You must get me one."

"Tomorrow morning, I'll drive to Akureyri, purchase a state-of-the-art laptop for you and set it up, so that after sunset, you can study what you like. Should I purchase a cell phone as well, madame? Then you can have this information at your fingertips, and even call someone a continent away if you want. Anywhere in the world, actually."

Fixated on the screen, her head bobbed. "Yes. Yes, and anything else electronic to connect me with the modern world."

"I suggest a smart TV, madame, a… a big-screen so you can watch up-to-the-minute news and movies right here, in the privacy of your home. You will love movies."

"Yes, Rune. Everything and anything else we may need." Yet she didn't want to pull away from the new pictures of Husavik on the screen. It took a fair amount of determination to say, "Let me not keep you from what you need to do."

"It's not an issue, madame. Stay and play around with the laptop if you like."

"No. I will read one of my books and then retire to prepare myself for tomorrow night. Set the alarm and go home to your son. But call Freya first. Ask her to come tomorrow night as well. I have so much to learn."

"As you wish, madame."

"Good night, Rune," she said as she stood. "And thank you."

Walking through the kitchen, Luna looked at the appliances with different eyes. Anyone would think a human lived here. A very old-fashioned human. She had no idea what all of these gadgets were for, except the refrigerator, which held tall glass jars of fresh animal blood.

What if Henri still walked the earth? What if, with the aid of these electronics, she could find him? Without a doubt, Henri would embrace modern technology. She scoffed as she walked through the living room, suddenly very ashamed about her lack of knowledge, her lack of interest in anything other than nights of passion in his arms.

She took the stairs to the second floor lost in thought. All the windows were shuttered tight against the outside world. She ran water for a bath and began to undress. Seeing no reflection in the vanity mirror, she realized that modern world or not, some things never changed.

She sank into the hot water, picked up a bar of scented soap. As one hand rubbed the bar across her breasts, the other slid beneath the water. "Henri, my love," she whispered, imagining his hand on her. She missed his deep, rich voice. She missed the way he made love to her. She missed *him*.

****

Freya closed the book she was reading and vacillated between holding off on the call to her brother or simply getting it over with. Rarely did she stay up this late, but the conversation with Luna kept rerunning in her mind. Very aware of the time difference, she picked up her phone and waited to hear her brother's voice.

"Tristan...I hope I'm not interrupting anything."

"No. I can spare some time. What's up?"

She sat back on the sofa and put her feet up on the coffee table. "How's everything? How's the family?"

"All's good here. The kids are fine. The wife is good. The crazy flu is behind us. Was it bad there when you returned?"

"No. It was never in the news and everyone here in the seaport is healthy and hearty as ever. Listen. Your healing circle, the one I attended at Mary Kendrick's brownstone." She heard a drawn out, "uh-hum..." and blew out a breath, "The three men in our mind-sight, who are they?"

"Two are mystical warriors associated with the Georgians. One is a vampire."

"Who is he?"

"You mean Draven?"

"Yes, who is he?"

"A pretty powerful vampire in the city who lords over the only known portal left on the continent."

"How is it he came to be involved with the Georgians and two mystical warriors?"

"I have no idea, only that he agreed to assist them in the Second Realm during the event. You know that. You were here with us."

"What's he like, you know, his temperament?"

"Well he wasn't going for their necks. You saw what I saw."

"Yes, but I focused on protection, not reading his mind."

"Yeah. That's a hard one. Mary and Sharon know more about him. Can't say what it is. You have Sharon's number. Give her a call."

"No. I want to keep this private… between us."

"Okay. It's your call, but listen, all I sensed is that what he did for the mystical warriors was obviously necessary. As for his temperament, I sensed arrogance, intelligence, and the ability to reason. I mean, he wanted to help. At least that's what I picked up from Mary's mind. He can't be all bad if the Georgians involved him in this last event. It was pretty radical, I mean, a hidden portal, which had to be closed by a good witch with all of us lending our powers. I recognized her in mind-sight. Didn't Mom know Bronwyn and her older sister?"

Very easy to go off-topic with him, she said, "Tristan, the vampire."

"He owns an elite after-hours club. I think it's called *Destiny*."

"Destiny's the name of the club?"

"Mary knows a lot more. She left early tonight, even though we're planning the gala."

"Oh. You must be pretty busy and I'm taking you away from your work."

"Nah. I always have time for my big sister."

She chuckled. "It was so good to see her again in October. You know, it's been years."

"And she's a sweetheart of a boss. You want me to ask about him? I can call you back. Whoa, it's like the middle of the night there, right?"

"It's very late, but I've got a lot on my mind."

"Freya, are you okay?"

"I'm fine. It's… something else. I'm asking this for a friend. I sense the need to help her. I don't know exactly how. But this vampire. I have to find him. He looks like someone she knows. An old boyfriend."

"You described a *vampire* to her?"

"Let's just say I'm still good with charcoal and colored pencil."

"You're sketching again, Freya! Good for you," he said with a thrill in his voice. It echoed through her psyche before she closed her mind to him.

"I am. Now and again."

"Send some to me. I'll frame them for display at the gala."

"Maybe. I'll think about it. When is the gala, by the way?"

"In a few weeks. You can come back to the city for it and stay for Thanksgiving. We can take in all the lights and decorations and Radio City before we go looking for this vampire."

"No. I need information on him as soon as possible. I'll send you a picture of the sketch. Tomorrow, maybe show it to Mary for me?"

"Sure," he replied.

She sensed Tristan's smile. She smiled as well. "Great. Call me after you show it to her. Kiss the kids for me and give your honey my best."

"Sure will. It's great to hear your voice again so soon. And send me those other sketches. I'm serious. Can't wait to see them. Love you, sis."

"Love you, too," she said.

Ending the call, Freya put down her phone. Then she picked it up again, searched the gallery app. She always took pictures of her sketches. Locating the vampire in billowed sleeves, she put in the text, "Are you sure his name is Draven? Great talking to you tonight. Stay well." Then she hit send.

Her spine tingled, her sixth sense hummed. Thinking about Luna and all she needed to know was mind-bending, and when her phone chimed, she actually jumped. Swiping across the green icon, even though not recognizing the number, she said, "Hello."

"Freya. This is Rune. I work for Luna."

"Yes. I know. How are you?"

"All is well. Luna asked if you are free tomorrow night to come to her home. I can direct you here or pick you up. If you are free, that is."

"Sure, Rune. And thanks for offering to pick me up. It would be appreciated."

"Good, good. I should tell you that she has requested I buy a laptop, a cell phone, and a television. But she'll need more than my help in learning all this. Will you help her as well?"

"Of course. I think it's a great idea, although pretty overwhelming."

"I do not want madame upset, Freya. We will take it slow and only give her what she can handle, a little at a time. Although, she appears very thirsty for knowledge."

"Of course, Rune. I sense there are many things she

needs to know."

"You can read her? Even though she is what she is?"

"Oddly, I can."

"It is a good thing."

"I sense that as well. What time can I expect you?"

"Six p.m. You will sense if she becomes distressed, Freya?"

"I will, Rune."

"Good enough. See you at six."

When the call ended, she stood and stretched with a yawn. Tomorrow was inventory day. She had new stock arriving. Perhaps she'd roll up her prints and take them to the post office to send them to Tristan. Many were of the whales, white seals, and tiny puffins. She'd leave it to her brother to pick and choose, although she highly doubted any of her colored pencil drawings would fit in at an art gala in New York City.

She saw Luna in her mind, sad but curious. She saw the vampire Draven in her mind as well. Yet she could sense nothing about him. Was he Henri? If so, why the name change?

"Too many questions, Freya," she said to herself. "Go to bed or you'll never get up on time tomorrow."

Chapter 8

Reality

Like an extra layer of security for humanity, the three immortal sorcerers of the Second Realm created a time warp when they updated the vampire realm. Should a curious blood drinker jump through a portal and find a way past a Gatekeeper, the distortion of day versus night would most likely end its existence by incineration. Only two portals around the world allowed in and out traffic. The North American portal was one of them. Draven found it highly amusing how the sires craved our world so viciously that they actually scheduled meetings at their noon hour, as if conducting business in conjured sunlight made some type of human statement.

Knowing this presentation would be brief, he had fed at sunset, drinking just enough to take the edge off blood thirst. The not-so-innocent gang member would need a transfusion, or a thick, juicy sirloin steak on the rare side. *Whichever, it's the idiot's personal choice,* he thought as he locked the vault door before stepping into the swirling blood-red mist.

Once through the portal, he jogged past miles of growing fields, then took his time strolling down the main street that led to the Vampire Council's Building. An arrogant stride in his new designer black suit brought him past the guards, dismissive and aloof as always.

Entering the cavernous council chambers with the thick folder tucked under an arm, Draven bowed to all seven sires, took his seat at the other end of the table with Herodotus a good nine feet away. Their "king" looked like an ordinary, forty-something businessman, only with deadly fangs and a penchant for sadism.

"Speak, vampire," Herodotus stated with both hands pressed to the carved, wooden table.

"I have properties for your consideration, Sire. Each has pros and cons."

"I was beginning to think a month with no blood while chained below in a dark, dank cell would be necessary to bring you back in line."

He wasn't in the mood for punishment considering it messy, beneath him and his acquired status. Clearing his throat, he looked down—in a humble way. "Yes, Sire."

"We should already be back in the human world. I suppose you will bring up that hidden portal business as an excuse."

"After thorough investigation, the report proved to be erroneous, Sire. Simply an insane warlock on a murderous rampage spouting nonsense." To further flaunt status and skill, not to mention a crucial steer away from the truth, Draven added, "The markets are still extremely volatile, which requires careful attention in order to keep your vast wealth from taking an unnecessary downturn."

"Yes. You're good with money. But this erroneous report… The sorcerers informed us that many Second Realm guards were run through the heart with a silver sword. Would you have something else to share, perhaps?"

Thrown by the question, he cleverly lied, "The use of a silver sword confirms it was not a vampire who killed them."

"Yes, I suppose had their necks been torn open it may have led to war between our realms."

"Exactly, Sire." To stroke the old bastard's ego, he tagged on, "and as we all know, you would be victorious in a war between realms, Sire."

Herodotus sat back, appearing appeased. "Proceed," came with a regal flourish of his left hand.

"As you wish, Sire." Draven began a somewhat vague presentation of the properties in an even tone. *Perhaps too vague*, he thought, taking question after question from Herodotus. Hours dragged on, which increased his thirst. When no further comments came, he leaned back and folded his hands on the thick folder, wondering just how much longer this would take. Like some internal clock chimed the hour, he'd need to feed soon, but only in the human world. Pushing the folder forward, he stated, "I leave this for your review, Sire."

Expecting to be dismissed, when no such command occurred, his jaw tensed, his fangs tingled. Yet he sat perfectly still, ready to graciously turn down the offer to feed from a blood slave—before getting the hell out of here in a hurry.

The seven sires appeared to be in a non-verbal tete-a-tete. These powerful creatures of the night were feared by all. If he were a lesser vampire, simply being in their presence would make him shake. But no. Not the Gatekeeper who could set them loose on unsuspecting humans. Once the missing persons reports began to grow, the Georgian Council would become suspicious of him. The unforgivable, evil act would positively be attached to his name.

"What about available properties with mansions?"

The question yanked him like a dog on a chain. Hoping Herodotus had not read him, an unquenchable thirst surfaced. *Yes, you fool, you should have drained that twitchy gang member.* After a dry swallow, he answered, "My search continues, Sire. I shall present them in one week."

Herodotus pounded a fist on the table. The thick folder jumped. As if by silent command, the other six sires abruptly exited through the massive doors to their private chambers. The click of shoe heels on marble sounded full of menace before the sire stopped behind him. One deep draw from his vein would reveal the collusion with Michael and Lukas Malone in early October. His other secret, too.

"I tolerate the threads of morality in you, Draven, the same as I did in eighteen-eighty-seven. Do you remember the gift I gave you? My daughter of the night?"

The greedy bastard will know it all! He'd burn in Hell still longing for Luna. But every second that his head remained attached to his shoulders was a good sign.

A brutal, "Answer me," echoed off the walls and Draven quickly whispered, "Yes, Sire, I remember."

"Now in the twenty-first century I am once again puzzled by you. All that sappy morality should have been tortured out of you when the portals closed years ago. Instead, you were chosen to be Gatekeeper by three immortal sorcerers, considered highly intelligent, trusted to grow our financials, yet weakened by the comforts of the human world!"

Grabbed by the neck, Draven came off the chair

landing yards away and hitting a marble wall. The back of his skull cracked open. Then the sire's immovable hand had him by the throat, flinging him across the chamber. His back hit the conference table and he slid across it to where Herodotus usually sat like a king. He rolled off, sprawled facing the ceiling. The heavy throne-like chair appeared to hover before it slammed into his chest like a block of cement. With a grunt, Draven shoved it off his cracked ribs.

Submission remained the only option, but the struggle to get on his knees was real, and the crawl to the bastard meant acknowledgement of a mistake. Precious blood oozed from his skull as he knelt in front of the sire with his eyes cast down.

"You are just as arrogant as your despicable brother in blood. Cyril reined Michael in with his fists. But never you, the quiet one, the respectful son. Always set apart, as if your passion and intelligence made you better than the rest of his progeny. Yet Michael remained Cyril's favorite. And look what his favorite son did to all of us! Cast into this miserable realm, without the thrill of innocent humans to hunt! Without the pleasant taste of virgin blood," Herodotus bellowed like an angry bear.

Gathering courage, he whispered, "Sire, I—"

"Do not speak. Do not move," Herodotus growled. "How arrogant to expect that I would be satisfied by a piddly crumb of information!"

Again, grabbed by the hair and thrown, his arms windmilled fully off-balance before he landed in a slide and turned aside to cough up even more precious blood. He knew what he had to do, because making a run for it wasn't possible. This crawl back was slow and unsteady. His body shook, but he bent low with knees far enough apart for support. Void of all arrogance to beg forgiveness, his forehead met the icy marble floor.

Yet the sire still circled like a killer shark. "I have led armies of men into battle. Every soldier followed orders and feared my wrath. Do you fear my wrath, vampire?"

When he whispered, "Yes, Sire," the click of shoe heels stopped behind him. Then a precision kick landed him face down and many feet away from where he had knelt. Unimaginable pain shot through his testicles. It had him speechless, wide eyed and shocked.

Crouched at his side, Herodotus used his tied back hair like a lever to yank his head up and back. "Look at me, vampire," the sire calmly ordered.

Barely able to focus, he obeyed. Those bits of coal flared with cruelty.

"Deliver my request or be stripped naked and carved until blood coats your skin. You have your one week."

When those massive doors to the private chambers slammed shut, the sound thundered through him. Cupping his groin, excruciating pain like nothing ever experienced had him unable to move. But staying curled on this floor wasn't an option. Terrified and thirsting for blood, Draven slithered across the floor and held on to a chair so he could stand.

But every step felt more agonizing than the one before. He limped and lurched past the vampire guards. As if some silent signal had gone out, the main street lined with vampires to witness his humiliation. With the last iota of dignity in this walk of abysmal shame, as if the entire realm knew exactly what had been done to him in that black marble room, every single vampire leered tight-jawed and odious.

At the edge of the city, he sank to his knees and crawled through miles of growing fields. Not a blood slave could be seen, not even a rabbit to grab and drain. Getting to the portal was his only hope of survival. If he stopped, then all bets were off. He could be staked by a vindictive blood slave. Or dragged back to Herodotus for more of a beating.

It took hours to reach the swirling blood-red mist of the portal. Fully nauseous, he flung his body through and landed on his stomach inside the vault. With the last ounce of strength, he unsealed the heavy steel and silver door, lurched into his office and pushed it closed before falling flat on his face again. Crippled by pain, he clawed his way to the desk and reached up far enough to push the landline phone. When it hit the floor, he pressed a button and heard Donovan whisper, "Yes, my lord."

In a shaky rasp, he ordered, "Bring a healthy minion from the club to me at once." He waited, curled on his side, and when a wrist came to his mouth, he latched on. Taking only two mouthfuls of thick human blood, keenly aware that a dead employee would cause unwanted problems, he sealed the minion's wrist wound and ordered, "Get him home. Now leave."

But Donovan reached for him, saying, "My lord, let me help."

He growled a sharp, "Do not touch me! Leave!"

The door to his office closed. Like a mortal man, Draven sucked air to fill his lungs only to cough up precious blood. He crawled into his home behind the desk, then into his room. Pulling himself onto the bed, pain knifed through his ribs, his head pounding, his swollen genitals screaming... Vicious pain.

It was a well-known fact that other-realm wounds

were very slow to heal. How long before he'd walk with some semblance of dignity again? He had no idea. How long before broken ribs knit together and precious blood stopped seeping out of his scalp? Again, no idea.

Never weepy, he couldn't stop blood tears clouding his eyes. Curled on the bed, he pulled the leather strip from his hair and hissed while touching his oozing scalp.

How stupid to believe I could control this sire. Trapped. I am trapped. No one could get him out of this dilemma—caught between the human world and the sire's realm, between morality and treason. His wants and needs held far more worth right now.

Without the title of Gatekeeper, he'd be expendable. And he enjoyed the prestige, not to mention the physical pleasures of sex, another perk. But his musical talents, business acumen, intellect and those threads of morality were distinctive. They keep him safe. He held them sacred—each impressive ability. True, the necessity for blood made him a killer, even though most of his victims were killers themselves.

Draven turned on his back hoping to lessen the throbbing agony between his legs. It didn't. *Stop this. Stop thinking. Take it like the man you profess to be.* He couldn't. Curled again on his side, he buried his face in the pillow. His body shook as his vampiric senses dulled. And like many a broken man, he wept. Each strangled sob stuck in his throat.

Chapter 9

Headaches

Mary Kendrick waited until seven a.m. knowing she had a decision to make. A: ignore the shooting pains in her head or B: barge in on her daughter and tell Lukas what she sensed. She chose B, threw on some clothes and hailed a taxi. Not one to visit without calling first, she kissed Martine's cheek as she entered the kitchen in Lukas Malone's brownstone. Although the ache that felt like someone was crushing her skull had dulled some, pounding in her temples flared in intervals reminding Mary why she had chosen plan B on a windy November morning.

Wrapped in a hug by Lukas, he whispered, "Are you okay?"

Mary smiled, appreciated the strong arms holding her up, sensing nothing but concern in the unique man her daughter loved. Still arguing with herself, she pulled away with the tepid remark, "I see you and Martine still haven't changed a thing." *So what if the brownstone looks just the way Michael had kept it?* Small talk wouldn't cut it, so she sat down in the kitchen, blew out a sharp breath. The pounding in her temples flared again and putting both elbows on the table, she reached up for another soothing rub.

"I like everything just the way it is, Mare, and so

does Lu," Martine answered out loud. Still in purple scrubs after a twelve-hour ER night shift at St. Francis Hospital, her daughter looked healthier than she had in a long time.

Blessed be, Mary thought, *and their love for each other is so deep that it radiates though their auras.*

Martine eyed her with a narrow glare. "So you just stopped by to be nosy at seven thirty in the morning?"

"Well, I waited until you got home," she stated with a shrug. Taking the cup of coffee offered by Lukas, she added a little milk, stirring counterclockwise before dragging the silver teaspoon through the dark liquid to create a pentagram. She took a much-needed sip. "I didn't sleep last night. And I've still got a first-class headache. Something's wrong."

Martine put down her coffee cup. "I don't sense anything weird."

And here's the issue. "You wouldn't. He didn't drink from you."

"Wait. What?" Lukas whispered. His shocked expression snagged her and didn't let go. His eyes, as deep-blue as lapis lazuli, wasn't the only feature that branded him a stunning man. Lukas's curly blond hair appeared rippled, worn long and tied back, yet full enough to frame a dimpled face even when he didn't smile.

Martine leaned into her. "Mom, who are you... Oh my God, is this about Draven? Jeez, he drank from you!"

"Many years ago. But something's *really* wrong with him."

Her daughter started to speak again, but Lukas's hand shot over hers. "Something has totally shaken you, Mary. Say what you sense. You have to tell me."

She looked away as the pounding moved to the top of her head. "Don't go to the Georgian Council with this, Lukas. This doesn't involve anyone but us."

"Yet," her daughter whispered, trying to grab it all from her mind, which wouldn't happen.

"Okay. Yet," she muttered before grinding her teeth. "It's not like he reached out to me. And I don't make it a habit to dream about vampires, either. Lukas, have you seen him?"

"Not for a few weeks," Lukas answered, "but he knows where to find me if he needs me."

"What about Guardians? Do they watch him?"

Lukas swallowed a mouthful of coffee before saying, "Not so much. Since the last event, things have been quiet."

"Maybe too quiet." She set the mug down and folded her arms on the table just in time for her temples to throb again. "I'm telling you, something's wrong with him. Sharon felt it as well."

"Sharon?" came from Martine and Lukas at the same time.

Now both of them were staring at her! Rarely did Mary roll her eyes, but it fit so perfectly. "It was twenty years ago for Sharon. Over forty years ago for me. Sharon called in the middle of the night with the same kind of banging headache I had and continue to have." Looking only at Lukas, she added, "Let's go to his club. Take a stake, just in case."

"What? Lu! No." Martine gripped his arm. "What if he's crazed or something. I don't want my mother—"

Mary clicked her tongue and huffed, "He's not crazed, Martine. If that's why my head aches and my spine tingles, I'd have come for Lukas in the middle of the night!" Pausing, she blew out a breath. "This is... different."

"How," Lukas asked, all business with a serious glare.

"Something's really off with him. Definitely not the Draven I know. Like he's reaching out for only God knows what. Even back then, I was never in his head and so connected."

"Reaching out how," he asked.

Her temples twanged again. "I can't see, but we have to go to him. I mean, it's not the same type of connection I had with your father, when he fought that army of Hell-beasts and we kept you safe."

"I was a kid in mortal danger, Mary," Lukas stated as he leaned back and crossed his arms. But his full lips were turned down and his jaw kept working in a tense way.

She held his gaze. "This is different. Let's go."

"I'm going, too," Martine said.

"No!" they both said at the same time.

Shaking his head, Lukas said, "I want you nowhere near him, M."

"Yeah, neither do I," Mary added. The next twinge came with a hiss, and her sixth sense went into Morse Code mode as if it could signal that damn vampire's distress.

Three door chimes sounded, and Lukas touched her daughter's shoulder just as she started to rise. "Sit. Drink your coffee. The Guardian will come to us if the visitor is important." And that he did, saying someone needed to speak with him right away. Lukas shot out of the chair and left the kitchen.

Her daughter eyed her. "Mom, what's wrong?"

"He's here about Draven. I sense it." Her stomach knotted. The next head pain came sharp and stayed that way.

"This shouldn't be happening. You don't love him, Mare," her daughter stated, using her name in an affectionate way.

"Of course not. Martine, I was young, head-strong, and infatuated."

"But once bitten, always connected, right? Isn't that what Michael says?"

"Something like that." She gave a nod, nervously rubbing her hands together, which were like ice. When Lukas came back in, he simply said, "Let's go."

"Why?" Martine asked.

"That was Donovan, the bouncer at *Destiny*. There is a concern. Mary?" he said, holding her arm as she stood. "You are to eat a good breakfast, M, and then go up to bed. We'll be fine. I'll fill you in later."

"No! No way. I don't want my mother—"

"This is not for you to worry about," Lukas answered. "This is what I do, what I'm here for. We'll check on Draven and if something needs to be done, I'll do it."

Her daughter's jaw dropped. "Oh my God! Don't stake him, Lu! Only a month ago, he carried you through that portal and home, back to me."

"I'm very aware," he replied in a gentle tone. "Whatever's wrong, I'll help if I can."

Her daughter was already out of the chair and in Lukas's arms, the tender kiss to her cheek ripe with emotion. It warms a mother's heart to see her daughter happy and healthy again. Mary sensed pure devotion between the two of them. *May it always be so and blessed be*, she thought. Martine's hug from behind made her smile.

"Ready," Lukas asked.

"As I'll ever be," Mary replied.

"I'll have a stake on me. But I swear, I won't destroy him unless it's necessary."

"I know." Reading her daughter, Mary replied, "Of course, I'll be careful. Do as he says. Eat and go to bed."

Martine shrugged. "I will. I promise."

Empty words, Mary thought, *because she won't rest until she hears from Lukas that everything's all right, and I know it sure as hell isn't. Paranormal threats don't have a time schedule. And evil never takes a holiday.* If that's what this was, then her daughter had to accept that only a mystical warrior could stop it. *That vampire could be dust and bits of bone within the hour.* With the same enhanced skills as his father, Lukas would destroy Draven—just like any other demonic threat to humanity.

Even though Martine had powerful witchy skills, Mary willed her a little strength. They were closer than most mothers and daughters. And a mother always had something extra she could share.

Even if said mother had a rip-roaring, mind-bending headache.

Chapter 10

Found

The November sun shone bright on a cloudless morning as the black SUV maneuvered through morning traffic. Lukas said nothing to Mary, but she sensed his apprehension, which made things more complicated. *Draven is a vampire. He may have the ability to act morally, but a vampire is a vampire. He can be clever, devious.*

The SUV pulled up to the curb, and neither of them waited for the Guardian to come around and open the back door. Then Mary eyed the huge, bald man holding paper shopping bags and pacing in front of *Destiny*'s door. Worry came off him in truck loads. She entered a hallway that used to have drab walls with chipped plaster. Well, it didn't look skeevy like it did in the 70s. Small security lights lit the bejeweled walls. She sensed more changes to a place long ago forgotten.

"Did you get exactly what I requested, Donovan," Lukas asked the worry wart.

"Yes, sir," the bull of a man replied.

He led them down a long flight of stairs, turned left into a wide black hallway with four unisex bathrooms kitted out with floor to ceiling mirrors before entering a very neat and masculine office. She scanned what had once been dark, dirty, and dusty before fixating on blood smears that started at a walk-in vault and ended at an impressive wooden desk with a thick slab of glass on top, an all-in-one computer and a land-line business phone. This bore no resemblance to the underground space she had frequented over forty years ago. Not one bit.

"I found him over here," Donovan said to Lukas, "I think he got himself inside." The chin-jerk indicated a door behind the desk where more smears of blood could be seen.

"Did you let him feed from you?"

"Oh no. Never, sir. He… he took a few mouthfuls of blood from a… a minion, but that's all. I swear."

"Thanks. We'll take it from here."

"Yes, sir. Anything else I can help with?"

"No. Go do your guard thing and don't let anyone into the club," Lukas replied.

Donovan placed the shopping bags on the desk, closed the office door behind him. Lukas crouched by the long smear splotched with gunk, rolled a bit of the grime between his fingers and took a deep sniff. When he stood and stared at the vault, a tight expression was on his face.

"You sense something, don't you," she whispered.

"Yeah. I sense something all right," he replied while looping his fingers through the bag handles.

She followed him into Draven's lair beneath the city. And what a lair it was! Dirty cement floors and cobwebbed beams had been transformed into a clean and modern everything! Recessed lights reflected off a black lacquer dining room set and a matching hutch with etched glass doors and backlit to boot. The displayed chinaware rimmed in yellow gold had a delicate floral pattern set against a crème-colored base. Hell yeah, she looked around!

At the far end, a comfortable living room with a dusty-gray, long sofa could be seen, along with a huge, big-screen for movie time. Wall-to-wall carpet the color of charcoal felt thick and cushy under her loafers. To her right, a galley kitchen with top-of-the-line, light-gray cabinets and black granite counters, as if vampires needed an area to prepare healthy meals. The open expanse to the left had been sectioned off into three rooms. Everything said excess and expensive.

"Oh Christ," she heard Lukas hiss.

Mary's sixth sense led her to the first open door. The master bedroom's décor looked masculine, stylish with a classy ebony dresser. She'd never seen that type of muted-gray paisley print on an upholstered chair before, simply stunning to her artistic eye. One entire wall was a closet, the other three were painted light-gray. At the side of the king-size bed with an ebony headboard, a classic ensuite tiled in crème could be seen.

Her eyes narrowed, drawn to what she assumed to be a trail of blood on the light-gray carpet, further evidence that something out-of-the-ordinary had happened—and curled on his side, Draven was on the bed. "What the hell did this to him?" she whispered, shrugging out of her coat, and draping it over the bed's footboard.

Lukas placed the shopping bags on the dresser next to the huge bed. "He'll be disoriented when he senses an intrusion. You'd better step back to the door."

It was a good ten, twelve feet away! "Like hell. All the bloody parts of him still look fresh, but I sensed something wrong hours ago! It was the middle of the night, damn it!"

"He wreaks of blood, dirt, and other things that aren't from the human world."

"Did he go back to the Second Realm? Did the sorcerers find out——"

"No. I know that scent. This is different. It has to be from the Third Realm."

"The vampires attacked him," she barely whispered clutching her neck.

"No. There's only one strong scent on him. I'm sure it belongs to an incredibly powerful sire."

Her heart lurched. "Who? Who the hell is that powerful?"

"My guess is the oldest existing vampire in Georgian records. It disappeared when the portals closed in two-thousand-five."

Her hand slid to her chest. "But Draven is strong."

"This vampire is stronger. It's a sire."

Unable to digest that, she went with what she sensed. "He crawled to the bed."

"Yeah. Leaving a blood-trail behind."

Lukas pulled his cell phone out of the back pocket of his blue jeans and took at least a dozen pictures of the messed-up vampire, some close ups from head to toe. Draven's dapper suit was shredded at knees and elbows, caked with blood and putrid smelly stuff.

"I'll get something to clean his face."

"No. Find a glass in the kitchen first. He needs blood."

"But if he wakes up——"

"I'm at full strength. He isn't," Lukas replied.

She hurried to the galley kitchen, too on edge to search the cabinets, and came back with a juice glass that was on the counter next to the sink.

Lukas looked at it, grinned with a drawn out, "Okay. So, we start small."

Carefully, she peeled the plastic lid off the container and immediately sensed it animal blood. Slowly, she filled the glass.

"Thanks. Now I want you in the other room, Mary, just in case."

"Like hell. I am not leaving."

He groaned a low, "I knew you'd say that. Then go stand by the door."

"I'll stand right here."

"And I always wondered where M gets her stubborn from," he said with a shake of his head. "If my father told you to stand by the door, you would immediately comply."

"Guess again," she said handing him the glass with animal blood.

Lukas turned Draven on his back and cupped the vampire's bleeding head in support before bringing the glass to his lips. As Draven's mouth fell opened, Lukas filled it. Some dribbled out, but the pillowcase already looked stained with blood. "Come on, help me out here. Swallow and drink, vampire," he said in a very clear, utterly gentle tone.

This time, Mary saw Draven's throat work, swallowing one mouthful after the other, until the juice glass emptied. She filled it again, handed it back to Lukas.

"Now you must go stand at the door, Mary. It's an order," he said in a much different tone. He sounded so much like his father that she immediately complied.

After the second glass emptied, Draven's eyelids shot wide. His warm-brown pupils turned an odd shade of yellow. His upper lip curled back exposing long, white fangs. Having never seen the transformation take place, it made Mary's scalp tingle and her heart race. The beast-within completely distorted Draven's utterly handsome face, morphed it into something sinister. She had to wonder which was real: his attractive features or this terrifying mask.

Lukas rested Draven's head on the pillow. He reached for the container of animal blood and then sat as close as possible. "Hide yourself, beast-within, or I will drop this and then shove a stake through your unbeating heart. Do it!"

A gurgled growl came with a leer of disgust, enough to make her shiver. A clawed hand raised with a distinct tremor and then dropped back to the bed. But the odd-yellow eyes remained defiant, so did the next gurgled growl.

Lukas's usual, friendly expression hardened in a way Mary never imagined it could. One hand held the container over the carpet while the other had Draven by the throat, pulling him up and eye-to-eye. "You defy me, beast-within? You dare to remain when I command you away. You'll go insane without this blood."

The beast-within looked ready to strike, but Lukas yanked it by the throat, lifting it higher with a shake. Those amber slits narrowed again with a sneer and a growl that sounded like a cornered animal's. Then the container hit the carpet, splashing blood all over the place.

Lukas suddenly had a wooden stake in his left hand—the tip aimed directly at Draven's unbeating heart. "Do it, vampire," he said calm and composed, "Control the metamorphosis. Force the beast-within back down as deep as you can."

What a shocker! She leaned against the threshold thinking, *such strength, such a lack of fear facing something so terrifying. You'd never know this ability existed in him.* Less muscular than his father, Lukas didn't have shoulders like a football player, looking lean but fit. He had an open, honest face with soft features. *Heads turn when he walks into a room. Those large, royal-blues capture your attention,* she thought, *and, boy, he sure as hell has Draven's full attention right now.*

Draven's eyes flickered natural-unnatural before staying their usual warm-brown. No sinister leers, just a groan close to a whimper sounded. Lukas eased him down until his head met the bloody pillow. "Damn it, vampire, I'm here to help," he whispered with a slow shake of his head, slipping the pointy wood back inside his leather bomber jacket.

"Leave me," Draven whispered, his voice gravelly and nowhere near the charming baritone—that hinted an exquisite European accent, that rumbled through his chest—that made you hope he'd keep talking.

"Like hell. We had a heart-to-no-heart last month, remember? I swore to be here when you need me." After a chuckle, he added, "Look what you made me do. A whole container of cow's blood soaking your Berber carpet." Then holding out his left hand, said, "Mary? No glass this time." She stepped around the splattered blood to pry open another plastic container before handing it to him.

Lukas's arm supported Draven's broad shoulders, and as he drank, added, "You're a literal bloody mess. The pillow is soaked, the bedspread is good for shit now. Then there's this pricey Brioni suit. It's like totally ruined. You either crawled or dragged yourself how many miles? Christ. For a vampire who never has a single black hair out of place, this tangled mop is a mortal sin against fashion. And in case you ever try to deny this, I took pictures… and I have a witness."

Draven's bloodshot eyes slid to her. Still shocked by that horrific transformation, she managed to straighten her shoulders and give a normal nod. Only after his lids drifted down did she breathe easier, taking the empty container from Lukas.

"Put the last one in the fridge for later." Then Lukas looked at her. "He needs stitches."

"He's a vampire. Don't they self-heal?"

"Yeah, but just like a living person, wounds from a different dimension don't close on their own. I can't call my personal physician. Doc Baker would have to report it to Deepa and the Georgian Council. Until we know everything, we shouldn't involve them. I think we need Martine. Christ. I hate for her to see this," he added in a tone ripe with disgust.

"She'll take care of him. I'm sure as a nurse she's seen worse."

"Can she suture a wound?"

"I guess so. And I'm sure she's still awake." Yet Mary felt hesitant. Her daughter would have to touch Draven to address his wounds. Would stitching his head bring the beast-within out again? She'd known Michael all her life and had never seen his face transform! Plus, over forty years ago on the night Draven's fangs sank into her neck, his beast-within hadn't surfaced, either.

"Make sure she brings a suture kit. Let Donovan know she's expected. Maybe go up and wait for her?"

"Sure," Mary replied before taking her coat and

leaving, much too rattled to send a mind-message. Walking the wide, dark hallway to the stairs, her heart lurched again. *All those years ago, months of flirting and then months together full of passion...* She couldn't help but wonder how close to death she had come... every time they were alone together.

****

Texting her daughter was the easy part. Waiting for her to arrive wasn't. Not after what she had just seen. Mary slipped her phone into a pocket and paced in front of the door to the after-hours club. She said nothing to Donovan, who stood right inside watching her like a hawk. Worry and caution were easy grasps from his mind.

The fresh November air felt good, though. Morning foot traffic mostly headed toward Broadway, and yet some odd, tingling sensations crept up her spine. She eyed the block up and down, pretty sure that someone tried to get into her mind. *Is there going to be another friggin' headache to deal with now? Not going to happen, because whoever you are, this is none of your business.* Discreetly sweeping her right palm, she began a specific spell. As pedestrians got the suggestion, everyone crossed to the other side of the street. Then she switched hand positions to a locator spell.

Her eyes lit on an old lady with an olive complexion hovering in the doorway of an empty storefront some three doors down. Close enough to watch, but far enough away to appear like just any other senior citizen taking a resting beat before continuing her morning walk. "Well, what do you know. A dark seer, a genuine rarity these days," she whispered. "Your type usually stays hidden or runs away when detected by good witches." *Not you, though. A brazen, blatant intruder like a nosey old busy-body on a fishing expedition.* Someone sensing something out-of-whack. Someone who uses her gifts for evil, not good.

Why be here? Why on this very block at this very minute? Mary snapped her fingers, and the old lady's head jerked up with a glare.

"Caught you, bitch," she bit out as the dark seer scurried away.

She'd remember that face. Those shifty eyes. Whispering words learned long ago from her mother, Martha, she cast a protection spell around the door to *Destiny*—just in case.

Chapter 11

Found Out

Less than agreeable, not to mention miffed that his expensive carpet had been spoiled by an entire quart of odorous animal blood, Draven watched Lukas place the empty container on his dresser. Every nerve twitched in agony, and he was still thirsty—even if it was only bland cow. Not about to offer a humble, 'Thank you for feeding me because I'm too weak to feed myself,' he wanted to be left alone. After a good sulk and a few muttered curses, he'd take care of the timeless need, one way or another. He could summon a minion he didn't particularly need and drain him or her efficiently, quick.

"Retrieve my cell phone from the desk, then leave," he rasped.

"No. You're not texting anyone to rip into a vein," the brat stated as if he was in charge.

"Has making love to a witch given you mind-reading abilities?"

"Thirst is so easy to sense when you're like… really under the weather."

"I could have added 'little boy,' you realize." That would have worked.

"Shut the fuck up. Christ, your demon side has one hell of a leer. Kudos to you for learning how to control the transformation the way my father could."

"I doubt you've seen anything like it before. Another tool for your toolbox," he rasped, hoping to piss him off enough to leave. Or retrieve his cell phone.

"I saw Dad's beast-within once. It was uglier than yours. What the fuck did you get yourself into? This screams of Herodotus, through and through. That's who I smell on you, isn't it? I don't see any slashed veins, so I'm guessing your balls are swollen like navel oranges."

He narrowed his eyes thinking, *they're more like grapefruits,* but replied, "Why ever would you say such a thing?" He moved his hips and agony knifed through his groin.

"Well, something down there hurts so much that you had to crawl... there's that. Then there's the Georgian files on sires we don't sense in our world anymore. Yeah. I've studied Herodotus. A particularly interesting read. He modeled his war career after dead Roman generals. You did something really choice to piss him off. He probably ended the beat-down with a kick that makes a man sees stars. Way back when, it was a Roman general's preferred punishment for disobedient recruits. They'd pee blood for weeks. And forget about getting it up and on. Even the slightest twinge is described as excruciating agony. You're fully out of commission, in every sense of the word. No walking, no hunting for a quick drink, and no sex. An ice-pack might help."

"Know it all," he groused. "Bring my phone and then leave me."

"I already said no. As for leaving, I don't think so. Your brother in blood would never forgive me—with you so messed up."

"You will not tell your father about this," he ordered.

"I do as I please, and if I think he should know, I'll tell him."

"What the hell were you thinking when you decided to bring Mary," he hissed. "And stop undressing me." His shredded suit jacket and shirt were already in a pile by the door. So were his shoes and socks.

"Wow. Look at these bruises on your chest. I'd say two or three broken ribs, and every layer of skin is ripped off both elbows and hands and, I assume…"

When his leather belt unbuckled, he growled a threatening, "Don't you dare." But the suit trousers came off, joining the pile of ruined clothes by the door.

Lukas winced with a whispered, "Ouch. Shit that has to hurt like hell." A thick, black silk quilt from the foot of the bed quickly came up to his waist. "Yep. Both knees, too, but Mary isn't going to see you naked. Martine won't, either. The old sire really did some damage down there. And you've got a fuck-load of contusions on your legs and chest."

"I am aware," he grumbled. "How did you know to come?"

"Mary sensed something. So did her friend Sharon. Both of them had bitchin' headaches You really get around—taking a nip here, a sip there."

"Those liaisons ended decades ago. It shouldn't be possible to sense me now."

"Thank your lucky stars they did. I can just imagine how many other unsuspecting women… I'm guessing more than a few already in assisted living places… woke up with headaches in the middle of the night, but don't know why. Mary saved your undead ass."

"That's how you knew to come." He scoffed, still thirsty and weak, still not convinced that somehow he had connected to two lovers from so long ago. Sharon had been a quick fling. But Mary, well, that affair stayed between them.

"Yeah. And then Donovan showed up on my doorstep."

"Pity. He's had a good ten-year run as my bouncer. I'll have to kill him now." When Lukas chuckled, he added, "Do not insult me with a laugh. It is uncalled for."

"You really are an arrogant bastard, aren't you, vampire? No one is killing anyone. Even though Donovan works for the likes of you, the man has a good soul. Might even go to church on Sundays."

He mustered a smirk. "And if I pull up his left sleeve will I find a certain tattoo?"

The slow shrug was another insult. "By that, you mean a dragon in an indigo circle with a sword identifying him a Georgian? I couldn't say."

"You're a clever bastard, little—"

Lukas's hand instantly clamped Draven's jaw. "Do not add the 'boy' word again or I'll crush these bones with one squeeze. Behave yourself. I mean it."

Hearing a soft, "Oh, Jeez," they both looked at Martine and Mary throwing their coats over the chair before coming to the other side of his bed. Mary clicked her tongue, placing her phone on the nightstand, but when the suture kit came out of a tote bag, Draven winced.

"Get a warm wet towel and a dry one for the back of his head, Mom. Lu, let's turn him on his side. Or better yet, can you hold onto him? Keep his head still?"

"This is unnecessary," he huffed as Lukas pulled him up. Very woozy and weak, his vision flickered. His chin hit Lukas's shoulder, obviously faced away from his neck.

Draven couldn't stop the moan. His long hair parted and a warm wet towel swabbed the gash on the back of his head—before he passed out.

Chapter 12

Musings

With Draven's scalp sutured, Mary washed streaks of blood off his face and then, the torn-up palms so Matine could start on them. *These talented hands aren't playing a Chopin ballade anytime soon*, she thought. All the lights were on, and as she aimed her phone with the magnifying light app on, her daughter picked bits of gravel out of each palm with a tweezer, disinfecting them before swaddling them in gauze. The pillow and pillowcase stained with blood had been thrown into a plastic garbage bag placed at the office door with the rest of Draven's clothes. A fresh pillow from the other side of the massive bed had a plush black towel over it now and cradled his head. Yet Draven kept moaning, not fully conscious.

With that task accomplished both women's narrow, knowing eyes lit on the quilt hugging Draven's trim waist. "Why is he still in loads of pain," she asked. Lukas didn't say a word, leaning against the dresser with his arms folded across his chest.

Martine's dark eyes flared. "It's not just his knees, is it, Lu? Be honest with us. Mare doesn't want to read you. Neither do I, so just tell us."

Staring at the carpet, Lukas replied, "The cruel sonofabitch booted him in the balls."

Seconds ticked on before Martine said, "We can put an icepack—"

Lukas cut her off with a quick, "He'll go ballistic."

"No worries. I'm a nurse, I've seen—"

"No, M. Let it be." After a sigh, he added, "I need him to tell me what the hell precluded this beating."

"Well, he can be arrogant and sarcastic," Mary offered.

"They're vampires. They're all arrogant. No. He was purposely humiliated and taught a lesson. Whatever went down between them is crucial."

"What about his legs? Any open cuts," her daughter asked.

"Check out his knees," Lukas replied.

Gingerly, Mary pulled up the quilt to expose his shredded kneecaps. "Oh Jeez," Martine said with a shake of her head. "All that crud has to come out. Mare, hold the phone close so I have better light?"

The sight of her daughter using that tweezer again to pick out bits of rocks and dirt deeply imbedded in raw, tender flesh made Mary's stomach turn. She handed the phone to Lukas and walked out of the bedroom holding the bloodied towel used on his scalp between two pinched fingers.

Heading to the kitchen sink, Mary really didn't want to go back into the bedroom. And she had to wonder when and *if* Draven would say what caused all this damage to him. She glanced around, thinking the kitchen a gourmet's delight, with a counter full of every cooking gadget known to man. A standing mixer the color of a Hibiscus, a state-of-the-art blender, even a stainless-steel stove complete with a grill in the middle. A coffee station to die for and an old-fashioned, ornate toaster, all of it useless because vampires don't eat. She scoffed as the crème-colored porcelain sink filled and began to soak the towel.

Martine walked in with her phone. "It dinged and you have an unread text."

"Thanks," she replied, drying her hands on a black kitchen towel with a designer logo embroidered into it. "I caught a dark seer snooping around while I waited outside for you."

Her daughter gave a huffy pfft. "You think she knows how this happened to him?"

"I'm sure she senses he's injured, but the old bitch got nothing from me, except wondering when you'd get here."

"Maybe there's always one on the block watching him."

"It's possible."

"And today she hit the lottery," her daughter muttered.

"I put a protection spell on the door."

"Good move, Mare."

"They won't be able to see what's inside no matter how hard they try." Unlocking her phone to read the message, her shoulders straightened.

"What," her daughter said.

"It's Tristan at the gallery. His sister wants to know who a certain vampire named Draven is. Look at the sketch." She handed over her phone, and her daughter sucked in a breath.

"Oh my. Jeez. It's like weird slides up the scale to weirder. And I was so happy settling into a quiet life with the man I love. Lu has to see this."

"He sure as hell does. Draven was dressed like that

when he went to the Second Realm with Michael and Lukas. It's a perfect sketch, exactly what I saw in my mind a month ago."

"So, who is Tristan's sister? How did she get this?"

"Oh, Freya moved to Iceland years ago. Pretty far up north, I think. In early October, she came with Tristan to the healing circle the night they went through the portal together. She always sketches in charcoal and highlights in colored pencil. Of course, I had a vivid mind-picture of the three of them stuck in my head the whole time they were in the Second Realm."

"Freya is like us? Like Tristan?"

She gave a nod. "She comes back to the city twice a year sometimes, to shop and visit family."

"Which is how she ended up in the healing circle during the event."

"Yeah. So why this text with a sketch, just as something happens to Draven?"

"It doesn't make sense, Mom."

"I agree. Go. Show it to Lukas." As Martine left with her phone, Mary gripped the sink and looked at the discolored water. Her hips suddenly hurt, and she had to lean back a bit to get comfortable. Putting a finger in the sink, she swirled it around and opened her mind.

A new event right on the heels of another. This is no coincidence. There's no such thing in the universe. In her world, it was a sign. *Do Georgian physics already know it's a here-we-go-again?* Michael and Lukas would be involved, and someone who stood in the shadows. She pulled her finger out of the water. At least her head didn't throb anymore. Now, she felt just plain tired from lack of sleep. "What the hell are you caught up in? Did you trigger another event," she whispered as she washed her hands with a good amount of dish soap and hot water. Draven knew how to shield his thoughts and if still unconscious, reading him was out of the question. *There's only one other way to find out if he started this or not,* she thought as she dried them.

When Mary entered the bedroom, Draven's eyes were half-open. She walked over, leaned down and slapped his face. Martine sucked in a breath, but Lukas didn't. Nor did he try to restrain her. "What did you do, you bastard?"

He didn't answer, but those warm-brown eyes brimmed with blood tears just itching to fall. Lukas touched her arm, a gentle pressure—just pulling her back far enough.

In an even tone, not at all surprised, Lukas stated, "I'm placing Guardians in your office and in the club. They'll be your best buds until I know more. Sustenance will be stocked in the fridge. And no. You can't have your cell phone." He turned to her, and his expression softened. "Martine needs sleep, while we question this individual, Mare."

"What individual," Draven asked in a flat tone.

"You and I will talk later. Concentrate on self-healing and get that swelling down. I suggest lying still. And keep your thoughts as pure as a saint's." With that said, Lukas ushered Martine out of the room, motioning her to follow. Then he turned back. "The vault is locked, I presume?"

"Yes it is locked. I am not an idiot," Draven replied in a thready voice.

"That's still to be determined. Don't give my men any problems you'll regret. Later," he said before leading them out.

Once in the office, Martine grabbed his arm. "What does all this mean, Lu, especially the sketch?"

"Nothing to lose sleep over. Mary and I will take it from here."

She and Martine walked behind him through the wide hallway, up the stairs, and then down the bejeweled hall to the front door. Donovan stood at attention until they were on the street. But Lukas stopped and turned to him. "Guardians will be arriving soon. I assume you know what they are."

Dipping his bald head, Donovan replied, "Yes, sir."

"Draven has been cared for. He cannot have his phone, so no calls or texts to it."

"I understand. Should we close the club down, like when we have a private party?"

"Yeah. That works for now. Only Guardians go in, Donovan. No minions. No one else. Let whoever is in charge of things know as well."

As Lukas eyed the bald bouncer, Mary planted the next question in his mind. "Do you carry?"

"Yes, sir. I'm licensed and ex-military. One never knows, right?"

Thank God, she thought as Lukas replied, "Totally. Who's your relief during the day?"

"No one, sir. My lord is very secure in his home during the day."

"Does he have a secret way of escaping his, uh, home?"

"There's a tunnel at the other end of the club that leads to the next block."

"Show it to the Guardians. Have one of them relieve you. Then go home and get some sleep. You'll be needed after sunset. And thanks for coming to me this morning."

"Yes, sir. Thank you, as well, for saving my lord."

Lukas gave an easy grin as he said, "Okay, ladies. Let's go home."

Once settled in the back of the SUV, Mary let out a throaty chuckle. "My lord? Draven must love being called that. I just can't believe it."

"*I* can't believe you slapped him, Mom," her daughter said. "Did you see the look on his face?"

"I did. And it was the right one. Right, Lukas?" she replied.

Martine's eyebrows shot up. "Want to clue me in… Either of you?"

"Mary," Lukas said.

"Oh, no. You're the wordsmith here," she answered.

His dimples deepened. "It's a visual clue. Not the non-verbal kind you and your mother use. His response wasn't anger. It was hurt. He's being forced into something that goes against his somewhat moral nature."

"I have to say, I really didn't know which way he would go," Mary stated. "Do you think he'll talk?"

"I'll get it out of him, one way or another. In the meantime, this Tristan person must be questioned as soon as possible. While the love of my life sleeps and dreams about me," he whispered to her daughter. "Once we learn why he sent this sketch, fact A should lead to fact B, which will then lead to C. Your mom and I will sift through everything, then I'll join you at home and upstairs," adding in a whisper, "in bed."

"Wow," Martine said, "I just love the way you lay it all out."

"I have many talents," he replied, giving her daughter a quick kiss on the cheek.

Seeing their fingers thread together warmed Mary's

89

heart. "I hate to interrupt you two lovebirds, but where do you want to do this, Lukas?"

"We'll drop her off and then head to Kendrick House. Is that okay?"

"You read my mind."

"Well, more likely you put it in there for me to say— again."

"He's got your number, Mare," her daughter said with a laugh in her voice.

"Sometimes you're a little too smart for my liking, Lukas."

"But you love me anyway," he replied.

Mary Kendrick most certainly did.

Chapter 13

Inquisitive

Luna had not rested well, which was odd for a vampire. There were no such things as dreams, yet she found herself floating to consciousness often as if somehow nudged awake. She rose before the four p.m. sunset and quickly dressed in a blue turtleneck and jeans. Hopefully, everything necessary for her initiation into all-things-modern was ready and waiting.

Against the wall that separated the kitchen from the main room, Rune had set up a table with the new laptop. Once he showed her how to maneuver the mouse, Luna brimmed with unimaginable curiosity and deep satisfaction opening tab after tab, typing questions into the query box that brought her to different websites. Full of anticipations about tonight, she buried memories of Henri, vowing to learn all she could at record speed. After Rune explained the cell phone, she gave a breathy, "What an incredible invention!" Her first text to Freya confirmed her friend's arrival later.

All this new technology was ingenious. It would take months of nightly reading to catch and understand everything. Why had none of this interested her before? It truly remained a mystery. *As a living woman, I must have been intelligent, perhaps formally schooled in reading and mathematics.* No. She had chosen to spend over eight decades enamored with memories of Henri. In the process, had she sold her intelligence short? The answer was a shameful yes.

Henri had been the center of her world, had provided a secure, secluded home in the French countryside. For night trips to Paris to view the marvelous Eifel Tower, the Opera House or the Louvre, he always reserved specific hotel rooms with shutters and blackout curtains. And he taught her how to be remarkably duplicitous around humans and other vampires. *Never were we questioned, simply appearing as lovers who preferred the solitude of each other's company.* Their undead "life" together had been perfect. "What a fool, what a fool, what a fool," she sighed, surfing the web like a pro. She couldn't wait for Freya to get here.

****

Many hours passed with Freya assisting Luna in assuaging curiosity. Glancing over at her friend, Luna continued to frown.

"Don't be so hard on yourself. You loved him. You followed him. It's understandable."

"No, Freya, it is not. I should have paid attention to the world around us. Henri did. That is how I came to be in this silent seaport. He researched. He planned, so I would be safe."

"Look," Freya said, "this is New York City, where my brother lives."

Her mouth dropped open as her eyes went wide studying the pictures. "It is so different, so vibrant this Times Square. Has he contacted you yet?"

"I hope to hear from him soon, you know, the time difference."

She sadly grinned. "At least this is one thing I understand."

"You understand much more than you think, Luna."

"I am fascinated by these pictures."

Freya leaned back in her chair. "Then perhaps you should read up on the city, just in case anything comes of the sketch I sent to Tristan."

"Why? New York is an ocean away."

"You could take a night flight."

Horror crossed Luna's face. "No. No. Never. I... I wouldn't know how. I will not be contained for hours in something that... that flies!" Glancing at her friend, Luna caught the covered yawn. "Oh. It's very late for you."

"Yes, it is. Not keeping my normal hours," Freya replied. "Plus, I have to open early tomorrow because the seaport will be flooded with tourists to see the northern lights. Some type of South American cultural group. I hope they brought heavy coats as well as gloves and hats. I might put a few more sweaters and winter gear out."

"Those hand-made by Icelanders," she said, glued to the webpage. "Perhaps raise the price since that type of souvenirs will be in demand. Add on five percent, then you can purchase more items from our local crafts people. That will help grow our economy."

Freya smiled. "You are certainly a quick study of modern-day capitalism. Yet you've seen so much in over a century. It's hard to believe you've lived through so much history."

"Obviously oblivious," she replied, embarrassed by the lack of current knowledge, but thoroughly enthralled with this Internet system. When Freya stood, Luna had to drag her eyes away from the screen. "I shall walk you out."

"No, stay and learn. I can see myself out," Freya replied.

"Will you come again tomorrow night?" Having a friend to talk to compelled the request.

"If you'll have me."

"Come for dinner. Let's say six. Rune will prepare a wonderful reindeer stew. The meat is fresh."

"You have hunted?"

"Yes. But this poor creature had a twisted leg. I believe I put her out of her misery."

Henri had taught her well. As cruel as he could be draining a murderer, he had been equally respectful of wildlife. She often butchered the fallen animal she fed from, leaving its meat wrapped on doorsteps of hungry villagers. Fresh, free protein was like manna from Heaven for the not-so-fortunate.

"That would be lovely. Oh. Rune can take me home tonight? I forgot he picked me up."

"Certainly." Luna walked through the kitchen and stood in the doorway to the office waiting until Rune looked up from paperwork. "Freya needs to leave."

"Of course, madame," he said as he stood.

"Can you prepare a reindeer stew for tomorrow night? I have invited Freya for dinner." He replied in the affirmative as she moved to let him pass. "You will take a good quantity of meat home for your own freezer as well."

Approaching the front door, Freya was already bundled up for the cold.

"Thank you, madame. I'll be back to prepare for tomorrow's dinner," he said as he keyed the alarm pad. The system replied in a female voice that the alarm was off.

Anxious to get back to her laptop and after the pleasantries of good nights, she closed the door and keyed in the security code. No matter how isolated her home, she knew the importance of safety. Henri had taught her that as well.

****

Mary welcomed her employee into Kendrick House, her brownstone blocks away from her daughter and Lukas. It had been in the family for four generations, decorated with class in an eclectic style that complimented her appreciation of art. In a traditional setting with the couch and coffee table facing the fireplace, burgundy, brocade armchairs stood at each side of the hand-carved mantel, as if to form a half-moon. A quaint chandelier lit the room as well as two Tiffany lamps. Lukas stood by the mantel. Tristan stood by the couch, shifting foot to foot as Mary sat in an armchair. After the men shook hands, the tall, blond and blue-eyed warlock studied Lukas.

She sensed that out of respect, Tristan made no attempt to read him. "Let me start out saying, no, there's no use denying the fact that Lukas was one of the three individuals we protected in the healing circle when your sister visited, Tristan." As leader of the healing circle, Mary used the formal expression of gratitude, saying, "Thank you for your assistance, young warlock, blessed be."

Tristan whispered, "Blessed be," his focus resting only on her. "I'm glad the event came to a successful conclusion. I, uh, want to apologize if sending Freya's sketch of the vampire and asking where to find him is off limits, Mary."

"No. Not at all. But I need to know why your sister is interested in him." *Okay. That was a bit too direct.* But Tristan was an honest man, an intelligent user of good magic like every witch or warlock she associated with.

"Her, uh, request is for a friend."

"What friend," Lukas asked.

"My sister didn't say. Just that Draven looks very much like someone she knows."

"So, you're telling me that there's a woman in Iceland asking about a vampire who is like one-hundred-eighty years old. And you know nothing else?" Studying Mary's employee, Lukas's eyes narrowed. "What do you sense?"

"You mean from my sister?"

"Yeah. This request sounds pretty urgent."

"Freya wants an answer yesterday, and she sounded very tired."

"She didn't sound frightened or put off, like something might happen if she didn't get info on him," Lukas stated.

"No, but my sister isn't a night person. She called close to eight-thirty our time." Tristan looked at her. "I stayed at the gallery to get the gala's admission tickets ready for printing." He looked back to Lukas. "I'm an artist as well."

"A very talented one, especially with water colors," she said to agree. "And gala preparations are always a nightmare."

Lukas nodded. "So it puts her call well after midnight. And that's not her way, correct?"

Tristan shook his head. "Is my sister in some kind of danger? I mean, she said she was asking for a friend."

With Tristan's fear quickly rearing up, Mary stated,

"There's no reason to worry, and don't wrack your brain looking for the connection."

Lukas started to pace between the fireplace and the dining area. "Will you agree to text her right now? It's afternoon in Iceland. I'll give you exact words. I promise. No harm will come to her." Tristan looked worried, the tight swallow visible. "Your heart's racing," Lukas added in a very calm voice.

Tristan's light-blue eyes shot back to Lukas. "I know you're not warlock."

"No. But my mystical senses are really humming right now. Your cooperation may be the critical piece of a puzzle. Ready," he asked with an easy smile.

After blowing out a quick breath, Tristan took out his phone, pressed the text icon and waited.

"Say hello the way you do and then type: I have a question."

They waited until he said, "She says: Hi. The shop's very busy. What do you want to know?"

"Type: About your friend and this vampire. Does she know what he is?"

Again they waited. "Not my story to tell. He just looks like an old boyfriend."

Very old, Mary thought as Lukas said, "Type: Oh, Okay. Mary told me where to find him tonight. If he gets curious, who can I say he looks like."

"She says: Try the name Henry... wait... she spells it with an 'i' not a 'y'."

Lukas's shoulders abruptly straightened, but his face remained friendly and open. "Great. The next text will be a bit lengthy. Here we go: Don't want to poke too much, but what's her name? I don't want to come up short when talking to a vampire. I mean, he'll want to know who's asking. I won't give him your name, just hers."

This wait seemed endless, but Tristan finally stated, "She says: tell him to think about the moon and the letter L. Text me his reaction."

Lukas went over to Tristan. "Text: Okay. Will do. Don't say anything to her until you hear from me. Now end your text the way you normally would. Then please hand me your phone. I'll give it right back."

Tristan waited for the text to *whoosh* before holding it out. Lukas took screen shots of the conversation between brother and sister. Handing it back, he said, "Thanks for your help."

"You need to swear that my sister is safe."

"I'll send Guardians to have eyes on her. I ask that you say nothing more to her and keep this meeting between us." Lukas extended his hand, and the men shook again.

Walking him to the door, Tristan turned to her. "Please, Mary. I trust you implicitly, but if Freya's in danger, I have to warn her."

"Don't worry. Lukas is a man of his word. He'll make sure she's protected." She paused. "I'll meet you at the gallery in a little while."

"I've got lots to do."

She gave a smile and a nod. "So do I. Hey. Listen. Keep this conversation out of your mind. Dark seers are lurking about. This is not anyone's business but ours."

As Mary closed the door, she hoped Freya really was safe. If anything happened, she'd feel responsible. As she reentered the living room, Lukas slipped his phone into his pocket. "Want to tell me about the dark seer thing, Mare?"

"I forgot you can hear the slightest whisper." She sighed before coming clean. "One was across the street from the club this morning."

"I'll keep an eye out and inform the Guardians."

"You can sense them," she asked, quite shocked.

"Their smell sticks in the back of my throat." Lukas shook his head. "This is moving fast. You're right. It's another event."

"You're certain?" she asked, touching the side of her neck.

"Henri is Draven's Christian name."

"Why am I not shocked? So, he was someone else for what, over a century, before I met him in the nineteen-seventies?"

"I have no idea when he switched to Draven, but his birth name is Henri LeVigne. As a composer in eighteen-forty-seven he ran with some pretty famous artists, many of them still popular today. Anyway, I have to do some research on female vampires."

As he started to leave, she said, "Lukas, wait."

"Sorry, Mare. Lots to do and I should talk to Dad."

She called out, "Your father's in this event. I saw it."

He stopped and turned. "Talk to me, Mary," came with a hell of a lot of concern.

"I sense it. And there's an unknown someone in the shadows who I can't identify. You need to get Draven to talk. He's hiding something important."

Lukas gave a nod and then hurried out.

Mary stood at the open door, saw him talk to the driver before taking off at a run. His speed was incredible, his form like a professional runner. *Why not take the car?* The answer was obvious. "Because he's worried. Because he's faster on foot," she whispered.

Chapter 14

Memories

After the text messages, the sketch, the info Mary shared, Lukas needed to chill before talking to Draven. *Iceland. A woman.* His father being involved meant trouble. The dreaded dark seers sneaking about meant danger. Just let one of those twisted sisters jump out of a doorway to get in his face, and all bets were off. This new event was blowing up fast, spreading like a goddamned virus and taking on a life of its own. Drilling down on Draven couldn't wait. *How do I play it with him?* He'd bet his silver broadsword that the vampire could put it all together.

"Damnit, what the hell is this about," Lukas mumbled in a worried way. The vampire's part in the early October event had been crucial. And although he hated to admit it, he had to honor his father's long, involved history with Draven. They were like carbon copies in the manner of speech, stance, facial expressions—the arrogance he knew how to punch through and get personal with.

As his mind raced, he slowed his pace to blend in with other pedestrians. *The moon and the letter 'L' are significant.* And he sensed more than just a thin moral thread in Draven. The vampire had totally prepared him for those harrowing days in the Second Realm with sound advice and flawless travel documents. Ample coin to purchase necessities, not to mention that vial of something minty to quelch the nausea of portal travel. Draven took out a good many palace guards, too. And although Lukas had raged against the vampire while injured and burning with fever, Draven carried him home to Martine.

That kick in the balls had been brutal. *Wouldn't wish it on your worst enemy. Yet even in utter agony and on the edge of starvation, Draven had control of his beast-within.* To harness such a powerful entity proved to be immensely difficult—never imagined possible. It took stamina, high intelligence, and a deep, driving desire to reject evil born within once sired. His own father, then a powerful vampire, needed Heavenly help in 1890 to dominate his beast-within. *No vampire, other than Dad has ever wrestled it into complete dormancy. Not once, but twice.* No other vampire has ever been given back his very own precious human life, either. When his father eventually told him the full gory story, respect and admiration soared.

Crossing Broadway with the noontime crowd of tourists and business people from all walks of life, Lukas recalled coming face-to-face with his father's beast-within. Just like any other eight-year-old, he had been off-the-charts terrified! It made a lasting impression. Then at age fifteen, he sliced the head off a sire, another one of Cyril's progeny. Through the years, he had tracked and staked many. This morning, being up close and personal with Draven's demon served as a jarring reminder. Vampires kill on a whim. Draven could as well, whether or not he had a moral thread—because he didn't own his soul anymore. No. The Heavenly Grace his father had been given in 1890 to master the beast-within didn't exist for this vampire.

Getting closer to *Destiny*, Lukas sensed no dark seers tailing him. No other outward threats. He had a troubled history with NYC, and he knew these streets as if they were on a dangerous version of the popular board game with get-out-of-jail cards. His little race car token had zoomed pass "Go" again and again. Turning the last corner, he cleared his mind and switched focus, tucking away memories that made him the man he was today.

Passing the Guardian who took over for Donovan, Lukas sped down the hall and jumped the staircase into the club. He nodded at the two Guardians stationed in the office and entered the classy lair. At the foot of the bed, he studied Draven at rest. He sat on the bed, brushed long strands of black hair off a bruised face and placed his hand on a cool cheek. Those warm-brown eyes eased open and instantly filled—again.

"Hello, vampire," Lukas whispered and caught the hard swallow.

Seconds slipped away before Draven said, "I must beg you to stake me now."

And just like that, the game is on, Lukas thought.

****

Even though Draven willed his eyes to clear, they didn't. *He may not look like Michael, but my brother in blood is etched in his demeanor.* He didn't like to be touched, and without asking permission, Lukas used both hands to pull him up, settling him against the ebony headboard without any effort. It did, however, produce a long hiss and a tight wince.

"Now, now, as Dad would say, don't go all dramatic on me," Lukas grumbled.

"I am not kidding."

"Can you stand?"

"I don't know. Haven't tried," he admitted both irate and confused, wanting to be left alone; wanting an end to this maddening battle within that had taken hold. He'd never forget the humiliation of such an excruciating kick. He palmed his face to hide the cluttered emotions he couldn't seem to control.

"Has the swelling gone down any?"

"I have no desire to look."

"Martine stitched your scalp, you know."

"I'm sure you only let her touch me because I was unconscious."

"Totally. So. Tell me why should I stake you."

His hands dropped to his side, but he turned his face away. "I do not have to disclose why. I am a vampire. You are a mystical warrior, whose reason for existence is to destroy soulless creatures like me. I'd much prefer that final death comes from your father's hand, but since he is not here, you will have to do." Irked by the chuckle, he added, "You think I am joking. Or perhaps, crazed. I assure you; I am neither."

"Tell me why Herodotus did it," Lukas asked, all business now.

He didn't answer, couldn't say it was none of Lukas's business because, in fact, seven sires' return to the human world was right up the mystical warrior's alley.

"Did he find out about the other event? Does he know you helped us?"

"*Mon Dieu,* definitely not. I'd already be dust and bits of bone. Not laying here wondering when I will be able to walk without pain again." Even sitting made his testicles scream, and although close to unhinged, he swallowed the pain.

"I never noticed your French accent before. There's more than a hint of it."

"I am in distress. It happens."

"So, what's the certain something you don't want to do?"

He narrowed his eyes thinking, *too perceptive for your own good.* "You are fishing."

Lukas shrugged. "Nope. I'm great at deduction. Mary's slap, or should I say your reaction, told me things."

"Ah, yes, dear Mary. Now you see where your soulmate gets her feistiness from."

"Don't dodge the issue."

"I am insulted that you would think me so devious. *Mon Dieu,*" he huffed again. The chortle came much too quickly, and his response was a glare. "Hand me your stake. I will do it myself."

"Draven—"

"It is in the inside pocket of your jacket. I smell the wood. It's oak." When he reached for it, a steel fist closed around his wrist to easily wrestle it away.

The warrior's expression turned serious, his eyes like sparkling sapphires with no trace of a dimpled grin. "This is so bad that you'd stake yourself? Christ, I'll have to put you on suicide watch. That friggin' sire asked for something. You refused."

Only partially correct. Had I refused, I'd already be in Hell. "Poking your nose where it doesn't belong will not end with me discussing it."

"Herodotus did all this damage. But it's only act one. He threatened something if you don't get him what he wants."

Far too perceptive and, indeed, very good at deduction. Visions of he, the Gatekeeper, an important vampire, being strung up naked and tortured, forced another turn away. "This is not your business."

"Like fucking hell, it isn't. I protect innocents from evil. Herodotus is evil."

"But I am not innocent. Don't try to bicker like your father. You simply come off bratty. Hand me your stake, child."

"Not a child," sounded heated.

So he added, "Still a brat."

"I'm thirty-one, vampire," sounded more heated.

He eyed Michael's son with contempt. "A mystical warrior who cannot stake a vampire."

"Not can't. Won't."

"So you tell yourself," he mumbled.

"What the fuck's the matter with you," Lukas fired back, his face tight, his brow creased. "Since everything I've read on Herodotus points to amoral, I'm certain it's the moral in you that asks for the stake. He wants something that bothers your conscience."

"What you've *read*?" Leering, he laughed, purposely exposed his long fangs. "What a little smart ass you are. I don't have a conscience. I have a demon in me."

"Yeah. A demon you control."

Now *there* was the edge of anger he sought, so he locked to those intelligent eyes and kept inching Lukas toward rage. Then, in a blink of eye, his undead existence would be over. *And all my secrets die with me.* To up the ante, he added, "Here's your chance. Step out of Michael's impressive shadow. Claim recognition as the new Georgian Champion. Add me to your trophy list. Do it. Shove a stake through my unbeating heart. Matter closed. Threat averted."

Lukas narrowed his eyes. "Yeah. Right. Then everything's peachy again."

"Exactly," he said with a snarl, "Just do it!"

"No."

"Then tell your father to come here and do it himself!"

"No."

He scoffed. "You are useless. Get out!"

"What does the moon and the letter L have to do with you?"

And more poking. But if his heart could beat, it would skip a few. "Get out."

"The moon. The letter L. Northern Iceland. I'm guessing a woman. What do they mean to you?"

Like nails drilling into wood, guilt pulsed in his brain. Weak and thirsty, he yelled, "Leave!"

"No. The moon, the letter L, some clueless woman," Lukas said in a sharper tone. "I've already sent Guardians to Husavik. On my order—"

Panic punched as he fired back, "How *dare* you do this! Call them off!"

"If it's vampire, the cunning female will be dust and bone."

His brain twisted with scenes of Luna. Stability and any form of control slipped farther away. "No! *Arrete-les*! It is… it is… *ne te regarde pas!*"

"What's the matter? Did you forget you've been in New York for fifty years?"

Furious, he spit out, "You little bastard. Stop—"

"Who the fuck are you to tell me to stop?" Lukas

pulled out his phone, held it out of his reach. "One text and they begin the hunt. In Husavik. Who should they stake?"

He growled like a cornered dog and struggled to grab it. "You have no reason to hunt her! She is of no concern!"

"Who is she, damn it," Lukas yelled. "Tick-tock, vampire, or the hunt is on."

As hard as he tried to pull it together, he couldn't. His eyes filled and his lips drew tight. "I beg you, put your phone away," he managed to say. His fingertips kept the insulting tears covered. He took a deep breath for no reason at all. The swell of both lungs put pressure on his cracked ribs, adding to his pain.

"Draven, talk to me."

Every vein spasmed. Like an addict, he craved thick, rich human blood. Yet he flatly refused to access the beast-within. He swallowed the sob. "You must not… not hunt her. *Laisse la tranquile. Je vous en prie.* She has no part in this."

"You love her," Lukas said in a soft voice.

"I *loved* her. Luna is hidden. Safe." Her name on his lips awakened an avalanche of memories racing through his brain, edging up his thirst.

"When?"

He licked his parched lips. "Nineteen-thirty-nine," he whispered.

"Why?"

"Iceland was neutral during the war. Luna never took a human life." Didn't *that* just rip the bandage off a gaping wound! Panic peppered defeat to up his primal need. "Michael will remember. He must hide her. Never tell me where. Now stake me."

Lukas gripped his shoulders. "Whoa, whoa, calm down."

But memories have a mind of their own, don't they? Uncontrollable. Unpredictable. Thirst flared like fire in his brain. "*Je t'en supplie.* He knows Luna!"

"How? How does Dad know Luna?"

"Eighteen-eighty-seven. Florence. Tell no one. He must not know she still exists."

"Now you're confusing me. Who's he? Wait," Lukas shook him, coldly added, "What aren't you saying?"

Heated, hungry and horrified... Draven fisted the lapels of Lukas's leather jacket. Just as quickly, Lukas clamped down hard on his wrists. "Stake me! Do it now! If Herodotus drinks from me, he will know!"

"What will he know?"

"Stake me, damn you!"

Jagged gasps of words, some French, some English tumbled out of his mouth. Then a hand had the back of his neck. Cow's blood came to his lips. He swallowed, choked every last drop down, then swiped his lips clean as his shoulders met the headboard. Animal blood didn't pack enough power to heal him, and not in the position to demand the human variety, his senses stayed dull. Focus evaded him, but he heard whispers at the door while his foggy brain teased out disjointed scenes of Luna before he deserted her.

Lukas came back and sat at his side. "Christ, Draven. What did you do? Steal her from Herodotus?"

"I say no more," he mumbled.

"You don't have to."

"You do not understand:"

"I don't have to do that, either."

"You are belligerent, and this is futile. Stake me—right here and now."

Lukas shook his head. "Fucking unbelievable."

"Vampires have existed as long as mankind. We are nature's way of culling the herd."

"People aren't cattle."

"You'll grow old, maybe live another fifty years," he snapped as he fought off lethargy. "I've existed for almost one-hundred-eighty years. Herodotus perhaps a thousand. Do the math."

"Are we going to philosophize about which is the superior being?"

Draven shrugged, closed his eyes. "Stake me, Lukas."

"And we're right back to drama. For the last time, it's a big N-O." A sharp breath punctuated that last vowel.

"Michael must move her. I have one week to comply."

"Comply to what?"

"Tell your father to hide her well. Do not have Guardians hunt her. I have much to do before I return to Herodotus. Unless you stake me now."

Lukas stood. Unlike his father, the son openly wore his emotions. The glaze over those royal-blue eyes filled Draven with more pain, more guilt. He had to turn his face away again.

"Swear that you're not going to do something stupid like rip a piece of wood off the dresser and do yourself in. I want your promise, vampire."

Tough talk didn't matter. It didn't disguise Lukas's concern for him, either. He was an undead thing that should feel nothing, but he grappled with so many damn emotions that he could barely mumble, "I promise."

After scrubbing his face, Lukas left without saying another word. Draven maneuvered through the pain until his head met the pillow. He curled on his side. Michael would honor the ask and then come to the city and end his existence.

Just as you gave me a choice on the first night of undeath, you, my brother in blood, will be here as I accept the stake. Winter. 1847. Huddled bloody and helpless. Alone in the clearing to face morning sun and burst into flames. Outside of Paris, beaten by Cyril. He slammed his eyes shut, but the recall unfolded...

The first drink and drain disgusted him. He, Henri LeVigne, a composer, an accomplished pianist, had been turned into an undead thing. Forced to quench the need, the act itself made him a murderer! Once the beast-within was sated, he turned to his sire and spat in his face. Cyril immediately retaliated with a ferocious beating, leaving him hogtied in the middle of nowhere to bleed out and face the morning sun.

Minutes before dawn, Michael cut him free. Dragged to a deserted barn, Michael buried him under bug infested hay that reeked of stale urine and manure. Then, with a mischievous smirk, he said, "Welcome to Cyril's brutal family. I suppose I'll be whipped for this. It matters not. I've survived worse. You will as well. Thus, you have a choice. Either accept what you are now or walk into the bright morning sun, brother."

With that, he left, and this existence is what I chose. Now, I will meet final death with open arms because I have had enough.

He buried his face in the pillow, unable to stop the bitter sobs as his eyelids grew heavy. Once Michael arrived, he'd be dust and bits of bone. Luna would be safe. Herodotus wouldn't be let loose on humanity.

****

After giving the Guardians specific instructions and burying Draven's phone in the bottom drawer of the huge desk, Lukas walked out with nothing showing on his face. Once the black SUV pulled off the curb with the partition up, he leaned back and palmed his face.

Christ, the vampire is way past stressed out and totally serious about being staked. Yeah. It isn't hard to do this math, either. He had been with Luna for fifty-three years. *That's a hell of a long time to love someone. For a vampire without a soul, that's unbelievable devotion.*

Lukas had always sensed his father's deep love for Alana. He reveled in the deep love he felt for Martine. *How would I feel if I had to turn my back on Martine and walk away to keep her safe?* It would rip his heart out.

He quickly exited the SUV in front of his brownstone. Once in the foyer, he texted his father to expect a video call after Martine left for the night shift at St. Francis Hospital. Trudging upstairs, he stripped off his clothes and snuck into bed next to the woman he adored. They'd wake just before sunset. Then he'd make love to her. Taste her, pleasure her, claim her once again as his alone. He pulled the coated band off his long hair and threw it, landing it on the dresser many feet away. As if sensing his need, Martine shifted to spoon against him.

He couldn't let go of what he had just witnessed in Draven. The desperation came from something far greater than physical pain. Even though the vampire's emotions were all over the place, it was obvious. He loved someone so deeply that he'd end his existence to keep her safe.

Love, devotion, and the need to protect weren't in a typical vampire's nature. But then again, neither was loyalty and trust. One short month ago, Draven proved he had both. Otherwise, his father would have been captured. Chris Forbes, an innocent man, wouldn't have his destiny intact. *And I wouldn't be in bed with the woman I love. I'd be dead.*

Chapter 15

A Tangled Web

Normally, Draven would be in a tailored, designer black suit, pressed black silk shirt and tie, as well as black socks and expensive shoes at sunset. The monotone look had been his signature for decades, which he carried off very handsomely. Ready for business, whether for the after-hours club or with investments for his otherworldly clients, he preferred to dress the part. *Definitely not tonight, thank you very much,* he thought. His rest had been fitful and uneasy, full of memories. Now, he had work to do.

Black silk pajamas would be an easy on-easy off. Plus, club business, along with other personal issues, warranted attention. And as far as he was concerned, Third Realm investments could be quickly manipulated to take a nosedive. That last one got him moving.

A Guardian stood in the bedroom doorway. Although young and slight of built, the mystical warrior could match a vampire move for move. So, Draven sat on the edge of the bed taking stock of his injuries. Broken ribs hurt like hell. Stitches stung his scalp. What continued to throb between his legs nauseated him. Frowning, he gave a narrow, sideways glance to his jailer.

"I intend to walk to my ensuite and shower. There is

no hidden escape passage and if you prefer to check, I will oblige, even leave the door ajar." He paused with a typical smirk. "Ah. You have already checked."

The slow nod confirmed that every square inch of his underground residence had been scrutinized. The club as well.

Not about to take a chance, he offered, "I shall stand very slowly and proceed to the shower."

The Guardian's heartbeat stayed steady with no indication of intimidation. Draven glanced down at himself. He stood, clenching his jaw as his eyes shot wide—he didn't utter a sound.

Stepping around the ugly pool of blood on the carpet, the short walk was pure agony. He unwrapped the gauze dressings from his hands and knees, then lifted a foot over the shower's short tile lip, which felt like jumping a hurdle. Having to brace his weight against the tiles was another annoyance, only relaxing when warm water soaked his damaged skin. And everything that followed: soaping up and drying off, pulling on the pajama bottoms and wiggling his feet into slippers took much longer than expected.

Like an obedient vampire under the watchful eye of a lethal prison guard, he downed a container of bitter animal blood before a slow shuffle into the office. To his dismay, yet another Guardian stood at the entrance to the hall.

Settling into the padded office chair felt like a new kind of torture. Thankfully, someone had replaced the landline phone on his desk. He pressed a specific button and waited for Donovan's "Yes, my lord."

"Put up the sign that says the club will be closed for renovations until further notice. Lock the door and come down." He hung up and waited, booting up his computer and scrolling through emails until Donovan stood front and center. "A notice will be sent to all employees. We will remain closed this week. Everyone will be paid normal wage to stay home. You, however, will remain on the job."

"Yes, my lord."

"I am contacting an industrial cleaning service for this floor and my bedroom carpet. You will bring them down and watch while they clean both."

"I was told that no one comes in or goes out, my lord," Donovan admitted.

He paused to study his trusted bouncer. "Yes. I'm sure you were." *What the brat doesn't know isn't my problem,* he thought. The sight and smell of the mess kept him on edge as if he had OCD. He needed clean and neat. "Bring them down when they arrive," he ordered.

"Yes, my lord."

"Thank you for locating Lukas Malone. Now explain how that thought entered your mind. I expect the truth."

Donovan's bald head bobbed once. "The driver knew his brownstone. I didn't think you'd want a minion tending to you—in your state."

"You thought correctly. Go on."

"Obviously, he's someone you trust." Then came a tentative, "I only wished to help, my lord."

"Lukas can be trusted." When Donovan's eyes slid to one Guardian then the other, Draven informed, "His men as well. One of them will relieve you when necessary. But the front door is to be manned at all times."

"Yes, my lord."

"That you will be well-compensated goes without saying."

"Thank you, my lord."

He watched Donovan leave. Not about to lean forward again, he sniffed the desk and located his cell phone buried under printer paper in the bottom drawer, then scrolled through the contacts for a specific cleaning company he trusted. They were discreet, excellent with getting blood out of anything. He sent a text stating what was immediately expected. Then he pulled his computer screen closer and began to go through more emails before checking the investments he managed for both the Second and Third Realms.

It didn't keep his mind off Luna. *Sending Michael is a gamble I must take.* He had no idea how to turn the odds in his favor. He forced his focus back to club business. It was more than necessary, especially with only six days before the end of his existence.

****

Aware of the time difference between New York and the Georgian Estate in England, Lukas whipped through family catch-me-up-chit-chat at lighting speed. He called Alana "Mom" out of deep respect for his father's soulmate. Plus, he loved the powerful ex-Guardian more than words could say. She was the mother of his twin teenage sisters whom he adored with all his heart. Alana had helped raise him through the troubled teenage years as though he were her own flesh and blood.

As if his father already had a suspicion, deep lines etched his face. Lukas heard genuine concern in Alana's voice as she said, "So, sweetie, why are you calling so late tonight? And we never video chat during the week,

117

either. Give it up fast. What's wrong?"

"Mom, I'm really sorry for the late hour, but I think there's another event unfolding. Deepa Chandra is already in the loop, but I asked her not to call the Georgian Council."

"Deepa agreed to that," his father asked.

"Yeah." He expected both the long pause and shocked expressions exchanged between his parents.

"Lu, sweetie," Alana said with more concern, "What happened and how serious is it?"

"I can't answer that second part yet."

"Then what's your gut instinct?" she asked.

"It could potentially be very dangerous."

"Just tell us what happened," she replied.

His father said in a no-nonsense tone, "Explain. Do not leave anything out."

He did so in one long, uninterrupted statement, ticking off Mary's headache through finding Draven and now, what he suspected—as detached as possible. "And he isn't going anywhere anytime soon. It's got to be painful as hell just to walk."

"Herodotus is not one to play with," his father said. "What a bastard."

"I'm assuming all the sires are cooking something up together. Draven won't say what Herodotus plans to do when he goes back, but I'm sure he'll tell you, Dad."

His father looked angrier than expected. "Seal off the bloody portal and let them all rot where they are."

"What if they really want out and decide to rush other portals?"

"Only two allow in and out traffic."

"Yeah, but there's a portal on every continent. Who's to say other Gatekeepers can stop a sire? Every one of those warlocks can be bought. And there's something else."

His father's dark eyes narrowed. "What kind of something else?"

"Maybe I should leave the two of you alone," his mother interjected.

"No, Mom, you need to hear this and I respect your input. Dad, who's Luna?"

There was a ripe pause before his father said, "Why are you asking?"

"Draven has her hidden in Iceland—since nineteen-thirty-nine. Luna might still be where he left her, in a town called Husavik."

"Oh my God," his father grumbled as his mother clicked her tongue.

Lukas told them about Freya and the sketch. He detailed the text he had Freya's brother send. "Of course, Tristan talking to Draven won't happen. *Destiny* is locked down tight with four Guardians on the premises. As for Iceland, I've sent Guardians to be on standby—"

"Keep it that way. She has never been aggressive. Not in the least."

"Yeah. I get it. But back to Draven. He went into panic mode talking about Herodotus. And he insists you move her and not tell him the location. I know it's a lot to ask, but I'm thinking you should bring her here instead of hiding her."

"Thank God the bastard didn't drink from him. He'd know it all. Not just about Luna, but also Draven's involvement in the October event."

"Which is why he wants final death. Christ, I can't believe I've got a suicidal vampire on my hands," Lukas muttered and shook his head. "He's convinced you're the only one who can protect Luna. If he sees her, maybe he won't keep asking for a stake."

"No. He won't. So Luna still walks the earth," his father stated.

"The country is very remote, my love," his mother replied, fully focused on his father. "We never had a large contingent of Guardians there. It's not heavily populated and there was no demonic activity ever suspected by the Georgian Council. Lu, she may be the only vampire in Iceland."

Leaning in, he said, "Draven swears she has never taken a human life. Is he covering for her, Dad?"

"No. That's one of the reasons why Veronique detested her."

"That despicable, horny bitch," his mother muttered with disgust.

"Mom," he said, drawing out the word with a chuckle. "I've never seen that look on your face before."

"It was such an enormous thrill slicing her head off. I can just imagine how cruel and spiteful she'd be to another female." She looked at his father. "Well, I can. That haughty, stuck-up bitch."

When he chuckled again, his father's next look meant stop-or-you'll-regret-it. Even though they lived on different continents, it worked. "Back when I knew Luna, she did not trust me."

Alana quickly said, "You weren't who you are now, my love."

He needed his father to say yes, adding, "That's totally true, Dad."

"No. Send a trusted representative from the Georgians instead of me, Lukas. Preferably a female."

"No-no-no," Alana replied with her beautiful hazel

eyes locked on his father. "That will spook her, my love, and a cornered vampire is a dangerous creature, even if she has no history of attacking humans. You, of all people, ought to know."

There had to be a way to persuade him, so Lukas said, "I've never seen anyone named Luna in my research on Draven, Dad. It's like she doesn't exist."

"He kept her well-protected, out of sight and scent of others like us. She may have been documented as simply an ordinary woman seen with him. Hiding her in Iceland was a very clever move."

"Husavik is near the Arctic Circle. Its population in the nineteen-thirties was under a thousand." Lukas tried again with, "You have to bring her here, Dad."

"I agree. It has to be you, my love," his mother confirmed. "He'll leave immediately, sweetie."

Lukas knew they were holding hands, and the kiss to his father's cheek was one of tender commitment. Then she looked at the screen again. "I'm going to pack some things for him. The two of you talk, okay? I love you with all my heart, sweetie."

"Love you too, Mom," he answered. Seeing pure devotion on his father's face as his dark eyes followed her out, Lukas waited. She had always been a strong, beautiful woman. Now in her mid-forties, she remained a classic Italian beauty.

His father looked at the screen again. "One event on the heels of the other. Not good."

"The timing is probably coincidental, not the universe warning us to prepare for an evil Armageddon. Look. I know you hate this city. I'm sorry."

"There's nothing to be sorry for. I'll find her and get her there." After seconds of silence, his father said,

"How bad is he?"

"Besides being a suicidal pain in the ass? Bruised, stitched and in a shitload of pain. He keeps slipping into French and gets kind of weepy."

"His sustenance?"

"Animal blood so he won't attain full strength. You know that if he returns and is bitten, we're burned. And then, who takes over this portal? Some sly warlock looking to make a fortune? It will be a fucking nightmare, with Guardians on surveillance twenty-four/seven."

"There's another issue as well. The Second Realm Sorcerers might search for any rips or tears on the edges of the realm to create new portals. Dark seers will assist with all kinds of spells."

Now to push him over the edge. "Then holy hell breaks loose."

"We'll be right back where we were sixteen years ago, damn it." Disgust entered his gravelly tone. "I'll find Luna. And you must be extra cautious, do you understand? Tell Mary I will stay at Kendrick House."

"No, Dad, this brownstone is still your home."

"Where I choose to sleep is my call."

"Martine would be upset if she doesn't get a chance to see you."

"Not as upset as she'd be if I were sleeping in the next room."

He winced, replying, "Oh. Right."

"Text me this woman Freya's address. Alert the Guardians in Husavik that I'm on my way."

"Gramps can get you faster transport and anything you ask for."

"I'll tell Miles exactly what I need to do this."

"Without council involvement, right?"

"Your grandfather can be diplomatic as well as persuasive."

"Thanks. I swear you'll be back with Mom in two days' time. Keep me posted. Take care and be safe."

The screen went dark. With that task taken care of, Lukas had other items on his agenda before returning to Draven. He stood and stretched before pulling up Georgian documents on Herodotus and Draven again. It would be a long night. This time, he'd be fully prepared.

Chapter 16

Learning Curves

Rarely did Luna experience a deep need to feed, and tonight was no exception. Earlier, she could hardly contain her excitement. The aroma of the hearty stew wafting through her home was like a reminder of human life in the 1800s. Had she hunted and cooked stews like this? She knew how to butcher. That was all she recalled. Lost in longing for life-memory, she had taken her time bathing and dressing, choosing a comfortable pair of jeans and another hand-knit forest-green sweater. Deciding to try something different, she let her hair dry naturally and then marveled at how the loose blonde waves felt on her shoulders.

Freya's arrival filled her with joy. Yet she found herself anxious, ready to learn more when they sat at the table during dinner, discussing all the new discoveries she had read about on the web. Gathering knowledge had been her sole purpose these past two days. Nothing else held her attention. Not even thoughts of Henri, which she pushed out of mind while clicking on video after video. If he had willfully abandoned her, then so be it. She'd move on, make it her mission to modernize, to explore this technical world she had finally awakened to. *The past is the past*, she told herself, *and I will no longer look back.*

Close to ten p.m., she and Freya were still exploring the Internet when Freya pulled out her phone. Noticing the crinkle of her brow, Luna asked, "Is something wrong?"

"No. Not really." Freya placed her cell phone back in her cross-body bag, she now knew the modern term for it, and refocused on the screen.

"Click this video and watch," her friend instructed. "Notice how the screen is grainy and there's no color to the moon landing." Mesmerized, Luna nodded once. "Now watch this video," her friend said.

As it played, she let out a long, soft, "Ohhh... Oh my."

"See how technology has changed? This happened about a few years ago. See the rocket booster return to its original structure? Look how the capsule is landing. These space travelers will simply walk out of it."

"You mean astronauts," she corrected, proud to know the term.

"Not quite," Freya said with a laugh in her voice, "They didn't go to the moon. And there is some controversy, whether or not to classify them astronauts. But this capsule as well as the rocket are reusable."

"Oh my," Luna said again. The simple, stunned reply had been uttered many times tonight. Lifting her chin off the palm of her hand, she removed her elbow from the table and sat back. "Henri has witnessed all of this. The advent of space travel, the unbelievable changes in music and art while I endured a... a boring existence safely tucked away in this remote seaport."

Freya shook her head. "You're being too hard on yourself."

"That I buried my face in classic literature and not

the modern novel is somewhat embarrassing. I'm sure there is a current psychological term for what I have done."

"Well, now you can google it, or download a book or just an excerpt right to your computer. I have a tablet, but my brother prefers to read on his phone."

And now I understand these terms. Before she looked up the most popular e-reader, she turned to Freya. "Have you texted him? Has he found out anything?"

Freya gave a thin smile. "I sent him a picture of one of the sketches. Although Tristan is very busy at work, he promised to have information soon. Perhaps tomorrow night."

"That is good. Modern communication is instant, isn't it? Not like writing a letter and posting it, which took days to be delivered so long ago. Maybe even weeks. It is simply astounding."

"You have a safe life. A peaceful one. You've never been hunted by Guardians here in Husavik, have you?"

With her eyes still on the computer screen, she replied, "I don't think I'd be of much interest to a Guardian. I have never sensed one close enough to discover me. But the world—"

"Is a dangerous place, my friend. Take all this knowledge in. Own it. But don't expose yourself if it isn't necessary. The world is not a kind place. There are conflicts in too many countries. There is crime."

"There has always been crime and other atrocities."

"Not like today. It's rampant. Iceland is one of very few countries without many problems. We rely on exports and tourists who want to escape their busy lives back home. They come to bask in the beauty of our hot springs and waterfalls. They want to see Iceland in its natural glory. Do you realize that the city this Draven is in has millions of people in it?"

She could give no answer. Simply nodded.

Freya sighed. "It's late. I'm afraid I'm not used to night hours anymore."

"Have you finished sketching the others you saw with this vampire? I am curious."

"No. I'm sorry. Haven't had the time," Freya answered.

"Can you describe them? I truly am curious," Luna said as she studied her friend.

Freya sat back and shrugged. "Well, one man is not as tall as the others. He has a stunning face, almost too beautiful for a man. His eyes are an incredible deep blue and his thick blond hair looks full of loose curls but it's worn like Draven's, you know, tied back. He's not as muscular. Slighter of build and his shoulders aren't as broad as the other two. Mary Kendrick, the good witch who hosted the healing circle in early October, was very worried about him during the event. Just before it drew to a close, he sustained an injury, but I didn't sense it life-threatening."

Her eyes searched Freya's. "And the other?"

"Oh, now *that* one is very interesting. Mary considered him family. I sensed something very familiar about him, but it escapes me. He's very handsome, the same height as Draven, with a head of dark wavy hair that brushes his collar. His eyes are intense, framed with thick lashes. His features are angular and his shoulders very broad. In fact, if I didn't know one was a vampire, I'd swear he and Draven were brothers."

Luna's back stiffened, recalling the vampire Henri often called his brother in blood, and she didn't like him—for many reasons. Freya softly called her name, which pulled her out of the memory of someone she feared. "You say they are not all vampires."

"No. Only Draven."

"How can that be? How can two mortal men stand next to one and not be bitten?"

"Yet look at us. I don't run screaming from you. Neither does Rune."

"Because I'm different," she replied, walking over to the fireplace. "Go back. This tall man who looks like Draven."

"It would almost be like describing Draven again, Luna, well, except for the wavy brown hair."

"Thin lips. Dark intense eyes."

"Why, yes."

"They often had the same expression on their faces."

"Yes. Why?"

Another shiver ran through her. "He *is* a vampire. And I know him."

Freya shook her head. "I honestly didn't sense two vampires when I sat in that healing circle. But I've seen him before, just can't place the when or where. And I sensed his constant concern for his son."

This made no sense at all. "His son? Who is his son?"

"The blond man, the other traveler I saw standing with them. Luna, what's wrong?"

She shook her head. Eased her brow because it couldn't be. *Michael was truly unpredictable, dangerous. He simply vanished after 1890. And of course, vampires cannot have children.* She shrugged the feeling off because it wasn't possible. Freya hid a yawn, and Luna frowned. "It is once again too late for you, my friend. Rune," she called, and he came into the room with car keys in hand.

"I'll finish the sketch and have it for you tomorrow night."

"Thank you, Freya. I look forward to our next visit." As they walked to the door, Luna added, "Rune, please go home afterward."

"Thank you, madame. I've downloaded more movies to the television for you."

"It is appreciated. I will see you next sunset."

She heard the door close, but her attention was drawn back to 1887, to memories of Henri and his devilish brother in blood. She had never felt safe around him. Always cautious around his vampire lover whose venomous comments were often palpable threats, nights spent at that Florentine villa with those two had terrified her. Henri's stern warnings to never be alone with Veronique or Michael came to mind.

She sank into the sofa, picked up the remote needing to switch focus to the big screen mounted over the mantel. *One news channel after the other… full of dire concerns.* Wars in various countries. Mobs of angry protesters all over the world, things called climate change, stock market fluctuations and economic warnings. Each crisis seemed bigger than the other. If she were human, it would have made her depressed and anxious.

Freya is right, this modern world is very complex. Well, enough of that, she thought, and found the musical entitled *My Fair Lady*. In 1912, she had enjoyed the novel it was based upon. Last night, she had been riveted to the classic drama, *Casablanca,* and another musical called *The Wizard of Oz,* based upon a book written in

1900. She had no desire to watch something called *Jaws*. The next title piqued her interest and produced a wry grin. "Why on earth would anyone in their right mind wish to interview a vampire?"

Chapter 17

Abducted

When Freya arrived home, she decided to finish the sketch of the two men standing with Draven. Although she honored her friend's request, she couldn't kick the feeling that Luna would never see it. *Odd and out of nowhere,* she thought as she closed the sketchbook and put her colored pencils away. Close to one a.m. she fought off the nagging feeling that something else would happen tonight. Instead of putting on a flannel nightgown, Freya changed into comfortable sweatpants and a loose sweatshirt before crawling into bed—only to be jarred awake hours later by pounding and the continuous chime of the security doorbell on the storefront.

She grabbed her phone, huffing out loud, "three-thirty in the middle of the night?" It was not only odd, but frightening. She opened the alarm system app, and seeing the person, she gasped. It was the tall man in her sketch! One hand went to her heart, but both feet went into her slippers, and she stood, not sure what to do. Hitting the microphone icon on the security app, she asked, "Why are you here? What do you want?"

The man stared directly into the doorbell camera, saying in a clipped British accent, "My name is Michael Malone. I must speak to you. I'm a very close friend of

Mary Kendrick."

Her eyes went wide recalling that name and thinking back to 2005. The Mayhem in Manhattan was burned into her memories. Hurrying through the store she unlocked the door. Hugging her elbows tight, she stepped back. "It was you in the event last month, the vampire with a soul? Oh my God, she was right!"

He walked in saying, "I am not a vampire anymore. It's a long-complicated story."

"Why are you here?"

In a rich voice, deep and mellow, he said, "Please, do not be frightened."

"I'm not." Which was strangely true. Her sixth sense remained calm, and she didn't feel threatened, but the look on his very handsome face read urgency.

"Your heart is beating very fast."

Blessed be all, it is! "You aren't a vampire, but you hear like one."

"Yes I can, Freya."

"You know my name?"

"Another long story. I'm here for Luna."

Sensing not a shred of malice, Freya said, "Please come with me."

Once in the living room, she indicated the sofa, asked Michael to sit, but he declined. Standing with his arms locked against his chest, his feet slightly apart, she sensed it a familiar stance, like a signature of the man he was. His coat wasn't heavy enough for the bitter cold, which appeared not to bother him.

"You have read me and know that I mean you no harm. You must take me to Luna. This is urgent."

She tried to read him again, but couldn't, which was incredible—that he could lock down his thoughts!

"Please. You must not hurt her."

"I intend no such thing. The Guardians now stationed in Husavik are here to insure your safety, should anything out of the ordinary occur. They will not intrude on your business, but they will remain close. Now about Luna."

There! She sensed it, and with certainty confirmed, "You're here to take her away."

"Yes," he simply replied, adding, "You've already read me," with a slight smile, which was as charming as the richness of his voice.

"You could pass for his brother."

"Many have told us so through the years," he calmly offered.

"Draven is Henri, isn't he?"

"Yes. He is. Please take me to Luna now."

Shivers ran from the base of her spine and tingled in her brain. She let out a small puff of air. "I've heard highly improbable rumors, but to meet you, well, this is just incredible," she whispered, full of awe. "All those years ago, you fought Hell-beasts and closed the portals!"

That charming grin appeared again. "No. What I did spurred them to close. I'm not a sorcerer, that's for certain." He paused before saying, "I have to get to Luna. Strangely, she leaves no vampire scent. You must take me to her."

"Yes, yes, certainly. I need a minute to put on my shoes."

"I must ask that you hand me your phone. Not that I don't trust you, but warning her may not be wise," he said with a hand extended.

"No, no, of course." After giving it over, she hurried

to the bedroom, pulling on socks and sneakers, sensing he had more to say.

"I have an SUV waiting. The driver will bring you back after you take me to her. Knowing Luna, assuming she hasn't changed, she will not consider this a betrayal by you—once she knows why I'm here."

Tying her sneakers, she caught his next questions. "Rune is the original family's grandson. He takes good care of her. Yes. I met Luna twenty years ago when I moved here. Yes. She has been comfortable and safe in the seaport."

"I hear this country is beautiful."

"It truly is and a great place to live."

"If you like isolation."

Entering the living room, she chuckled, "Some of us do, Michael. My gifts have deepened here. There isn't any turmoil, just clean air and quiet." Buttoning her coat, Freya led the way out through the store. Michael opened the black SUV's door to the front passenger seat. "I can sit in the back, if you prefer."

"You will need to direct the driver, and then he'll return you home."

Clicking her seat belt, she asked, "And what about her home?"

"Rune will be instructed to keep her property and investments running smoothly."

"She will not return," Freya said very softly as a sad feeling ran through her body.

"Is that simply a statement of possibility?"

"I think it's fact, isn't it? Luna still loves him."

"She loves Henri, not necessarily Draven," Michael seemed to suggest.

"Fate will run its course," she stated, and then

indicated a left turn onto a narrow road with a private property sign clearly visible. Its incline steepened for a while and then leveled out. The driver stopped yards away from the house made of concrete and wood with all windows shuttered and a porch lamp lit. She turned and looked at Michael. "Be gentle with her. And make sure Draven knows to do the same."

"Thank you for your assistance," was his reply before he left the SUV.

As the driver turned it around and started down the narrow road, she murmured, "So it is, so shall it be." Luna would be in the Georgian Champion's capable hands. That she'd be reunited with her Henri was a given. But how on earth would he get her to New York? Whether or not he needed it, she sent a protection spell Michael's way.

Luna will reshape her destiny. She couldn't remain secluded here in Iceland. Freya sensed it. Whether ready or not, her friend would enter a changed world, foreign and full of uncertainties.

Although it was never easy to lose a friend, she again intoned, "So it is, so shall it be," when the SUV came to a stop in front of her shop.

****

As the movie ended, Luna shook her head. Children didn't survive turning, sinking into madness within hours and drawn to walk into the sun. That a vampire had no reflection, and cried tears of blood rang true enough, though. *Perhaps I will download the book,* she thought, *and I can do so right now, perhaps buy that latest e-reader.*

Just about to get off the couch, heavy knocks startled her. Standing, she turned and stared at the front door

135

before she approached it. *The scent of a man, a stranger.* No one in the seaport came up the private road, and like a fool, she hadn't turned on the alarm when Freya and Rune left. *Have the dangers of the outside world suddenly arrived on my doorstep, in a home hidden so far up the volcanic mountain?* Vampire strength meant she'd neutralize the threat in seconds. But then what? *Do I call the police? Where is the nearest station?* Luna wrung her hands, bit her lip, and decided she'd worry about that next step later, perhaps call Rune back here to handle it with the humans and keep herself hidden when they arrive.

Standing at the door, she heard a steady and strong heartbeat, and then the whisper of her name, followed by, "It's Michael. Let me in." Full of terrified memories, her head jerked back. She shook it off and took a deeper sniff, but no scent of the arrogant vampire ran up her nose. "Go away. This is private property, and you are trespassing!"

"Luna. You know me."

"I do not," she barely whispered, fully certain that only another vampire could hear her.

The door handle jiggled with a firm, "Yes, you do. Open this door."

"I am not alone," she stated, standing her ground.

"Yes. You are."

"I'm calling the authorities."

"No. You aren't. Luna, let me in. Right now. I have news of Henri."

My Henri... Could it be true? Hesitant, but curious, she stopped wringing her hands and turned the knob. When the door opened, her eyes shot wide, and she ran the other way. He was on her in a split-second, locking her to his chest. Using every ounce of vampire strength, the struggle to pry his arms off went nowhere, his hold rock-solid.

"Where did you hide the human with the heartbeat," she shrieked.

Michael moved back with her tight against him, kicked the door closed and growled, "I've hidden no human. Stop fighting me."

That fear inside skyrocketed. She tried to summon the beast-within, something she'd never needed to do. Only a pitiful growl escaped. Twisting her head, ready to sink her fangs into his shoulder, he grabbed her chin turning her face away. "No biting. I swear, I won't hurt you."

"Henri never trusted you!"

"Henri sent me."

Drawn back to a different century, she wanted to scream for the one she loved, but it would serve no purpose. Knowing how Michael could go from charming to lethal in seconds, she hissed, "Liar."

"I'm telling the truth. Please stop struggling."

The silky baritone whisper had rumbled through his chest. Warm, steady breaths bathed the back of her neck, and she heard a healthy heart beating in his chest. Captivated, shocked, she soared far beyond confused. His grip loosened and she turned, pressing both hands to his heart, which did, in fact, beat? Fully fascinated but still unsure, she whispered, "This is a trick. It cannot be."

"It's no trick. But you're calmer now. That's a good sign."

She studied his handsome face, remembered mannerisms so similar to Henri's. The width of his shoulders—so similar to Henri's. Blood tears filled her eyes, whispering, "This is impossible." He pulled her into a gentle embrace, as if she'd break in his arms.

"It's important that I bring you to him. We must leave right now."

Luna pulled back and searched his dark eyes. Unlike the mischievous twinkle she remembered so well, these eyes were wise, full of concern. His palms held her cheeks. His warm thumb captured the next blood tear before pulling her close again.

"I know. It's a lot to take in," he whispered.

"Yet you are as strong as a vampire."

"Vampiric skills have not left me. It is all quite complicated, this mystical gift of life. Luna, we must leave immediately. He needs you."

"I have waited decades for his return! Now you say he needs me? Why?"

Michael slowly shook his head. "I will explain on the jet. A helicopter will take us to a private airstrip, but we must leave at once."

Henri needing her… A human Michael staring back at her? She started to shake. *Helicopter? Did he say an airstrip?* "No. I am not… I cannot leave."

"We must go. Put on your coat."

She looked away, walked to the laptop and picked up her cell phone holding it in a two-fisted grip to her chest. "No. Henri would have come himself. You are lying."

"I said put on your coat. It's bitter outside." He glanced down at her phone and then walking over, held her gaze. "Come Luna. Your coat." Walking her to the door, his hold on her arm was firm.

"I have been here for eight decades. This is my home."

"Luna. Now," he said in a sharp tone.

"You were always unique, but—"

"You have no idea," he replied.

"Explain how you are made different?"

"Right now. Let's go." He took her coat from the hook beside the door and held it. The fur slipped up her arms. Then he fastened each button and pulled up her hood. "You are frightened. Confused. I understand. But you must trust me."

"But this is my home."

"Rune will see to everything. Freya will assist if you like."

"How do you know about Rune and Freya?"

"Luna, please." Taking her arm, Michael escorted her outside to a dark SUV. He got in the back seat beside her and closed the door, leaning into the driver and saying, "Inform the team at the airstrip that we are enroute." Then he sat back and pulled out his cell phone, his fingers moving across the screen.

"What airstrip? What team? Who are you texting?"

"My son. He's with Draven."

Freya's description of the second sketch came to mind. "How do you have a son?" Michael didn't answer. "He... he is blond, not as tall as you and Henri." He glanced at her and put away his phone. As the SUV turned onto the main road, Luna grabbed his forearm. "Henri is Draven, isn't he?"

"That's what he goes by now."

She should have been overjoyed that he still walked the earth, not this confused. "Then why, after so many decades apart, would he want me again?"

"He needs you, Luna. My foolish brother in blood has done you a great disservice. He left you vulnerable and clueless. Not even a bloody bodyguard," the human Michael grumbled.

"I have no need for one!" Miffed by his comment, she huffed, "I have been on the Internet, and I have watched five movies! And I know how to text."

"I take it all the electronics in your home are new, then?"

Proudly, she replied, "Purchased two days ago."

"Bloody Hell," he muttered. "When he's back on his feet, I may have to slap him around a bit."

"Why is he not on his feet? This reply puzzles me."

"This and everything else, I imagine."

She tried to process such strange replies, not to mention this abrupt abduction in a vehicle moving very fast on a dark road lit only by its headlamps. "Unlike you, Henri was never aggressive. Is he injured?" When Michael didn't respond, she pushed. "Who would dare to injure a vampire?"

As if lost in thought, Michael said, "Herodotus."

She flinched. Her hand flew to her neck, whispering, "My sire still walks the earth!"

"He is truly a bastard, a sadistic one at that. You will not see him. You will not be near him. He's in another realm."

"Freya spoke of different realms. If Henri walks the human world, then how could my sire injure him?" Recalling Michael's brutal ways, she shook her head. "No. You have injured him."

He looked at her in a most unsettling way. "Don't be absurd."

This is all wrong. All a lie. Her eyes slid to the side window. "Take me home."

"That, I will not do," he stated without emotion.

She huffed, crossed her arms and planned her escape. But when the SUV stopped in a flat, isolated expanse, she didn't move, gaping at the beastly thing just yards away. It appeared so intimidating, so big, so foreign.

Chapter 18

Fight and Flight

Terror slithered through Luna's veins. Unfamiliar sounds assaulted her ears and strange smells filled her sinuses when the door opened. Michael stepped out of the vehicle, but Luna didn't move. When he said, "Give me your hand," she shook her head. Then he leaned further into the open door. "I said, give me your hand, Luna." Pressing her back against the opposite window didn't seem to matter. He reached in and pulled her out of the SUV. As it raced away, fear of the unknown hammered at her. Still resisting, he stated low and sharp, "Not making this easy, are you?"

With a rough cinch of her waist, he handed her off to a man inside the beast. The human's grip wasn't as strong as Michael's. *This one I will fight*, she proudly thought. But Michael angled at her side and closed the door.

Whirring sounds drove her deeper into panic. When she screamed, he returned a menacing growl. A wide red strap crossed her lap, her chest and clicked. She fisted the buckle but didn't know how to unlock it.

"Just sit still and stay put," he ordered. Covering her ears with her palms, she bucked against the harness. "I said, sit still, damn it," he bellowed, gripping her wrist in a painful way.

Not even this new level of fear released her beast-within! No clawed fingernails, no pupils morphing a feral-yellow, but she drew back her lips, bared her fangs and hissed.

Over the dreadful thumping, she shrieked, "Henri never raised his voice with me!"

"I am not Henri," he stated with an intimidating growl. "Now settle down."

"Don't speak to me as if I were a child!"

"Then don't force me to treat you as one, because I will not hesitate if you keep this up," he countered.

She scrunched her eyes and scoffed, "How dare you!" Her right fist connected with his chest. Then he wrestled it to her lap. A mortal man would be rubbing the sting, unable to breathe. But no, not Michael!

"Do that again and you will regret it."

"Henri will bite you when I tell him how you treat me!"

"I highly doubt it. Now sit still," he ordered so harshly that she pushed into the seat and screamed again. The vibration of the behemoth thrummed in her chest. He snagged her chin and glared. "I don't react well to tantrums. Shrieks and screams, either."

The sway of the beast, the sense of lifting into the air frightened her as much as he did. Squeezing her eyes shut, she swallowed the next scream.

****

The helicopter flight seemed endless, and when it touched down and the whir slowed, Michael unbuckled his harness first. She let a wild glare light her eyes, although he didn't seem to care. Standing outside it, he said, "Well, come on then."

Pulling herself up, she left the behemoth. But what

appeared next was even more intimidating! Sleek, white, wide and long, it was much bigger then what she stepped out of. Lights embedded in the paved way looked endless. Icy arctic wind whipped all around, as if singing a caution. The smell of fuel stuck in her throat.

Michael took her arm. She yanked it away. "Luna," he said, slowly drawing out her name like a warning. Her eyes slid one way and then the other. Only a flat emptiness appeared, for as far as she could sense, but she dug deep within and hissed.

"Walk to the jet or I will carry you."

She scoffed at the absurd challenge. "You will not!"

"I absolutely will. Walk."

"No! Henri brought me to Iceland. Here I stay. I will use my cell phone to text Rune. He will come for me." She fumbled in her coat pocket and got it into her hands.

He took it, flung it so far that she didn't hear it land. "You will cross the tarmac and board. This is your last chance to do so with dignity."

"You are still an arrogant bastard!"

"Do not try my patience. Put one foot in front of the other and walk, damn it."

"You are taking me to Herodotus, not to my Henri!"

His dark eyes narrowed with a tight lean in. "Good Lord, you are pushing my buttons!"

When he reached for her arm, she ran. Total darkness in an unknown area of Iceland was less terrifying than that winged monster. Not thirty feet away, he caught up and threw her over a shoulder. Her feet kicked air and she punched his back, slapped his backside, but his long strides continued up the metal stairs into it. The door sealed, and as a high-pitched whine hurt her ears, she kicked and slapped again. Two men were seated and silent, staring straight ahead—ignoring her plight as if it didn't matter.

They entered a space lit from above without windows, and as soon as her feet hit the floor, she glared at her kidnapper. Calm and smug, Michael leaned against the only door with his arms locked to his chest and his feet crossed at the ankles. When her back hit the far wall, she brushed her long hair away from her eyes to study her prison. Two sets of high-back, upholstered chairs faced each other, the wide aisle carpeted in the same indigo blue.

"Take off your coat," he ordered as he threw his jacket over a chair. She unbuttoned her fur full of defiance and flung it, hitting him in the face. He placed it on the same chair as his and then slowly approached. "This behavior is infantile and insane. I swear to God, had I known you'd be such a handful, I'd have sent Guardians to drug and drag you without so much as a glare from those big blue eyes."

"And their hearts would have beat like wild drums when I bit their necks!" She put her hands on her hips, blowing more wisps of hair away but locked to his glare.

"So you drink human blood now, do you? I recall how it nauseated you. Tell me, is that when your beast-within will surface, vampire? Because I've not seen one little fingernail turn into a claw. Not a flicker of feral-yellow in your eyes. You have no defense without the transformation. Now sit down and figure out how to buckle yourself in. It's the law for take-off."

What is take-off? What does it include? How will this huge, heavy thing fly through the air? So many questions she definitely wasn't about to ask him. "You will regret the decision to kidnap me. You are still as cruel as I remember."

"Really, Luna," sounded full of sarcasm and arrogance.

"Nothing but a vicious thing that insults me with empty threats!"

"My threats are never empty. You should recall. Now sit down. I will not tell you again."

"I choose to stand," she countered with a rebellious jerk of her chin. And she had no idea why she said that!

"For five hours," he stated with a smug smirk.

"You are strapped in. I am not. It will be easy for me to attack."

"Then go on. Have at it. Let that demon loose. I'm waiting, vampire."

A small growl escaped. "Cruel. Mean. Full of menace! You haven't changed at all."

His eyebrows rose, the expression dark and dangerous. "Do not push your luck, Luna."

"Do not glare at me like the lascivious beast you truly are, Michael."

The jet suddenly lurched. A strange vibration hummed under foot and rattled up the bones in her legs. When the beast came to a stop, he appeared perfectly relaxed in one of the leather seats with a seatbelt across his lap and his eyes closed. "For the last time, Luna. I am ordering you to sit down and shut up."

She growled, "Ordering me? Do not tell me what to do, human!"

"Suit yourself," he replied as if too bored to bother.

That did it! Even though human blood was like sour milk in her mouth, she bared her fangs—just as a tremendous roar reached a deafening pitch. Both hands covered her sensitive ears. Strong vibrations hammered her body.

Thrust back with a force never experienced, she was too stunned to scream. The jet moved at a tremendous speed before the metal monstrosity angled in a way that made it impossible to walk forward. Sinking to her knees, she huddled at the bottom of the wall, shaking and shrieking. Only when the force against her body lessened did her eyes ease open—to see Michael's shoes.

He pulled her up. She twisted and flailed, but no beast-within surfaced. And when he let go, she hauled a hefty slap to his cheek, screaming long and loud right in his face.

An odd expression appeared and his right eyebrow lifted. "I haven't addressed a tantrum in many years. Yet you carry on like a wild brat. Don't say I didn't warn you." He held her arm with one hand and smacked her backside with the other. Hustled into the armchair, he belted her in—which further fueled her fury. When he leaned in, she drew her face back. "Stay quiet or I will do that again, with vampire strength."

What an offence, she thought, pounding the chair's padded arms. "How dare you! Henri would never—"

"He absolutely would. Now get control of yourself."

"You purposely meant to insult me!"

Taking the chair across from her, he looked aside. "This is all Henri's fault. You know absolutely nothing about the world we once shared." He paused and studied her. "There is much I must tell you. If you ask questions in a civil tone, I will answer every one of them." He paused again. "You cannot access the beast-within, and you still refuse to drink human blood."

There is no escape. Her head settled against the cushioned seat. His tone had changed from sharp to soft—like Henri's.

"Please talk to me, Luna," he said.

"It has always been dormant. I don't know why. And yes, the few times Henri forced me to drink from him, it was nauseating," she confessed.

"Absolutely unbelievable. Your canines are long enough to tear into a vein. You have speed and strength, heightened senses and self-healing?" She nodded, noticing how his wide hands gripped the chair's leather arms. "I am truly sorry for the insult, but I had to be sure."

"I will still tell Henri what you did."

"He will agree it was warranted."

"Warranted?"

"Well, I wasn't about to grab you by the neck and throw you around the cabin. I again apologize. I've been intimidating. You've been terrified."

When he looked aside, she studied his handsome profile, so very reminiscent of Henri's. Michael never was one to apologize for his outrageous antics. This man with a heartbeat, however, came off sincere, somewhat concerned.

"You are aging like a human, Michael."

He gave a nod. "I'm in my mid-forties now. Does it show?"

"Not really. Just in your tone, perhaps in your demeanor—and around the eyes."

"Raising children will do that to you. And I have a beautiful wife."

"You.... You have a family?"

An easiness was evident as his heartbeat slowed. "It is a complicated story, but yes. We can talk about that later. First, I must tell you about Henri."

"Who now calls himself Draven," she replied, interested in what he had to say.

In a caring way, he disclosed fact after fact, including Henri's status as Gatekeeper. There were no sarcastic comments or witty barbs. She asked questions, sometimes not believing him and saying so. He answered with clarity, saying how Henri would go into detail. Simply knowing that soon she would be in his arms and under his protection gave her comfort.

The change in Michael was truly astounding. He told her what had happened to him in 1890, which explained why they never saw him again. For a vampire to regain conscience and soul was unheard of. Then he vaguely described what had happened sixteen years ago. To be mysteriously gifted with human life was something not to be believed. Yet here he was, a living, breathing, aging man. Every word kept Luna riveted to his soothing, deep voice.

How had the impossible been made possible? Yet his strong, steady heartbeat, his obvious need to breathe, and his color no longer pale like mine says he tells the truth. His mannerisms may not have changed, but there is a palpable depth to him now. As hours passed, up in the air and still unnerved, Luna realized she was in the presence of someone very different. A singular human.

If Freya had been correct about the other man in the sketch, then his son had been born to the vampire, not the man, years before he regained human life—another unbelievable truth! She wouldn't ask how it was even possible, but she didn't doubt it, either. When he grew quiet, her curiosity piqued again. "Tell me about your son. Does he know my Henri?"

"Yes, he does," Michael replied.

As he told her about the strange October event, she realized that Michael Malone had always been a measure apart from other vampires. Different, not only singular. During their time together in the late 1880s, she had no idea how truly unique he would one day become.

Until now. In a jet. Strapped to a blue leather armchair. Thousands of feet above the Atlantic Ocean. Soon to be united with her eternal love in a city far, far away.

Chapter 19

Devious Decisions

Lukas had argued against the cleaning service. Draven had taken the hostile comments on the chin and grumbled an apology for going behind the brat's back. But being watched like a hawk didn't sit well. Although outraged by Lukas's company, he wore an intentional smirk. "Aren't you bored sitting across from my desk and watching me work my magic with investments in European markets?"

Of course, he was curious about the numerous texts that came in and went out on the man's phone for the past three hours, each little ping an additional annoyance. After no reply, he tried again. "Shouldn't you be home thinking about what you will cook for Martine when she comes off her shift at dawn? Perhaps fold a load of laundry or vacuum the living room, so the lovely, good witch does not have to work her fingers to the bone."

Finally, the brat looked up, that mischievous grin in full view. "I employ a cook and a housekeeper. Martine wants for nothing. Any other questions about how I provide for her?"

As if dared to continue, he returned a similar look. "You feed her nutritious meals, I hope."

"Speaking of feeding, when was your last intake of blood?"

"Ah, you worry about my well-being." He'd ingest less and less. By the time he returned to Herodotus, the first slash to a vein would drain him quick. "Very compassionate, indeed."

"Well, look at you. All back in control and as arrogant as ever. How's the swelling? I could have Martine bring a jock strap when she comes to check your stitches."

"No thank you. I am healing."

"Not fast enough to walk back into the Third Realm with a nice long stride and a steady gait. Time keeps ticking on, vampire."

"The sires couldn't care less whether I limp or skip. As long as I return." *To face unimaginable agony.* "Which reminds me. I have an important business meeting tomorrow night."

"Good to know. I'll be right here."

"No. You won't. Nor will these Guardians. It will raise suspicion, and I do not care to explain who you are or why you're in the meeting."

"Then my father will sit in."

He leaned forward and swallowed the discomfort in his balls. "You have torn Michael away from the eternal love of his life? Are you not able to handle one weakened vampire's all by yourself?" His shoulders relaxed, cautiously leaned back thinking, *is Luna safely hidden away already?*

"He's agreed to honor your request. So no, nix the meeting and your skip back to the sires. Maybe use these last hours on earth to clean things up. That should keep you busy enough unless you've changed your mind— about being staked, I mean."

No. He had not. But he had to be sure. "You've

convinced him to hide her?"

"Yep. Service with a smile." The phone slipped into Lukas's shirt pocket. "Let's cut the shit. Drain two containers of animal blood. Maybe get a little introspective about final death and meditate. It's just a thought."

"Luna is safe. That's all that matters." Finding it odd that Lukas's expression gave him nothing, his jaw tensed.

Then those royal-blue eyes flashed with authority. "Cow blood. Now Draven."

The brat wasn't about to bring it to him, and he braced the chair's arms. When he stood it was... excruciating. He did the shuffle of shame to the galley kitchen, drained one container but dumped the others down the drain, leaving all three rinsed out and ready for inspection.

Animal blood didn't give him a high, and it left a gritty residue on his tongue. During the pathetic shuffle back, Draven stopped at the rolling server cart with every type of expensive liquor. He washed the taste away with mouthfuls of seventy-year-old vintage whiskey. Then he entered the office and sat down—with care. "How many more hours before you leave me alone?"

Surprisingly, Lukas stood and put on his jacket. "I'm off."

"Thank you."

"I'll be back with Martine."

"You need not bother to return. I will not harm her."

"Yeah. No. I'll be right there up close and personal with a stake when she checks out your stitches. If I were you, I'd get some rest because it's going to be a long morning tomorrow. You might get cranky."

"I have remained awake many mornings."

Lukas clicked his tongue, which irked him even more. "I insist you take my advice."

"I assume Luna is hidden somewhere safe." He held up a hand. "No. Do not tell me where, but I am correct, am I not?"

"She's with Guardians right now. Fully protected and out of reach."

Narrow-eyed, he studied Lukas's bland expression. Guardians could be male or female. Hopefully, Luna was in the care of the latter. Hopefully, females were less aggressive. But something nudged at him. "Why would your father hand her over to Guardians? What guarantee do I have that one will not become overzealous and use a stake?"

"You have to trust me that she's safe. Now go to bed."

"I will consider it," he replied, not at all satisfied.

Trust was a human trait that vampires didn't hold near and dear to their unbeating hearts. But his brother in blood owed him too much to cross him. *Yet, if he does, what can I do about it?* Nothing, which made him feel powerless again, and added to his physical misery. And he didn't like it.

Expecting to be left alone, when a stout Guardian walked into his office, Draven rolled his eyes. Another took a post in his dining room—looking very much out of place in a vampire's home. They didn't speak or move, reminding him of cardboard cut-outs, yet watching his every move. Not one whiff of fear came off them. He assumed they were near the end of their mystical mission, not like the over-eager sixteen-year-olds who were newly called. *Too young at age sixteen, committing to ten years of fear and courage with no guarantee of survival when destroying a vampire.* He could easily smell them near—and avoided them the way a human avoids stepping into a tornado. Guardians were that lethal. And now, more than one would be just steps away.

Standing up to leave the office had been an agonizing decision, and the shuffle into his home made him feel like a fool. He snatched that open bottle of whiskey on the rolling server and lurched into his room. Thankful for the soft landing on his bed, he gulped down one mouthful after the other until his senses dulled and the bottle emptied.

The carpet no longer had the sight or scent of blood that had saturated it for hours. And the whiskey bottle made no sound as it slipped out of his hand. Stretching out, he centered himself with one pillow behind his head and pawed around until he had the quilt in hand and up to his waist.

Perfectly aged, pricey liquor to drink in a room full of pricey furniture. He had amassed a fortune, especially over the last decade and a half. Who to leave it all to crossed his mind. Final death loomed like a demon, just as real as his beast-within. He felt compelled to guarantee Luna's continued existence in hiding. Like Martine, she'd want for nothing. Even if the family entrusted with her safety had invested well, he'd provide extra.

Another slab of guilt piled on what he already carried. How many times had he talked himself out of sneaking into Husavik to see her? He assumed he had eternity. He could afford to hire a private jet for a night flight. It would have been so very easy. Now, time had run out.

The powerful role of Gatekeeper had made him rich. He enjoyed every pleasure affordable. Had spent an easy million renovating the space beneath these buildings, turning *Destiny* into something of a novelty. He owned half the block. Prime New York City real estate. Personal tailors, private chefs when entertaining necessary businessmen, human minions of all kinds and in every profession to do his bidding—you name it, he had it. Not to mention those high-paid courtesans, like his own private harem to satiate sexual needs that had nothing to do with love.

The alcohol buzz made his mood feel like a mudslide in a downpour and he snickered. *I don't deserve love. I never have.* "Well, boo-hoo for me," he grumbled. Again obsessed with Luna, Draven shook his head, or at least, he thought he did. She had always been terrified of her sire. The last time they crossed paths with Herodotus at the Paris Opera House in late December 1889, the scent of fear radiated around her like an unusual aura. He closed his eyes and saw it all.

Spotting Herodotus in a similar private box across the concert hall, I pushed up my shirt cuff, and forced Luna to drink deeply from my wrist. Even though she gagged, she met my demand.

During the first intermission of Wagner's *Tristan und Isolde,* the curtain of their box suddenly opened. "And there stood that beady-eyed bastard with a look as cold as the night," he muttered with a slur. The sire ignored her, snidely saying they deserved one another, both of them "atypical" like some monstrous experiment gone haywire.

Luna was so shaken that we left immediately, barely

making it into a dark alley before the human blood I forced her to ingest spewed from her lovely lips. The next sunset, we left France to spend years in Switzerland and then Greece.

"Ah, sweet, lovely Luna," he murmured with more of a slur, and welcomed the numbness that far too much whiskey provided. *Nothing matters anymore. Everything has changed. Perhaps it's time to give up and give in.* This new persona he had created after he left her on that icy shore was most definitely coming to an end.

****

Why was he moving? Draven's chin hit a shoulder, but he couldn't scent a thing. His throat was dry, his limbs loose and floppy. A tight arm held his back. In a lazy way, his eyes eased open. "The cow's blood is drugged," he slurred out.

"I wouldn't do that to you, vampire," Lukas whispered.

"Why am I so groggy?" he got out, but it took too much energy to talk—or think.

"Do you want me to spell it out?"

He groaned a slow, "mmm…hmmm," willing his eyes to open, which they wouldn't do.

"You don't have any human blood in your system to absorb so much alcohol," sounded too condescending, as if he were intellectually challenged.

"Lu, be nice," came softly from a woman. His long hair parted, pushed aside. Something cold stung his scalp and he hissed.

"It's just an antiseptic. The gash is almost fully healed and very nicely at that," she added in a soothing tone.

"My dear Martine," he slurred.

157

The arms across his back flexed. A bit more pressure and the rest of his ribs would crack. "She's not your 'dear' anything. How quickly you forget," sounded tense, uneasy.

"I ap... apologize," he replied, less than interested. Scissor snips, slight pulls to his scalp felt ticklish, and he shivered.

"Put him down gently, Lu," sounded so sweet and caring. As Draven's head met the pillow, the lovely nurse fixed the quilt under his arms as if to tuck him in. Her raven-black hair looked to be pulled up in a loose bun, her complexion much healthier than a month ago, her face no longer hollow and drawn.

He felt the dopey smile on his face and didn't care if his fangs were exposed, saying with half-closed eyes, "He feeds you well?"

His reward was a beautiful smile. "He certainly does."

"Good man," he murmured with another slow blink.

"I'm surprised you can focus at all," Lukas replied.

"Do not get cross with me. I'll tell your father."

"Sure you will. He'll be so proud of you being hell-bent on self-destruction."

"Should I make him a cup of coffee," Martine whispered.

Enthralled by her, he answered, "No. I like all the fuzzies around the edges and two of everything... two of you."

Lukas frowned. "Oh, Christ, he's too drunk. Coffee isn't going to sober a vampire who downs a four thousand dollar bottle of whiskey. He'll have to sleep it off."

As the brat's voice faded, Draven tried to catch

another look at two beautiful Martines. Then his lids drifted low and lower still. Strands of hair brushed from his face by a soft and feminine hand.

Luna loved it loose, not neatly tied at the nape of his neck. "Only when I'm with you, *ma chere*," he whispered.

****

Before leaving the club, Lukas had spoken to the Guardians on the dayshift to ensure that the damn fool had no access to any more alcohol. He wanted Draven taking sustenance every four hours, which obviously, he had not been doing. Then he and Martine got in the back of the SUV driven by a Guardian.

"You're frustrated and worried about him," Martine said as he put an arm around her and drew her in close.

"Now I have a suicidal vampire with a fucking feeding disorder on my hands." He let out a groan, slammed his head back on the headrest in the backseat.

"Jeez, you really think that's the case? It can't be good. Not even for a vampire."

"He's purposely weakening himself. Take a look and see it all." He closed his eyes and let her walk his mind.

She blew out a puff of air and shook her head. "Michael will get through to him."

"Christ, he better. This plan has to change. The lover's reunion has to wait." He pulled out his phone and sent a quick text.

"What you said back there, I mean, can a vampire sleep it off?"

"I have no friggin' idea. I'm having Dad take Luna to Kendrick House instead. You have a finished basement, right?"

"Great-Grandmother Morgan had it done in nineteen-twenty-nine. You know, just in case Michael needed a place to stay or hide, or whichever." Her shoulders shrugged. "He used it a lot the year you hunted him."

"So that's where he was. I couldn't scent him. Like he just vanished into thin air."

"Granny Martha's protection spells were super-powerful. Mare and I helped sometimes… when we sensed you on the block. We cloaked Kendrick House. You're just lucky Granny Martha didn't catch you."

"Good to know," Lukas said with a laugh and then kissed her hair. Martine's face tilted up and he captured her lips, the kiss deep, sensual, and long. Her hand went immediately to his fly, her finger running up and down it. Yeah. He was already hard.

She chuckled as they kissed again. "I could make it so nobody sees us," she whispered.

God, he wanted her. She pulled far enough away to see it in his eyes. "We can't, although I want to. I've got to explain this to your mother and make sure everything's good. Do you think she'll take Luna in?"

She rubbed his chest, replying, "If you ask her nicely. I know I'd say yes. To anything you ask. Every time." Leaning away, she knocked on the partition. When it slid open, she said to the Guardian, "We'd like you to drive around the city. Say, loop through Central Park before you take me home? Would that be possible?" Of course, the driver complied, and when the partition closed, Martine raised an eyebrow and kissed his lips. "So here we are. All comfy in the back seat with tinted glass all around… All alone and private."

Her tone said pure seduction. "I'm very

uncomfortable in my jeans," he said tugging at the waist of her purple scrubs.

"I can just imagine," she said, unbuckling his belt, unbuttoning his jeans and sliding down his fly. When Martine had him in hand, he hissed and his hips jerked. She added a soft, "Oh my," sexy and slow.

Lovings the feel of her on him, he whispered, "This is very naughty. The driver might be able to see us."

"He'll just see the two of us talking, so don't stop undressing me while I play with this."

He eased a hand into her scrubs. She lifted enough to get them and her panties down. One sneaker clunked against the floor of the SUV and with a leg free, she was exposed. "Yeah, very naughty," he whispered.

"Thrilling, too. A little dangerous even. Suppose we're stopped. How would we ever explain our state of undress to a cop? You all high and hard. Me all wet and ready."

"Just the way I like you."

She came out of his arms to straddle his lap. Looking down at his erection, she bit her lower lip with a very sexy grin. The scent of her intoxicated him. The expression on her face made him harder still. When she gripped his shoulders, he took hold of her hips and brought her down on him. Her head fell back as she moaned.

The way she rode him, tight and slow had him holding back release as long as possible. Hearing a low whimper, his finger slid down. The lower it went, the more she panted. Then he touched the tip of her and the thrill felt spectacular when they climaxed. The scent of coming together filled the enclosed space.

Slowly, they untangled. By the time the driver

pulled up in front of their brownstone, they were fully clothed. Lukas followed her in. After kissing his cheek, Martine went into the kitchen. He ran upstairs and took a cold shower.

****

After Lukas dried off, he took the time to send two important texts. He pulled on a clean pair of jeans and buttoned a crisp dark-blue shirt. Ten minutes later, he had the answers he hoped for. He came into the kitchen, took the mug of coffee from Martine's hand but didn't join her at the table.

"I couldn't wait until we got home. And I love making love to you, Lu," the woman of his dreams said as she buttered a piece of toast.

"Change the subject, M, or I'll get hard again."

With a sexy squirm in the chair, she gave a mischievous cackle, but he was totally serious. And the way she bit into that toast, well, all he had to do was look at her and he wanted to take her on the kitchen table. Unfortunately, there were more pressing matters. "Thank God Dad's staying at your mother's. I think I'd go off the deep end if we had to be totally hands off for a few days."

"And I'd join you right off that deep end." She took another bite and chewed. "You're less frustrated now. I sense it."

"Yeah, let's switch that subject, too." Lukas swallowed a mouthful of coffee and shifted into low-gear. "Christ, it pisses me off that Draven's hellbent on self-destruction. And it *really* pisses me off that we're going from one event right into another. It's never happened before. At least not that I've read about in Georgian History. There's an ebb and flow in the universe."

"There's no ebb and flow with evil, though. Maybe what happened in the Second Realm was only part one. Maybe this is part two." She wiped her hands on a cloth napkin.

"Is that what you sense?"

"No. It's just an observation," she replied as she stirred her coffee counterclockwise, dragging the silver spoon around in a pentagram with the whisper of "blessed be." He knew the routine, sensed the gravity of those words like a prayer.

"I'll think on it, but I don't see a connection."

Her head tilted to the side. "I don't, either, but it's kind of odd, though."

"What do you mean by odd?" He studied her beautiful face, feeling blessed that a month ago, he had made her his. She completed him in so many ways.

"I don't know, but odd is the only word that comes to mind," she said. "That Freya sketched Draven during the last event, that a female vamp decides to tell a good witch who senses a connection. That Freya just happened to be in the city to sit in on Mom's healing circle a month ago, not to mention her brother works for her. Plus, here's another thing. If the last event hadn't occurred, you wouldn't know how to handle Draven. You wouldn't even know he existed."

She has a point, a very good one, but where's the connection? "You think Draven links the two events? Until he's on his feet, it's shut down portal travel, you know."

After a sip of coffee, Martine shook her head. "I have no idea, but sorcerers are tricky."

"And vampires are cunning. This keeps the

continent safe for a while, but what about the other six and those gatekeepers?"

She asked, "You mean what if the vampires decide to make a comeback in our world?"

He shrugged. "Maybe that's what Herodotus hopes for."

"You'd need an army of Guardians to go and clean out the Third Realm, Lu. The number of human blood-slaves coming back here would create a major problem. They'd all need complete medical workups while in quarantine. Then there's the mental health component."

He shook his head. "Years as a slave. Bitten and fed on by multiple vampires."

"I hope the Georgians have thousands of psychologists and social workers because they're going to need each and every one of them. There aren't enough healing circles in the city for good witches to wipe their memories clean."

Finishing his coffee, he thought about Herodotus. *How many other sires reside in the Third Realm?*

"Why are you thinking about sires?"

Lukas looked at Martine and shrugged. "I honestly don't know. I've got to go." He put the mug in the sink, went over to kiss her cheek. "Later."

"You promise?"

"Always. I'm a man of my word." They smiled at one another, and he left the kitchen, putting the conversation out of mind. Luna and his father would arrive soon. Transit was in place. He had no idea what to expect.

Chapter 20

First Impressions

Standing in the parlor of Kendrick House, Lukas accepted the tight hug, already wincing at the term of endearment sure to come. "I've missed you, little boy," his father whispered.

"Missed you, too," he replied, letting it go and pulling out of the hug.

"I'll visit Draven first, then I want eight hours of peace in a bed. No texts full of drama. No interruptions. Just sleep."

The raspy tone full of exhaustion was worrisome, but the "ask" had been for something only his father could provide and would never be denied. No matter what. "How the hell did you get her from the van to the house?"

"Covered head to toe, under an umbrella, and flanked by four Guardians."

"Smart move. I don't sense any injuries on you. Did you drug her?"

"No. She's docile."

His eyebrows shot high as they each took an armchair. "You're joking, right? Docile and vampire don't go together."

"She cannot access the beast-within. I've never seen anything like this before. She exists solely on the blood of animals. Guardians cannot scent her."

He sniffed the air and had to agree, but said to be sure, "No way. Seriously?"

"I'd venture to say Luna is… something else, like an inactive vampire."

"Like an anomaly?'

"It absolutely fits." His father sighed, ran both hands through his brown wavy hair. He only did that when frustrated or exhausted. Or both.

Trying to process the idea of an anomaly and now very curious, he'd have to accurately document the female vampire for the Georgians. "I'll stay with her while you see Draven."

"Why did you decide to bring her here instead of delivering her to his lair?"

Lukas blew out a long, slow breath. "Besides starving himself? A few hours ago, he was off-his-ass drunk."

"Idiotic sonofabitch. He'll be so fucked up when he goes back to Herodotus that it will be an easy kill."

"He can't see Luna like this, Dad."

"No. He can't."

"You know him better than anyone. Maybe force him to see reason?"

"I truly hate the role of enforcer. First Luna, now Draven."

He leaned forward. "You just said she's docile."

"She panicked. Terrified of a helicopter, terrified of the jet… Screaming, punching, hitting and acting out. You know how I deal with tantrums, how my patience goes only so far when those buttons get pushed."

Shifting with a chuckle, he couldn't imagine his father getting parental on a female vampire. "Oh no, not *those* buttons."

"Every last one of them. Let's go. I'll introduce you," his father offered as he stood.

Lukas followed him down to Kenrick House's basement. Like his brownstone, it had the washer and dryer under the kitchen, but here it was hidden behind a sheetrock wall. The rest of the windowless space had a small living room with a sofa. His father opened a door, revealing a room with a twin bed, a desk and a dresser.

The female vampire, dressed in blue jeans and a forest-green sweater, sat on the bed. Lukas could tell she wasn't petite, with long legs, a healthy build, and elbow-length, loose hair a natural white-blonde. Her features appeared delicate, her lips full, her eyes like light-blue prisms. She stood, sniffed the air to take in his scent, and without hesitation walked over studying his face. He stood perfectly still, showed no aggression, but as she circled, he scented her as well. *Not even a trace of human blood in her, and yet, except for a heart that didn't beat, I'd never know and walk right past her. Think her just a pretty woman.*

"Luna," his father said, "this is Lukas. He'll stay with you while I visit Draven."

Her gaze swept down to his work boots and back up again. "Your human son does not look like you, Michael. His eyes so dark-blue that they rival sapphires. Just a… a stunning face."

Hearing that word made him grin. It seemed to be a favorite when describing him—too many times to count. Yet he kept his guard up, regardless of her compliment. Luna's voice was soft and gentle. He couldn't believe what he was seeing.

She sat on the bed, folded her hands in her lap—in a

timid way. "You are a mystical warrior, as strong as a vampire?"

"I am. Yes."

"He won't hurt you," his father stated in a tender tone, touching her shoulder. She looked at him the way a child would to a parent. "You can ask my son anything. He'll be honest with you, the way I was on the plane."

"Be gentle with Henri, Michael. He only meant to keep me safe."

His father sank down on a knee and took her hand in his. "We talked about this. He left you defenseless and vulnerable. It's abandonment, not love."

"It *is* love."

"I'll deal with him the way he understands."

"He is your brother in blood," came out like a gentle reminder to a trusted friend.

Christ, she really is docile. No aspect of the beast-within shown or sensed. In fact, if her demeanor was authentic, the term "inactive vampire" made a hell of a lot of sense.

When his father left, Luna stood and walked over to the desk, quiet for a while before she turned to him. "If you have questions, ask away."

"Your hair is the color of sunlit sand on a tropical beach, but very thick with loose curls."

"If I don't tie it back, yes."

"Henri only wore his tied back when we were in public."

"He still does," Lukas replied.

"There is the scent of a woman on you. Do you love her?"

"With all my heart."

"Is this her home?"

"Why do you ask?"

"Her scent is here as well," she simply replied.

"This is her mother's home. She lives with me now."

"Oh," Luna said with a nod. "She is your lover." He opened his mouth to reply, but she quickly added, "I must apologize. That is a private, personal matter."

"No worries. You're just... curious." *So am I,* he thought.

She smiled, pulled her hair over a shoulder and began to braid it. "Very much so. Do you know this electronic device called a laptop? I wish to study modern things and watch movies."

He now understood exactly what his father meant. "I can have one brought here."

"Thank you. And a mouse, please."

He pulled out his phone and texted his driver. "Perhaps you would prefer to rest until it gets here."

She shook her head and rolled her light-blue eyes. "There is too much to think about. Michael told me how his existence has changed. He is a good father?"

"Dad's one of a kind." *Just like you are,* he thought. Female vampires weren't gentle or sweet. She seemed something rare, like a delicate wildflower growing in the midst of a lava field. He was fascinated by her.

"I know how to text. I had a cell phone in Iceland, but your father threw it away."

"Yeah. He can really overreact sometimes." *I mean, what else do you say to that?*

"I do not like helicopters. Have you ridden in one?"

"A few times."

"I do not like jet planes, either. The noise of the engines on take-off hurts my ears." She stared down at her folded hands. "Your father showed no concern for my fears. He was excessively firm."

"I'm sure he had a reason."

With a frown, she replied, "I will still tell my Henri."

Sensing the need to shift her mood, he asked, "What else have you studied on the Internet?"

Looking up at him, her light-blue eyes went wide. "Oh. Many things, and there is still much to discover. You would be right to think me out of step with modern times."

Just out of step? "I understand what it's like to suddenly see the whole world and not just a little slice of it. It's a lot to take in." Saved by the ping of his phone, he pulled it out of his pocket and read the message. "I'll set the laptop up for you when it gets here."

"You are kind, not like your father in manner and tone. Yet you have mystical gifts."

"Yeah. I do."

"You scent things, like a vampire."

"That, too."

"You are not rough like Michael."

"I can be, if necessary. But I have a slower fuse."

The slightest smile appeared. "Henri has a slow fuse as well."

He gave a charming grin, which seemed to work, still thinking this one of the weirdest conversations he'd ever had. "You've had sustenance?"

"Yes, thank you. I need very little. When I hunt, I share the meat with… friends. Human friends."

"Good to know," he replied, still thrown off by yet another anomaly. "Air travel and fear of the unknown can be tiring. Unless you have more questions, you should rest."

"Do you like to read?'

"I love to read."

"Do you like movies?"

"Sure."

"So do I."

She spoke with joy and animation. And now he was discussing movies with a female vampire? He draped his legs over the desk chair and folded his arms on its back, totally intrigued.

After a solid sixteen minutes of conversation, Luna sighed before looking down at her hands again. "I have much to process about your father. In eighteen-eighty-seven, Henri cautioned me never to be alone with him. Michael is now very different."

He knew all about his father's past—with and without a soul. "He's a good man."

"Yes. But much more formidable than Henri."

"Henri can be quite formidable as well."

"But my Henri is always quiet. Very kind. Like you."

He wasn't about to discuss that arrogant vampire who had a good amount of cynicism infused in his personality. How would this gentle creature react when Draven's typical sarcasm surfaced? Thankfully, his phone dinged again. Looking at the message, he said, "The laptop will be here in thirty minutes."

"Thank you, Lukas." Stretching out on the bed, Luna curled on her side, facing away from him.

The researcher in him remained wildly intrigued, but the man in him grew more furious. If his father didn't stake Draven, Lukas highly doubted that Luna would recognize the vampire "her Henri" had become.

Chapter 21

Stake Me!

The aroma of strong coffee wafted through Draven's room. "It's just the two of us in your lair now. Open your eyes. I'm here to stake you." The clipped British voice had not a trace of humor in it. "Bloody Hell. Will you wake up and sit up," sounded even less pleasant.

Draven's eyes opened. His hands gripped the tucked in quilt at his sides. "Why is the room spinning?"

"You are truly a clueless fool."

Distinguishing the signature stance, the fuzzy form glaring down came into focus. Dressed in a black shirt and jeans, Michael's longish, wavy hair framed a face similar to his. Anger simmered in those dark-brown eyes. He used his elbows to support the unsteady slide up until his back hit the headboard, which caused a great deal of spasms between his legs.

"Luna is safe? Well-hidden and under your protection," he inquired.

Michael pulled off the quilt. "As per your request. Now put your feet on the carpet. We will have a little chat in the dining room."

He'd not be able to match the long steady strides, but needing to know details before meeting oblivion, Draven's toes gripped the carpet. He buttoned his black silk pajama top before slowly standing and settled the waistband of the pajama bottoms higher on his hips before the rather halting trip to the closest dining room chair. He had to brace the table to lower himself with a hiss. Raking his fingers through his loose hair, when it settled behind his ears, he picked up the fine china, drank the tepid but tolerable coffee before silently setting the expensive cup on its saucer.

"With all the bonding between us during the last event, why the hell didn't you tell me they want out of the realm?"

Michael's glare knifed right through him. That low, cutting tone as well. "You'd have immediately gone to the Georgian Council and blacklisted me. I am no fool. You are on the side of all that is good. I am not." He shrugged adding, "well, perhaps I am sometimes, possibly, *marginally* good. I had hoped to keep the sires at bay, locating land that will take years to build on, after many unforeseeable delays."

"How long have they been asking to leave it?"

"How long have they been there, brother?"

"Ever since?"

He relished the look of amazement. "Of course. Lately, it comes up every time I update them on their investment portfolios. I held off as long as I could."

Sitting back with his legs crossed at the knee, Michael eyed him. "They have no suspicion about your involvement with the side of all that is good—to use your own words. No suspicion about the early October event?"

"No. I shield my treason very well. I won't be able to do so now. It will be a very slow, very painful end. Which is why I want you to have the honor of staking me." Shocked when a pointy piece of oak hit the table,

Draven had to blink and refocus on it.

With his mouth turned down and his gaze averted, the man all but lashed his arms to his chest. "It's no fucking honor," sounded derisive.

"It is the only way."

"Why?"

"Because I prefer a quick poke in the chest to hours of torture, brother."

"Bullshit," Michael bit out.

"Before you do it, I need only to make a few clicks on the computer that will ruin them financially. The sorcerers won't be paid their monthly millions to keep the vampire realm in its current state of habitation. Once the human slaves die off, they will have no blood source, which will force them to eye the Second Realm."

"You're not touching those accounts."

A thin grin slid across his lips, a quick glance at the pointed wood followed. "Thus, either you stake me, or I go back to face the end to my existence."

"Animal blood will bleed you out quick."

"Only after the humiliation of being hung naked for all the other sires to see while he tortures me."

Michael's low, whispered, "Jesus Christ," matched the futility Draven felt.

"I will not be able to shield my mind, brother." His throat tightened saying it out loud, his grip on emotions elusive again. Craving human blood like a junky, the alcohol did a nasty job on his nerves, too. "Herodotus will see everything in my mind: How Luna still freely walks the good earth. My traitorous connection to you and your son. How there may be hidden portals to find and open for their return to this world." His hands began to shake. "Shove that piece of wood through my unbeating heart. I am begging you."

"How long since you've fed? I want the truth."

"A pint of animal blood plus a bottle of fine whiskey put me out quite well for a rather long stretch of time," he mumbled, somewhat proud of himself.

"Nice. Real smart," Michael said with another tight glare. "Thank God I didn't bring Luna with me to see you like this. You're a fucking mess, screwed in the head as well."

Unable to stand fast enough, he leaned in with narrow eyes. "You bastard! You brought her here. To this city? How dare you! And you call yourself an honorable man."

"And what do you call yourself? Tell me. What kind of protector are you to leave her exposed and vulnerable for eighty years? She's like a frightened child, Draven."

"The family I hired still protects her," he bit out through shakes and twitches.

"They are humans. If she had been discovered by another vampire and challenged, she would have no ability to defend herself. She'd become a blood-slave, a crazed female to fuck and abuse," Michael shouted with a finger pointed his way. "You are not only weak. You are absolutely delusional!"

"Stake me," he fired back.

"No, damn it! Now pull yourself together." Michael shot up and walked into the office.

Too shaken to hear the hushed conversation, too uninterested to care and too focused on the stake, shivers ran through him. His elbows hit the table. Like a human, he hugged his shoulders, shaking with tight, dry swallows. Pure misery. That's what he felt. His head hung low like a disgraced creature.

Then, the exquisite dishes rimmed in gold rattled in the hutch as the door slammed. Although his teeth chattered, he got out, "Take her far away and hide her, damn it! I give her over to you for protection from her sire, from… from all who would do her harm."

Michael paced the dining room once, twice, three times before finally saying, "You turned her into some kind of mutant who knows nothing, not a single thing about our world or the modern human world. There isn't the slightest sign of the beast-within. No feral-yellow glare. No metamorphosis. *Nothing!* She cannot protect herself."

"How am I to blame? It obviously saved her from being hunted by Guardians. It obviously kept her safe."

"Yes, and longing for your return. But did you return? No. You selfishly moved on, drinking and draining, amassing millions and basking in the prestige." He paused. "Are you proud of what you've done, Henri?"

"Do not call me that," Draven hissed. Both thumbs shot to his temples to hide the swell of blood tears. His fingers laced across his eyes. He simply sat there trembling, thinking, *I have been betrayed. It was a simple request. But the arrogant man brings her here!*

Minutes passed, saying nothing to each other because there was no more to say. He didn't have the strength to argue. He didn't want to go on like this, either. The sires would find a way out of the Third Realm, eventually. *Let the rest of the world deal with the chaos to come. I'll be dust and bits of bone.* A knock on the door sounded. Still emersed in his internal rant, he didn't bother to look up, thinking, *Maybe a Georgian must witness the staking. Let them document my final death. I do not care.*

He sensed Michale move around his home before leaning against the table. A tall tumbler was placed on the table before him. The heady scent filtered through a sniff. Healthy, human blood… Draven moaned low and long.

"Drink it down."

"You bring me to a crossroad. I do not wish to travel either way."

"You need to drink."

"You do not know what I need."

"I absolutely do. I promised Luna I'd bring her to you at midnight. So. You will drain every glass I put here." Michael's voice stayed low, full of control. "Tonight, you will give the award-winning performance of your undead existence. You will sleep until one hour before midnight. Then you will shower and dress in the finest suit you own, comb your hair and neatly tie it back in a leather band as always. You will be at your massive desk, perhaps finishing business that needs attention when she arrives. Because tonight, Luna will only see the intelligent, well put-together vampire I know you to be."

"It will be a cruel lie," he offered, truly tempted to reach for the glass and drain it—even more tempted to reach for the stake and drive it through his own chest. The tightening of his swollen balls made him very uncomfortable.

Michael gripped his shoulder. "Let's call it a necessary deception. Come on with you. Take your hands away from your face, drain the first glass and let it filter through your veins."

"What if I attack you?"

"You won't."

"Would you stake me then?" *It's a plan, a good one, at that.*

Michael's hand slid around the back of his neck in a pressured grip. "I'm getting impatient, Draven, and I'm close to exhaustion. I'll bloody well haul you to your feet and throw you into the exquisite hutch across the room. All that glass and broken dinnerware. I might cut myself getting you up— to throw you into it a second time. My blood is powerful. Our sire said so the night I was turned. When I staked him as well. You'd drink if my blood dripped right into your mouth, wouldn't you?" The unexpected shake was merciless. "Wouldn't you," he barked. "Now fucking drink."

Once freed Draven winced, couldn't hold the tumbler steady, let alone lift it. Michael helped guide it to his lips. It tasted fresh, clean of alcohol or drugs. At first swallow, his eyes closed to savor the taste. The process repeated until the time came when he felt strong enough to take the next, and then the next without assistance.

His vision cleared. His senses hummed. The scrapes on his hands and knees faded. His broken ribs began to knit together. Carefully pushing off the table, he felt fragments of control return. Face to face, they locked eyes. Draven swallowed, then cleared his throat about to speak, but Michael fisted the lapels of his pajama top and yanked him in close, a mere breath away.

"Pull this shit again and I swear, as sure as I am glaring into your bloodshot eyes, that swollen balls and all, I will beat you until you beg for mercy." Then, fixing Draven's collar, added, "See you tonight, brother. You had better play your part well. For Luna's sake. Not yours."

The arrogant bastard picked up the pointy wood and strode out the door. Two Guardians entered his dining room. Draven scented hard, oak stakes on each of them. He straightened his back and carefully walked into his room. Of course, they followed. Once in bed, he pulled the quilt up to his chin. *Let rich human blood work its own kind of magic, but I know how this ends,* he thought as his teary eyes closed.

Chapter 22

The Right Thing to Do

Sensing the late afternoon hour, Lukas shifted in bed beside the woman he loved. He had just read two emails from his father. One briefly outlined this morning's visit with Draven. The second simply said: *"Come to Mary's at eleven-thirty."* He read the first one over again, not at all satisfied.

Mary's text confirmed his father was still asleep and that she would have Luna ready a half hour before the midnight reunion with Draven.

Perfect, he thought. Much had been accomplished, and he agreed with the switch-over to human blood. He didn't want to plead his case and beg the Georgian Council for approval, but he could trust his personal physician, Doctor John Baker, to tap the veins of Georgians. Healthy wholesome human blood would speed up self-healing, maybe alter Draven's depressive state and give him a fighting chance. To insure the vampire's cooperation, seasoned, male Guardians were stationed at *Destiny*. Two female Guardians were with Luna at Kendrick House. So far, no out-of-the-ordinary texts had come in to disrupt the status-quo.

Next to him, Martine stirred. When she turned, he kissed her cheek. "How long have you been awake," she asked through a yawn.

"About fifteen minutes," he replied, kissing her neck.

"Everything okay," she said as his mouth traveled down to her breast.

He pulled back and looked at her, replacing his mouth with his hand. "Dad didn't stake Draven, and not a nip or growl from Luna. Now back to the matter in hand," he whispered with a mischievous grin.

Throwing her head back, she laughed, which thrilled him. He never kept anything from her but coveted this private time in bed. Plus, a certain part of his anatomy had already gone into high-gear.

"Did I ever tell you how much I love waking up with you like this?"

"What. Talkative and all business," he whispered as his hand slid lower.

"No. All hard and ready," she replied.

He kissed his way down in a slow sensual way. When his kiss found where he wanted to kiss more, he repositioned for a better taste. A hand traveled back up to her breast as her hips slowly gyrated. She arched against him, running her fingers through his long, loose hair. He heard her heart race, felt the heat flushing her skin as arousal began to peak. She whispered his name as he guided his erection in, and then he reveled in the ecstasy written across her face. The rhythm of making love to the woman he treasured with all his heart took over. He simply couldn't get enough of her.

****

As the November sun set, they were both showered and dressed. Martine wore a fresh set of purple scrubs for her ER night shift at St. Francis Hospital. "Aren't you going to wear something special for tonight?" she asked while twisting her raven-black hair up and into a bushy bun.

Lukas chuckled before saying, "No, why?"

"It's a special event. Wear your soft-blue shirt and like, regular shoes instead of work boots. Meet you downstairs," she said as she left their bedroom.

He pulled off his boots and put on casual shoes, not really seeing the need. It was an important night for Draven, not for him. After tying his hair back, he slipped the Kendrick amulet over his head and under his shirt to settle against his heart.

Meeting Martine in the kitchen, Lukas kissed her cheek before preparing her favorite sunset breakfast, two scrambled eggs with a lot of butter and toast on the side. She had already started the dark-roast coffee, freshly brewing in the coffee maker. Even before the pot filled, he put his cup under it, added a dollop of milk and a heaping spoonful of sugar. He swallowed his coffee, thinking, *things can go either way tonight.* Setting breakfast before the woman who owned his heart, he also filled her purple mug, but didn't join her at the table.

"Is this going to be a three-cup night for you, Lu?"

He gave a shrug, took another sip before setting his coffee down. "I have no idea."

"So. Tell me all about Luna."

Relaxed with his back against the counter, he answered, "I swear to God, there's nothing like her in any research I've studied."

"Doesn't she appear in Georgian records or something? I mean, they know every undead thing on the planet. They journal everything."

"There's one questionable entry from the late eighteen-eighties in Paris. Even though the description fits, it doesn't identify the woman on Draven's arm, and that's just it. The entry states woman, not vampire. There's no tangy scent to her, not even enough to warn that I was in a room with one."

"You were alone with her?"

He saw the tense expression and slowly rolled his eyes. "Yeah. I was."

"That's taking a chance. Suppose she bit you."

He started to smile. "Really? First off, I'm stronger than her and second, it was like babysitting a twelve-year-old."

"Yeah, a twelve-year-old going on a hundred and a half."

"One-hundred-thirty-something is more like it. Look into my mind and see her."

Martine put down her fork, narrowed her eyes before closing them. "Oh, wow. Very attractive. Lovely long hair. Pretty tall for a woman. I'd say five-nine maybe?"

"Just about," he said as he sat and folded his arms on the table. "Inquisitive the way my sisters often are. She speaks soft and polite. Comes across sweet of nature. Yet her sire is the sadistic bastard who did all the damage to Draven."

"Oh my God," she murmured with a slow shake of her head. "How could something so evil sire something so… so not evil? Maybe she keeps her dark side hidden."

"I don't sense a dark side. The word 'evil' doesn't fit in the same sentence with her name. You can't call a vampire an innocent, but in this case, well, Dad used 'inactive vampire' as a possible tag. Animal blood shouldn't assuage her thirst, which is another anomaly."

"Now that's just weird. And she didn't try to bite

Michael on the plane?"

"Nope. Even after, you know, typical overbearing dad stuff. And she flatly refuses to believe *her* Henri could be, in any way, a problem."

"Even the intimidating version of Michael didn't get her riled enough to attack?"

He shook his head, watched her finish the scrambled eggs. "She only managed a bit of a growl."

After a bite of toast, Martine eyeballed him. "Nothing else?"

"Nothing. You know, female vampires are crafty, unpredictable. I swear, I'm stumped."

"So... you're taking a sweet, gentle vampire to Draven, the suicidal, feeding-disorder and drunk off his ass version of what he once was. Jeez, Lu."

"Dad put him on human blood."

Toast in hand, she leaned forward. "Do you think that's wise? Suppose he goes nuts and bites someone?"

"We can handle him. I sure hope he taps into his mature-and-put-together side tonight. What I've seen lately would fascinate a demon shrink—if there were such a person."

"But is it wise to feed him human blood?"

"In a way. The sires will only scent his normal diet."

"You're not serious about letting him go back there?" She searched his face for a reply, and when he didn't give one, she added, "Draven helped you and your father in the last event. He carried you through the portal and watched over you like you were his own son in the hospital. He proved his moral side isn't just something he puts on to impress, Lu."

"He has to go back. He brought this on himself."

Her hands shot into the air. "How so?"

"He should have told me what the sires want. I would have brought it to the Georgian Council in a very careful, diplomatic way that didn't indict him."

"So because he didn't come clean and spill his guts, you and Michael are just going to stand down and let them destroy him?" She dabbed those lovely lips with a napkin, picked up her purple mug.

He brought the empty plate to the sink and then leaned against the counter again, watching her. "He has to go back, M."

"Then why bring Luna to him, only to send him off in a few days—to never return? That's cruel, Lu."

He looked aside. "It's not cruel. And as for Luna, the Georgians will need to study her."

Her hand flew into the air again. "Pfft! Like some poor, caged animal in a lab."

"Georgian scientists aren't heartless. They'll document her. Possibly place Luna above the Law of the Kill, the way they did years ago with my father."

"The Georgians needed him as a champion for their cause. They don't need a female vampire who speaks softly and survives on animal blood."

He leaned forward, uncomfortable with the accusation. "They won't hurt her."

"Are you sure about that? And then what? Happily return her to Iceland? Yeah. Right."

"Martine, this is complicated. She has to be studied. Then they'll decide what to do with her."

"Tagged like an animal. Probably thrown back out where some vampire will see her as easy prey. I don't accept it. You shouldn't, either." She stood and put her mug in the sink.

"Protocol is already in place."

She turned to him with fire in her eyes. "And you're comfortable with it?"

"No. I'm not comfortable with it. Not in the least. Look. I don't want to get ahead of this."

"Don't give her over to them, Lu. Find another way."

"You're worried about a female vampire?"

"Yeah. I am. And I'm worried about you. The man I love isn't cruel or deceitful. It's gonna work on your head. I know it will. Don't let them touch her. Find another way."

He gave a nod, kissed his cheek. "I didn't make you dinner. I'm sorry."

"Look. You've got a lot on your mind. I'll grab something from the café, or maybe Dottie will bring enough for two, like she usually does." Martine came into his arms and touched his cheek. "Please be gentle with her. Be the person you are. If she's been secluded and sheltered, then she's vulnerable."

"You're the second person to use that word."

"I know you'll do the right thing. You always do," she whispered and pulled out of his arms. "Find a way to get Draven out of this mess."

They said, "I love you," at the same time, as if they read each other's mind.

Lukas pulled out his phone before walking into the dining room. Sitting in front of his laptop, he checked for any new emails. He linked his phone to the screen. One text from Mary appeared. She had a dress for Luna to wear tonight. Luna liked it.

He typed back: *"Great. Thanks."*

Opening a new word document, what happened this morning had to be journaled. The Georgian Sovereign

Council would eventually request a full account. He'd make sure to give them one, which would include his honest take on Luna. Martine's words rang in his ears and played in his brain. He wanted to protect Luna. He wanted to keep Draven safe, as well.

It was the right thing to do.

****

Draven awoke in less pain than before he laid his head down. Healthy human blood in his veins had definitely sped up self-healing, and, he supposed, Michael's threat helped as well. But his mood remained unstable, with too many highs and lows that surfaced like a warning of impending doom. Luna, right here in this dangerous city, had him anxious. Dark seers, cloaked by dark magic, had him edgy. They were into secretive cults, worshiping sorcerers and sires like deranged groupies. What if they got a whiff of Luna? A whiff of his liaisons with Michael and Lukas? What if they had already made contact with Herodotus?

I'm in no position to protect her or myself like this. And that made him miserable.

Two pints of human blood waited on his dresser. His eyes shifted to the Guardian who stood like a sentinel in the doorway. After planting his feet on the floor, he stripped off his silk pajamas before draining the glass bottles, and then shuffled into the ensuite. Less swollen but with everything too tender below the waist, he let hot water drench his body. Careful not to rub his scalp while washing his hair, he had to clear his mind. All the emotional clutter felt like bleeding scabs in his brain. Yet, at midnight, a reunion that threatened to expose every rawness within was something he couldn't avoid.

The insolence of Michael bringing her here! He yanked the lever and then dried off. He dried and tied back his hair, and then walked across the bedroom to the closet. He eyed a particular suit, one worn a few nights ago, and his lips settled in a smirk. Well, he could be insolent, too. But the black silk shirt and tie would be fresh.

Dressing wasn't as difficult as expected, although running, hunting, and getting aroused were definitely not happening yet. After putting on black socks and shoes, he stood with more ease. That he no longer shuffled leaving the room gave him more confidence.

Entering his office, typical arrogance showed none of the internal conflict pulling him every which way but forward. Carefully, he sat at his desk and texted Mallory to meet him tomorrow at sunset. As his computer whirred awake, he couldn't stop thinking about Luna. His hand balled into a fist before gripping the mouse and opening the Internet. He had hours until he faced her. In the meantime, global stock markets had to be checked, buy and sell orders to give.

An hour later, he switched to club business. Open or closed didn't matter. Liquor orders had to be placed and payroll had to be approved, which got him thinking about his impending final death. He leaned back in his chair, ignored the Guardian's shift in position with a dismissive glance.

Who will run the club? Who will inherit my assets? Weeks ago, Lukas had handed him something precious. His only child, his son born in 1835, had followed in his footsteps as a musician. Julien LeVigne had also been a composer. On that October night when holding his son's original compositions, his eyes had filled with blood tears. They were payment from Michael, for his assistance in the Second Realm. Instead of immediately contacting a detective to search for any living descendants of Julien, Draven had immediately locked the manuscripts in his closet's private safe. Why?

Because when you believe you have eternity, you simply put things off.

Had Julien married? Could there be a great-great grandchild, perhaps a direct descendant still alive in France or Italy? *You will never know, you fool.* And none of this mattered because he was quickly running out of time. Angry at himself, Draven stood. The Guardian at the door to his home stepped aside. In the room next to the master suite, he sat at his treasured grand piano. The musician in him chose Chopin's *Grande valse brillante in E flat*, said to be the composer's favorite. It filled the room with drama and joy, but sixteen bars in, it didn't suit his emotions. He switched to *Nocturn, Opus 9, Number 2* in the same key. *Yes, much better.*

His hands mastered the keys. Unlike this current situation, he alone controlled every facet of the instrument, the very weight of each finger, the chordal destinies of harmony or dissonance. He alone manipulated everything in his performance. The emotion, the passion with unparalleled brilliance, vibrated through him. When both hands rested on his lap, he released the *sostenuto* pedal and closed his eyes. *Control. I must take control of my existence as well.*

He left the room, and when passing the Guardian stationed at the office door, the look on the young man's face finally showed something—like awe. "And you thought I only excelled at the drink and drain," he stated with an arrogant smirk, "Well, think again."

Miserable within, he sat at his desk, opened a blank word document and began to type. He could fix a lot of what bothered him with his own, personalized version of a last will and testament. Donovan, his trusted bouncer, would inherit *Destiny*. His staff, faithful minions all, would be assured a full year's salary with health benefits and dental, even if they chose to not remain with the new owner.

A grin began, thinking that if he had to leave this world, he'd do it in style. Except for Luna, he had never supported anything but himself during the many decades of existence. Perhaps now, knowing the end drew near, those moral threads within had thickened. Why couldn't a vampire donate anonymously to great causes, or piano performance scholarships? He made a list of renowned music schools and other charities he'd heard advertised on a particular news station.

He then set aside a hefty sum to back up the financial support for Luna. In the event that Michael passed of old age, Lukas would take up Luna's protection. Then he paused, knowing he would have to trust Lukas to hand her over to someone else, once he reached the end of his own life.

Closing his eyes, he took a moment. Mary Kendrick should get a portion of his assets. Had the good witch not told Lukas, he'd have completely bled out, gone insane. *Or*, viciously drained the first minion who dared to enter his bedroom. Martine would inherit a portion for stitching his head and caring for him. Then, Lukas would be tasked with researching any living descendants of Julien, and he or she would inherit a fortune.

Reading over the document and admiring his prose,

a sense of peace settled within. Once printed, he saved the file, reached over for the papers. *Yes,* he thought, *this is the right thing to do.* On the last page, his signature was, as always, a graceful flourish. He placed it in a crisp, white envelope, put Michael's name on it, and put it in the top drawer of his desk.

The simple act of completion, the sense of finality hit like a punch to the chest. Indeed, he had amassed millions. He thought about the Third Realm's investment portfolio, still itching to obliterate their holdings, or, at least, send them into a downward spiral to eventually wipe them out. He was tempted. Very tempted.

Turning off the computer, what he would do later fully crystalized. *Tonight, I will give a uniquely different performance.* He'd bask in Luna's beauty one last time, and then she would want to leave immediately. After the beating that was sure to follow, his brother in blood would hide her where she'd never be found. Not by anyone, especially Herodotus. Because Luna couldn't survive her sire's cruelty. She'd be better off staked through the heart.

Chapter 23

Lovely Luna

Lukas sat across from his father and Mary in the living room at Kendrick House. "What I found should fit perfectly," she said, glancing back and forth between them.

A smirk crossed his father's serious face. "We're dressing vampires now. Fucking odd. Not to mention feeding and stitching them up. All of this is far into the I-can't-believe-it zone."

Thinking it almost funny, Lukas swallowed the chuckle and asked, "How do you think Draven will react when he sees her?"

When his father didn't answer, Mary said with a loose shrug, "Who the hell can predict? I'm right there with you, hoping for a strong love-conquers-all vibe."

His father looked at her. "Do you sense anything, Mare?"

"My sixth sense isn't humming, But Luna is pivotal, unless Draven's too far gone."

"An 'inactive vampire' holds the key," Lukas whispered with a shake of his head.

"Well, it's an appropriate tag," his father answered.

"What if she tells him not to go back to the sires?"

"She doesn't have it in her to make such a demand, Lukas," Mary said. "I know Draven can be devious, but

I don't want to see him meet his end, either."

"This isn't a live and let live situation," his father interjected. "We're talking about vampires. Whether or not she drinks human blood, whether or not he has a significant moral thread, it makes no difference. He should have told us what they wanted last month."

Mary quickly huffed, "That's no reason to let his head sail across a room from a slice with a sire's silver sword," adding a shocked, "I can't believe I just said that."

"You, of all people, know he cannot be trusted," Michael shot back.

Acutely aware of how guarded his father looked, Lukas sensed the black and white of his words. They sounded as immovable as a thick, brick wall. But Martine had said something similar to her mother's comment. "Did talking with Draven this morning hit a nerve?"

His father crossed his arms and looked away as if he had just shut down, closing both of them out. "Sullen is one thing. Irrationally despondent is another."

The description of this morning's conversation had been generic. *Maybe too brief. He is totally not a man of many words, giving the 'what happened' without the 'how' most of the time.* "But you told Draven to put his best foot forward tonight. You didn't have to play the enforcer."

"Not until just before I left."

"And you showed compassion," Lukas suggested, waiting for more.

"To a vampire, to two vampires—in less than twenty-four hours. What *is* our world coming to."

Mary sat forward. "Listen, up until sixteen years

ago, I could have described you as sullen and despondent, too. So you were a different type of vampire, already tagged mystically-enhanced. One of a kind since eighteen-ninety. Many people showed *you* compassion."

"These two didn't reclaim their souls the way I did, Mare."

"But they somehow manage to access moral values, Michael, which isn't easy to do when there's a demon possessing your soul," she countered.

Lukas quicky held up a hand. "Whoa, whoa! The philosophical question of soul or no soul is one that holds no worth at this point. We'd be here all night if we started to discuss it. They aren't like Dad, Mare. And neither of them are powerful sires nor similar to any other vampires I've staked, for that matter. So how do we use the lovers' reunion tonight?"

"Let it go as it goes and then we react accordingly," his father said. "Seeing her again has to affect him. One way or the other, he will go back to the sires. If they destroy him, then so be it. At least he gets to say goodbye to Luna."

Clear and succinct without one emotion. Whatever transpired between them this morning must have hit a nerve. Or two. *There has to be another way out of this, damn it,* Lukas thought.

"She's coming," whispered Mary.

Everyone stood, signaling an end to the discussion. Luna came through the door and into the living room with two female Guardians flanking her. Lukas couldn't help but stare. No one would guess that a beast-within owned the soul of the striking woman who looked from face to face, as if seeking approval. Lovely white-blonde hair loosely curled around her shoulders and ended at her elbows. The emerald-green flowing dress fit perfectly and complemented such a pale complexion and light-blue eyes. A touch of lipstick, the shade of a ripe raspberry covered her full lips. The plunging neckline accentuated her breasts in a sensual way.

"You look beautiful," Mary said, "and the shoes fit?"

Luna glanced down at her feet. "They do, Mary. Thank you."

His father approached her and the Guardians stepped back. Her stare into his eyes was bold, intense, and yet searching in a tentative, innocent way. "Henri will be pleased," he simply remarked.

He sure as hell better be… enough to get his ass in gear, Lukas thought. It was a chance they had to take.

Mary followed them to the foyer, placing a black woolen shawl over Luna's shoulders. His father shrugged on a suit jacket, which hid the stake at his back. After putting on his leather bomber, Lukas slipped the stake into the left side of his belt. There was no earthly way that Draven would not be moved when he saw Luna. Of that, he was sure.

Chapter 24

Reunion

Thinking back to how she had fought Michael made Luna feel embarrassed and full of regret. Mary Kendrick treated her with dignity. So did Lukas and the female Guardians as well. With Michael, however, she felt different. He was supportive in a silent way; someone well-respected as a leader, not a follower. She began to understand the daunting role he had played in getting her here.

Seated in the back of the black SUV between the two men, she leaned forward with her head snapping left and right to see out the tinted windows. Neither Michael nor Lukas said a word, which was perfectly fine. Too enthralled with the sights of this city at night, she studied the architecture on blocks full of brownstones, then tall buildings and busy crosswalks.

The way the bright signs blinked and flashed mesmerized her. Huge, high billboards like giant television screens showed events around the world. Seeing this place called Times Square, she realized how pictures on the Internet couldn't fully capture the thrill of the crowds, the excitement of being right in the midst of it all. *Although unable to scent the scene, what a magical place this is*, she thought. For more than a moment, she wished she could get out and walk this street called Broadway and take in all that she could only glimpse from inside.

Still perched forward and, curious about everything, Luna felt the lean as the vehicle turned off the main thoroughfare and down a one-way side street before pulling up to the curb in front of a dark nightclub, not lively as one would expect. Then again, she really had no expectations. None at all, except Henri holding her tight, whispering words of love in a place of security she had missed for over eighty years.

Lukas's hand, firm but gentle, helped her out of the high vehicle. His grip wasn't like Michael's during her journey to this city, whose hold had been anything but kind. Then again, whether or not it showed, Michael came across as fiercely protective of them all. In a way, Luna appreciated him for pushing her to the limit of tolerance. It fostered a deeper understanding of who she was, of what she had the capacity to handle—on her own.

Flanked by the two handsome men, they approached a smokey glass door with a large, bald man standing like a watchman. Once inside, dim security lights lit their path. Michael led the way down a long, bejeweled hall, and then, they took a flight of stairs down. She had scented Henri the minute they entered the building, and when they approached the door at the end of a much wider hall, who stood behind it heightened her excitement.

So many questions, so many feelings. Had I a beating heart, it would race. Will he take me in his arms and hold me tight? Will he expect a tamed kitten, something to play with only when he chooses? Before she could pull out of her thoughts, without so much as a word of warning, Michael opened the door. Two men glanced at her before they left the office.

Lukas's hand was still in hers, and her grip tightened. He leaned in with the whisper, "I'm right here, and I won't let go until you do."

No. She couldn't let go. Yet, as if she were moving backward in time, eight decades worth, she gave a nod, searching Henri's warm-brown eyes, stepping toward him with Lukas at her side.

My Henri. Tall and broad-shouldered. His black hair pulled back, accentuating his widow's peak, his angular features with lips like a slash drawn across his face. In a tailored black suit, black shirt and tie, he looked commanding, his arms crossed at the chest and his feet slightly apart. And behind her Henri, Michael took up the same stance. They still looked like the brothers in blood they were in the late 1880s. Michael's hairstyle had changed, and yes, he now had a heartbeat, but they looked beyond handsome, beyond formidable, like unique, unnatural forces to be reckoned with.

Lukas walked forward and she found herself moving as well. She hesitated when they stopped an arms-length away from the object of her eternal addiction. She let go of Lukas's hand as he took the shawl from her shoulders.

Henri stood in front of a massive desk. Reaching out, her fingertips gently ran down his face. Their gaze locked to each other, drawn like magnets as he took her hand away and kissed her open palm. His touch trembled through her. Blood tears glistened in her eyes. They both stepped in at the same time, falling into an embrace she had yearned for every single night of this undead existence. Her head rested on his shoulder as his hands pressed to her back. Anxious to hear his rich, deep voice, she whispered, "My eternal love."

"You should not be here," he whispered in reply.

She heard just a trace of a French accent, yet his tone sounded like a scold, like she'd done something wrong. Her body stilled. Something inside shattered. It felt as if invisible shards of glass ripped open every vein. His hands braced her shoulders, pulled her away from the place of comfort she had longed for throughout decades without him. The study of his face told her nothing, the hollow look in his eyes, as though she stared into an abyss. The vampire standing before her appeared to be less about who he was and more about who he had become.

She took a step back. "Is this what the modern world has done to you, or was I so blinded by love that I did not see this coldness, Henri?"

"One sees what one wants to see. And please do not call me Henri. I prefer Draven."

"Ah, yes, Draven," she said with a tilt of her head, "The Gatekeeper of the portal, the owner of a trendy club, the worldly investor for sorcerer and sire alike. So many facets to this new persona. I suppose you had to destroy—to rebuild yourself."

He appeared distant, disengaged. The reunion she had hoped for didn't seem right. Instead of hearing a profession of love, perhaps even an apology, she'd been admonished for coming to him? Michael had said he needed her. Oddly, she didn't see or feel his need at all.

It wasn't upset that snaked through her. Not disappointment, either. What bloomed within felt like anger, at herself and at him. Had her romantic fantasy of this reunion been distorted by love and longing? Had she failed to realize that he had experienced many, many things while she stubbornly held on to the security of sameness? After eighty long years of waiting for his return, which had never happened, perhaps anger was bound to surface.

"Do I remind you too much of your past? Is that why I shouldn't have come here?"

He replied without emotion, "You were safe where I left you."

"Really. How would you know? You never returned. Yet every Hunter's Moon I stand on the very spot where you left me to search the sea. How foolish I've been." The realization caused another revelation, and her shoulders straightened.

"You have had a protected existence, which I have provided," he said in arrogance.

"I have had a sheltered captivity, thanks to you." She aimed the comeback perfectly and oh yes, she had much more to say. "Michael is right. You abandoned me. Left me vulnerable. That is not love. Seeing you now, I question why you ever chose to be so burdened with me."

"You will stop speaking at once," he snapped at her, as if he were in command.

"I choose to continue. Eighty years alone is more than a lifetime for most humans, and no, I will not stop speaking." She eyed him from the top of his pulled-back hair down to the shine on his shoes. "Look at yourself. Put together in an ensemble that foretells the darkness in you. It is worshiped, isn't it, this new persona? You, the lord and master over minions with your pockets overflowing. It gives you the thrill of power, of displaced ownership. I am thankful that Michael was candid, instead of coating the truth like honey coats a spoon." Yet on the plane, she had *insisted* that he could not possibly be talking about her Henri. Well, she had been wrong.

"My brother in blood has loose lips," he growled with a sneer.

"Oh, were that true. I should have listened more and defended you less. You take what is offered and crave more. You suck dry the victims and then thirst for more. Calculating. Cruel. No mercy is in you because, indeed, you believe yourself lord and master. This office screams of wealth and power. So does what I see through that door behind your desk. Yet all of this is barren. Just like you." Her eyes slid to the side before coming back to his. Then, one strong sniff told her more about him, something he'd regret. "I smell her... The last woman you had. Do you think so little of me that you clothe yourself in the scent of sex?" She let the remark sink in, took in another nose-full of female coming from the front of his trousers. "I have remained faithful, but to what, I ask myself. Decades of dreaming of your touch, your mouth on me. For what? From the moment of awakening in undeath in that room beneath Veronique's villa only *you* have touched me."

"You expect me to believe that you have never taken a human lover?"

Thinking his smirk rude, she stepped into him. That question fueled her anger. "I do. There were never lies between us. You may have changed, but I have not." Yet again, that annoying smirk angered her.

"I have provided financial security. Had I known, I would have gladly provided that type of service as well."

"You would have paid a man to be used for sex?" Her eyes narrowed, yet he continued to show nothing on his face, kept an arrogant stance as if he were above her.

"It would have suited you to see me in someone else's arms, with someone else's mouth on me, yet you show no shame? Like a common pimp?"

"There is nothing common about me," he replied with a lift of his chin.

"Oh, I believe that underneath this impressive display common thrives in you. So does emptiness because that's where you reside. You might have made the suggestion to take hundreds of lovers. We had all that time on the ship together. You could have sat me down and said that you'd never return, that it was goodbye forever. I might have taken the next ship back to Europe. I'd be a very different vampire, wouldn't I?"

"No one stopped you from leaving."

"Do you recall the journey to Iceland, or is it too long ago to remember how we spent those last days together on the ship?"

"I'm sure you will remind me," he said as if bored.

She slapped his face. Hard. And then she slapped him again. Just as hard. Blood dripped from his lip, which he didn't lift a finger to swipe away. With his eyes cast down, he looked as if those shards of glass in her veins had somehow magically transferred to his. Letting out a shriek, she pounded his chest. He did not move, nor defend himself. The next slap, a back-handed one, sent him reeling to the side and grabbing onto the desk's edge.

Suddenly she lifted off the floor with Lukas's arm banding her waist. She continued her assault on the egotistical vampire who stood like a stoic, who took every blow until she was pulled farther away and he was out of reach. Fully furious, she fought to pry herself loose.

"Enough," Lukas whispered as if he understood, "Please calm down, okay?"

But then a low growl sounded. Draven's eyes flashed back and forth between feral-yellow and their natural warm-brown. The change looked like a strobe, a subtle flicker as his features hardened. "Take your hands off what is mine," he growled and bared his fangs.

"I don't think she's yours anymore," Lukas replied.

"He will attack you," Luna screamed.

"Then he's dust and bits of bone at your feet," came from Michael's son.

Her reply, "No. No, no, please," sounded like a cry and a plea. When Lukas let go, she closed the space between them and studied his profile. Her Henri remained speechless.

****

That type of flicker had never happened before. He was unable to accept how the mere sight of Lukas holding Luna brought him so very close to losing control of the beast-within. Draven kept his back to everyone, held the desk to steady himself. His eyes filled, his jaw clenched tight, forcing what owned his soul far, far down where it belonged. *I am literally seconds away from getting my last wish to meet final death. Right here. Right now. In front of Luna and disgraced for all to see.* He fully expected to be thrown across the office, to feel Michael's brutal fists. And yet, Luna's reaction felt more painful than any beating he'd get.

He couldn't continue the aloof façade much longer. Now, with the beast-within back in its metaphorical prison, those despicable blood tears trickled down. He sniffed the next ones back, squeezed his eyes tight. *What now*, he thought. His plan to drive her away, in spite of

Michael's warning, had cut her too deeply, had been overly vicious, even though her verbal comeback sounded as if ice ran through her veins instead of blood! Every word rang true. Including the fact that he purposely wore this suit with the scent of sex all over it.

Luna's hand came over his. She pried his fingers off the desk and slipped her hand into his. He shook his head as his shoulders lowered, hoping to discourage her. His throat closed, making it impossible to speak. Blood tears kept drip-drip-dripping to the desk. Almost inaudible pings, yet he heard each one land. She turned his shoulders, cradled his head to her breasts as he sat on the edge of the desk. She stroked his hair, began a gentle sway as if to soothe him.

I am less than dirt beneath her feet, a disgrace. Creatures like him didn't deserve love. They didn't deserve loyalty. That she had never sought the arms of another was a shock that only proved him more undeserving. And through the years, what had he done? Denied his love for her and fucked his way through Europe, through multiple American states. The drink from a woman's jugular heightened the act of sexual penetration. Rarely did he drain one because they were his conquests. His trophies.

Then in the 1970s he settled in this city. Not long after his arrival, he found Michael, the only vampire who had the power to reclaim his soul. Jealous of how his brother mastered the beast-within, he hoped those threads of morality he kept hidden would give him a similar outcome. Of course, they had not. *Where are those moral threads tonight? I have caused significant pain, enough to have her slap, punch and kick. I have damaged her in a way I never thought I could.*

Luna whispered his name. Draven refused to move. She pulled the black silk handkerchief out of his suit's breast pocket because no, he would not soil her with his touch.

Perhaps the merciful God above will grant me the gift of a quick end. Broken. He felt the same as he had right after the humiliating kick from Herodotus. Now, he was broken in front of Luna, Michael, and Lukas, fully certain they were not pleased with the way he had treated her. And yet, not a sound came from either man.

Luna whispered, "Come with me. They will respect our privacy and allow us to be alone together."

Yes. He needed to be alone with her. To apologize. To grovel at her feet and beg forgiveness.

She pulled back, again dabbed below his eyes. "They are sitting in the armchairs with their backs to us now. Come."

Holding her hand, he slowly stood. He let her lead him into the privacy of his home. Instead of the bedroom, Luna walked through the dining area and into his living room.

Chapter 25

What Now?

"Bloody hell," Michael hissed, running both hands through his hair. He didn't have to look over to see the shock on his son's face. "I was one breath away from grabbing that fool by the back of the neck to fling him across the room. I warned him to be civil."

"Of all the reactions I expected, that sure as hell wasn't one of them," his son mumbled, as though hesitant to respond.

"Let's hope we don't have a double suicide-by-stake on our hands now," he hissed.

"She'll talk him down."

"I hope you're right. If you're not, the only benefit to this is that seven deadly sires are stuck in the Third Realm."

"Until they bribe a gatekeeper on another continent to open a portal," his son replied.

"No. The Second Realm sorcerers would sense it. This one must stay bloody locked."

"I'm certain they'll find a way to open it if they sense Draven's gone. Think of all the fucking conjured things that'll be walking city streets again, playing with humanity."

"Then sixteen years ago after the Mayhem in Manhattan, all I accomplished simply gave the human world a tease of peace, not forever, but fragile. It absolutely felt permanent at the time." Pissed to Hell, Michael cursed under his breath, not at all comfortable with any outcome but a final one. "And let me add, I do not like the idea of sending him back to the sires. God only knows what he'll do or say if he isn't stable." He paused. "How many days do we have?"

His son shook his head. "Two."

"It's not enough time, even if we double his sustenance. His ribs and the crack in his skull might be healed, but that fucking kick did damage, much more than just physical. I'm sure Herodotus knew the effect it would have." He raked his fingers through his hair again and began to pace the office.

"So basically, we're screwed."

"In multiple ways. Seven sires with all kinds of unknown skills, most likely far above those of a normal vampire. Cunning intelligence, possibly the ability to read minds, like our sire could."

His son leaned forward with an elbow on a knee and his fist supporting his chin. "We can't ask the Georgians for assistance this time. We have to act on our own."

He looked at Lukas in disbelief. "Guardians are already keeping an eye on him and Luna."

"But we can't ask Guardians to assist us in a fight with the sires, Dad."

"Unless we get them here, through the portal. Then they must engage."

"And probably die in the fight. You said it yourself. They could have all kinds of abilities." His son sat back and let out a sigh before saying, "Nope. They have to be destroyed in the Third Realm. Every last one of them. Then the realm will be in turmoil, looking for new leadership. The vampire population will most likely drink and drain every human blood-slave before turning on each other, culling themselves."

"You're getting too far ahead in this. The sires are the main problem."

"So let's explore what you said before. What if we find a way to get them here. Then we don't let them return to their realm."

His eyes narrowed, trying to follow the logic. "Keep going."

"We have them all in one place with no exit, right here in this office. We'll have half a dozen Guardians protecting the hallway."

"They'll sense the Guardians."

"Not necessarily because they'll be so focused on being in the human world, they won't sense us a threat."

"Us? Who exactly is 'us'?"

"You and me. With silver broadswords in each hand."

"There are seven of them and two of us."

"No. There are three of us, counting Draven. That's two apiece."

He eyed his son. "I know you're bright. Three times two is six."

"Well, Herodotus is already dust and bone," Lukas replied with a loose shrug.

"And how is that?"

"We have Draven bring him through first. By himself. The old sire won't even make it into this office. Once he's dust and bone right there in the vault, the rest is simple."

Michael scoffed. "Nothing about any sire is simple."

"It is, though," his son argued. "Draven could say

that he can only bring two through the portal at one time. He walks them into the office. We slice off their heads. They won't think it necessary to bring weapons."

"Only their fangs, which are deadly enough." He didn't like the sound of this. Not one bit.

"We can totally do it, Dad."

"Don't even think it. There are so many unknowns, it could end in disaster."

Lukas foolishly threw his hands up. "Then we have some seasoned Guardians as backup, right here in this office. Should you or I go down, they'll continue the slaughter."

"And if a sire manages to get a Guardian's broadsword in hand, not only bites, but it slices and dices through human flesh before leaving the club to drink and drain the first innocent human it sees walking down a dark street. No. Not an option."

"No. Wait. Just hear me out…"

And there it is, stubborn conviction, far too naïve and premature. He leaned against the vault's door, crossed his arms and closed his eyes thinking, *one sire is deadly enough. Seven sires, well, it would be absolutely absurd.*

Years ago, he had spit in the face of fate with outrage in his unbeating heart and a single broadsword in hand, destroying sorcerers and an army of Hell-beasts for retribution. This was different. No. *Destroying seven sires at one time is far too dangerous.* He could lose his son, which was an unbearable thought, no matter what the consequences might be.

"…and I doubt there's a tooth fairy. I mean, at least Santa has some correlation to good old Saint Nick."

Snapped out of his thoughts, he asked, "What the

bloody hell are you going on about?"

"You didn't hear a word I said! I could see it on your face." Lukas shook his head, stood up and approached. "It all comes back to one thing. When are you going to get it through your head that I'm not about to sacrifice myself? Just like you, I go into a fight with my eyes open. I've taken on vampires without so much as a scratch. And if I get wounded destroying seven fucking sires, at least I'm in a world where I self-heal." His son stopped in front of him pointing to the vault. "Taking this fight to the Third Realm isn't happening, either, because when you jump through that portal, I do, too. We won't have back-up. We'll be in a realm with thousands of thirsty vampires. Not even *two* mystically human men could possibly survive. And we accomplish nothing," his son added in a sharp tone.

Michael fully glowered. When he stepped forward, his son took a healthy step back. "You can babysit the lovebirds by yourself. I'll take the day-shift. Maybe when I come back you will have come to your senses, little boy," using those last two words on purpose. The flush coloring his son's cheeks was exactly as expected. *Let him swallow it, rethink it all through, because I'm not about to sanction something that could get us both killed, in any dimension.* Once again, he felt as though the weight of the world landed on his shoulders. This time, however, it felt a much heavier, personal burden. Love for his son was an endless abyss. Love for his wife, Alana, and his twin daughters knew no end as well.

Chapter 26

Womanly Persuasion

It took a while, but Luna swallowed her nervousness, not her nerve. Draven deserved every slap and much more for his decision to be insulting. His home said he had spared no expense on luxury. Everything she saw confirmed that Henri was no longer visible. A very different vampire had taken his place.

She had guided him to the sofa, had held his arm as he sat. As the argument heated up between Michael and son, Draven unbuttoned his suit jacket. She slipped it off his shoulders and hung it on the back of a dining room chair. His hands hid his face, and she knew she had to do something out of her nature to help, something to jar him into action.

Taking the small towel in the half-bath off to the right, she soaked it with hot water before going back to him. She wiped streaks of blood off his hand before prying the other free to dab his cheeks. His eyes stayed shut, his handsome face lined with defeat. Leaving him to rinse and wring out the towel, she wished she could wring her hands and be rid of each wavering feeling within. Neither of them had spoken, and she sensed it would have to be a radical move to get through to the one she still loved so deeply.

Returning, Luna sank down on the thick carpet, sat

back on her knees and studied everything about Draven. When the argument in the office finally stopped, she never expected his broad shoulders could hunch any lower. The planes of a handsome face she had dreamed about for decades hardened, the downturn of his lips, the expression he wore said he was grappling with something untenable—a look never seen on Henri who had a steady personality, like a glide over smooth ice. *Has the creation of Draven removed the shackles Henri had kept in place?* She intended to find out, so she knelt tall, leaned forward and kissed his furrowed brow.

"I have horribly wronged you, *ma chere*," he whispered. "Can you ever forgive me?"

"Open your eyes and look at me, Draven." Pulling his handkerchief from the suit's breast pocket, she dabbed away fresh blood tears. Those warm-brown eyes that had always reminded her of melting milk chocolate were bloodshot.

"I do not deserve your love, nor your kindness."

She sat next to him on the sofa. "You will not tell me what you do or don't deserve. Any and all decisions are mine and mine alone now. At this moment, I choose to soothe you." She tugged him forward until his head settled on her lap. His long frame slowly repositioned across the sofa with his knees bent and on his side. She freed his hair and ran her fingers through it. There were no natural waves, the black strands coarse, just as she remembered. Studying his profile, she whispered, "Why are your eyes closed again?"

"I cannot bring myself to turn and look upon you. I am fully embarrassed at this display of weakness, yet I cannot seem to stop."

"Why? Weepy isn't weakness. It says so on the

Internet, a new place to search for so many different types of information."

His lips curled hinting a grin. "The Internet has been around for decades."

"Yes. I've missed so much—tucked away like a country mouse." He actually smiled, a true rarity. The glimpse of a long fang excited her. Not giving in, she asked, "Do I amuse you?"

"I'm sorry. I mean no disrespect," he quickly replied, his profile once again grave.

"Abandoning me in Iceland was a great disservice."

"You are well taken care of?"

"Yes. The same family still cares for me. Rune is exceptional."

"And who is Rune, may I ask?"

"The original caretakers' grandson. He sees to all my needs."

His eyebrow raised. "I thought you were faithful to me."

Her jaw actually dropped, but hopefully she had found her "in" replying, "You believe I lied before?" Unsure of what to do next, she shoved his shoulder.

Draven rolled off the sofa and landed with a thud, sprawled at her feet and groaning in pain. He mumbled, "I deserved that."

And much, much more, she thought. With her hands clipping her waist, she stepped over him and glared down. "I blame you for my naiveté! You purposely kept me unaware, like an over-protected child. Now I understand Michael's roughness with me."

Propped up on both elbows, his eyebrows knit, "Rough? In what way?"

Here's the switch that needs to be flipped. But how?

All those book excerpts she browsed… steamy words, stimulating scenes and graphic sex. Some of those movies came to mind. The strong female characters… Their melodramatic monologues had purpose. She straightened both shoulders and channeled her "inner actress," describing every detail of her journey back to him, from opening the door and seeing Michael to boarding the plane. His reactions, every facial expression fueled her drama. By the time she got to Michael's final insult, the tight lipped, flared-nostril look confirmed success.

A low, long growl rumbled. "I will kill him."

She leaned down and wagged a finger in his face. "You will do no such thing! At least he tried to bring out the beast within me. You never did!"

"Luna—"

"Not even for my own protection! Even our last day on the ship, you chose to wallow in regret at the loss of your possession. Me. A possession. How infuriating! How demeaning!"

"Luna, I—"

"Do not 'Luna' me!" She knelt at his side. "You could have written the line Rick used on Ilsa in *Casablanca*. But he stood on a foggy airstrip, not the freezing shore of lonely Husavik. You were so self-absorbed, so unaware of me and my needs—with that sullen look on your face, just like the one Louis wore in that interview movie."

"What on earth are you talking about?"

"Pull it up on one of your big screens," she fired back.

He grabbed her arm and pulled her down. She teetered on her knees, his face a mere inch away. "You were not my possession. I loved you. I love you still."

"So you say. And what's going through your mind right now? To kiss me?"

"Yes," rumbled through his chest.

"To take my breast in your mouth?"

He growled a slow, "Yes."

"What else?"

"I pull up your dress and taste what is mine."

"Why should I let you?"

"You will not stop me."

Draven growled, but he wasn't there yet. He went in for a kiss. Luna jerked back and turned her face. "I do not give you permission. Stop this... this useless assault."

In an instant, her back hit the floor, with him on top. The scent, the weight of her immortal lover had her ready, but she wouldn't give in—yet. *Fury has to boil in his veins. One more hard push,* she thought. Henri had been a gentle lover. She had been at ease and willing. *Well, not anymore! Draven needs a challenge, not submission.* He tried for another kiss and she pulled back. Gripping her chin, his lips slammed into hers. She locked her teeth, refused his tongue. Twisting away, she coldly declared, "You will not have your way. You cannot take me...so severely injured."

"There is much more I can do to you besides kiss," he gruffly replied.

His quick reach unzipped the flowing green dress. He pulled her out of a flimsy strapless bra, pinned her arms down teasing the tip of a breast with his tongue.

"Let me go," she ordered to push him over an edge.

"Never," he growled.

The cap sleeves came down, the soft material

exposed her waist and more. She gasped, and he captured her open lips to accommodate his darting tongue. The struggle felt liberating, titillating as well. When his lips left her, she sucked in a breath. "All those years, at the very first touch, I gave in to your every desire."

"As you should have," he replied in arrogance.

"What a misogynistic reply. No. Not tonight and nevermore! What I freely gave you—" Another plunge of his tongue before a rough kiss had her wriggling beneath his weight. Electric excitement shot through her core when his hand raced up her dress. But she clamped her thighs. "You might be strong, but I'm no weakling, either." With one good shove, he fell on his back. "As I was saying—what I gave so willingly every time, I will not give you now."

"Let's just see about that," was punctuated by another long, low growl.

She quickly crawled away. He snagged a shoe, and it flew off her foot. Grabbed by the ankles, her breasts hit the carpet, but she kept her thighs locked together. The dress slid up exposing her back as if the soft material couldn't tolerate her skin. She fought to get it off her head. The push-up bra quickly unhooked and then his finger rimmed her panties. Another jolting current hummed as she clawed at the carpet. He pulled the lacey undergarment down but couldn't get it off. The splay of his hand across her bottom gave a new kind of thrill.

"Open your legs, my dear," he growled.

"Like hell. You get nothing," she argued.

"Very well. We'll do this another way," he said in a tone she'd never heard from Henri.

This Draven persona came off very sexy, unpredictably erotic. He licked the small of her back, and her eyes shot wide. His hands gripped her hips. She swallowed a moan. Then her bottom jacked high in the air, and he had her knees wide apart to tease the damp lace that barely covered her. Pushing up with her palms, her back arched. A squeal escaped with the next tease.

"I like your beautiful body in this position. Now hold still," he whispered in her ear.

Pressure on the lace spiraled into erotic. She had to peek between her thighs and moan a shaky "Ohhh...." He tugged the lace lower, gripped her thighs and flipped her flat on the floor, face to face.

He growled, pulling the delicate panties off. "You are glistening and slick."

Digging a foot into the carpet, she scooched back. "How observant. Yet you can't do a thing about it."

His eyes were hooded—full of menace. "I will have you in ways you've never dreamed."

Off came his tie. He undid both cuffs and shrugged off his shirt. The roll of his bare shoulders had never thrilled her like this! She scurried back using both feet this time, reaching the dining room table. Like a lion on the prowl he crawled, his long hair a thready curtain to partially hide a hungry look. Her thighs pried open. His lips crushed against her core. Every demanding nip and lick drove her wild. She fisted his hair drawing him in deeper and craved his next move.

Then squirming and wiggling, her hips thrust at nothing. *Brought to such arousal and left?* She glared at his amused grin and clamped her knees together.

"Pull them apart right now."

"I will not!"

Looming over her, he looked unstoppable, and his hand slithered down her belly until he touched the tip of her sex. As her body hummed and loosened, two long fingers slid in deep.

"Now you will come in my hand," he ordered.

How could his voice go so deep? Better yet, how had he turned this around? About to protest, a slow swirl of his thumb brought about an inner explosion, and she rode shockwaves surging through every part of her.

"Ah, finally you understand," he growled.

Her bottom lifted in his hands, her throbbing core met his mouth again. His eyes bore into hers as his fangs grazed each thigh. *Henri never made love like this!* Not a hint of love lit his lusty expression that promised another erotic delight.

"Did you like that, *ma chere*?" Completely boneless, she moaned, but then he added, "Now we move on because I am not finished with you yet."

Dragged across the carpet, Luna's eyes shot wide as his back met the sofa. The caveman move landed her face down and across his lap. He had a hand at her waist while the other ran up and down the back of her legs. Bold and bothered, she asked, "What do you think you're doing?"

"This is how I want you. This is how you will stay."

"No. Let me up."

"You are in no position to make a demand."

"I said let me up."

"I like the feel of you like this. The view as well. Let us now address the verbal assault in my office. You brought me to tears for all to see. I've already been humiliated once. You couldn't wait until we were alone to express such outrage?" He smacked her bottom with such force that she shrieked.

She furiously scrambled to kneel at his side. "How

dare you!"

Sweeping his hair back revealed a murderous expression. "You meant to insult me!"

"Wearing that woman's scent insulted *me!*"

"She means nothing."

"Really? All this bought-and paid-for-sex has made you an aggressive lover."

"Sex is sex. It doesn't involve love." His eyes blazed as never before. "I have loved only you. That I cannot do to you what I want fully pisses me off. Do you know the stamina it takes? The incessant ache to not become erect with you so inviting, so beautiful?" He slowly stood, moved away before stalking back. "Your sire did this to me! That I cannot bury myself inside you is infuriating!"

Softly, she replied, "You will heal—"

"I do not have enough time to heal!" Like a caged animal, his chest muscles flexed. Throwing his head back, a bitter laugh exposed his long fangs. Heated and harsh, he yelled, "His despicable demand. His useless realm. With six other sires sniffing at his heels, waiting for the right moment to send him to Hell! I hope they fucking stake each other!"

As she sucked in a breath, a strange chime came from his suit jacket. Still shocked by his outburst, she stood, quickly found her bra and panties. He handed her the green dress, and then shrugged into his shirt, buttoning it but not tucking it into his suit trousers. Although disheveled, he radiated power, intense sexuality. The sound began again, and she asked, "What is that?"

Fishing through a jacket pocket, he pulled out his phone, swiped it with a muttered, "little brat bastard." Walking to the kitchen, he buttoned both cuffs. "It's an alarm. I'm on a fucking feeding schedule."

Worry consumed her as she slipped into the dress and met him there. He pulled two different sets of containers out of the classy refrigerator and put them on the counter. When she turned, he zipped her up.

"The plastic containers are yours and these bottles are mine." He unscrewed the cap on his and removed the lid of a container for her. "*Porter un toast, ma chere.* To seven auspicious final deaths. May they all rot in Hell." He raised the dark bottle before drinking it. She sipped the cold animal blood finishing only half. After draining the second bottle, he swiped at both landing them in the sink. "As soon as I am able to run again, I will drain the first malevolent troublemaker I see."

Righting the bottles, Luna found it ironic that her actions and reactions tonight had not taken her to Henri's side. They introduced her to someone new. They brought Draven back. Not whole, perhaps, but more than enough to rise above humiliation. Maybe just enough for him to begin soaring toward revenge.

Chapter 27

Bicker or Banter

In the office, Lukas thrust his head back and blew out a slow breath. "Aaaannd mission accomplished. Wow. Talk about a steamy reunion. Way to go, Luna," he whispered. It's not that he wanted to eavesdrop. He had the same enhanced senses as a vampire. Doors or walls didn't matter. If far away, it took some concentration. But just forty feet or so? Not a problem.

Documenting everything he heard including the make-up sex—now that would be the real kicker. If he used his deductive skills, he could map their moves, too. It might be the first X-rated Georgian entry.

But yeah. Luna did it. Broke him down and built him right back up. *Incredible what heady sex can do for a man... a vampire... whichever. How the hell Draven didn't get hard is beyond me.* Did the vampire feel about Luan the way he felt about Martine? Even though he'd had his share of sex partners, only with Martine did that leap from dear friend to dearest lover pulse through every cell in his body. Plus, no man breaks apart like that if he doesn't feel a deeper kind of love.

In the last event, Lukas sensed a deeper depth in Draven. He had categorized it as high intelligence that allowed for a few moral decisions. But after this, the ability to love deepened that depth into something unknown.

The sound from a piano had him sit forward. It was a slow song, sad, not jazzy or modern. A mournful, steady melody. It reached an emotional frenzy and sped up like it had to drive a point home before the slowdown to sad again. Three bold splashes of sound ended the experience. *Breathtaking, beautiful and full of passion before a final sigh.* How could a chilly vampire express all that warm emotion? *No way is it all technique. Christ. Another anomaly.*

The door behind the desk opened, and Lukas sprang to his feet. Draven was tying his hair back with a leather strip, but his shirttails weren't tucked in and he looked lost in thought. The frown wasn't his typical, arrogant smirk. "And here I thought two Guardians with average hearing were stationed here. I should have known better. And no. I didn't slit my throat and bleed out all over the carpet."

"Wow. You really rocked it."

"*Rocked* it?" Draven glanced over and shook his head.

"Yeah. And the song—"

"Composition. *Opus Twenty-Eight, Number Fifteen* by Frederic Chopin. And before you ask, yes, we knew each other in Paris before I was turned. He was a shy, quiet man, yet a poet at the piano. Often melancholy."

"Oh. Good to know," he replied, still highly impressed as he changed the subject. "You've both taken sustenance?"

"I'm surprised you didn't hear us swallow. Oh, and thank you ever so much for that irritating alarm you put in my phone. As if I cannot sense the need."

"We aim to please and I like to be thorough."

"Yes, I'm sure your report will be quite specific as well. Shall I add voyeur to your many talents? The flush is creeping up your face."

Yeah. He could feel the embarrassing reaction. "Okay. So we're even."

"Not even close." Draven crossed the office, stood directly in front of him. At the door, Luna whispered his name, but the vampire didn't respond. "Not a flicker in your eyes. Not a skip of a heartbeat. You are that comfortable with one such as I so near your jugular? Perhaps, a quick sip of your mystical blood might put me over the top."

Getting even closer, Lukas grinned. "Not a chance in Hell because I fight dirty. You'd totally end up with a bloody nose and multiple contusions. You can't spare the loss of one little drop if you intend to go back to the Third Realm. In fact, let's up your dose tonight. Why don't you back off and go chug down another bottle right now."

"That throbbing vein in your neck is much more tempting, but I shall honor my bond to your father. Luna will stay here with me."

As Draven stepped back, Lukas turned to her. "Are you sure you're okay with this?"

"Yes," she replied, still fixated on the vampire.

"Have one of your Guardians bring over her belongings. May she keep the laptop you purchased while she is here?"

"Why? Is she going somewhere?"

The grin appeared friendly enough. "Perhaps my question was off a bit."

"Yeah, just a tad. Sure. I'll have it sent over."

"Thank you, Lukas," Luna replied in the gentle tone he had come to expect.

"I will acquaint her with the rest of my home and then come back to complete some tasks."

"After draining another bottle of blood," he said.

That thin-lipped smirk appeared, just like his father's, and it gave you that fuck-off feeling. "But of course," Draven stated before they left together.

Shaking his head, Lukas turned the comfortable armchair to face the desk, then brought it closer. He shot off a series of texts, including one to update his father. Some seven minutes and forty-two seconds later, yeah, he was counting, Draven set two cups of freshly-brewed coffee down on his desk. "I presume you take it black like your father?"

"That's fine."

Draven clicked his tongue and groaned, walked back out and returned with a small glass of milk, a bowl of sugar and a spoon. "Next time, just say how you take it," he said in a dry tone.

"I didn't want to put you out." Lukas added a splash of milk, two heaping teaspoons of sugar as the vampire eyed him. "Okay, so I like it sweet."

"Yes. I can see."

The computer gave off a soft whirr and once again, Lukas went back to his phone. Neither of them spoke until a Guardian walked in with the laptop and a large tote bag. Draven took both items in to Luna. Then the television turned on and a brief explanation of the remote followed. Hearing the movie title she requested, Lukas grinned.

As Draven sat at his desk, Lukas said, "That's a pretty heavy movie, *Legends of the Fall*."

"She finds a certain actor quite interesting, having seen him in another movie recently. He has a certain look about him."

Now he grinned. "Yeah. I get it."

"I'm sure you do." Picking up his phone, Draven sent a text before putting the landline on speaker. "You have the list of items to be purchased as soon as the boutiques on Fifth Avenue open. You will bring them down yourself."

Donovan's serious, "Yes, my lord," had Lukas biting his lips to stifle the chuckle.

Seeing his reaction, Draven's eyes narrowed. "He is my minion."

"Oh I get that."

"My Luna needs proper clothing for this time of year in the city."

"You know, Martine would put some kind of crazy ass spell on me, like maybe a trip-and-fall if I chose her clothes. Shouldn't do that without asking her first."

A shocked look came before an uncharacteristic shrug. "Everything is returnable these days."

"I could send a female Guardian with her after sunset."

"No. No Guardians. If she does not like what I purchase, you will take her to return it. She may get exactly what she likes—if that is the case."

"And when you present her with whatever you buy, do so with a very contrite apology because you didn't ask what she likes before you sent Donovan," adding a dramatic, "my lord."

"Please, do not be a nuisance, young man."

"What is it with this young man shit. I'm thirty-one."

"Yet you come off a bit of a brat at times."

"In living years, we're the same age."

Draven smirked. "Not even close, considering the decades I've lived. By the way, I was a month shy of thirty-three when Cyril sired me. It is odd that I catch you in a mistake. Perhaps you need a nap."

"Nope. I'm good." Staring into each other's eyes, they both sipped their coffee.

"Chit-chat will cease. I have important business that requires concentration."

"No worries, vampire. So do I."

Both of them went back to their devices like two sparring partners jogging to assigned corners of a boxing ring. God only knew what the next round would bring.

****

At precisely five o'clock in the morning, Draven announced, "I will retire now."

"Good. Down another bottle before you sleep. It's an order; not a suggestion."

"Perhaps you should leave your assignment early, since you've become bossy and quite cranky."

"The smug retort and sarcastic smirk after hours of peace is so very uncalled for, vampire."

Draven's head fell back with a laugh. Lukas quickly thought, a*nd what a set of fangs you have. Long, white and pointy.* His father's fangs were shorter, less obvious, although by no means your average canines.

"There is a reason for the slight grins and thin smirks."

"Yeah. If anyone caught a glimpse of what's in your mouth, well, he or she would either scream or pee their pants. Or both."

"Your comebacks are indeed amusing."

"Glad to oblige." Leaning back, he took a swig of cold coffee and set the cup down on the desk. "So. I'm waiting."

"For what?"

"A thank you."

"Thank you for what?"

"Bringing Luna back to you. After all that drama tonight, I'd think you'd be a bit more humble and appreciative."

"Ah. This was your idea."

"Yeah."

"Did you have a difficult time convincing your father to leave Alana's arms?"

"Nope. In fact, Mom convinced him."

"Mom? Is Alana still the stunning Italian beauty, as she was, when a young Guardian?"

"She's still exceptionally beautiful, inside and out."

"Yes. The way your father protected her... I never strayed too close."

"That was very wise because you'd have been dust and bits of bone at her feet, never getting the chance to experience all this luxury and power you now possess."

"Yes. Luxury and power," Draven replied staring at his desk. "I would appreciate not having Guardian's stationed outside my bedroom."

Lukas shrugged. "As a man, I completely understand, but then there's that drunk-off-your-ass incident. Who's to say you're not planning something stupid?"

"I am not."

"No? No more emotional outbursts with suicidal tendencies? You totally had me worried, vampire."

"I am not an idiot, little boy."

Instantly irked, he replied, "You just had to slip that in, right?"

"Yes. And watch your tone with me. I know how this ends. Two more nights of holding her in my embrace is your assurance of my equilibrium. Then she is to be hidden in an unknown, safe place while I meet my fate."

That had him on his feet with his fists on the desk, leaning down. "Christ, you're thick. Luna's not going anywhere. Just like you, she's here to stay. And as for meeting your fate, I'm working on something."

"Really."

The word dripped with arrogance. *At least that part of his personality is back.* "Yeah. Really," he replied in the same fashion.

"Not you, nor your father, nor an army of Guardians, which you do not have at your disposal, can alter what is already set in motion."

"We can destroy them. All of them. Herodotus included—if we work together as a team."

"We are not a team."

"We were a month ago. That worked out just fine. We can do it again."

Draven held up a hand as his nostrils flared. "I am not interested. Your father will honor my wishes to hide her. You, *little* boy, will not dream up any more heroics. Am I clear?"

Okay. That does it! Lukas leaned in hard. "You really want to piss me off? I told you I fight dirty. Now look who's bossy and cranky."

"And look who is smug. This is not a game. I am not a member of your team. Discussion over." Draven stood, turned and walked through to his home. The door shut with a loud thud. A hushed exchange began with Luna. Then the television went silent. Minutes later, and through two closed doors, Lukas could still hear them talking.

"What a fucking pain in the ass," he mumbled, texting the Guardians in the hallway. When they entered the office, he said, "Keep your post in the hallway tonight, not in the office or at the bedroom door." Both men nodded. "Take a break and go grab something to eat but stay alert in case dark seers are sniffing around. Be back by seven."

After they left, Lukas moved to the cushy desk chair. On his phone, he brought up his notes and added to them. There would be no "Round Three" tonight. But that arrogant vampire would see the error of his logic. Eventually.

Chapter 28

The Warlock

Relieved by a Guardian at eight a.m., Lukas couldn't wait to get home. Dog tired and anxious to hold Martine tight in his embrace, he entered their brownstone. After hanging up his bomber jacket on a brass hook, he came to a dead stop and sniffed the air. The Guardian standing at the living room arch started to talk, but he held up a hand. "Not necessary. I recognize his scent." Surely, Martine had made it clear that their guest was welcome, but he wondered why the warlock had come here this morning.

As he entered the kitchen, Martine graced him with a lovely smile. He went over and kissed her cheek before his gaze rested on the blond warlock who put down a mug of fresh coffee and stood to shake his hand. "Wow. You look great. Back from the UK already?"

"I've got a good reason," answered Christopher Forbes, Martine's former patient whose life had been saved in the early October event. Chris gave a smile as he sat again. Well-built and three inches taller than Lukas, he sported a neatly trimmed beard covering a strong jawline, an impressive look on him.

"I think you need to hear him out, Lu," Martine said as she fixed his coffee the way he liked it.

After a slow sip, he replied, "Sure. What's up?" He

sensed a healthy heartbeat, caught the twinkle of power in such ice-blue eyes.

Chris sat back relaxed. "I want to thank you in person for finding the dark witch in the Second Realm. You gave me back my destiny. It's been a very interesting month at the Georgian Institute, learning how to use my psychic powers, learning that I have other skill sets. That place is extraordinary."

Lukas chuckled. "Yeah, like a grownup, scaled down version of Hogwarts."

Chris grinned with a shake of his head. "Is it ever. You know, I can't shake this weird hyper twitchiness, like there's a threat happening across all three realms."

Lukas glanced at Martine. "Now that's some wicked perception, so soon after figuring out who you really are. Downright cool. What is it you sense? Feel free to speak. I hide nothing from her."

Clutching his coffee mug, Chris cleared his throat. "It took not a day to connect the feelings I've had for like a week. Just before I left the UK, I got a strange call from an old friend of yours, Martine. Celia's your aunt. Right, Lukas?"

His eyebrows rose. "My very powerful aunt. Her psychic skills are legendary."

"Yeah, well, something's off in the Third Realm with the vampires. Celia thinks there's a shift coming. It'll impact the Second Realm as well as this world. I sense it, too, but I can't see it." Chris swallowed a mouthful of coffee before adding, "Georgian psychics helped me tap into my gifts. I'm not fully schooled in spells and such, but my sixth sense is doing a really sloppy dance, which I can't ignore."

"Nor should you," Martine said. "Never look away,

Chris. Bits and pieces of what it's trying to show you will eventually coalesce."

"Yeah. That's what Celia said when she met with me."

Lukas beamed with a shake of his head. "You went up to the Scotland mansion?"

"Right before I left for New York—at Celia's invitation."

"Wow. My aunt actually agreed to meet with you?" Not that she was an introvert or antisocial. In the four years living at the Scotland Estate, he could count on one hand the visitors who weren't family, much less those who came at her invitation.

"She's one powerful psychic, and sends her love, by the way. Thorn's as well. Uri says he misses sparring sessions with you."

"Oh, I'll bet," he muttered. He deeply loved his aunt and uncle but had little patience with his sixteen-year-old cousin. For all that unnatural muscle and brawn in one so young, the kid's mood swings made you dizzy.

Chris eyed him. "I sense the very strong attachment to your aunt."

"Both my aunt and Uncle T were instrumental in helping me with things after the Mayhem in Manhattan, and then the event in Siena."

"You were Uri's age?"

"Fifteen, a year younger," Lukas replied.

"There's a ton of documentation on your father, the portals closing as well. Paige filled me in a little on what happened in Siena the following year."

Changing the subject, he said, "Wow. You're still seeing her?"

Chris grinned. "I know the two of you have some

back-history, Lukas."

"That was a really long time ago. It is what it is." *And let's leave it at that.*

"I didn't mean to go off-topic."

"No worries." But Lukas's mind went wild. With most paranormal events, random connections fleshed themselves out within hours. They were days into this one already. And the warlock's connection to it totally stumped him. "So, what's on your mind?"

Chris leaned in, folded his hands on the table. "I swear to God, as soon as I picked up a broadsword, I knew how to use it, like an ancestral instinct was jarred awake. The instructors I worked with—"

"Nigel and Neeb?"

"Yeah. They were pretty impressed. I'll admit, so was I."

"It's a great skill to discover you have."

Chris studied him, saying, "An innate skill?"

"Totally. So where's the link to what's happening now?"

"I need to be in on whatever the hell this is, Lukas."

Now he eyeballed Chris. "Why?"

"Instability means a threat to Second Realm dwellers from those vampires." The tall warlock shifted in the chair. "Celia gave me a broadsword, said it would be put to good use and very soon. I believe her. I want in."

"But this event involves powerful sires. If it comes to a fight, it won't be like training. Vampires bite necks. Broadsword wounds are real, and unlike me, you don't self-heal. Are you sure you're willing to literally risk life and limb? Think on it a while."

"This is happening soon. You need me."

233

"And believe it when I say, we can use another warrior, but you have to understand the dangers. Plus, you've got Paige to think about. I mean, if you're getting closer, does she understand that you might sustain a permanent injury? A clean strike to your face can lead to the loss of an eye or even disfigurement."

"Look, I know yours is an inherited mystical gift—"

Lukas held up a hand. "Hey, I've been nicked and stabbed. It stings like a bitch and the pain is really bad. Plus, I won't take you into the field without first assessing your skill level. Don't get me wrong. A warlock's ability to, maybe, read a mind, would be a Godsend. But reading a vampire's mind is tricky."

"This could be a life-altering decision, Chris," Martine said. "Maybe talk it over with Paige?"

"M's right. If you still want to stand with us, we'll have a go at broadsword etiquette. You'll also need to be trained in how and where to stake a vampire."

Chris gave a slow nod. "Sure. I'll discuss it with her."

"But very discreetly, I mean, you don't want to freak her out," Lukas added.

"See?" Martine said, "I told you Lu would listen."

"That you did." Chris gave an open smile, and then they locked eyes.

"Do yourself a solid. Put all personal matters in order. Leave a letter for Paige saying what you need to say to her because there's no guarantee you'll survive. There never is."

The warlock stood. "And yet, last month, not even knowing me, you risked your life in the Second Realm to save mine."

"It was the right thing to do," Lukas replied.

"Yeah. Now I understand the words you live by."

He nodded once. "Above all, protect and save the innocent."

"If I've been given these gifts, then I'll do the same."

Still cautious, Lukas answered, "Talk it over with Paige."

Chris extended his hand. Lukas stood and shook it. The energy that passed through his palm revealed unusual power in the warlock, their sense of purpose in alignment. *Another warrior in the fight that is sure to come might just tip the scales.*

The warlock leaned in saying, "Enough so, that good has a fighting chance to overtake evil," which finished his exact thought.

As Martine walked Chris out, Lukas sat down, pulled a blueberry bagel off the plate in the center of the table, ripped it open and buttered it. As the fridge door opened and closed, he thought, *reading a mind is easy. Facing a set of fangs is not.*

"Chris won't get in over his head, Lu," Martine stated. "A bagel's not enough. You need scrambled eggs. With such a super-fast metabolism, you're fading fast."

"You just worked a twelve-hour shift. I'll be fine."

"Pfft," she huffed, shaking a metal whisk at him.

He grinned as his stomach growled. "I can't believe he met Auntie Celia and Uncle T."

"I can't believe she gave him a broadsword!" As four eggs cracked in a glass bowl, he started to stand. "Don't you dare lift that gorgeous butt off that kitchen chair."

"I can cook. You've been on your feet for hours."

"Yeah, so? You reunited lovers who've been apart for like eighty years. So what was it like?"

"Just grab it all out of my head," he said, too tired to talk.

As Martine cooked, scenes played in his mind, complete with dialogue. He heard a few "Oh my Gods" and then a breathy "No, he really said that to her?" Then she turned to him with a hand over her heart and gasped twice before filling his plate. "No kidding? Really?"

"Draven was an emotional nightmare."

"Luna's instincts were dead-on, though. That's exactly what he needed."

"I agree." He dug into the scrambled eggs. Martine sat at his side sipping coffee, and he kissed her cheek. "Thank you for feeding me, for putting up with this craziness... for loving me."

A pretty smile was his reward. After the last bite, he put down the fork and took her hand. Their fingers threaded together. With a lift of an eyebrow and a sexy smile, she said to him, "How does a bubble bath sound? I'll wash your back. Your front, too. Then we can fall into bed together."

"And pick up where we left off in the tub?"

"Ooh, you read my mind. What do you say?"

"With the state I'm in, it's hard to talk, might be harder to climb the stairs as well."

"So, you're up for it?"

"In a totally uncomfortable way."

"Jeez, I love that dimpled smile. You are such a cutie," she said wrinkling her nose.

Acing the stairs, he couldn't wait to shrug out of his shirt, but mostly, he had to get out of his jeans. Some slow, slippery sex with the love of his life before falling asleep with her in his arms had his undivided attention.

Chapter 29

Reminiscing

Unlike his son, Michael was not at all convinced there was any way to save Draven from torture and final death. These six unknown sires had to be powerful. And yet, Herodotus had them under his thumb, acquiesced to his dictatorship like Simon Says for vampires, only much, much deadlier. That sadistic bastard would sense Draven's deepest fear and run with it.

He had seen the legendary sire in action just months before reclaiming his soul. Even Cyril kept his distance from Herodotus. And Cyril had no morals. *Well, neither did I back then. Not a shred.* Cyril's beatings were no joke, enough to make any vampire break down and cry, but Herodotus gave new meaning to the word punishment.

What he had seen stayed imbedded in his memory, gross beyond belief. Just before boarding a freighter back to New York that sailed out of Civitavecchia, he and Cyril attended Herodotus's massive gathering in the Roman countryside. The sire had a vampire strung up. They saw it skinned and partially butchered. Hours passed before the sadistic sire finally cut off its head to end its misery.

Literally shaking, ready to vomit, Cyril had gripped his arm and led him out of sight of Herodotus. He wretched and then took the brutal slap as his sire scolded, "Had he seen your reaction, my son, you would have been the encore performance, and I would not have been able to stop him." Even now, a chill ran through him.

Swallowing a mouthful of coffee, Michael's eyes slid to Mary as she entered the kitchen. Dressed in a dark-brown tailored suit with a silk, frilly white blouse, the statuesque woman didn't look in her late sixties. Her hair, only peppered with gray, was styled perfectly to touch her shoulders and accentuate her intense, dark eyes. He loved her like a sister. Always had.

"What are you doing here? I thought you had the day shift," Mary said as she poured a cup of morning coffee and joined him at the table.

"With seasoned Guardians on the premises, Draven isn't going anywhere. And if they need me, they'll text."

"How did the reunion go last night?" she asked.

A low groan and a long growl seemed a fitting answer.

"That bad, huh?"

"He pulled some arrogant shit on her. Then she slapped him silly and made him cry. Yes, you heard correctly."

Considering Mary's history with Draven in the late 1970s, the look she gave, thin eyebrows high and the edges of her mouth turned up, was just as expected. "Did you want to stake him right then and there?"

"No. I wanted to throw him up against a wall and slap him much harder than Luna did." She had a throaty laugh, and hearing it made Michael grin. "But Luna accomplished what we couldn't, according to my son's text. I imagine they are currently tight in each other's arms, in that massive bed of his."

"So he's back on track. Love will do that to you."

"Don't I know it. Dreams of Alana saved me sixteen years ago. Had it not been for that fantasy, I'd have given up. Then my boy would have been killed. Her love rescued both of us." He paused at the recollection. "I know what it feels like, wanting to finally face the fires of Hell by ending your own existence. And no matter how together Draven now appears, it's still what he plans to do." He sat back in the chair and folded his arms across his chest with a slow exhale.

"You think he's playing her?"

"No. I believe he loves her. Maybe not the way I love Alana, of course."

"You protected Alana throughout the ten years of her mystical mission as a Guardian."

"And I fell head over heels in love the first time I saved her from six vampires who thought they'd take out a seventeen-year-old Guardian, like a trophy-kill. She was already so stubborn," he added with a slow shake of his head.

"But there you were, an eternal twenty-seven, the mystically enhanced vampire with a conscience, to rescue her. Handsome beyond belief and twice as stubborn."

"Yes, and years later, she comes back to this filthy city, puts her life in danger to rescue me from the bowels of that fucking building—before they incinerated me."

"That you actually survived those eight days, poisoned and bled dry, still shakes you, doesn't it?"

He scoffed. "Draven gets a brutal kick to the balls, and he wants to end it all."

Mary leaned forward with her arms laced on the table. "He doesn't have your stamina, Michael. He doesn't have a soul. That's why he needs your help."

"Henri was never a fighter," he said.

"Draven has some fight in him."

He shrugged and looked away. "I have centuries on him, Mare."

"I'd say that he's somewhat envious, maybe looks up to you like a... a big—"

"Brother." He met her gaze as it softened. "So, this self-destructive bender he's on?"

"He knows his existence is going to end," and softly added, "Michael, you cannot let him go back. You cannot let him face this Herodotus beast. He's aligned himself with good, not evil."

"I must ask you something. If it is too personal, I apologize beforehand." He leaned forward and her head bobbed once. "All those years ago, Mare, when you were with him, what drew you in?"

"You mean, besides his drop-dead gorgeous, good looks?"

He gave a soft 'Yes," and held her gaze.

"Draven had a tender side, and there was a sadness in him, like I often sensed in you. When we were alone, he'd perform an intricate piece on the piano, and I'd sit at his side, lost in its beauty. It made me think he was human, Michael, full of emotions, like a... a colorful palette of feelings artists often sense in one another. When he played, I couldn't accept what I knew to be true, that he was a vampire with a beast-within. We flirted with each other a long time—before we acted on our mutual attraction."

"Then he bit you,' he bitterly stated. "I should have staked him then."

She looked away and shook her head. "We were

241

very passionate for months with each other. That night, I think he forgot I wasn't like him. I wasn't an immortal."

"Or he forgot *he* was."

She closed her eyes and touched two faded scars that looked like freckles on her neck. "The bite was incredible pleasure and pain all at once, beyond anything I could describe. And when I cried out, he pulled back, immediately licked the wound before he turned away."

"He said nothing?"

"No. Not a word. I got out of his bed, grabbed my clothes, and left."

"That happened over forty years ago."

"I remember it like it was yesterday, and I never spoke to him again, not even during the October event, although I had him vividly in my mind. I confess to sending extra protection his way, because his part in it was integral—to safely get you and Lukas through that hidden portal and returned to our world."

With a gentle touch to her hand, he stated, "You sense we must assist him?"

"As sure as I'm sitting here with you. I mean, can you even imagine how much harder it is to do the right thing when you don't have a soul? Would you have been able to?"

"That is an absolute no," he slowly whispered. "Had it not been for the mysterious Divine Intervention in eighteen-ninety, I'd have continued draining innocent victims."

"Then open your heart to him, just a little."

"I will not promise anything, though," he answered.

"That's understandable. Look. I've got to open the gallery. The gala's only weeks away and there's a pile of prep work to do, even with Tristan's help." Standing, she added, "You should call Alana, Michael. Get her take on things. By the way, what does Lukas say about all this?"

He bristled. "He wants to help him, only God knows why."

"I'll tell you why. I saw how he interacted with Draven right in front of me and Martine. He sees the other 'you' in him—before you had a pulse again."

He gave a hooded glance. "My son gets his emotions involved."

Mary frowned. "What I just said isn't an insult, and yeah, Lukas has a tender heart. Think about what I've said, not as the ramblings of an old lady, but because I happen to have wicked witchy skills." Walking away, she said over her shoulder, "And call your wife. Right now."

Michael leaned back in the chair and crossed his legs at the knees. After staring at his phone for thirty seconds, he pulled up the number, hit the green icon and pressed speaker. His wife's first words were "Hello, my love. I miss you."

"I miss you, too," he whispered. Like a balloon about to burst, devotion swelled in his heart.

"What's wrong?"

"Nothing," he said, and then had to admit, "everything." He gave a rundown of what was happening with Draven. As always, his wife's questions were astute, forcing him to think deeper about the situation. Then he gave a sigh. "I've taken up too much of your time."

He heard a quick "pfft," and winced at the clicks of her tongue. "I'll pack a few things and text when I'm on the way to Mary's brownstone."

He sat up. "No-no-no, you will not come back to this

miserable city! I will not have you anywhere near this, Alana!"

"Just try and stop me," she replied in that feisty tone he rarely heard these days. "I still have all of my Guardian skills intact. I'm an asset."

"But the girls—"

"Love staying with my parents who totally spoil them."

"Alana—"

"Are we going to bicker now? I love you, Michael. I want to help, and I miss you next to me in bed every night. I followed your wishes with the last event and crawled the walls until you and Lu were back in our world and safe! I flatly refuse to do it again. Maybe I'll book a swanky hotel room. Ooh. What a perfect idea!"

"My Guardian—" he said, low and firm, reminiscent of the tone he used with her years ago when he watched over her staking vampires.

"Try to stop me and you'll sleep on the couch for a month! Then you can explain *that* brood to our daughters, all by yourself. Be nice, Michael, or you'll have me to deal with, to borrow a favorite phrase of yours."

He stared at the bloody phone when his wife ended the call—seething and seeing red.

Chapter 30

Brothers in Blood

There was no reason to wear a suit. Knowing he'd be behind his desk, Draven dressed in a clean black cotton shirt and rarely worn, pressed, black jeans. The thick fabric kept a certain part of his anatomy tight and better supported than loose suit trousers. On second thought, he shrugged on his suit jacket and added a black tie.

The walk to the galley kitchen to drink three bottles of human blood didn't feel too uncomfortable. And oddly enough, timed feedings kept him steady and thinking rationally. Why hadn't he tried something like this instead of waiting until the need overwhelmed, and he had to immediately hunt down some miscreant? Best answer: Because that's what vampires do.

"Also, because you don't own a fucking blood bank," he muttered as he grabbed a container of animal blood for the love of his eternal existence. After he elbowed the refrigerator door closed, he leaned against the stainless-steel beast. "I could raid one nightly, although it would be risky. Or... I could turn the other bedroom into a secure place for my minions to donate. I could hire a nurse to draw and bag the blood. It could work."

Then he frowned. Who was he kidding? He had no

reason to plan. He didn't have eternity anymore. Even though murderers and gang-members were everywhere like a verifiable buffet, he'd never hunt again. Final death was only a day away.

He entered his room and sat next to his sleeping beauty, softly called Luna's name. When her pretty blue eyes opened, he couldn't help but grin. She eased herself up to sit against the headboard. "My pajama top looks enticing on you, my dear." He wanted to rip it open and tease a nipple, but instead, he abruptly changed his thought pattern and held out a container.

"I do not need sustenance, my love." He placed it on the dresser and then came back to her side. "How is your injury?"

"I am less uncomfortable today." It was true, which gave him hope.

"You will not go back to Herodotus." she stated with her eyebrows knit tight.

"This is not for you to worry over." Draven ran a gentle hand down her cheek. "Rest, my dearest, it is still hours until sunset." When she lay back down, he tucked the heavy silk quilt around her. He captured her lips, letting their tongues tease each other, but before another desirous thought and a very uncomfortable swell between his legs, he pulled away. "I will come to wake you later. I will touch you and taste you until you quiver in my arms," he whispered.

She sighed low, as soft as a kitten's purr. "I will dream of you."

Thankfully, her beautiful eyes closed. Trying not to be aroused took more self-control than he had. Sharp pains in his balls had his jaw tight and his fangs tingling.

****

Walking into the office, Draven glanced at Michael sitting in the same leather armchair that Lukas had occupied hours ago. If looks could kill, the man with a familiar arrogant smirk would be about to take his last breath.

"What's got you bent out of shape?" Michael asked.

"What indeed," he replied as he sat down at his desk with care. The twinge in his jeans hit hard and he hissed.

"I feel for you, brother. That fucking bastard."

"It's torture having her in my arms. To give pleasure without entering her is madness. I can walk but cannot run. I can bring her to orgasm but dare not become aroused. I will rip him limb from limb. I swear it, so help me—"

"God," Michael said.

His nostrils flared wanting to choke the man. "Yes, so help me *God*. I am not afraid to say the word. It doesn't set me on fire, the way I thought it would."

"I'm sorry. I didn't mean—"

"Ah, but you did. The first time your son went through the portal, when I was down on my knees with my hand searching for his through the mist, I even dared to pray, something I'm sure you never did without a soul." He glared, not about to let Michael off so easily. "What! No sarcastic comeback? *I* never dared to enter a church or a convent the way you did. I feared the sacrilegious repercussions just as I feared a stake. Not you, though. The more outrageous the act, the more of a thrill."

Michael looked down. "I swear, that December night in eighteen-ninety, when I took those innocent women's lives—"

"Nuns, dear brother, not just innocent women. Holy

sisters were your last sacrificial virgins."

"Afterward, right there in the convent's chapel, I craved final death."

"How ironic, is it not? To have been rewarded with your very own soul and the ability to dominate the beast with-in as none of us could. Maybe before I return to face final death, you will find it within your power to sneak me into the cathedral where I'll fall to my knees, and then lay this body out in prostration at the foot of the altar and beg the Lord's forgiveness." Leaning back, he shut his mouth, licked his lips, and after a quick intake of air, blew out a sharp breath. "This is my fate. This is my punishment."

"Don't say that," Michael whispered.

He held up his hands. "I will speak of this no more. As I told your son right before dawn, we are not a team. You owe me no loyalty."

"The fuck I don't." Michael came around the desk, leaned a leg against it with his arms locked to his chest and his feet crossed at the ankle.

The mortal man, mere inches away, stared down at him. He flatly refused to look up and meet those dark brown, too-intense eyes.

"A month ago, I trusted you with my life, with my son's life. I trusted you to do the right thing, and you came through, killing those first four realm guards when I couldn't. You brought me food. Let me sleep. You eased my mind when I worried about Lukas. I saw your distress when he was unconscious. You even backed down and left the dark witch to her own fate instead of ripping into her neck. Without access to your soul, you have much more self-control than I ever had. It is absolutely admirable how you control the beast-within.

Lord knows, I never could."

"It is a learned skill." The compliment stunned him, but before something sappy came out of his mouth, he said, "You were never so loquacious. That long proclamation, made all the more distinct by the crisp British accent, makes one wonder."

"Deal with it, brother."

Putting sarcasm aside, he replied, "You honor me with your trust."

"Honor you? With something you earned? Luna said something very perceptive last night. You have indeed rebuilt yourself."

"She is my eternal love," he whispered, and yes, thank you, he had. *And it damned well does me in—to shove that beast-within down deep, to thicken that moral thread. To create a metaphorical conscience with my intelligence and feed only on the tarnished humans sniffed out like a hunting hound.* It took a certain stamina that Michael never had.

"Over a century ago, you wrapped yourself in loving Luna, just as much for your own survival as for hers, and our sire let you go."

"Because after you returned to New York, I planned my escape from Cyril. Little villages in the Pyrenees, always far away from cities and other like us."

"I must say, it was both clever and wise beyond reason."

He still wouldn't look up, recalling Cyril's wrath—until he learned to shield his moral threads. "I wanted what I had with Luna more than I wanted the acceptance—of others like us."

When Michael rested a hand on his shoulder, he felt the reality of loss like never before. Draven willed his eyes to clear because once again, his emotions were all over the place. Like he had shattered a jar of pennies and couldn't pick them up fast enough without cutting a finger or two. And he didn't trust himself not to go all weepy right now.

He realized that although human again, Michael didn't gush with tenderness. In fact, you could rarely predict what he was feeling, how he would react. This man stayed guarded, kept everything neatly tucked away, tied up tight and to himself.

"You aren't going into this alone," Michael stated in a soft, steady baritone. "You don't call yourself a team member. Well, too bad because we are not leaving. And another will join with us."

Slightly baffled but overly curious, he had to ask, "What do you mean 'another'?"

"Christopher Forbes has offered to help."

His face snapped up, searching Michael's eyes. "Why?"

"How should I know? My son's text said that, strangely enough, Christopher can wield a broadsword, and he has warlock abilities that might be useful."

The list of humans to worry about just grew longer. "I do not see how."

"Perhaps he will sense something. In any event, a little back-up is a good thing. I'd say the odds are tipping in your favor."

Not nearly enough, Draven thought.

Michael walked away, sat down and crossed one knee over the other with his arms locked to his chest. "Have a little faith, brother. Try it for once. It might suit you, you know, and compliment that thickening moral thread. We have a chance, four against seven."

As their eyes locked, his narrowed. "I do not follow."

"All seven sires will enter Hell together."

No. Not possible. Fully unsettled, he said, "You are not seriously considering this."

"I absolutely am. We go with you and take them on together. It sends a clear message to all inhabitants of the Third Realm. No sire will come back to our world for the drink and drain. The Gatekeeper will not allow it. Now, don't you have a meeting soon?"

Trying *not* to see Michael, Lukas, and now, Christopher, drained and dead on that black marble floor, all he could say was, "Yes, a meeting."

"Make it a quick one. The real estate agent has been cleared. I'll be in your dining room listening." Michael pulled out his phone and remained silent.

To focus on business was impossible, yet Draven had to steady himself and do what had to be done. Then he thought about his last wishes, all typed out with his signature attached, folded in an envelope and hidden in his top desk drawer. If this was the plan, would Michael be alive to read it? Would anyone—including Lukas?

****

After showering, Luna tried on the clothes Draven had purchased. Most of them would be returned. In her own jeans, which had been washed and actually pressed, she decided on one new sweater, a soft, fine knit with various muted hues of blue. It felt heavenly on, and she liked the boat-neck collar. Then she recognized Michael's scent before opening the bedroom door—barefoot and enjoying the feel of thick carpet.

"He's meeting with the real estate agent," Michael informed in a low whisper.

As expected, he sat at the far end of the table like the head of the household. She took the chair at his side. With her hands folded tight on her lap, what she really wanted to do was pound on his chest, to cry and scream and beg, to insist that Draven be kept safe. Would Michael understand? Could he make it happen? After all, he wasn't a commanding vampire anymore, just a man, perhaps stronger than others, but now, entirely human.

In a clear, soft voice she stated, "He will not return alone to my sire."

"I'm certain he won't be alone," Michael said folding his arms across his chest.

Her eyes went wide, a bit relieved. "So you understand why I must go with him."

"You what!" The glare continued, very penetrating, as if his eyes could drill through hers. "Absolutely not!"

"I will offer myself to Herodotus. He can do to me whatever he pleases."

"Does Draven know about this idiotic idea of yours?"

His whisper rivaled a hiss, and insult had her in its grip. "It is not idiotic. He will take me as his slave and allow my love to continue his existence as Gatekeeper."

"You will not go with him into the realm, Luna. Is this clear?"

As if that could stop her! With her head high, staring straight ahead, she said, "I will go with him."

"Absolutely not!"

"Your heart is racing."

"I wonder why? Do you truly think that nasty bastard won't torture and rape you in front of him before cutting off his head?"

"That will not happen," she bit out and started to

leave.

Michael held her wrist with a tight expression on his face. "I have more to say."

She sat back down with dignity. "You will not change my mind."

"Like hell I won't. If you think for one second that Draven will allow this, then you're terribly mistaken! He'd tie you to that chair and lock that bloody vault door behind himself. Then, those of us who can help him will be unable to get through! Get it out of your head, Luna. I swear to God, I will interrupt his meeting and tell him right now."

Would he do that? Was there even the smallest possibility that others could help and he'd survive? Her eyes filled. Her lips quivered as she shook her head. No. She'd follow him through that portal. "I will not lose him. I will not exist without him. You cannot stop me. You will not interfere!"

Suddenly pulled off the dining room chair, Michael took her into the half-bath, shutting the door and turning on the faucet to muffle the sound of endless sobs ratcheting up her throat in despair. Both of her hands stayed clasped to her mouth.

Holding her tight against his him, Michael whispered, "He must not hear you cry. He cannot see your distress." When she peeled off, his palms held the sides of her face in a tender way. Only then did she realize that his eyes were glassy and moist with clear tears. Human tears. "I swear on my soul, I will not let Herodotus destroy him." He swiped the corner of an eye, and then dampened a patterned, paper hand towel to wipe away her blood tears. It turned to mush under hot water. Throwing it in the toilet, he flushed away any trace of it.

He led her back to the dining room table, but this time, sat with his back to the office door. The sound of a woman speaking and papers rustling continued as he leaned in close. And he still looked upset. Then the blank mask he wore reappeared. He was a master of purposeful deceit to hide his emotions. "What just happened stays between us, is that clear? He cannot lose focus, Luna."

"We have less than a day left, Michael. One day after eighty years apart! It isn't enough. Not nearly enough." Afraid she'd cry again, she closed her eyes and said no more. When the conversation in the office ended, Michael touched her hand. She eased tension out of her expression and swallowed her feelings like a master of purposeful deceit as well—and waited.

Minutes later, her immortal love came through the door and walked to her. Draven's gaze slid from Michael and back to her. "I did not expect to see you awake, my dearest."

Michael stood and that familiar thin grin appeared. "I'll be in the office. Put some loud music on, would you please? I'd prefer my report simply states that I heard nothing." Locked on Draven, he added, "When my son arrives, we have matters to discuss."

"Noted," Draven replied while walking across the room. He picked up the remote and pressed a button.

But misery consumed her. "I remember how you would often play Chopin's nocturnes whenever we came upon a piano. Will you play again for me, my love?"

"Later… only for you," he said with affection. Then he turned to Michael. "The sound system will loop through a series of compositions. I'm sure it will suffice."

Luna watched Michael leave and close the door.

Locking her arms around Draven's neck, all he offered was a tender kiss. But after that conversation, not to mention last night, she didn't want tender. Outraged that she'd lose him thundered within. She traced his fangs with her tongue, rubbed her hands down his chest and then played with his fly. Suddenly lifted into his arms, her lover's growl turned erotic.

In their room, he placed her in the center of the bed. The sight of him locking the door, taking off his suit jacket, throwing it over the chair in the corner, and then the way he unknotted his tie, had her crawling to the edge like a stalking tigress. Her eyes swept down his body in a lusty way. He came to her. She unbuttoned his shirt, pulling it out of his jeans while he unbuttoned both cuffs. Sweeping the soft blue sweater over her head, her hands worked her breasts. When he leaned in for a kiss, she dodged his lips and tugged at his belt.

Those magnificent hands replaced hers on both breasts, leaving her free to pull the belt out of its loops and drop it to the carpet. He groaned, whispered, "This is truly torture. I want to be inside you."

Her hand ran down the front of his jeans. A low, long hiss began before he recaptured a breast, teasing and nipping. What he did with his tongue felt maddening, and she continued to rub and cup him. He moaned when she brought her body closer and knelt before him. Her hips rocked against his, her jeans unzipped. One hand splayed across her bottom while the other snaked down to tease her core, greedy and provocative, until she squirmed and whimpered.

Then she was naked down to the knees. "Oh, my dearest, you are a temptress."

"Only for you, my love," she answered, knowing

she'd do anything he wanted. But she also had to know. "Tomorrow night—"

Draven cut her off with a kiss. She gripped his shoulders and stiffened as two long fingers possessed her. The heat of his growl echoed through her bones. She wanted his thick erection in her in a wanton way. "We must stay in the moment, as if there is no tomorrow. That is an order. Should I sense distress in you, it might anger me. I might get rough."

Just the thought made her throb. "I so like you rough. Ohhh, yes, yes please."

His expression promised more pleasure. Just the sight of his sharp fangs, the very idea of them running up her neck stood her on a cliff of passion. She eased back on the bed and let her imagination run wild. Her jeans came off her feet, but he fondled her through the thin silk panties in a way that had her panting.

"Do you like this, my love?" Her response was a teasing moan, the mischief in his eyes an unspoken challenge. "Good. I intend to do much more."

"Tell me what you will do." She wanted the feel of his mouth on her again, the thrill of his tongue taking what was his alone.

His fingers ran up the damp panties, but the way he eased them down had her undulating. "I prefer to show. Never tell," her eternal obsession growled as he knelt between her thighs.

No. She would not lose him. And should he be taken from her, she vowed to end her own existence. No one would talk her out of her decision. No one would be able to stop her.

Chapter 31

Unexpected Arrival

"Sorry I'm late. Got caught up with Chris, had to go back home to shower and change. Shit. My hair is still wet," Lukas muttered already out of sorts, adjusting the cloth-coated band Martine insisted he use. "You should have just gone back to Mary's. The Guardians could have handled—" He stopped talking, studied his father reading a file full of papers. *Okay, so yeah, he's a tad agitated.* "Wow. I haven't seen you sit at a desk in a very long time."

"I don't care for desks."

Lukas shrugged off his bomber jacket, laid it on the couch and sank into the armchair facing the commanding man who lived a life of action in a world very few knew to exist.

Then his father glanced his way. "You look like you're somewhere else."

"I'm just remembering the only other time I saw you sitting in an office like this, reading something."

"Yes, after a year of peace, knowing you were finally safe. It was the eve of your fifteenth birthday."

"I burst into your office at that evil place, and you blathered on and on, throwing around some useless techno-talk. Then everything changed that night."

A weary sigh sounded. "Look at us now. Trying to

save a vampire instead of staking him."

The last four words came out a grumble. Yet without Draven's help last month, he'd have been hung from the palace wall in the Second Realm. "So. What are you reading?"

"Descriptions of properties Draven thinks he's presenting to Herodotus tomorrow night. Over my dead body he does this alone."

Some weird tension lined his father's face. "So that's what bothers you?"

Leaning back with his arms laced across his chest, his father's face resonated disgust. "This brings us full circle, right back to the way it was when you burst in on me that fateful day. When Draven goes through the portal to present this, there's no bloody guarantee he will come back, damn it. Herodotus will grab the incantation from his mind and then open the portal to return, to drain innocents and sire an undead army."

"We have to get them all to come through to this office. It'll be easier to stake them."

"Nothing having to do with any sire is easy. And with seven of them, six being unknowns, there's no guarantee any of us will survive a confrontation. Once again, he's as good as dust and bits of bone. There's just one way to do this. I will go with him."

"Wait. What? No fucking way, Dad. That's suicide."

"Well, death and mayhem wasn't on my to-do list this November, either."

"They have to come through the portal. Look. I pushed Chris to the limit during our work-out. He's capable with a broadsword, and he easily picked up what I showed him with a stake. It's inherent in him, like it is in me."

"He isn't mystically human, Lukas. He won't self-heal when injured."

Both hands flew up fast. "Neither will we, if this goes down in the Third Realm."

"There is no 'we.' I go with Draven. Alone." His father's tone turned resolute, his face and posture, well, basically aggressive.

"Not gonna happen. You go. I go," Lukas shot back. "I have wicked skills."

"But you don't have fangs. These sires do, their inner demons always thirsty. And they can move like a blur, even around *you*."

"Yeah, and their lust for your blood is equal to their lust for power."

"My goal is to keep Draven's existence intact—so he continues to monitor what comes in and goes out of this portal."

"And my goal is to keep the innocents in this world safe from all things evil! You know, sometimes you really get under my skin," he fired off. Just like years ago in the Siena event, he saw his father dead and gone forever. "I won't have Mom a grieving widow and my sisters fatherless because you want to save a vampire." The next look meant watch-your-step. *Too bad, I don't care,* he thought facing that glower.

"I know Herodotus. I can anticipate his moves."

"And what about the other six sires, Dad? And that's only if you get through a realm full of vampires. You think they'll take a step back and watch? It's fucking suicide and you know it! We have to get them here or else... Christ! They'll kill both of you!"

Shooting up, his father threaded his fingers through

his hair with a sharp, "We cannot let seven sires walk through the portal! I swear to God, Lukas, open your eyes!"

"My eyes *are* open—all the way! At fifteen I took out Zoltan, that maniac of a vampire, right in front of Cyril's bony body. Then you cut off Cyril's head. Mom took out Veronique, another powerful sire. No. We get them here. We trap and destroy them, one by one!"

"That's if we can get them here, which is a fucking enormous if," his father said with a shake of his head.

"Four against seven," he yelled, "In the human world. That should be our goal."

"Make that five against seven," they both heard.

Lukas jumped up and turned to the unexpected voice coming from the hallway door to Draven's office. Hell, his eyes even shot wider saying an astonished, "Mom?"

His father's furious "Damn it, Alana," hung in the air at the same time.

She laid her jacket over his without saying a word. Dressed in black leggings and a dusty-rose colored sweater, her hands clipped her waist looking back and forth between them.

Totally speechless didn't describe it, even though his first instinct was to wrap her in a hug and give thanks to God that she was here. If anyone could talk his father out of something stupid, it would be her.

But the shock of watching her familiar habit of pulling her long, brown hair over one shoulder had Lukas rooted to the floor. His father didn't make a move, either. Because her expression read *really* pissed off— something he hadn't seen in years.

His parent's eyes stayed locked on each other, as if they were the only two people in the room. "I told you not to come, my Guardian."

"Deal with it," she replied with a hand brushing the air. "Now both of you, sit down and let's all take a breath." Turning on her heels, she shut the office door. Facing them again, she waited until he and his father did as she asked, then she picked up the other leather armchair as if it weighed less than a step-stool, setting it down next to his. She leaned over and smooched his cheek before sinking into it like a queen. "All right, so now, let's discuss this as a family," sounded cool, controlled.

Hoping to cut the tension between his parents, he softly asked, "When did you get in?"

A blunt "Not now," came from both of them at the same time, and he shut his mouth.

Glaring at his father, her leg crossed at the knee and a foot tapped freely in the air. "I'd ask you to lay it out for me, my love, but I heard the argument as I came down the hall."

"Alana," his father voiced in a slow warn, "they are sires. Very powerful. Very dangerous."

Her hand brushed the air, as if they were about to discuss something mundane like a goddamn grocery list. "A vampire is a vampire, Michael. They all turn into dust and tiny bits of bone in the end. You know my mystical skills didn't go *poof* when I left the mission. So... five against seven should work just fine, when we get them through that portal." She pointed to the vault door at the other end of Draven's office. "Steel and silver, I presume?" His father nodded, still locked to her big hazel eyes. "Perfect. The sires won't touch it. But this Draven character is a vampire. How does he manage it?"

"I've only seen him turn the handle, Mom," he

chimed in, very respectful.

"Good to know, sweetie." She granted him an easy smile. "Mary and I stopped at the ER to see Martine. She looks healthy again. Love will do that to you, right? Oh, and don't bother checking your texts. I told her I wanted to surprise both of you."

"That you certainly did," his father stated in a rumbling tone. "All seven sires will not walk through the portal, Alana."

"Yes they will, my love," she replied with a slow nod. "You know you're going about this all wrong, don't you."

His father cleared his throat. "Am I, my Guardian?"

"Yes. You see, it's the mind-set that matters here. Think like someone who has been denied what you truly, deeply crave. Now? It's in reach. You'd do anything, even act on a spur-of-the-moment temptation. Because it's right there, for just little old you. Look over those properties, my love, and describe the best one fit for a sire." She leaned forward, settled her shoulders. "Let's pretend it's up in New York State, like two hours north of the city."

His father looked ready to go ballistic, but he scanned the real estate listings. Paper shuffles collided with the sound of his soaring heartbeat. He slapped the listings down and spread them across the desk. Didn't say a word until zeroing in on a particular page. "Fifty-two million should make a nice dent in their assets."

Mom bit back an I-told-you-so smile. "Describe it, my love."

"Five hundred acres bordering state forest and protected land. A stable for eight horses. Hi-tech video security system around gated property. An obscene number of bedrooms. Formal ballroom, movie theater, indoor heated pool and a solarium."

"Uh-huh," she slowly drew out.

"Ten fireplaces, two kitchens. Library, great room, and poolroom."

"All furnished?"

"Furnishings included. The mansion is set deep within sculptured gardens and far away from the private road. A six-car attached garage with two apartments above. Wine cellar beneath the main house, a cigar room and windowless, climate-controlled storage rooms. I don't believe I need to go on," he said and threw the listing down.

Her hands flew up with an excited, "Sounds perfect."

His father's dark eyes bore into her hazel ones. "Alana darlin',' talk to me. What are you thinking?"

"Hopefully, the same thing you are... finally. This Draven character says it's awaiting their visit this very night. I can see the stunning, dramatic lighting around the entire property. I'm sure the electricity is on. Oh, it is vacant, isn't it?"

"If you want it to be," was his reply in a much softer tone.

"So, should he go through to the sires with such fabulous news of a perfect place so close and ready for immediate occupancy, why, they would be dying to see it. Pun intended."

"I see where you're going with this, Mom," Lukas slipped in because it could work.

"And I'm not even close to finished, sweetie," she replied, reaching over to squeeze his hand. "Here's your plan. Said vampire Draven, who I can't wait to meet, goes through the portal exhibiting confidence and pride in what he has to present. Let's say there are three bids on it already, but since it's so perfect, he really hopes the sires will grant him the humble request to have them come through the portal immediately to approve the purchase of the property. Why, they could take possession within a week! Think about it," she said with an easy shrug and an innocent expression. "Seven days until the freedom to drink and drain. The freedom to walk the human world again. They can be roaming among us looking for long, lovely necks to bite—as soon as the paperwork's signed and the money transferred. Draven says he has a stretch limousine waiting right outside his club, this very night! It's only a short drive and they'll be back in their realm before our sunrise. They can give approval tonight, and tomorrow morning, bam! He'll have the deal signed, sealed, and delivered. I assume he can put on a dramatic performance, can't he?"

"Totally," Lukas answered, "Drama is his middle name."

Leaning back in the office chair, his father stated, "They won't fall for it."

"Oh, they will," she replied with confidence. "Lu, can Draven pull this off?"

"Yeah, Mom, he can."

"My love," she said, only looking at his father, "is our son telling the truth?"

"Alana, darlin'—"

"Great. So we have a plan. Just to be certain we can slice off their heads, said dramatic vampire escorts three through the portal at a time. We slay, and he goes back for the next three. Now six are history. Then he escorts Herodotus through, because we save the worst for last."

"Draven might want that kill for himself, darlin'."

"And you'll be right at his side to assist." She relaxed back in the armchair. "Well, Lu, what's your take on this? I already know how Dad feels. Don't I, my love?"

"Yes, darlin'," his father answered as he laced his arms again.

She snapped her fingers and when she pointed to him, he said, "Better than brilliant, Mom. I should have thought of that."

"Sometimes it takes a woman to put it all together for you. Well, now that it's a go, when do I get to meet this Draven character? My curiosity is off the charts."

As if on cue, that slow, soft, groin-grinding music stopped. Draven came through the door dressed like his father, in black shirt and jeans. His father had his sleeves rolled up. The vampire didn't. And as arrogant as ever, the vampire came all the way into his office.

Standing next to him, his father simply said, "Alana, this is Draven."

****

Of course, he had scented her. Captivated by the ex-Guardian who still looked to be in her late-twenties, Draven placed a hand over his unbeating heart and dipped his head in respect. He made no move to touch her or lift her hand to his cold lips. The classic Italian beauty's gorgeous, almond-shaped hazel eyes were framed with long, thick lashes. Even casually dressed, she reminded him of royalty, of a young, vibrant Sophia Loren. In a voice oozing with charm, he said, "I am most pleased to meet you, Alana."

"Same here," she replied in a soft lyrical voice.

Moving like a dancer, she came around Lukas.

Standing before him, no one would ever believe this curvy, five-foot-three woman had the mystical skills of a fierce warrior. Yet, it would simply take a slight thrust of her dainty wrist to shove a sharp piece of wood through his unbeating heart.

Her head inched up to expose a lovely long neck. "I know what you did in the October event, and all I can say is thank you. I believe my husband left out really big chunks of information—about you." She glanced at Michael, then studied him again. Her one eyebrow rose. "He could definitely be your brother, my love. The likeness, well, except for the straight black hair, is uncanny. I'm guessing it's just past your shoulders, right?" He gave a slow nod, still marveling at her ease with him. "And you like to wear all black the same way my husband does. Wow. You even stand the same way. Who would have guessed?"

Michael cleared his throat, before saying, "It's always been a bit of a throw off when seen together."

"Wow. Cyril really did choose a specific type. Oh, my-my-my," she added as they stood shoulder to shoulder. Alana's hand came to rest right below that lovely long neck. "How is it that we never crossed paths in the city during my ten-year mission?"

He allowed a thin but genuine smile, insuring his long fangs definitely did not show. "I was acutely aware that you were under my brother in blood's protection, and I valued my undead existence more than my curiosity."

Leaning in, Michael whispered, "You know that thing you feel with Luna? Rein in the charm because she is mine. Only mine."

He clearly understood. Wouldn't dare to question it.

"And to what do I owe the pleasure of your presence? It is a most dangerous time. Perhaps you should not be in this city."

Michael held out a hand and Alana took it. She molded to his side, and Draven understood that move quite clearly, too. "Did you two talk or something? He said the very same thing to me—about this city being dangerous. I'm not about to miss being in this showdown. My husband is worried about you. Our son is as well. This is right where I belong. As a matter of fact, we have loads to discuss."

Michael seemed softer as he held his wife, more than Draven would have expected. Then her head turned ever so slightly. She took a quick sniff.

He stated, "That scent is my Luna."

"She doesn't have the scent of a vampire. I don't get that tingle that usually happens, either."

"It's another anomaly, Mom."

Alana looked at Lukas. "You didn't scent her, either, sweetie?"

Lukas shook his head, saying, "Yet she is vampire, existing exclusively on the blood of animals. There's no documentation of another one like her."

Draven quickly offered, "Michael can confirm that human blood nauseates Luna."

"And the beast-within?" Alana asked him.

He looked only at Michael. "No beast-within surfaced when she was threatened by your husband. I believe it occurred on the jet right after takeoff from Iceland. My Luna is truly unique." He paused and refocused on Alana. "Perhaps we should move to the dining room, where you will be more comfortable. I should like you to meet her."

267

As strange as it was to invite three lethal mystical warriors into his home, he didn't feel anxious. Something swelled within at the thought of being accepted as part of Michael's life, both past and present. It touched him in a way that had he a beating heart, it would be pounding with pride in his chest.

****

As Alana and Lukas sat at the table, Michael pulled him aside. "You have taken your sustenance?"

"Yes, of course," Draven replied.

"And Luna?"

"She has minimal need but finished a container—before I came into the office." He got a friendly pat on the back for that reply—before walking over to crack open the bedroom door. Dressed in blue jeans and that pretty blue sweater, Luna was brushing her hair. "Will you join us, my dear," he whispered. Granted an easy smile, for the first time in his undead existence he added, "We have company, someone new for you to meet."

Yes, once again he forced his eyes not to tear. They had been doing this weepy thing much too often this week. At any given time. Like he had no emotional control. When Luna whispered his name, he took her hand. "Yes. Come," he said.

Michael sat at the end of the table by his office door with his wife at his side, Lukas at his other side. Conversation ceased as they approached. "Luna, this is Alana, Michael's wife."

"So beautiful," Luna softly said, "It is a pleasure to meet you, Alana." She smiled at a woman who could turn his eternal love into dust and bone before he'd be able to yell a desperate, "No!"

Michael's wife offered a care-free but gracious,

"Pleased to meet you, Luna. As soon as Lu told us about you, I had my husband leave immediately for Iceland."

Seating her like a true gentleman would, Luna settled in the chair next to Lukas, who leaned into her with the whisper, "Everything's okay? He's been treating you right?" Her soft, "um-hum," produced a thin grin.

At her side, Draven took his place at the head of the table. Having no idea what to say, he folded his arms across his chest and stared at his brother in blood—for help. Alana continued to take in everything about the two of them, but he didn't mind, just as curious about the unique family now in his home.

Then she shook her head. "I never, ever expected to say this, but we're here for both of you. Luna, you're under our protection, and we'll do whatever it takes to keep Draven safe. So. There's a lot riding on how we approach this, and I have a plan." Her gaze zeroed in on him alone. "If you play this right, we can change the world as we know it."

Luna's hand came over his. *I simply have hours left to hold her, to show my devotion to her.* The thought was sobering, to say the least. "I'm aware of what I must do. I have no regrets."

"Regrets?" Michael groaned. "Do not push my buttons, brother. I told you before, we are a team. Me, my son, my wife, Christopher Forbes, and you. Five against seven is doable."

"Six against seven," Luna stated. Everyone looked at her, Draven as well. "I have speed, skill, and the ability to track, Alana. My sire humiliated him. I will be the one to exact revenge."

Before he could object, Alana quickly said, "You

don't have to explain yourself, Luna. If it were my husband, I'd feel the same way. So. We'll put your skills to good use. We'll train together and be ready as an attack team. You'll be with me. Michael is with Draven, and Lu is with Chris."

Draven shook his head. "No. Please rethink this. You are a mother with young daughters at home. I cannot accept nor will I allow it."

"You don't have a say in it," Michael stated, staring at only him. "You are not at full-speed, nor capable of taking on seven sires. But you are capable of bringing them through the portal to us."

"Impossible," he insisted with a tight look.

"Very doable," the man replied with just as tight a look. "Now sit back and listen."

"No. I will not allow—"

"I said you will listen. Remember our little chat at this very table. See yourself crashing into that hutch. All the precious blood spilled. Replay my words in your intelligent brain for a bit."

Alana shook her head and clicked her tongue. "Did you threaten him, my love?"

"Absolutely," Michael arrogantly replied. "My wife will lay out the way this goes down. And you will simply listen."

Draven sat back, not at all happy. Not at all convinced that whatever this was would work. Luna took his hand and squeezed it. Lukas, the little know-it-all, gave him that mischievous grin. And Alana? The power radiating from her sparkling hazel eyes told him it had been very wise to stay more than fifty feet away from this particular Guardian of Souls when she patrolled the streets of the city all those years ago. Very wise, indeed.

Chapter 32

Much Needed Breaks

The restaurant in Little Italy, known for its homemade pasta, was owned by a trusted Georgian. After a veritable Italian feast, Lukas sat with his parents and Mary enjoying family catch-up about his sisters, life with Martine in this city, and anything else non-vampire related.

Before Mary arrived, they had ironed out details about how to proceed with Draven and Luna. His parents agreed with him that once this was over, the immortal lovers should be placed above The Law of the Kill by the Georgian Sovereign Council. Luna exhibited no threat to human life. Draven exhibited unique control over his beast-within and, for the second time, had proven his ability to choose good over evil. If Draven could get the sires curious enough to walk through the portal, then he'd deliver seven unsuspecting evil things, and they would send them home to Hell. Then he'd be able to make a highly compelling case to the Council on their behalf.

A fresh frothy beer arrived, along with an expresso martini. He smiled at the waiter saying, "I didn't order this."

"I did," Martine said as she kissed his cheek before sitting next to him.

"How did you get off of your shift," he said, fully delighted to see her.

"I have my ways," she said with a smile. She sipped the martini, her favorite kind, and set it down as her other hand rubbed his thigh. *So much for table-talk,* he thought, *hello to what I'll do to her later on in bed.*

Then Mary looked at his mother. "Say the two of you will stay for the charity gala."

"That's coming up soon, isn't it," Martine replied, still having her way with him under the table. "I can't wait. I have the perfect gown. You own a tux, right, Lu?"

"A what," he said and cleared his throat. "Oh, no. I don't think so."

His father's eyes shifted from Martine to him. "Proper dress is a morning coat. I'll give you the name of a tailor I used years ago. You won't be disappointed. As for staying in the city—"

Alana cut him off with, "We'd love to, Mare."

"We would?" his father replied.

"Uh-huh. The girls are in good hands with my parents. This event will be behind us, so why not? I love the way you look in tails, my love. And we haven't been to anything like a fancy gala at a swanky hotel in such a long while. I can have your suit, shirt and shoes sent over. Ooh. I have the perfect gown in mind. It'll be fun to dance and enjoy ourselves, to waltz the night away." She pulled out her phone. "Let me text the housekeeper right now."

"Alana darlin', maybe we should—"

She held up a hand. "Almost done. There," she said putting down her phone. "We'd love to attend, Mare. And the suite at the hotel is so comfy."

"Let's call it a night, darlin'."

"It's not even midnight. It's been too long since we've spent time with Lu. Not to mention Martine and Mary. Besides, Martine hasn't ordered yet."

Still having her way with him, Martine answered, "I had a roast-beef sandwich on my dinner break. I'm good with just this delicious drink."

Lukas shifted in the chair, didn't trust himself to enter the conversation about gala gowns or its elegant venue. He reached down, squeezed her hand before placing it on her lap. Martine smiled, continued chatting like nothing was happening under the checkered tablecloth. He glanced her way before picking up his beer glass. If she did it again, there'd be no way he'd be able to walk out of here.

"I'm thrilled you're staying," Mary said. "We might even get to have an old-fashioned Sunday dinner."

"Five on the dot," his father stated. "We will bring dessert."

****

Michael had the love of his life pinned to their hotel room wall. The only light came from stars in a clear November sky and the bright cityscape outside the wide window. His wife unbuttoned his shirt. With her sweater already off, he flicked open the clasp of her bra. "I've missed you, darlin'. Now about the way you took over tonight." He kissed her neck, working his way down to her breasts.

"You know you love it, have come to expect it..." her voice trailed off with a moan as her hands ran down his chest.

"I swear to God, the way you still get to me is incredible." Carrying her to the bed, he placed her down gently before removing her ankle boots, then everything else that touched her supple skin. His Guardian's beauty had grown over their years together, her embrace always a place of comfort. Pleasuring her remained his sole purpose when they were alone. "Now this is much better."

"Let me help undress you, my love," she whispered in a low sexy voice.

He sat on the bed as her arms came around, rubbing his chest, working lower until she had his belt unbuckled and his black jeans open. He pulled off his boots and socks and everything else off. Turning to her, she fell back and held out her arms like a siren calling to him through the mist of desire.

"So you were saying?"

"About what," he asked between kisses up her body.

"That you love the way you get when I take things over. All hard, hot and bothered," she said and then gasped at the way he touched her. "It makes you so aggressive, like you can't wait to do what you want with me, like right now."

The next whimper did it. He was done talking, preferring to tease his way up to her luscious lips in silence before he made love to her. With the first powerful thrust she cried out his name. Her skin felt like silk beneath him. She called him her commanding lover. Tonight would be no exception.

****

Martine sighed as Lukas traced the tattoos on her back. Little purple flowers in a sweet bouquet with a scrolled name, Madeline, in memory of her daughter. An ancient symbol that meant healer and then an owl perched on a tree limb, each one artfully done. The newest was the symbol of infinity with his name intertwined in vibrant green ivy vines. Unlike the ugly scars crisscrossing his back, hers told a beautiful story of who she was.

They had shucked their clothes in a heated blur and made love sideways, across the bed. He loved to watch her orgasm, and what she did had him hissing and panting. When they came together the second time, every quick breath she took echoed through his soul.

"This thing tomorrow night," she softly said.

He drew her closer with a kiss. "What do you want to know?"

She played with the hair on his chest. "How dangerous is it, Lu?"

"It's five against seven. Six if we include Luna. Mom said she reached out to certain ex-Guardians who train newbies at the Georgian Institute. With any luck, they'll want to assist."

"Why don't the Georgian's order them here?"

"Well, first, they haven't been in the field for years. Second, this isn't a sanctioned event."

"How so?" she asked, snuggling closer.

"It wasn't run past the Georgian Sovereign Council for approval because there were no innocents attacked. And since Draven is the Gatekeeper, the Council would order that he doesn't go back."

"What are you not saying?"

"The Georgian Sovereign Council doesn't provoke a war. It's not their way."

"Guardians take orders from you. They're our drivers, even our security."

"Only because of who and what I am, a mystical warrior born with these gifts, my father's son. I wasn't a Guardian, M. I don't have a tattoo of a dragon in a circle on my wrist."

"But you're a part of them."

"And I'll always be. Their mission is my mission. But this time we're, more or less, on our own."

"It's too dangerous. Call it off."

"No. We can do this. I know we can. And the world will be a safer place because of it. If the ex-Guardians coming are who I think they are, well, Christ, Dad trusted them with my life in Siena. I have years of history with them." He had to lead her away from questions, already sensing her upset. "It might be wise to reach out to Paige before this goes down."

Her brown eyes narrowed and the flecks of gold in them appeared to brighten. "I know what you're doing."

"What am I doing?"

"Switching my focus away from this. Just so you know, I'm taking a couple of days off until this is over."

"Wouldn't it be better if you were busy at work," he asked, hoping to change her mind.

"Not a chance in Hell this time. I'll call Paige first thing in the morning."

Yeah. He could have predicted that. "Thanks. I'd do it myself, but talking to you is better, especially if she and Chris are serious."

"I sense they are. Just like you and I, it's their destiny."

Not about to question her witchy ways, he answered, "Wow. Good to know."

"And I'll invite them to join us at the gala. This one should be fabulous with you and your parents there. So," saying as she kissed his chest, "what is it you want Paige to know?"

Where to start. "Broadsword wounds are ugly. Even

a graze from a sire's fang could be possible. She has to be prepared."

"*I* have to be prepared," she said pushing off his chest. She fingered the Kendrick family amulet he always wore. The leather strip had been replaced with a sturdy silver chain. "It's too soon after the last event. You have a scar on your thigh from that one."

He sensed her whispering a protection spell, always caught it when she did. "This is happening in our world, not theirs, so I won't scar. Neither will my father. But Chris, well, that's the danger, warlock or not."

"And what about Alana? What if she gets hurt?"

"Mom has the ability to heal very fast, and she's incredible with a sword."

"So you're worried about Chris, but not yourself or your parents?"

"I'm prepared. So are they." Lukas sat up as she knelt by his side. "I stay focused and use all my enhanced senses."

She gave a one-shoulder shrug. "That doesn't mean I can't worry."

Love thundered through him as he studied the serious expression she wore. He blew out a slow breath, tried to make it better. "How can I say this and not come off sounding like a jerk? I'm quick and steady, but not Superman. I don't fly, fucking forget the cape and tights thing, and I don't have those wonky eyes that cut through steel."

Her hand rubbed his cheek. "No. Yours are so dark-blue and beautiful, and the way women gawk at you."

"Yeah, yeah, I know," he replied throwing that aside. "But seriously. Not one of those sires will be let loose to walk God's good earth after they come through that portal. Every single one of us knows what has to be done. I promise to call as soon as it's over. Then I'll come home, shower off the stink of them and make love to you over," he kissed her lips, then her forehead, "and over again. And if I find out you've worried yourself into a frenzy after I'm telling you not to, I will deal with you. You won't like it."

She grinned with a wiggle. "Gonna get all bad ass on me, huh?"

"Totally," he replied before he positioned her beneath him. "Christ, I'm hard again. See what you do to me?" She bit his lower lip in a very greedy way.

Then they both said, "I love you," at the same time.

Chapter 33

What Is Love?

After hosting his human, well, mystically human company, and completing his necessary work in preparation for sunset, Draven opened another file that Lukas sent via email. He studied the contents carefully before sending a series of numbers back via email. Then he closed the computer, bid a terse "Good night" to the Guardians standing at the outer door to his office and entered his home.

He came to the dining room table and kissed Luna's cheek as she scrolled through different items for sale on a popular website with a look of awe on her face. Of course, she had access to his credit account on the site. He left her "oohs" and "ahhs," undressed in the master suite and took a hot shower.

So much bothered his mind, including Alana's plan, which was actually brilliant—if he played his part like an Oscar-winning actor. He had to pull this off. It was the right thing to do. Many reasons jolted him, some more than others.

First and foremost, none of the humans helping me should die. Those pesky emotions surfaced, causing his eyes to tear and his head to hurt. The tragedy would be so immense that he'd never forgive himself. A unique warlock, a beautiful mother, a son any father would be proud of, and most of all, his brother in blood, a true champion. Had he a human heart, it would be trembling from the fear that snaked through his veins.

The human world must not change. He liked it just the way it was, thank you, with all its flaws, even with those pesky dark seers. Humanity didn't need to be subjected to sires creating a new army of vampires, nor the drink and drain of innocents just for the thrill of it. Nor the untimely deaths of healthy young people who should be living life to the fullest, marrying and making babies. These types of meaningless slaughter were fully unconscionable.

The sires, and who the hell knows how many other vampires are in the Third Realm, should stay there and be grateful in their conjured world—for their kind, not my kind. They showed no thread of a moral code, had learned how to feed off of each other, or paid for a quick drink from a blood-slave. Should those blood slaves suddenly flood this world, there would be questions, investigations, and rampant hysteria. The confirmation that vampires exist would be exploited by the ruthless media. No one in their right mind will believe so many humans were abducted by aliens or some other nonsense. The exposure would cause suicides, weird cult worshippers, and every other type of mania, not to mention knowledge of other realms. In the grand scheme of all his worries, vampires going to war with those witches and warlocks in the Second Realm bothered him the least.

It was the human world and specific individuals he cared about that worried him the most.

After drying off, Draven pulled on a pair of black silk pajama bottoms and kept his long hair loose. When

Luna came into the bedroom, he smiled, held up his pajama top with one finger. As if this were the new-normal, she took it, stripped out of her clothes, except for the silk panties low on her hips. He buttoned the top as he kissed her.

"Perhaps some sofa time with you in my arms," he whispered.

"Can we watch movies?" she asked as her hands slid to his hips.

"Of course, my dearest."

"After your sustenance. Three glass bottles."

"Yes, yes," he replied with a fretful sigh. He'd be forever grateful to Lukas and Michael for bringing Luna back to him. Whether he had hours or decades, Luna in his arms, in his bed, comforted him.

They took care of his need in the galley kitchen before settling on the sofa. He sat against an arm with her between his legs, her beautiful blonde hair spread across his chest. The screen came to life, and she fiddled with the remote to scroll through an array of titles.

"Why are you so quiet, my love," she asked.

Where to start when there is so much to say. "I am ashamed of myself for not sending minions to bring you to me decades ago."

"Perhaps you weren't ready to be faithful to only me. My existence has not been awful, Draven, boring, perhaps, but not a horror. I've been cared for, allowed to do as I chose."

"Yet I see you fully engrossed in that laptop and hungry for knowledge."

"And I love movies. Ooh, and on-line shopping! It's addictive! No. The desire to stay as you left me is on me. Only me. The world did not touch me, and maybe, I did not want to touch the world. Had this not occurred, no one would know I exist except for Rune and Freya. It is good that Lukas decided to reunite us. It is good that you asked him to send Michael, who is protective of you, Draven, as if you were truly his blood. Lukas has a tender heart. I like him. I like Alana as well. A very truthful, strong woman."

"In more ways than one. She is still quite lethal to those like us."

Luna turned to snag his gaze. "We are not like other vampires, mindless and driven by thirst. Your personality has strengthened and your passions have reignited. You have good in you, Draven. We are different."

"We turn to dust and bits of bone the same as the others," he replied with a shake of his head.

"No vampire would go up against a sire. No vampire but you."

"Michael did. He destroyed our sire. When I arrived in this city, I watched him stake any vampire he came across."

"Yet he didn't stake you."

He laughed before saying, "I made sure to take care of my need long before I met up with him. Had he seen me drink from a human, after he beat me, he would have staked me."

"Back then, you saw him protect Alana?" she asked before settling on his chest again with the big screen's remote in hand.

"Yes. In the nineteen-nineties. He was always at her side, until the night she turned twenty-one. Then I didn't see him for months. Nowhere to be found. But one night, there he stood in the shadows watching his Guardian again. I never saw them speak to each other after that absence. Nor touch her, for that matter. He never gave a reason for why he disappeared, nor did I press for an explanation. But how intriguing, to protect someone who could slice off your head with a silver sword or push a stake through your unbeating heart at any given time."

"They have deep love for one another. It is visible, the meaningful human life they've built together, having children and watching them grow. What an astonishing twist of fate. Did you see Lukas with him back then?"

"Not until two-thousand-three. The boy was a hellion. Full of rage and quite dangerous pursuing Micheal. I sense it's a complicated story. One I have little knowledge about. Then, like Michael, the boy suddenly disappeared. I didn't see him again until a month ago, quite grown up and formidable like his father." He stopped talking and closed his eyes. "I... I had a son in my human life. His name was Julien."

She turned again in his arms, her wide blue eyes beyond beautiful. "How? How do you know? Except for what you told me, I remember nothing of human life. I sense loss and sadness, but that is all I recall."

"During the last event, Michael threw tidbits of information at me, about my life, my wife and my son Julien. He said Cyril had been fascinated with my parlor performances in Paris. Perhaps that's why he sired me. I'll never know. And when the last event came to a conclusion in mid-October, he sent Julien's original compositions and a daguerreotype of him as a grown man. I saw it as payment for assisting him and his son in the Second Realm." He began to smirk, recalling those last harrowing hours before coming back through the portal. "Lukas has quite a temper, very reminiscent of that dangerous child I once saw. I experienced it firsthand right before we returned to our world."

"The past molds us," she said in a soft voice.

"I know he was imprisoned in the Second Realm. Any innocent child that survives such a horrible thing would be feral."

"You must have provoked him."

Aware of her defending Michael's son, Draven replied, "No. Lukas had been injured at the time. Became feverish and belligerent, and he flew into one hell of a tantrum."

She secured his long hair behind his ears and then cupped his cheek. "Yet Michael trusted you with him, which proves you are truly valued by both of them."

He looked away, fearing he'd tear up again. "I do not deserve your love, Luna. Had I told them about this a month ago, I might have saved myself a brutal kick in the balls."

"Then I'd still be alone in Iceland. This cannot be our last night together."

"We will not discuss it any further."

"We will discuss it, and you will say what you must say to me."

He sighed, in awe of her caring nature, in awe of the determination on her face. The reality of this situation was something he couldn't ignore. She had to know how he felt. "There is a good possibility that I will not return."

"I will not lose you, Draven. I love you so very much."

Although he found it hard to continue, he owed her more. "Should I fail to return, I've made provisions with Michael for your safety. If I manage to con them and they come through the portal, should you see that the mystical warriors are no match for the sires, you must immediately get away and find Mary Kendrick. Tell her you are to be returned home, protected and hidden."

She shook her head with a firm, "No. I won't go back to Iceland."

"Yes, you will go back and do as I say. Your safety is paramount."

"This issue is larger than me. It's larger than you. The sires cannot be let loose on this world. I'll fight to final death. I will not go backward anymore."

"Then I go to my final death knowing you are lost as well," he replied more bothered than before. Whether or not fate would intervene and allow his survival, he couldn't know. She had no idea about all the issues weighing heavily on his mind. "Luna, I will not—"

Cutting him off with kiss, full of passion, Luna held his face studying him. He felt so unworthy of her, and at the same time, so desirous of her that words left him. If things went wrong, if this was his last night on earth, he had to make love to her. He'd endure the pain and discomfort to please her, to please himself. Deepening the kiss, he embraced each jerk and twinge. He wanted her. He wanted to be in her.

As if she sensed his need, kisses trailed down his chest. Draven gripped the couch, unwilling to stop what was happening below his waist. His fingers dug into the top of the couch as well as the cushioned arm beside him, his chest expanding as he filled his lungs with air like a mortal man. One foot dropped to the floor. She leaned down and kissed him through the silk pajama bottoms as his arousal hungered for her attention. With a growl, his head fell back. A hand ran up his thigh and then parted the black silk to expose him. Feeling the uncontrollable stir, her tongue teased as he hissed and hardened.

Her eyes flashed to his. "Are you in pain?"

He swallowed hard, whispered the little lie of, "Not yet." Her slow grin read sexy as hell. She licked again, the sight and the feel of her tongue on him producing another thrilled jerk of his hips. What if he couldn't hold an erection or even perform? "Luna, you must stop. Come rest against my chest."

"No. I do not want to," she replied before another lick. She moved off the couch, and as he turned, she knelt between his legs. His cock throbbed again and this time, she took him into her mouth, slowly slid up and down.

How much more could he stand without letting his body fully respond? "Is this because you want me to get rough with you again?"

She pulled back as if his question finally registered. He fixed himself, as best he could, and then she stood and held out her hands, which he immediately took. "I have decided I don't want to watch a movie anymore. Come to bed, my love."

Standing with a growl, he couldn't talk his arousal down. "I will not be gentle with you after what you just did."

Her hand shot to his groin cupping him, balls and all. "This is mine. Only mine from this moment on. Am I clear, Draven? No other lips will ever kiss you. No other mouth will ever touch this again."

The harsh tone, the narrowing of her sparking eyes, well, he loved every minute of it. He groaned as the pressure of her hand stoked those damn twinges again. "Yes, my dear," he replied, still somewhat shocked at such an erotic, bold hold. Then she placed his hand on her core. A growl raced up his throat because of this brazen move, a thrill beyond belief.

"This is yours. Only yours. No other hand has touched me in this existence. No other mouth has ever teased an orgasm from me. None ever will. Am I clear, Draven?"

Barely audible, he replied another, "Yes, my dear."

"Now, come take what is yours alone to have." Luna untied his pajama bottoms and they raced down his legs as she straightened her shoulders. Forget about fumbling with buttons. He ripped the pajama top off her and wallowed in an edgy moan, a sensual lift of a shoulder. "I like it when you pull my panties down." Which he did immediately. On his knees. All the way, so she could step out of them.

Then his face burrowed into her belly, his arms shot around her as she stroked his hair. "If I survive this, I vow to be at your side throughout the rest of my sorry existence. I have wronged you beyond belief."

"You will survive this, my love. We'll see about the rest of your sorry existence."

What a tease you are, he thought. Standing, he devoured her full lips. During the slow dance to their bed with twinge after twinge, desire deepened. By the time she sat on the bed he was hard, high up and ready. She eyed his erection in a wanton way, so unlike the Luna he left on the shores of a faraway country decades ago. Hunger flared in her gaze with the glow of sensual heat, a look he'd always remember.

He put a knee on the bed, expecting her to sidle back. Instead, she held his thighs and took him into her mouth, worked him gently, but oh yes, just the tantalizing feel of her made his hips rock. Pain didn't matter. He craved her desire. When she left him and licked her lips, one thin eyebrow lifted in a come-on look that pleased him. Draven wanted more.

Luna draped across the bed. He spread her legs farther apart. She tasted heady and rich, the arch of her back enticing. Supported on his elbows with the tip of him poised to take her, she panted. He pushed into her, instantly coated, demanding full union with the immortal love of this existence. She let out a cry as he pulled out and slid in again, to love her slow and gentle, filling her with all of him, kissing her breasts and then possessing her mouth.

Her knees came up. One leg rested on his hip. He dismissed the pain. For her. Only her.

With the tender whisper of, "I love you," he knew he was finally home.

Chapter 34

What Ifs

As day dawned, Lukas sat at his computer with a cup of strong coffee in hand. Today would be busy. After sunset? It would turn dangerous and deadly. With an event imminent, he required little rest. Dressed in black sweats and T-shirt, he rolled tension out of his shoulders and scrubbed his face as if those two things would make what he had to do easier. He'd do texts and emails first, hoping what he needed had been sent.

His father's text stated a workout session would take place at *Destiny* this afternoon. *Good call,* he thought as he sent a text to Chris with time and place. Then, Draven's email contained the crucial info he needed. Once downloaded from Georgian files, he studied the pictures before texting six photos to his father.

Like research, journal entries were part of Georgian protocol, but rarely uncomfortable the way this personal reflection would be. The Georgian Sovereign Council would have to know why they did what they were planning to do, even if tonight's action had not been sanctioned—especially if there were casualties or say, he and any of the others didn't survive. So… he'd start with the easy, or rather, eas*ier,* since none of these were run-of-the-mill issues.

Last night's discussion around the vampire's dining

room table would be a breeze to enter, but the different scenarios that could occur tonight required objectivity. The importance of spelling out everything was a critical part of his thought process. Would the sires take the bait? Would Draven trick them and bring them through? Was including Chris Forbes in the event detrimental or instrumental? Were there enough mystical warriors to overtake three sires at a time? He typed and answered each question, and many more, with the required analysis.

The next document, the personal component, had him anxious. Putting Alana at risk clutched at his heart. His sisters, only fifteen, led a shielded life at the Georgian Estate in England. Alana might be feisty and brave, but she hadn't been on a mystical mission in years. He didn't doubt she could handle things. It was the unidentified abilities of the sires that would be the crucial factor between success and failure.

Reopening the first document, he added more questions: Would the sires sense mystical warriors waiting? What if they refuse Draven's invitation? The element of surprise, silver broadswords ready to lop off heads with swift, sure strokes was a given. Would the sires use their fangs or carry swords? Possibly. Would the sires go for their necks? Definitely. With six known military leaders in life, this wouldn't be a walk in the park. All were lethal.

He went back to the second word document after another scrub of his face. The fact that he could lose one or both of his parents made his chest ache. More than just his world would shatter if that happened. The loss of his father would send his life into a tailspin. He couldn't even imagine it. If something happened to Alana as well, her entire family would be crushed. So would scores of Georgians and others who knew and respected both his parents. He'd have to bury his personal grief, his abject anguish, before he told his sisters in person, unable to face his personal grief let alone care for them. Which meant relocation to England. And he couldn't even imagine how Martine's life would change. He trusted in their love. They were each other's destiny. What if she wasn't ready for this type of ready-made-family commitment? They'd only been together a month, even though they'd known each other for years. Time alone, just the two of them, was important. Just the idea of raising the twins terrified him, made his gut twist.

Which led to another fact. He could self-heal but couldn't regrow a hand or an arm. He'd be a burden on Martine. Would have to come to grips with the fact that his days as a mystical warrior, possibly the only reason for his existence, had come to an end. Taking it a step further, what if he didn't survive? Thank God Mary had strength and resilience. The woman who owned him, heart and soul, would need her. Martine's grief, like it had been with the loss of her baby, would be bottomless. Would she stop eating again? Would she crawl so deep inside herself that nothing and no one could bring her out of it?

Oh yeah. That really rattled him. He had to take a minute, swallow his emotions, his worst nightmares, and digest it all. Seeing the words typed on a page, the black and white of it all, he palmed his face, willed his vision clear and took a deep breath. *Christ, I really hate doing this.*

He forced his attention back to logistics. Guardians would surround the club on high-alert. Four handpicked, seasoned Guardians would be with them in the club as back-up. He scanned their profiles, not about to lose even one of them. In the event the sires escaped the ambush in the office, they'd be met by wooden stakes and silver swords in the club. If they got outside, they'd meet their fate on the street. He made another decision to insure everyone's safety, ordering all mystical warriors in the club, including Luna, to wear training tunics made of reinforced fabric. The vests as well as a trunk full of extra weapons would be waiting for the fight session this afternoon.

His phone dinged, and his eyes shifted to the text panel that came up on the side of his word document. He leaned back with a grave expression on his face. Reinforcements of the retired-Guardian kind were on their way. He knew each and every one of them. How their mystical skills had remained intact was a mystery, not one he dared to question. All of them were experts with trusted weapons used to destroy vampires. *The odds of success just skyrocketed.*

Truly grateful for their involvement, tonight's strategies had to change, and Lukas opened the first document again.

****

At Kendrick House, Mary had the living room set up and ready to go for tonight. Her nerves weren't completely raw yet, but they were well on the way. This healing circle would include many more than just the regulars. Specific good witches, whose power on their own were formidable, had been asked to attend. Not one had turned her down. Furniture and every folding chair she owned lined the walls with the dining room table moved to the center of the elongated oval. Beeswax candles stood on every flat surface, ready for the flick of a Bic to the tallest one.

In spite of what could happen once it all started, the gala, a yearly fundraiser she had created decades ago weighed heavy on her mind. What if something disastrous occurred in the event? What if their plan didn't work? No matter how it played out, she'd have to be strong enough to pull the charity benefit off without a hitch.

Sitting on the couch, she pulled out her phone and waited for Tristan to answer. "Are you good without me today?" she asked, and then let out a sigh of relief hearing his confident response. Taking in the newly created open space, she listened with a grateful grin, and hearing Tristan's respectful ask, replied, "That's fine. The more power we have, the better. Freya's always welcome here. Tell her the gala ticket is comped. Be here before midnight."

Ending the call, she walked into the kitchen, put on a pot of coffee, and waited. Then she took her cup and sat at the table just as her daughter came in. Martine poured herself a cup of coffee and joined her. They both added milk, stirred the silver spoon counterclockwise before making a pentagram, whispering, "As it is, so shall it be."

Shielding her own concerns, Mary sensed frantic worry as Martine blew out a breath, her hand sliding up and down the mug. "So here we are again, Mare. Another crazy wild ride with no idea how it ends, and I won't be on shift in the ER to keep my mind off it."

That frantic worry was growing stronger by the second. Leaning both arms on the table, she folded her hands. "How did you manage to leave without Lukas seeing this in you?"

"He was glued to his computer screen until noon."

She narrowed her eyes. "And?"

Her daughter flicked a wrist. "Okay. I used a couple of strands of his hair to do a teensy-tiny 'let M sleep in' subconscious suggestion. He was gone before I came down."

"Take a breath and trust his skills. He's got it all together, honey." she said, in a calming voice.

"Jeez. Michael and Alana, not to mention Lu."

"I know. So many we love are in this."

"It's never happened before. I can't help feeling like I've been sucker punched. Nothing can happen to any of them, Mom, not even a scratch."

"That's why you'll be with us in the healing circle tonight." Her daughter shot her that challenging look. "It's been over five years. That's too long, Martine. Come share your energy with us."

Her daughter looked away. "I don't know if I'm ready to see everyone again."

"Well then make yourself ready. It's where you belong. Look how your life has changed. Look how *you've* changed." She paused to let that sink in. "You can't be alone tonight. Trying to cast that kind of personal protection spell around him will drain you like never before, especially distracted with someone else there."

"Paige can't be alone, either, Mom. I'm sensing she's already passed I-really-like-Chris and is creeping closer to some deep, deep love."

"So bring her here. We aren't heathens, you know. Whether she prays or joins in our chant is up to her. Positive energy is positive energy. She'll want to help, and she shouldn't be alone, either."

"Maybe. I'll think about it."

"Martine, don't make me insist."

Her daughter rolled her eyes and frowned. "We'll need suture kits at the club, just in case."

"Already done."

"Jeez," Martine sighed. "Doc Baker's in on this? Are you certain?"

"You're kidding, right? My senses are weirdly tuned into this event, ever since the Draven-headache that got me involved so fast."

"Then count on me and Paige to be there as nurse assistants for him." Putting the mug down again, her daughter leaned forward. "Not fair, Mare. Why didn't I sense it?"

"Because you're too close, loving Lukas the way you do."

"You love Michael."

She smirked. "Not in the same way."

"And Draven? Are you including him in the spell tonight?"

"Naturally. I have to admit, though, protecting not one but two vampires might make some of them in the healing circle uneasy, but it's the right thing to do."

"Lu is completely bewildered by Luna."

"So am I. And I'm baffled about Draven." After a slow sip, Mary added, "It's been a hell of a lot of years."

"But you don't love him."

"No. So why is the connection is still there?"

"Once bitten, always sensed," her daughter whispered.

"Even after forty years?"

"Sometimes connections are intertwined with fate."

"As it is, so shall it be," she simply replied.

"Yep. So shall it be," her daughter whispered. They sipped their coffee, both women deep in thought, both good witches getting a jump on protection spells, even with the dangerous event still hours away.

****

"I despise wearing sweats," Draven said while tying his hair back. He wouldn't even comment on the sneakers, certainly not his idea of acceptable footwear. But the ugly things had been brought down by Donovan, no doubt sent by Lukas. *If I survive this, my trusted bouncer will get a healthy raise and a healthier warning to never speak to Lukas again.* In his book, those two had become too chummy.

Luna giggled. "We look ready for a jog."

"I don't feel ready for a jog. Not at all," he replied, more irritated. "At least he had the good sense to purchase the sweats in black, not some horrid shade of iridescent green." Yet no matter what the love of his existence wore, she looked beautiful, so tall and statuesque. Luna held his waist, kissing his cheek. "You know I will have to scrub my skin raw before I dress tonight. Herodotus must not scent you."

"I'm sure we won't train all afternoon," she replied as her hands ran down his chest, completely avoiding his statement about her sire. "You will need to make love to me after we train."

"Over and over," he whispered like a private vow. Feeling more like himself, he'd accept the limitations and keep that part of lovemaking slow and careful. As for today's irritating but required workout, he'd be cautious as well. But once dressed for his traitorous trip to the Third Realm, creating the necessary distance from

Luna would take every ounce of self-control.

Dear God, please let me come back to her, he thought as if it were a prayer. He'd look like a fool falling to his knees right now, especially since his soul had been invaded almost two centuries ago. *Nevertheless, I wasn't a murderer in life.* That had to count, right?

Chapter 35

Chills and Skills

Exiting the blacked-out SUV, Lukas eyed the closed club. His senses, already sharp, honed in on people standing across the street from the club, people who appeared unusually interested in his arrival. They weren't Guardians. He was sure of it. He felt eyes on his back as he left the vehicle. Instead of heading into *Destiny*, he crossed the empty roadway, which sent a chill racing up his spine and a peculiar scent up his nose.

Like a pack of wolves no longer interested, they turned their backs on him with heads down, walking toward Broadway. All except for one. The old lady's olive complexion reminded him of the Romani people, someone who detested gorgers as if anyone not of their ancestry were scum of the earth. The shine of her pitch-black eyes intrigued him when locked to his, the expression on her wrinkled face similar to a zealot's.

He approached with a steady gait. "Wow. What did you do? Put out a group text to every dark seer in the tri-state area, just to get a heads-up on what's going on across the street?" Her chin raised as those black orbs narrowed. "Don't even try to penetrate my thoughts. Not happening, bitch."

"The Gatekeeper is a traitor." She spit on the ground, never unlocking her glare.

"So you think you'll do a telepathic direct-connect with the sires, and like a loyal puppet, send a warning?" He leaned in closer. The evil oozing out of her smelled like acid from an old crusty battery. "You have no idea what you and your gang are up against."

"No, they don't," Chris said, walking over, stopping at his side. "I felt the dirty dark seer air as I came around the corner. Oh yeah, and the way your friends suddenly scattered sent my senses into a nosedive."

Lukas held her gaze, grateful the warlock showed up when he did.

"Don't mention it. That's what friends are for," Chris whispered.

"So the question is, what do we do with you?" The scent of hate filled the air, but the old lady's racing heart had him wondering just how juiced her powers really were.

"The Gatekeeper is a traitor," she hissed again in a breathy tone.

"I heard you the first time. Is that all you're programed to say, because I've got somewhere to be." Lukas gripped her arm. With a wince, she turned her face away. "Hear me, dark seer, and be sure to mind-message your cronies. All the cowards had enough sense to shuffle away and leave you to stand alone. We are a force you don't want to tangle with. Should our plan go haywire because your loyalty is to the sires, I will hunt you down. Your stench is ripe enough to easily track. When I find you, like every other evil thing I see, I will end you."

When he let go, she found her footing and pointed a bony finger. "You have made a powerful enemy, Lukas Malone."

"Yeah. I'll add you to my current list. Chris, can you—"

The warlock snapped his fingers and the dark seer went rigid. Stepping closer, Chris pressed his thumbs to her temples and closed his eyes. Ten seconds after that, she collapsed.

Lukas caught her before she hit the pavement. "Whoa... what did you do?"

"Just planted a picture and made an urgent call for help of the human kind, which should arrive any minute now. I'd say a trip to the psych ward at St. Francis is in order."

The screeching of brakes and the *whoop-whoop* of a siren drew his attention to the police car at the curb. One cop came over. "What happened here?"

Chris looked directly into the officer's eyes. "We were walking by, and this woman was all, like, ranting and raving about how aliens are after her, and then she fainted."

"I'll call for an ambulance," the police officer said.

But then, the dark seer roused, screaming, "They're here! They're after me! No. Let go. I have to time travel away!" Her eyes flicked wide, and when she lunged, hissing and beating on the cop, well, that put a different spin on things.

"Cancel the ambulance," the cop said into the devise on his shoulder. But both cops had to wrestle her into the back of the police car.

"What's going to happen to her, officer," Chris asked.

"We'll take her to St. Francis for a psych evaluation after the ER checks her out." With that said, he got into the police car, never asking their names or how to contact them.

Lukas whispered, "Fuck. Did his body cam record us?"

"Nah," Chris stated. "It'll be all static and no picture."

"Nice move. How long do you think they'll keep her?"

Chris shrugged. "The spell will lift after midnight. Depending on what drugs they pump into her, I'd say she'll slide back to reality somewhere around dawn. By then, this will be over, right?"

Lukas nodded as they crossed the street. "You're fucking powerful."

"With the fate of humanity at stake, I dug down deep."

"And your arrival was perfectly timed."

"Sometimes you just have to trust your instincts."

Donovan held the door. Walking through, Lukas kept his voice low. "I don't believe in coincidence. Neither do you."

"Not anymore. Nothing can interfere with what's going down tonight. And should any of those assholes I passed decide to send a warning to the sires, they'll be thinking about close encounters and little green men, too."

"I sense she's their guru."

"Yeah, let's pray they don't make a move without her."

Once downstairs, Lukas leaned in. "And keep this to ourselves for now."

"No. I'm calling Mary, just in case. A wider spell of protection around this place couldn't hurt."

"Good idea," he replied, taking in the training space.

He gripped Chris's shoulder while looking around. The empty dance floor was perfect. A laptop had been set up on the bar and ready for him, the lights turned up as bright as they go. The leather couches were set in a u-shape up against the wall closest to the hallway that led to Draven's office. An open trunk stood off to the side.

His parents arrived first. After a nod to his father, Lukas stayed in his mother's rib-crushing hug long enough to sense that her mystical strength had never lessened. *Thank the good Lord up above and good to know*, he thought. Walking back Chris, who kept shaking his head, he asked, "Does being here bring it all back?"

"Yeah. Didn't think I'd ever be standing here again, though. Wow." Chris slapped a marble column. "This is right where I stood in October… when I noticed the dark witch."

"Get it all out of your head now because once we start, you can't lose focus. And as for what happened outside? Bury that as well." He sniffed the air and walked back to Alana. "Thanks for calling them, Mom."

"Phil's here, too," she whispered. "You should have been the one to ask, sweetie."

Just like after every other scold through the years, a rumble of guilt started, and he offered, "I know, Mom. I'm sorry."

Gripping his chin, she kissed his cheek and said, "It's been too long since you've talked to them," before she went to his father's side.

Lukas took a deep breath and turned. Not only did his favorite four people in the world come down the stairs and into view, but a fifth person, someone he totally didn't expect, ignored him and bee-lined directly to his parents. Yeah. He'd have something to say about it, for sure. All dressed in black sweats and work-boots similar to his, the four retired Guardians put their own personal weapons on the bar. He took the first hug with deep respect.

"Well look at you all grown up. A lean six-foot and incredible form, I hear." The blond monk had a powerful grip and a wiry body that belied his lethal ability fighting vampires and Hell-beasts. Still studying him, Philip gripped his shoulders.

"It's been a long time. Great to see you," Lukas replied.

"I've heard all those mystical warrior skills have grown some."

"That would be the truth," his father said as Philip traded hugs with him, then his mother.

Lukas swallowed feelings that took him back in time and faced the other three retired Guardians, whose mystical skills had been put to the test in Siena some fifteen years ago. They knew more about him than he cared to admit, and their friendship had solidified over the years while living at England's Georgian Estate. It had been a troubled goodbye four years back. He had been totally torn up over Martine's icy put down that all but shattered him, but he needed distance from everyone and moved to the isolated mansion in the highlands of Scotland.

"I should have reached out to you guys myself," he admitted with a sheepish grin.

"And me too, of course," replied Petula, the only female warrior other than Alana in this event. Neeb, her husband, a huge, bald Scot had him in another bone-crushing hug.

"I can't believe you came," Lukas when he kissed

Pet's cheek.

Before she could answer, Nigel grabbed his shoulder and slapped his back. The warrior still had white-blond hair, now cropped neat and short. "What, mate, and miss all the fun taking out some nasty sires? We trained you right proper at the Institute, didn't we now?"

"And what a handful you were, Lu," Pet said as Neeb, a man of very few words, nodded.

Nigel's legendary sneer appeared. "Stubborn as a mule and full of mischief. It was always a pleasure to kick your bratty bum when you didn't listen."

"I remember all too well, thank you very much." They all laughed because it was true. Too stubborn for his own good, he'd argue with Nigel until flushed with rage. Then his father would find out and get painfully parental on his ass. Made him apologize every damn time, which he did very fast.

Lukas took them all in, still brave mystical warriors now in their mid-forties that helped mold him into the man he was today. Like Alana, their skills hadn't vanished when they turned twenty-seven and were relieved of the mission. Another thing no one questions. After a brief catch-me-up conversation, Lukas could no longer avoid the straggler who stared at his feet with his hands in his pockets, towering over his mother like a giant.

Already pissed off, he walked over thinking, *fucking six-foot-five and strong as a bull, far beyond what he should be at sixteen.* Uriel Thornwell had a head of messy red hair complimenting prominent cheekbones and a strong jawline, his eyes as green as a cat's and just as bright. Nope. Seeing his young cousin here didn't sit well at all.

Grabbing his arm, Alana whispered in his ear, "Be nice, sweetie. Remember what you were like at his age."

Yeah... no, he thought. "Who said you could be in this, Uriel?"

"Me Da. Mum came with," the teen mumbled. "I'm ready. It's what you trained me for."

The kid probably had no idea how intimidating he came off. Yeah, he had mystical skills, but an unpredictable nature. Lukas glanced at his father. "Did you agree with Uncle T?"

"There's always a place to start. Now is bloody perfect."

I'm not letting this go, he thought. "He isn't a Guardian, Dad."

"Well, neither were you," his father answered in an edgy tone.

Lukas pitched his head back and looked Uri in the eye. "If you don't follow orders, you're out. If you sneeze wrong, you're out. One step over the line and I shut you down. Got it, cuz?"

"I get it," the kid mumbled with a shrug.

He eyeballed him again with an aggressive, "You sure?"

"I said I get it," the kid said, a skosh louder.

"We have one inexperienced fighter already. I can't afford to lose focus and babysit you." The flair of the kid's nostrils meant he was ready to blow, and equally, Lukas felt ready to wipe the floor with him.

His father gripped Uri's arm, walking the kid back a few feet. "Lukas is correct. These are sires. You won't like the old-fashioned way I deal with even one little step over the line."

"I know, Uncle Michael. Da warned me," Uri said—with respect.

"Good. We understand each other." That no-nonsense tone was one you'd be a fool to challenge.

Everyone stopped their conversations, and as if they had taken a collective sniff, all eyes turned to Luna and Draven who stood in the middle of the dance floor.

"I like what you've done to the club, Lukas. That corner conversation pit is an improvement," Draven said locked to his gaze with Luna held tight to his side.

Lukas could just imagine their discomfort. Two vampires surrounded by mystical warriors and a warlock with wicked mind-walking skills. Yet he scented no fear on Luna. And what he scented on Draven was, more or less, apprehension.

"I assume there is a stake on every single one of you, and that trunk is full of more silver broadswords."

"A few silver daggers as well," Lukas informed.

Chris went up to the vampire. "I want to thank you. Without your help, I may never have regained my life a month ago." He offered his hand.

Draven shook it as a thin smile crossed his lips. "I am pleased to see it all worked out. You are obviously healthy once again."

"I am. And tonight, I repay you."

"It is not necessary that you place your life in danger for me."

Chris inclined his head. "But I've learned that a little back up is a good thing."

"Yes, I've heard that before," Draven replied. "No doubt, this group is much more than a little of a good thing, providing stakes and silver swords are not aimed at our unbeating hearts."

Between the sideways glances and tilted heads, Lukas introduced everyone. Petula was the first to cave. "I know she's vampire. Why is it that I cannot scent her? Can anyone else?" Every warrior joined in the chorus of "no's" or "I can't, either's."

"Luna exists solely on animal blood and her thirst is minimal, at that. I know. It's an anomaly," Lukas said.

Alana stepped forward, took Luna's hand from Draven. It came off a tender gesture of acceptance. "The sweats fit you perfectly. Luna will spar with me and Pet."

The three of them moved a few feet away, with Petula still ogling Draven, who stood next to his father. "How very interesting," Pet whispered.

"We had the same sire," Michael stated.

Nigel sneered, saying, "Bloody hell, you two could pass for brothers."

"Since you're the first to make the comment, you'll be with us. Uri, you as well," Michael added.

"Right," Lukas said. "I'll work with Chris and Neeb." Knowing Philip preferred to work independently he added, "Phil, you're the swing when we spar. As per protocol and always stated before an event, I've got to say it: If anyone at any time chooses to stand down, let yourself be known." When no one spoke, with a click of the remote, the first photo came up. Lukas stood by the laptop. Everyone moved in close. "Let's meet the sires. These Georgian Archive photos are old, but vampires don't age, so there's that. There's no info on the seventh, so only six photos will be sent to your phones."

Knowing his father had first-hand knowledge on some of them, he deferred the briefing. "All six were soldiers in human life," Michael said. "Most likely, the unknown sire as well. First, we have Ramon, turned in eighteen-seventy-eight. He developed his talent with a sword during the Spanish-American War. I met him once and wasn't too impressed. He's not so much a leader as he is a follower."

The second came up. "This is Kiko. Notorious for his cruelty during the sixteen- hundreds, he was a fierce warlord in Japan, and just as brutal in death. He did not roam Europe, in fact, it's reported that he preferred Japan and Korea." He pressed the remote again. "Alfred began to sire in the late seventeen-hundreds. He was originally a British general sent to the colonies to destroy the Continental army and sired on American soil. I met him in New York during the War for Independence. I didn't like him, but he was very capable with a blade."

The next face appeared. "I never crossed paths with James, but I've heard stories. He's been around since the early seventeen-hundreds. My sire went to great lengths to avoid him, calling him coarse and aggressive. Craving power, James created a clan and called himself a laird. They mostly roamed Scotland. But if you've ever fought a highlander like Neeb, you know what you're up against. The next is Armadad, well-known for cruel executions of weak vampires in the early eighteen-hundreds. In life, he was thought to be an African prince. In undeath, he ruled that continent, but often liked to roam the city of London as if he were on holiday. I witnessed his allegiance to Herodotus in eighteen-eighty-nine and kept my distance. That brings us to Herodotus."

"Any questions so far," Lukas asked.

Petula raised a finger. "There are no pictures of the seventh sire?"

"I did not see his face in any of the photos. All I can

offer is that he is quite tall, he has long blond hair worn loose and is blue-eyed," Draven stated.

Lukas replied, "Look, it's anyone's guess how old or crafty that one is, so be prepared for anything. Now for Herodotus." The sire's face appeared on the screen. "This was taken from the video feed in here about a month ago."

"Bloody Hell. You let him loose with humans," Nigel said in a heated tone.

Draven's head snapped to him with a leer. "He was not let loose, as you so rudely state. The club was kept closed for a private party."

Before anyone asked, and very aware of Nigel's trust issues, Lukas said, "Give them more."

The vampire glanced at his father before continuing. "I had been summoned before the council due to the portal breach. To appease Herodotus, I offered him a night of pleasure. Be assured that the entire time he was in the club, the entrance was locked, and security was exceptionally tight, the courtesans highly-paid and slightly drugged to insure that any sips of their blood would not entice the sire to drain the woman."

"And this is allowed by the Georgian Council, Michael?" Petula asked.

"It is tolerated," his father replied. "Draven serves a purpose."

"And the council sanctions it," Petula said with wider eyes.

Before this went any further, Lukas said. "In a way, yes, but—"

Draven cut him off with, "I do not touch my human clientele. I maintain an agreement with this particular service. The courtesans know what I am, and their survival is insured. Should your moral high ground find this too hard to accept, think of it another way. You will find no drained female corpses rotting in any streets of this city."

"Did it ever cross your mind to stake the sire," Philip asked in his usual, calm voice.

Draven studied him as his nostrils flared. "Ah, frankincense and myrrh. You are a man of the cloth." He put his right hand over his heart and bowed his head before saying, "I thought it many times."

"What stopped you?" Philip asked.

"I value my head on my shoulders." His eyes slid to Luna and then back to Philip. "I believe that is all I will say."

"Let's get back to Herodotus," Lukas stated with a click of the remote.

All eyes went to his father as he said, "He is the oldest sire known to exist. I've been in his company, and what Draven didn't say is that he dabbles in dark magic, the way our sire did. Unlike Cyril, Herodotus has been known to skin vampires, disembowel them with a smile on his face. Other sires often deferred to him; most likely feared him."

Lukas closed the laptop and looked at everyone assembled. "That's why he comes through last so we will all be fully focused on him. Don't underestimate these sires. Once within reach, strike to slow them down and then lop off its head. Everyone's in black tonight. There are training tunics in the trunk. Be sure to take one before you leave. There are no exceptions. Sliver daggers stay tucked in your boots unless needed. Stakes within quick reach. Please, no nicks or cuts during this session. And when sparring with Draven and Luna, definitely no slip-ups. As per protocol, I ask again: Anyone standing down?" He gave them thirty seconds, studied each warrior, especially his cousin. "Good. We're fighting in our world. Those of us who self-heal have an advantage. Nevertheless, Doc Baker will be stationed right outside in a van, should he be needed. Any questions?"

"What if Herodotus goes for Luna or Draven when he gets through," Uri asked.

"You are to protect them as if they were innocents."

"But they're not," his cousin replied.

As everyone else walked away to form groups, Lukas fisted his cousin's shirt and locked to his eyes. "They're both under our protection, so deal with it. If what I just said wasn't clear enough, I'll be glad to find a private space where you and I can have at it."

The brat jerked his arm away and backed down, which was a good thing. Because being held captive in the Second Realm had taught Lukas well. If pushed into a rage, all bets were off. Uri would be incapacitated— totally *not* able to fight tonight.

Chapter 36

Confessions

Draven left directly after the sparring session, but Luna sat with the two women in the corner of the club. They were a good team, and she had picked up broadsword techniques quickly. Petula, the English woman, had purple streaks in her light-brown hair. The look fascinated her thinking it attractive. She could hear the men conversing in a friendly manner, many feet away when Alana said, "You did very well today, Luna."

She smiled at Michael's wife. "Thank you for teaching me, especially the stances. I know it sounds strange, but I enjoyed this. You and Petula are very strong."

"It's Guardian strength, and we are blessed that ours never left us when the mystical mission ended," Petula stated. "It comes in handy moving couches or cleaning behind the fridge."

Alana said, "It doesn't normally happen, but ours is not to question why. By the way, you picked up defensive moves really fast."

"I'm also highly competent with a bow and arrow."

"I'll bet," Alana stated with a chuckle. "But it's swords and stakes tonight."

"May I use a dagger instead? I feel I have more control."

"Your height and strength would be perfect with a broadsword," Petula said. "Bloody hell! I cannot believe I'm saying this to a vampire, but I mean no offense, Luna."

Alana's warm hand touched hers. "Sure, if that's what you want. As for weapons, I know what you mean, Pet, but Luna has to feel comfortable with it, the way we do. Michael told me you were sired at Veronique's villa in Florence."

"That is correct," she replied, studying his wife's beautiful, serene face.

"Really," Petula said. "That is an incredible piece of real estate in Florence. I especially liked the marble staircase. So very posh." She waived to Neeb and quickly added, "Ooh. Time to go. Hubby and I want to join up with a walking tour. See you tonight."

Luna waved as the perky female warrior left the couch, but curious and rather shocked, she said to Alana, "You've been to the villa?"

Alana moved closer. "Many years ago, and oh yeah, I remember it well. Pet and I were there during the Siena event, but she didn't get to meet the haughty bitch up close the way I did."

"Veronique is deadly, often malicious and always cruel to me. I don't know what Michael saw in her besides sex and lust."

"I totally agree. That's why it was such a rush slicing her head off."

Luna's eyes went wide. "*You* destroyed her?"

"Uh-huh. With a silver short sword. That deceitful creature tried to have her way with him, and then I arrived. Well, the bitch flew at him, and *swoosh*, off went her head. She got exactly what she deserved, princess or not."

They studied each other, a vampire and a retired Guardian, equally strong. Two females on the same wavelength, equally disgusted by Veronique's antics. "I never enjoyed our visits to the villa. She couldn't be trusted, and Michael was very different back then."

After a quick glance at her husband across the dance floor, Alana grinned. "Do tell. I'm all ears. Not that I'm into gossip but… getting anything out of him about his time with her is like pulling teeth."

Luna leaned in. "Well. To begin with, Veronique was truly a terror. It showed on her face. As for Michael, he could be utterly charming and frightening at the same time."

****

"He did fine with me. Show some patience," his father whispered. They stood off to the side, watching the conversation between Uri and Nigel heat up. The seasoned warrior's short fuse was happening, any time now. With a little luck, one stupid reply would have his cousin grounded and out of tonight's event.

Then Nigel stormed up the stairs, and Lukas frowned. "Keep a tight rein on him."

"Are you talking to *me*, little boy?"

The last two words, spoken like a threat, snapped Lukas's head back. He stared into dark, narrow eyes. "You don't have to get testy. You know what I mean."

"He's a mystical child, just like you were. Thorn believes he was born a warrior for the cause of all that is good."

"He's untested in the field. There are too many unknowns." *Christ, yet another family member to worry about*. "If things go wrong—"

"Things will not go wrong. See the outcome you want and make it happen."

"Yeah. Sure. What if Draven doesn't come back through that portal?"

"Then I go in and bring him back."

And right there's Plan B, Lukas realized. If his father thought, for even one brief second, that he'd go it alone in a realm full of vampires to find Draven, well, the man was totally out of his mind.

****

Very aware that he had been followed to his office, Draven made a gentlemanly gesture as he sat in an armchair. Philip sat in the other one. "I remember you as a Guardian in this city. Your movements were quieter than most, even when you trained Alana."

"That was many, many years ago. We never crossed paths."

"No. I never had use for confrontation of any kind, as I am sure you noticed when we sparred. I prefer to bite, not fight. Perhaps a silver dagger and a stake would be enough."

"If you intend to use them."

Why bother to lie, to a man of God, no less? "I will not survive this. I know Herodotus well enough. He'll somehow change the game and reenter this world."

"Then let's insure that he meets final death instantly," the calm monk said.

Draven looked away, and before he could stop himself, said, "There have been times when I have prayed." No scent of disgust came at him. In fact, the monk looked serene.

"I can say what I sense, but I'd rather hear what you have to say."

He nodded once. "I take control over the beast-within. It will not rule me or my actions. Innocents are never hunted, nor are children. My fortune has been made through legitimate investments; my employees are paid well. I may not own my soul, but what is right is sensed, and I act accordingly. This bond between my brother in blood and his son… I honor it as a gift, a… a blessing." He paused, searching for the right words. "If I am to face final death, I want someone clean, someone close to God to know this."

Philip stood in front of him. Placing his left hand on Draven's head, the other raised in an unexpected way. He sensed the sacred Christian symbol moving through the air over him. Without a spoken word, the monk left the office.

How is it that I did not burst into flames? Stunned by such an act of calm compassion, Draven closed his eyes knowing how only hours from now his fate would be sealed. Once he scented Luna, he pulled himself together and stood, drawing her into his embrace, his kiss tender, reverent. Hand in hand, they went into his home.

In comfortable silence, both took sustenance in the galley kitchen. Then, he led her to the room with the grand piano. He chose a soulful nocturne in a minor key by Chopin—just for her. He poured his passion into the piece, his love, his distress and his joy that she was again at his side. After releasing the pedal, he stood and watched the keys disappear as the lacquered lid came down.

"Just beautiful. The song of lovers talking," she whispered.

They entered the bedroom and he locked the door. His kisses were unrestrained passion knowing this would be the last time he touched her. They shed their clothes, and when she came into his arms, their tongues danced to a new rhythm, a slow one, full of devotion.

She untied the leather strip at the nape of his neck. They settled under the quilt and tight against his chest, she whispered, "Perhaps you'll consider cutting your hair shorter like Michael's."

Hearing playfulness in her tone, he said with a rare laugh, "Never, my love. I don't have those soft waves to pull it off."

"Perhaps I'll cut mine like Petula's and add purple highlights the way she has."

He growled. "Do that and you will regret it." He kissed her long, blonde braid, so soft against his lips.

"How will I regret it," she asked in a sexy tease.

"I will pull you across my knee and it won't be playful," he replied. She laughed in a sexy way, which thrilled him. Then he pulled her chin up and managed a tight glare. "I am not joking. No short hair, and most-definitely, no purple highlights."

His next kisses worshipped her breasts. His immortal love fisted his loose black hair. The slight tug shot right down, and instantly he was high and hard. With an urgency like never before, he captured her mouth. Making love would be incredibly erotic. Then he'd thrust deeper, faster, harder until he filled her. There would be no regrets. He'd show singular devotion to his eternal love. Luna would know she belonged to only him. Then he'd take his place in Hell, having experienced genuine love with every fiber of his being—in this ungodly existence.

****

Sensing sunset, Draven refused to leave his bed. He

watched Luna at rest, held her close. There was nothing more to say to each other. Yet, the fear he would face at midnight kept interfering with memories of their fifty years together—before that Hunter's Moon night when he abandoned her, punishing both of them with his cruel decision.

As evening hours trickled away, he knew he had to leave their bed, leave her. He took his time in the shower, scrubbed every inch of his body and lathered his hair twice before rinsing off in the hottest water his skin could tolerate.

Herodotus would not scent Luna on him. Not at all.

He stood far away from his bed to dress in a dry-cleaned black suit, a fresh black silk shirt and tie, black socks and new shoes. When her eyes eased open, he studied her beauty, gave a single nod, and closed the bedroom door when he left.

In the galley kitchen, he took additional sustenance of healthy human blood and rinsed out five glass bottles. He walked to the Steinway grand, studying it with reverence before he sat down and played his fellow composer's famous *Polonaise*. Paying attention to every note, his passion soared with determination. The composition raged at a destiny that could not change before redemption thundered through furious, resolute chords. Hope lingered in the air until utter silence.

This musical gift had given him comfort—created from a complex combination of wood, steel, keys of ebony and ivory. All earthly things. Every vibration touched that unseen place within, turning raging emotions into controlled sound. It was pure agony to turn away, always thinking of a piano as his oldest friend. He may not have access to his soul, but when his fingers touched the keys, he felt human again. Yet he braced his broad shoulders and walked through the door without looking back. Willing blood tears back into the wells of his eyes, he took a deep breath, even though he didn't need to breathe.

Apprehensive about his next performance, he sat at his desk. Opening the leather folder, he studied the lie created to ignite curiosity in seven deadly sires. Then he turned on the computer to review his financial affairs one last time and to interpret the markets and move his investments for a higher yield.

Club business came next. Payrolls were approved so that when *Destiny* reopened without him, all would run smoothly. He checked the sealed envelope hidden in the top drawer of his desk, hoping that Michael would be alive to open it.

With nothing left to do, he sat back and let memories of Luna wash over him. His first glimpse of a woman about to die. Her first night of undeath in his arms. Fifty years of loving and protecting her. Finding a young couple to care for her and then booking their costly passage on a French ship in 1939. He had meticulously accomplished it all and had felt like a living man so in love with a living woman that he was willing to walk away from her. For her safety. He let himself relive every scene—then tucked them so deep down that no one, not even her sire, would find them in their hiding place.

****

Hours later, Draven scented his visitor, probably for the last time. Without looking up from his desk, he stated, "A bit early, brother?" Michael turned a leather armchair to face the desk but didn't pull it close. *One last private conversation, with someone I've known since eighteen-forty-seven.* They were both arrogant but in different ways. Always the leader with keen intuition, Michael often had witty comments and enjoyed the banter and bicker before getting what he wanted. He, on the other hand, observed everything through an artist's eye and preferred to remain quiet.

"Are you ready for this," Michael asked, his expression serious, the lines on his face more pronounced. "I want honesty. Now talk to me."

Draven leaned back, crossed his arms and let out a sigh. "It doesn't matter whether or not I'm ready. This will happen. I will play my part as best I can and hope that I am rid of Herodotus and the fucking sires for good. But it won't mean a collapse of the realm."

"Explain."

The one-word, arrogant command didn't even rile him tonight. "I'm sure the captain of the guards will assume power. It might be bloody, and a few heads will roll before bursting into dust and bone, but the understudy is always waiting in the wings."

"You'll deal with whomever it is."

"If I still walk the earth, which I highly doubt." He held up a hand. "No. You asked for honesty and I shall give it. There are no guarantees. If I am there too long, it means I failed. Should good fortune be on our side, and you take out a few sires, but I do not come through with Herodotus, I am instructing you to lock the vault door to keep the human world safe. There's a document for your eyes only in the top drawer. My affairs are in order, so to speak." He paused before adding, "And please, no heroics. You have two young daughters, a strong son who still needs you. So does your wife, a true beauty who loves you. All I ask is that you protect Luna."

"Lukas is petitioning the Georgian Sovereign Council to place her above the Law of the Kill. You as well. But let's not get ahead of ourselves tonight."

That was a shock, specifically how quickly such a decree could be set in motion. "Your son has a tender heart, a good soul. You've taught him well, brother. So. Why are you early?"

"I'm still bloody pissed you didn't confide in me about the sires request."

"It would have made no difference. Sensing a betrayal, all fingers would have pointed to me. I'd still end up tortured."

"You are truly dwelling on that happening."

"Because it will. You and your mystical warriors can fight the other six, but Herodotus destroys me tonight."

"Over my dead body," Michael huffed out in a growl.

"I certainly hope not. There is so much vibrant life to live within you, brother. So many who love, respect, need you. It was thoughtful to send the monk in for a private conversation with me, oddly comforting. Another experience I never thought I'd have."

"I'm sorry. It wasn't possible to get you to the cathedral in daylight."

"No. Not at all," and then added with a sneer, "I'd like nothing more than to watch the bastard gurgle as I stake him." He stood. So did Michael. They met in front of the desk, both with their arms locked across their chests. "If it were you, you'd fight to win. When I lose, please don't think less of me."

"I don't think less of you. I never did."

"Oh, come now. Honesty. Remember? It works both

ways. You were always the fighter. Sometimes broody, but always triumphant with your fists."

"You could sit at a piano, and without saying a word, have a room full of women panting and swooning at your feet. We made quite the pair."

"You challenged Cyril like a true alpha male. Look at us now. You're still fighting my battles."

"That's not where your talent lies."

"Nevertheless, it is true."

"You can do this, brother. Be just as cunning as that bastard is. Let the beast-within loose. Don't have me come in there after you."

"No. You will not do so, Michael. Call it my last wish if it eases your conscience, but you will not put your precious life in danger. I want your word."

"Well, you won't get it." They locked eyes. "Say it, damn it, say you will fight like Hell."

The man's heart pounded like the roll of a tympani, still an amazement to hear. Knowing the next move would be him being grabbed by the throat, Draven dipped his chin. "You have my word."

"And I will hold you to it," Michael replied in a calm, controlled tone.

At the sound of footsteps and scenting the mystical warriors coming down the hall, they both turned, stood shoulder to shoulder, until everyone assembled. Luna entered, and after a long, silent look, Draven stepped away from everyone.

She kissed Michael's cheek, his son's as well, before going over to Alana. Michael's wife helped her with the training tunic, and once the last snap secured to cover her neck, the love of his existence stood hand in hand with her. They positioned at the opposite end of the office—as far away from him as possible.

****

Right after Chris called, Mary enlisted a slew of healers and Georgian psychics thwarting any dark seer who tried to connect to any other realm. That old sire and the other six wouldn't have much magic to draw on tonight.

Close to midnight, she swiped at her eyes as she pulled a close friend, a powerful psychic into the brownstone's kitchen. They hadn't lent each other support like this in a long, long time. On the counter, a huge urn of coffee continued a rhythmic perk. Celia Thornwell stood an inch over five-foot, which always made Mary feel like a giant. "My God, it's been years since we were in this kitchen together, hasn't it," she managed to say.

"Your mom's funeral. Martha was such an incredibly powerful woman."

"Yeah, a powerful good witch as well. Wow. That's almost five years ago, Celia."

"Uri was still a scrawny little tyke. Then all of a sudden he shot up, like, overnight. I need a step-stool to look my son in the eye, Mare," she said with a sweet laugh in her voice.

"They'll all keep him safe."

"I know he'll be fine. I would have come to help, whether or not he was in this."

"You don't mind sending protection to two vampires?"

"Nope. Not at all," Celia said as her bright-green eyes almost twinkled. "Uri couldn't scent the female. And as for Draven, well, I trust Michael's judgement any day. Nope. I'm on board a hundred percent."

"Can you link your mind to your son?"

That sweet laugh erupted again. "I can link to any mind, see through another's eyes as well, which I fully intend to do when this starts. Ooh! I can give the healing circle a play by play!"

"I don't think we should share too much."

Celia snuck a peek through the doorway. "Yeah. About that. Kendrick house is packed!"

"Suppose you send what you see to only me, maybe to Martine, too?"

Her hand went over her heart. "Oh Mary, she's coming back to your healing circle. Thank God! I was so concerned when she closed herself off from everyone. It just hurt so very much."

"Lukas brought her out of it."

"And with him is where she's meant to be."

"It took her long enough to see it," Mary replied.

"Yeah, but hey, true love and destiny go hand in hand. When Lu came up to Scotland and moved into the mansion, he was beyond miserable. The way he kept to himself, well, I told him it was unhealthy. No matter how I pried, he wouldn't talk about her, but I felt the dark, abysmal hurt in him."

"You always could."

"He's a very special sweetie in my book. Wow. Now I'm overjoyed for both of them."

"So am I. It's a blessing," Mary replied.

Then Celia sucked in a breath and stood perfectly still. "They're ready," both gifted women said at the same time.

Mary grinned. "It's been a long time since we did something like this together."

Celia whispered, "Once this is over, we need to

discuss Chris Forbes. He's got wicked skills, Mare."

"Funny. I've yet to sit down alone for a talk with him."

Celia touched her arm. "Oh boy. Just wait. I sense that he has an awesome destiny to fulfill."

They walked back into the living room, took their places next to Paige and Martine, who spent almost a full minute hugging the little slip of a psychic, as Michael always called her.

Conversations drifted into silence. Windows were cracked open. Beeswax candles were lit and the lamps turned off. Like last month's event, it was standing room only.

Chapter 37

Going Back

"Ready," Michael asked.

With the leather folder tucked under an arm, Draven gave a nod replying in a whisper, "As I'll ever be."

"You've got the stake and the dagger hidden well?"

"Of course," he answered in his own arrogant way. Draven walked to the vault door and then turned back to look at the mystical warriors in his office. They were dressed like a special-ops team on one of those television shows about war. *Yes, this is war. A very different type of war. Man against Sire. Good against Evil.* If he could get all six through the portal, then these brave individuals would destroy them. The heavy, glass-topped desk had been pushed against the wall along with both armchairs, creating enough room to lop off the sire's heads.

Draven keyed in the code. He grabbed the handle and the vault door swung open until it covered part of the wall. He met Luna's eyes, gave a deep bow with his right hand over his unbeating heart, and then entered the eight-by-eight dark room to face the portal. The swirling vortex began as he whispered secret words, and the mist morphed to blood-red.

About to step through, Michael grabbed an arm. "Look in my eyes."

Beyond edgy, he asked, "Is this really necessary!"

"There's a tiny slip of a psychic who wants to see you. So just do as I ask."

He complied with the unusual request, compelled to do so in a mysterious way, staring directly into Michael's dark-brown eyes that appeared more intense than usual. A shiver raked through him and settled in his brain. His eyes wrenched wide, and then, just as quickly, the feeling left him. He jerked his head back, pinched the bridge of his nose, repeatedly blinking. "What the hell was that?"

"She's a powerhouse of goodness, that's all I'll say." Michael took a breath and blew it out. "You've got the stake where you can easily reach it?"

"We already went through this," he said. But as if he were a toddler, the man's hands patted him down to check for both.

Then Michael gripped his shoulders. "Stay focused. Act up a storm. You've got this."

The last back slap was unnecessary, but he took it in stride. Stretching out his hand, it slipped through the portal's vertex. Then he stepped through.

****

Standing right outside the vault, Lukas felt the draw of the portal deep in his chest, the thrum of the hum assaulting his ears, the scent like wet dirt. The blood-red vortex continued to swirl, and he lurched back. His father had actually crossed himself, barely whispering, "Good Lord above, I know it's strange to ask, but please watch over that vampire." Entering the office, his father stated to all assembled, "He's through. Celia sees him now."

"Way to go Mum," his cousin murmured.

"Way to go is right. Now let's keep our senses sharp." His father eyeballed Chris. "If you have the power, link to her mind."

Lukas fastened the last snap at the neck of his tunic as every mystical sense hummed. No tension. No fear, either. Each heart beat its own rhythm, each warrior's skills revved and ready. "Everyone, broadsword in hand. Any sire that comes through is fair game. Take your posts against the wall. All local Guardians are in the club, protecting the stairway up at all times. Now we wait."

He thought about the last event, the crucial role Draven had played, the loyalty he had shown. Lukas whispered his own prayer for that vampire's success in a realm full of predators.

****

Red mist swirled around Draven's ankles. Ignoring discomfort in his groin, he jogged past the empty planting fields, taking an arrogant stride down the center of the main street to the War Council Building. Strutting past guards who had scoffed at him one short week ago, he kept his gait steady, not as wide as usual. His shoulders lifted in the deserted lobby, and entering the black marble cavern, a quick glance noted the huge hook dangling from a thick chain on the far wall. He had a good idea why it had been added to the cave-like ambiance of the room. All seven sires were already seated at the long, carved table. Standing at the empty chair with his left hand over his unbeating heart, he bowed deep as "My Sires," rumbled up his throat.

"You may sit," Herodotus announced.

Draven caught the sneer as he sat with the file perfectly positioned. He then waited and waited. Had he been human, sweat would trickle down between his shoulder blades like a dripping faucet to drench his silk shirt. His collar felt like a noose and his bruised testicles tightened, producing a quick twitch at the side of his mouth. Out of the corner of his eye, he saw guards line the chamber doors, standing at attention like good little vampire soldiers. Would they witness his torture and final death, or catch him if he ran? Either way, he was fucked.

"You may begin," Herodotus finally stated like a king, certain that "off with his head" could come at any given moment.

With his mind clear, he made eye-contact. "I have extraordinary news for you, Sire, and the perfect property." The listing stats were handed out, and he waited as the sires read.

After several tense minutes, as if on cue, he was ordered to speak, and rattled off praise for the property, describing each nuance with as much passion and animation as he could muster. Using so many adjectives was out of his comfort zone, but he kept a charming grin plastered on his face.

Was it working? The six sires kept glancing at each other, then at Herodotus, who showed nothing. Once or twice, all eyes went back to the real estate listing. When they all studied him, it felt suspicious—being the speck of something under the proverbial microscope. Yet he didn't react. He had no idea how long he had been talking, but it was clearly time to bring the grand finale home.

"Most honored sire, I could continue to praise the many superior aspects of this perfect mansion, but my eyes are not your eyes. Thus, I have a limousine waiting outside my club in the human world, so that all of you may visit the property, to walk from room to room before purchase. This is the human world's night, and it is under a two-hour ride from the city. All the magnificent lighting is on and the security codes for entry are in my phone, which is on my office desk. Rest assured, if what you see is acceptable, the bid will be placed with the listing agent immediately. I am assured our cash transaction will be accepted. Once the paperwork is signed, you will take up residence within days." *Or right now*, he thought, hoping at least one of them sensed it.

He heard quick murmurs and had to wonder what non-verbal conversations were also taking place. And yet, Herodotus kept his eyes closed. Grunts, moans, a few rumbling growls erupted from the bastard. "Is the portal open?"

"Yes, Sire. I left it so—for us to return."

When his burning black eyes eased open, Herodotus turned his head, nodded to the guards, who left. Then those empty orbs bore into his. Unsure if the nod had been some type of signal, Draven quickly stated, "I truly wish to please you, Sire. It is my hope to usher the sires through three at a time. Then I will personally usher you through the portal, as I have the time before."

"How very noble of you."

The reply dripped of sarcasm, and Draven glanced around the table. "Last through guarantees your protection, Sire."

"Yes. My protection," Herodotus said with a scoff.

He had to bring this home and now was the time. "I have another gift for all of you, a rather exciting one. After the visit, I shall have courtesans with willing wrists waiting to be tasted, waiting to entertain each sire, specifically as he desires. Only if it is your wish, Sire."

Heated murmurs began again, tight glances between the six extremely noticeable. And what do you know, this time, not a one looked at Herodotus.

"Perhaps you have something else up your sleeve. Perhaps I did not kick you hard enough a week ago."

"I only mean to please, Sire, to prove my loyalty." With eyes cast down, he added, "It is a perfect, secure home in the human world. I walked the magnificent grounds. I visited the spacious underground rooms for all of you to avoid daylight. My apologies if I have been too bold."

Through the endless wait, Draven sat perfectly still. Not a shake in his hand, not a twitch to his lips, and not a stabbing pain in his balls. He kept a vivid vision of the fictitious property in his mind as if the descriptions he had just stated were true.

Without a word, all six sires stood at once and walked out the doors to the lobby. He allowed himself to hope. He had no idea where they were going. He had no idea whether or not he had been successful.

Yet Herodotus sat at the other end of the table—like a chiseled slab of granite.

Chapter 38

Treason

"This is taking too bloody long, damn it," Michael hissed.

"I'm right there with you," Lukas answered, close to nauseous with the thrum of the portal still hammering at his chest. Thank God his stomach was empty. Seeing his father reach for his broadsword snapped him back to attack-mode.

"Message from Celia. We have trouble. I don't know what's happening, but it isn't the fucking sires."

Now what the hell does that mean? Against the wall and out of sight from the portal, Lukas's left hand tightened on the broadsword's leather hilt, his feet slightly apart to insure perfect balance. All the other mystical warriors did the same. His father's hissed "And here we go," meant some type of game was on.

What came through the portal and staggered into the office like disoriented rats to a puddle of dirty water were four vampires—dressed exactly like the filthy guards in the Second Realm. The sight of billowy gray shirts, thick belts and loose black pants made Lukas want to kill.

They weren't sires. Deadly? Maybe. Skilled? Perhaps, probably prepared to find a few terrified human minions with exposed necks to bite. Their swords were at their backs, still sheathed. And as if they had no ability to scent danger, they simply stared straight ahead.

"Going somewhere," his father asked in a casual tone.

Three of them turned to look at the same time and bared their fangs. One idiot sprinted to the other end of the office and opened the door, only to meet Petula's stake. The others lost their heads within seconds.

The next ones through the portal looked just as unprepared. Some of them showed form with sword in hand, but their fangs didn't get to any necks. The screeches were ear-splitting before heads flew. Dust and bits of bone choked the air before coating the floor. Another six hesitated in the room with the portal before entering with drawn swords and fangs bared—like they had finally had that 'uh-oh' moment. These had even accessed their beasts-within, with feral-yellow eyes and looks of madness. Yeah. They kept every mystical warrior on his or her toes, but none of these vampires stood a chance.

Luna, along with Alana and Pet, held the wide hall that led to the club with confidence. No guard made it past the trio of females. When the office filled once again, with very little room to maneuver, Lukas and the others sheathed their broadswords and grabbed their stakes. A thick residue of final death clogged the air.

Lukas grabbed a guard by the throat and pinned it high on the wall, staring directly into a face with feral eyes and discolored fangs. "Where are the sires?" he asked, raking the stake down its pale neck. A steady stream of blood began, the smell, worse than rancid meat. The idiot hissed just as Lukas inhaled. "What the fuck! Is this what you drink from each other smells like?" With the stake at its unbeating heart, he repeated,

"Where are the sires?" The next hiss came with a clawed hand reaching for his throat, so he let loose his rage and shoved the stake through its heart.

Brushing off its remains, he turned as his father asked another asshole the same thing. Now *that* vampire guard looked totally terrified, but his father had always been a master at intimidation. The question had come in a murderous tone. Not getting an answer, his father slammed it into the wall again and again, finally getting a sputtered out, "They await a signal."

"Now, now, don't stand here shaking and tell me the signal," his father asked in a casual tone. When it hesitated, the punch broke its nose. One hand gripped its jaw ready to break it until it mumbled, "Open hand... through... mist."

"Well, what do you know. Could it come from a hand with broken fingers?"

Lukas sneered as he threw the next charging guard to Uri, who made quick work of staking it. The steady stream of vampire guards continued until the lull came unexpected, with only the guard held by his father left. He signaled the mystical warriors to stand down as everyone eyed the last terrified vampire too stupid to access the beast-within.

The sounds of hand bones crunching came with a long howl of pain. His father stated a friendly, "Well, you have two. Let's have you signal with the good one. And do not fuck up. Do it right, and I will let you go back to your realm." Lukas followed as it was walked right up to the swirling red mist. The struggling thing hissed but stuck its good hand through as ordered. "He may come in 'handy' again," his father said.

"I agree." Lukas grabbed its arm, holding it steady.

Tense minutes passed. Then his father stated, "Celia says they see it, so get ready."

Ready for what, Lukas thought. He flung the guard in his cousin's direction. "Put it in the dining room and hog-tie it tight. Stay clear of its fangs." Looking at the other mystical warriors, he said, "It's anyone's guess what comes through next. Line the vault walls so we're out of sight."

Then they waited for the inevitable as well as the unpredictable.

****

It had been a full thirty minutes, but Draven sat still and silent, his eyes down, listening to the sire's boots click, pacing the black marble floor. From time to time, he heard a grunt or a growl, as if the bastard was lost in thought—or sensing something? Like treason, perhaps.

More minutes ticked by, and just when he thought he might actually survive this charade, Herodotus grabbed the back of his neck and flung him across the room. Hitting the wall face-first, his nose bent at a funny angle. Righting himself against the wall, he gripped the hidden pointy piece of wood under his suit jacket and waited.

Some kind of perverted glee lit the nasty sire's face. "What fools they were, two dozen guards lost in a planned deception. How long has your allegiance been compromised?"

He lunged, sinking the stake into the bastard's chest, but missing the heart. Swifter than any move imaginable, the sire pulled it out. The gaping wound stopped bleeding right before his eyes. Then like a tit-for-tat, Herodotus drove it through Draven's own chest in the exact same spot, the pull out just as fast, and flung the stake across the room. Except his gaping wound didn't close and shockwaves of pain vibrated through his nervous system.

"You dare to wield a weapon against me, as if an inaccurate jab of wood can stop me? I could have aimed better, but no, a quick death is too good for a traitor."

"Rot in Hell," he hissed clutching the bleed, spitting out a mouthful of blood. *How many dark magic spells protect Herodotus?*

"More than you can count, vampire, and far too complex to win against."

He knew he hadn't said that out loud, which only meant one thing. Final death.

The sadistic bastard stepped back and raised his hands. Draven's vision flickered, but no beast-within emerged. Then, the room slanted, off-kilter. He felt himself pulled across the floor. His suit jacket peeled off. His shirt slithered up and ripped off as well. His black silk tie snagged a hand and then the other to bind his wrists. Both arms ratcheted up and over the dangling hook to lift him off the ground. Shoes and socks left his feet, which searched for floor, and the back of his head slammed against the cold marble wall. His suit trousers tangled around his ankles. The hidden silver dagger clanged against black marble.

There he hung, naked and exposed. Like a mortal man, he panted and panicked. The glint of the dagger he had agreed to carry said what came next. His eyes bulged in their sockets as the sire slashed his veins. His long, piercing screams echoing through the room.

"Collusion. Deceit. Tricking sires with lies! Why is that?"

He spit out what filled his mouth. "I'll be waiting for you in Hell."

"Yes, coated in blood and bled dry," Herodotus stated with a sneer.

His body twitched and jerked. Leering at the bastard, his fangs bared. He howled in anguish but refused to allow the metamorphosis. He'd meet final death like a man, not a demon. Then his executioner dropped the dagger and picked up his hand-made Italian leather belt with his right hand—while his left slashed the air. Nothing happened. Herodotus cursed under his breath and studied his hand. Then the sadist walked over and gripped his thighs.

Suddenly his bloody chest slapped against cold black marble. His head lolled back. The bite of the buckle, shocking and hot, carved into his flesh from twitching shoulders to curling toes. He screamed until no sound came out.

Closing his eyes, "*Mon Dieu, pardonne moi*," lingered on his quivering lips as blood gushed from his veins.

****

Lukas felt restless. The inactivity had to be a false lull for sure. They kept the door into the hall open. His colleagues, his parents and Luna stood with him lining the wall with the vault, out of sight and at the ready. Joining them, he said to his father, "It's show time, isn't it?"

"Don't let your guard down, not for a bloody second when this starts," sounded murderous.

He nodded, and when they heard murmuring as if someone was very inquisitive about the vault room, his left hand clenched the broadsword's hilt. The unmistakable sound of short swords being unsheathed sharpened his mystical skills. So did the hisses and growls.

The sires rushed the office as one powerful entity, and every mystical warrior engaged the evil enemy. Deadly fangs were bared, their eyes a feral-yellow. To dodge and maneuver around six sets of fangs and short swords clashing with broadswords left little room. They crossed the floor and continued the fight. This was not only a battle of strength, but a battle of wits. Yet each mystical warrior had the same mission in mind. They maneuvered through the wide hall and into the open area of the club. Like some macabre tango, mystical warriors sidestepped the sires, twisting away fast with fluid moves of disengagement.

They can't be taken out one-on-one. It had to be a group effort.

Just as Lukas thought it, the mystical warriors switched tactics. Using herself as bait, Luna leered at James. His father and Neeb sprinted forward. His head rolled as both parts of James's body turned to dust and bone with an awful shriek. Ramon and Kiko were fast and deadly, their form with the short sword meticulous, their fangs bared and just as deadly. Nigel, Chris and Philip edged them to the bar. With a quick turn, Kiko's sword ran through a Guardian. The mystical warrior went down immediately. In a gutsy move, Luna's short sword sliced across Kiko's back. The sire shifted his stance with an angry growl to face her. Luna slowly walked backward, giving Neeb time to switch Kiko's attention, dodging and striking with his broadsword before slicing off Kiko's head.

Ramon, snarling like a rabid dog and ready to bite, lunged for Nigel. Philip used the hilt of his sword to break its nose. As the sire reeled, Lukas leapt forward and lopped off Ramon's head. Dust and black bits of bone rained down to settle on the floor at his feet. Scenting blood on another Guardian curled in a ball by the stairs, Lukas's rage heightened. The warrior's tunic had been ripped open and he bled from a sire's bite. Another lay not far away with a slash down his right arm from shoulder to wrist. After that quick glance, Lukas locked on the sires still fighting with fangs bared and precise sword strokes. Neeb and Nigel engaged Armadad, who moved like a tiger, making its way to Luna. The sire's short sword dripped with human blood, but the final *whoosh* came from Alana's blade after sneaking up behind and striking.

Hearing Pet scream, Lukas leapt at Alfred. Matching its every cunning move, keeping his neck away from the bastard, he sensed an opening and went for it. With a twist of the wrist and a tremendous upstroke through its shoulder, another head left an undead body. The damned thing screeched like a tortured owl before dirtying the floor with dust and black bits of bone.

Nigel's sword pointed to the last sire, a tall one with striking features and a mane of blond hair like a magazine model. It slashed at Chris, whose sword went airborne, and then it leered at Uri, its lips peeled back, its long fangs bared. With a sweep of his huge hand, Neeb sent Chris flying and out of harm's way. Both he and his father sprinted across the club at the same time. He tackled his cousin, threw the kid to the floor shielding both chest and neck, as his father took off the unknown sire's head.

The sudden silence, except for heavy breathing, mixed with the scent of human blood. The floor looked gritty with the residue of six undead things.

"You okay?" Lukas asked.

"Yeah. Thanks," Uri mumbled.

Standing, he offered a hand and pulled his cousin to his feet. As the adrenalin rush subsided, Lukas looked around the club. Many were bent forward, taking in a lungful of air. Petula hissed in Neeb's arms, cradling her wrist. Some of his friends had been nicked, but nothing life threatening. All four Guardians had been injured, with three on the floor not moving. He and everyone else were in the stand-down stance, taking in the aftermath. But it wasn't over. Not yet.

His father came to his side. "Six sires taken out. At least two dozen bloody vampire guards dust and bits of bone as well. This whole place needs to be fumigated."

Walking back to Draven's office, Lukas kept cursing under his breath. "But no Herodotus."

"He's not coming through."

"This is fucking bad, Dad. We have to go in."

He got a tense, "I am aware." His cousin came into the office and stood at the door where Draven's desk should be. "Uri, get the guard."

Chris entered with broadsword in hand. "I'm going with you."

Lukas walked over, took a quick sniff. "You're bleeding." He grabbed the warlock's upper arm, then the snaps of Chris's tunic pinged as he ripped it open. "Yeah. Once that jacked-up stuff inside that gives you a high settles down, this will hurt like a bitch. Your face is only nicked but check out your chest. A sire's blade cut clean through to flesh, right over your heart."

"I owe Draven my life," the warlock argued.

Shaking his head, Lukas stated, "Not an option. You're not going."

Uri entered the office with the vampire guard held by the throat. The kid totally dwarfed the trembling thing. "Too bad we can't defang you," Lukas stated as he got in the guard's screwed face. "Ewww, the stink of that shitty blood you drink makes me want to puke. And I hate to puke." He glanced at his father leaning against the vault door, running his hands through his hair. Alana stood at his side talking fast and not looking relaxed.

"We bring Uri with us, Lukas," his father stated.

Not about to argue, he eyeballed his cousin. "Stay close and stay focused, okay?"

"Yeah. I hear you."

The casual, almost indifferent reply took him back to sixteen and stubborn. "Remember what I said before, cuz, and pay attention. Anyone else injured?" he called out as more warriors gathered in the office.

Nigel threw down his sword and unsnapped his tunic. "We've got some, but only one is life-threatening. Not bad for a night's work."

"Pet has a graze on her neck and a broken wrist, I think," Neeb stated calmly in that deep voice of his.

"And what about Luna," Lukas asked, looking around the room. "Luna," he called as he walked past them, back into the club and locked eyes with Philip. The monk shook his head.

On a run, he came back. Panic shot through him, thinking, *Oh Christ. She went through!*

"I don't want to hear it because you are not going," his father loudly argued with his mother, adding in a low voice, "I will be fine. So will Lukas and Uri. End of discussion."

"Dad. Luna's not here," he said.

Alana grabbed his father's arm with a whispered,

341

"Oh no! Michael."

"We will get her. Take over, my Guardian. Everyone should engage if anything else comes through. If it's Herodotus, do what you did to Veronique." Then he kissed her, picked up his trusted broadsword and said, "Get a move on, Lukas. The flunky will lead the way to the War Council Building."

Lukas turned back to the mystical warriors gathered in the office. "Tunics on and swords in hands. There's still a sire to send to Hell." At the vault, Lukas said to his cousin, "It's yours to walk through. Keep its fangs in sight. Go." With that, his father stepped through the portal first. Then Uri and the guard. Alana grabbed his arm and kissed his cheek. Lukas gave her a loving look before stepping into the blood-red swirling mist.

Chapter 39

Dust and Bits of Bone

Fully disoriented after coming through the portal, Luna swayed before falling to her knees and clawing the ground. There was no going back—not only because she didn't know how. She made a vow to herself and she would keep it. At first, she stood to sniff the air, to filter out the scent of her eternal love. Then one step led to another, and although skeptical of the afternoon sun lighting the growing fields, she began to run. No one tended the crops. Not one vampire showed itself, as if the entire realm was deserted.

The dirt road turned into a paved one, resembling an old-fashioned street with brick houses lining it on both sides. No cars. No sounds of birds in the trees. Just a willowy wind brushed her cheeks. She stopped running, took in the silence at a time of day when any normal city would be abuzz with activity. Nothing. *Shutters are tight on every house, but hundreds if not thousands of vampires scent an intruder.*

With shoulders straight and chin high, she began to walk. In the distance, less than a mile away, a black obelisk stood against a cloudy sky like an ominous tower. She knew her eternal love was in there. She'd throw herself at her sire's mercy and beg. Yes. She'd grovel, offer her body in exchange for his.

Then, as if someone had wrapped themselves around her, she couldn't move forward. No matter how hard she struggled against whatever it was, she couldn't break loose. Was it fear that had her in its grip—or something else?

****

Wooziness always plagued Lukas after portal travel. But this time, it dissipated within seconds. And he wasn't hunched over puking his guts out. Oddly enough, the air in the Third Realm seemed very similar to the human world's.

When had Luna gotten past them and through the portal? How much of a head start did she have? He had no idea, but he had to get to her, and with that goal in mind, he sprinted ahead of the others, letting his mystical senses lead the way. The blood-red mist thinned until it swirled around his ankles and completely dissipated. Reaching the growing fields, the dirt road beneath his boots became clear. He picked up inhuman speed.

Later on, it turned to pavement beneath his feet. The city, if that's what you could call it, looked deserted with not one vampire on what appeared to be the main street. Then the council building loomed in front of him, like some kind of out-of-place monolith. No guards were visible, but they were surely hidden somewhere and watching. Was it a trap? Or was Herodotus so engaged in torturing Draven that he simply didn't care?

He hauled Luna off her feet as she jostled with a scream. "No. No. Stop fighting me. Christ," he spit out, wrestling the dagger from her hand. "Dad's not far behind. We'll handle Herodotus."

"No. I will do this myself," she said with a growl in her tone.

"Not happening," he replied, seeing the others running toward them.

"I'm going to put you down and you will—" But she shot out of his hold and ran like a gazelle. He couldn't catch up. Then she shot through the tall glass doors with him still too far away.

****

Luna flung open another set of doors and let out a piercing cry that reverberated off black marble walls—like the scream of a banshee. The sight of Draven placed her on the precipice of insanity. Her eternal love hung off the floor, naked and coated in blood as if it were a second skin. The image, forever branded on her brain, made her scream again. The sour scent of human blood stuck in her nose. The scene was an unimaginable torture, with a bright-red pool beneath his feet and his head lolled back. Herodotus stood next to his handiwork, glaring at her, a belt dripping flesh and blood in hand.

Her sire. The one who turned her into an undead thing in 1887. His empty eyes nailed hers, sending shivers up her spine and fury up her throat. Letting out a long, low hiss and baring her fangs, she stood there, well out of his reach.

"But of course. The misfit who walks the human world while I, your sire, remain prisoner in another realm. My blatant mistake comes to me now, like a pitiful pup who should have been culled at birth. Had you arrived an hour ago, the traitor could have seen me play with you before cutting off your head."

The pool of blood below Draven filled her with defeat. That no more blood dripped and splashed was the final insult. When her sire took a step forward, she sank to her knees, resigned and ready. Yes, they would exit this existence together, in this dungeon-like room of natural stone.

Through the haze of horror, she heard, "I see you've been busy, Herodotus. Your penchant for gruesome has not changed." Michael walked past her, as if he were now her protector, and Luna knew not to move.

****

Throughout centuries of undeath and decades of life, he had witnessed a hell of a lot of ugly things. What Michael saw right here and now sickened him. He didn't hide his contempt when he stepped in front of Luna, still a good twenty feet from her sire. He sensed Lukas and Uri behind him but at his sides. As if he had given a signal, they did not move.

"I recall how you would put on a spectacle. Those undead observers didn't threaten you, did they, Herodotus? First humiliation. Then unspeakable torture. It always ended in bloodcurdling screams before bits of dust and bone fluttered down to dirty your boots. I see you still go in for the same ghoulish routine, the bloodier the better."

"Ah, the biggest traitor of them all. You have the audacity to enter my realm with your smart mouth and that beating heart in your chest, Michael," the bastard growled.

"I absolutely do."

"And who are these humans you brought to witness your brother in blood's demise—before I send him to Hell."

"I brought family with me because taking out evil things like you is a family affair."

"Ah, yes, the troubled child who destroyed the powerful Hungarian sire, another one of Cyril's progeny.

He is now a man."

"And my nephew, called the fire of God."

"Ah... But it matters not. The three of you will die. And as for this groveling simpleton, you may all watch as I make her scream."

Herodotus leered at Luna, and Michael said with tact, "No-no-no, look at only me, Herodotus, not anywhere else."

"Such an arrogant creature. Cyril put up with you. Had you been mine, I would have skinned you, then set you afire—long, long ago."

Lukas mumbled "fucking bastard," and Michael watched those beady eyes rake up and down his son. The hand holding the bloody belt suddenly rose, pointing to Lukas. "Because of you the portals closed, locking us here like caged rats. Your father's retribution set this prison in motion."

"I wasn't intimidated by Cyril and I'm not intimidated by you, either." his son replied, far too antagonistic. "You'll turn to dust and bits of bone just like any other vampire."

It's not time yet. So Michael growled out, "Mind your manners. Not another word."

His son scoffed, mumbled, "Yeah. Sorry."

But that bastard still eyed Lukas and dared to flick a wrist. Nothing but a faint breeze occurred. He sensed all the juice the sire had counted on wasn't happening, and as if the action had been an afterthought, the sire snickered. "I will drink deeply from that one's jugular before I drink from yours, Michael."

"I highly doubt it. My son's not as sweet as he looks. And my nephew? He may be young, but he's all muscle. Just look at the size of him, a full foot taller than little

347

old you. So, no. You are not biting any necks. You will not touch who are mine. We came for Draven. You'll use that silver dagger lying in his blood to cut him down and then step aside."

"I give orders, not follow them," the sire bellowed. "No?"

"No, traitor. I have the power here. You, a mere mortal with a death wish, do not. Perhaps I will send for my guards. All it takes is a thought."

"Why ruin this reunion? We are all family here. Let's keep it that way. Cut him down."

"Your heroics are too late. The traitor is exsanguinated. For quite a while now. I took the time to admire my handiwork—before I gut him neck to balls. Now you will watch, of course… you and your family," it said with a righteous sneer.

Michael stepped closer, itching to use his words, then his broadsword to destroy the damned thing. "You're fucking fascinated by his balls, aren't you? I never thought you to be into anyone's balls but your own. Do you miss your harem and now swing the other way? I mean no disrespect… or maybe I do, but it is a personal preference, isn't it? Or has being king of the realm, perhaps, gone to your head—not the one on your shoulders. I could go on and on, but you truly wear down my patience, shorty. So, you've got your rocks off with the humiliating nakedness, slicing veins, and beating my brother to a bloody pulp. You have, no doubt, scratched that sadistic itch in those little, tiny, miniscule balls of yours. We shall be magnanimous, oh mighty little king. We mean your subjects no harm… at least, not today. The realm is all yours now, since the other six are already home in Hell. Go on now… Tip-toe away like a good little sire and plan out your singular reign." Then his voice sank low and murderous. "In other words, get the fuck out of here."

The sire's ugly beast-within morphed its eyes a feral-yellow. Its lips pulled back to bare long, deadly fangs. Then it flickered back to human and stayed that way—as if it couldn't maintain the transformation.

When Herodotus flew at him, Michael stood with open arms and took the brunt of its weight in his chest. As they hit the floor, his trusted broadsword clanged on the marble floor and slid away. He dodged those deadly fangs, channeling his outrage over what had been done to Draven, what could still be done to his son, his nephew.

His mystical senses hummed, but unlike his own sire, Herodotus was well-fed, which made him incredibly strong. "Get Draven and Luna out of here," he shouted, hoping to God his son and nephew were quick enough to grab both of them and flee.

As the two of them rolled on the floor, Michael took punch after punch, needing both hands to keep those sharp tips away from his neck. He wasn't about give Herodotus a chance by letting go to grab for his stake. With its lips peeled back and its fangs closing in on his jugular, he used both hands to push the sire's jaw away. But they ripped through the tunic and his shirt anyway, sinking into his right shoulder. He bit back the yowl of pain, knowing it would only take one deep suck and one quick swallow of his unique blood to jack up its strength even more.

Gritting his teeth, he gripped the bastard's narrow shoulders, pushing with all his mystical strength, and managed to lift the snarling thing up a good foot. A huge hand closed around the sire's neck, and Herodotus rose even higher.

His nephew had the sire, choked and flailing, a foot off the floor and still gripped tight by the neck. Even before Michael found his footing, its hands began to rise. If the sire had any dark magic left in him, they would all suffer. He shouted, "Lukas, now!"

Staring straight into the eyes of death, his son shoved a stake directly through its unbeating heart. As its face registered shock, the screech of the beast-within was deafening before dust and bits of bone rained down.

Only Luna's jagged sobs breached the silence—as she hugged her body, still many feet behind him and far from the pool of blood under Draven.

Chapter 40

Blood Bond

Michael grabbed his bleeding shoulder as he stood. "Nice work. Cut him down and let's get the hell out of here. I'll take care of Luna."

Focused behind him, his son's eyes narrowed. "Shit. We've got company."

Cursing under his breath, Michael turned. Six guards bared their fangs, hissing like the snakes they were. "Three against six. A piece of cake," he stated as he picked up his trusted broadsword. They started to cross the room.

Luna sprang to her feet, and in a blur of a run, blocked their path. Her arms spread high and wide; her feet anchored slightly apart. She bared her fangs growling low and long. Then, she crossed her arms, straightened her shoulders and held her chin high. Not one vampire guard made an attempt to rush her.

Absolutely impressive, one second on the floor sobbing and the next, an entirely different creature of the night, Michael thought.

She stated with authority, "You will not touch the humans. You will not touch *me*. It was witnessed. The realm is bequeathed to me, the daughter of Herodotus. Let your captain step forward." The idiots looked at each other but didn't move. "You dare to have me ask again?

You dare to defy me?"

One guard finally stepped forward. "We are equals. Our orders came from only Herodotus, my queen. What is your wish, my queen?"

Without missing a beat, she stated in a tone Michael had never heard before, "It is your task to inform blood slave and vampire alike: No harm comes to me and mine. No fangs are bared. Now leave!" They pounded their chests, bowed and backed out the chamber doors. When the doors closed, Luna swayed with another sorrowful sob. Lukas caught her before she hit the marble floor and tucked her to his chest.

Michael stepped through the blood pool and slid up Draven's suit trousers. "A little bit of dignity at least, for the journey home, brother," he whispered so full of concern that he couldn't hide his emotions. At his side, Uri choked and gagged before reaching up to get Draven's bound wrists over and free of the hook.

As his nephew placed the vampire on the floor, he said with pride, "You have the strength of two, don't you?"

"Da and Mum say the same thing."

"And neither Thorn nor Celia lie. Lukas trained you well."

"Yeah, but he really rides my ass," the teen mumbled.

"Good. He should. You followed orders tonight. It better stay that way," he added in a tone refined after years of handling his son. "Tell Lukas and Luna to give me a few minutes alone with him." His nephew started to open his mouth and he warned, "That's another order. Do not ruin the compliment now."

The massive doors closed. Michael knelt, rested

Draven against his chest and grabbed the vampire's slack jaw. What he was about to do was risky, but it had to happen. "Dear God, you are a mess," he whispered. He unbuttoned a cuff and rolled up a sleeve. "Come on. Scent me, damn it." Getting no response, he bit into his own wrist and put it to Draven's mouth. His unique blood coated the vampire's tongue. "You must swallow." His lifeforce, ancient and mystical, flowed freely, and he rubbed the protruding cartilage of the vampire's throat to encourage a natural reflex, pleading, "Swallow, brother. Please swallow." Even unconscious, the all-powerful need for survival would still be there, and he'd give as much as he could spare. Seeing the shallow reflex begin, he kept his wrist tight to Draven's lips.

After hours of tension, battling guards and sires, not to mention the tussle with that bastard, he felt the physical drain. Major blood loss wouldn't help, either, but he didn't pull away until a sense of lightheadedness began. With his wrist still bleeding freely, he lay Draven back on the marble floor. He unsnapped, shrugged off the damned tunic and ripped off a wide strip of his shirt to bind his own wrist.

As if he had called out, Luna, Lukas and Uri rushed in. Kneeling at his side, Lukas clicked his tongue. "Christ, he's a mess. So are you."

Cold beads of sweat dotted his forehead. "I'm fine."

"Yeah. Sure." Lukas unwrapped his wrist, motioned Luna close. "I know its repulsive, but can you seal his wrist with a lick?"

"I... I'm not sure, but I'll try," she barely whispered.

Her tongue felt ice-cold, but seconds later, the bleed lessened. Michael took a deep breath before letting it out slowly. He didn't look forward to the miles-long hike back to the portal in a realm full of vampires, no less. He wasn't even sure if his legs would hold him up.

"Nice move, Dad. You could have told me what you were going to do. Thank God your wrist is, well, sort of, sealed."

"I said I will be fine, but there is no guarantee he will come out of this with his mind intact. We have no idea how long it's been. Torture and total blood loss makes this rather dicey."

Softly crying, blood tears raced down Luna's cheeks. Biting her lower lip, she looked away. He glanced at his son, who quickly said, "No worries, Luna. We'll get him out of here." Grateful for Lukas's firm grip, Michael stood, very pleased that he didn't sway too much.

"Want me to carry him?" his nephew asked.

He nodded once. "Sounds good to me."

As Uri settled Draven over a massive shoulder, Luna also stood. They made it out of the lobby. But once beyond the tall glass doors to the street, a dozen vampire guards stood waiting.

"I'm not up for another fight," Michael had to admit.

"There will be no more fighting. I will deal with them," Luna whispered.

She stepped forward. With fists clipping her waist, she bared her fangs and gave a guttural growl. Immediately, every guard jerked a left fist to its unbeating heart, thumped twice, and formed two lines with a wide path in between. Her carriage stayed royal, clearly a don't-mess-with-me as she led the way.

The main street lined with hundreds of vampires appeared to be the next challenge. They stared at

Draven's bloody body, at the three humans—being led by their new "queen." Not one hiss, or lunge, or snicker came at them. But when the paved road turned to dirt, Luna and Uri broke into a run.

His son stayed close as they jogged at a slower pace. "You look a little pale, Dad, and that bite needs to be disinfected."

"Nope. I'm good."

"Do you think guards will follow?"

"I highly doubt it. I mean, there has to be at least an ounce of intelligence among the lot of them." *And certainly not after the way Luna handled herself back there.*

"Why don't we see any blood slaves?"

Michael had no idea and wondered the same thing, but answered, "Let's stay in the moment, shall we? That's a problem for another day."

Fading fast, when blood-red mist finally clawed at their ankles, he wanted to get down on his knees and thank the good Lord above. But once fully in it, more tense minutes began searching for Uri and Luna, searching for the portal as well. Out of nowhere and standing a few yards to the right, Chris Forbes came into view. "The three of them are safely through already. I came back for the two of you."

"How'd you pull that off," Lukas asked, sounding just as relieved as he.

The warlock grinned. "Wouldn't you like to know. You two ready?"

Really feeling the blood loss now, he and Lukas locked arms with the warlock. As one entity linked by flesh and bone, they shot through the swirling void until stepping inside the vault room. Chris raised his hand and the poral sealed.

They both eyed the warlock, his son the first to ask, "How the fuck did you do that?"

"Celia's helping me."

"That little slip of a psychic has always packed enormous power," Michael stated.

His son closed the door to the vault, twisted the lock mechanism until a click sounded. When they both eyed the office, Lukas shrugged. "It doesn't look too bad, just lots of ashes."

"I'd still have it fumigated," he replied. Then Alana had him in her arms. He whispered in her ear, "The way you jumped out of that chair really turns me on, darlin'."

"Uh-huh. Baker's tending the wounded out in the club. We didn't lose anyone, which is great. Celia's been giving Chris a play by play through Uri's eyes. Oh, Uri took Draven straight to the bedroom. Guardians are giving blood. Martine's on her way with Paige to help. As soon as you had him, we started to prep. Oh, and my sister wants her son back, so after he donates a pint, we have a car and driver waiting. That's the end of my first update." She kissed his lips, then held up his bandaged wrist and studied his shoulder.

"I had to. He was bled out." She pulled him into Draven's home, forcing him to sit on the couch.

Her right eyebrow rose as she again eyed his wrist. "You know I'm okay with it."

"And only the tips of that bastard's fangs pierced my shoulder."

"Uh-huh."

He started to stand, but his wife pushed him back down and took his hand before sitting at his side. "Lu and Phil are tending to him. You're not going in there.

Baker will have a look, you know, see what he can do. Neeb and Nigel are getting their veins tapped as we speak. Phil was the first to give a pint. And Pet has a broken wrist. Is that enough of an additional update for you, my love?"

"Absolutely, my Guardian. Lukas will want to donate."

"You need rest. Your face is bruising and I'll bet you gave him more than a mouthful of your blood."

"I'm fine."

"Uh-huh. Don't even try to hide all those aches and pains. Let me move a bit this way," she said in a calm, soft voice. "Great. Now stretch out on the couch and put your head on my lap. I won't take no for an answer, so just do it." Of course, he complied and turned on his side. "Now close your eyes." She stroked his hair and rubbed his arm. God, he truly loved her. She always knew what to say. What he needed.

Chapter 41

Helping Out

There had been a rubber sheet already spread out to protect his bedding. Lukas helped Philip clean Draven's face, chest and legs the best they could. Oddly enough, the cuts to his veins looked to be healing, which confirmed that his father's mystical blood had sped up things—more than just a bit. Lukas looked at Philip, then over at Luna who sat in the upholstered chair across the room. "Can a vampire go into shock?"

"Let's turn him over first and then maybe try to soothe her," Philip whispered.

Lukas nodded. They rolled Draven onto his stomach. Lukas knew what a belt buckle felt like. He had scars to prove it. But flesh had been gouged out, the wounds much, much deeper. His scars stopped at his waist. Draven's would be shoulder to ankle.

He went to Luna. Her eyes were bloodshot with ribbony red streaks down her pale cheeks. She'd been wringing her hands non-stop. He pushed the long blonde braid off her shoulder as another sob sounded. He took her shaky hands in his. Her grip was weak.

Crouched down and eye-to-eye, he said, "I know the smell of human blood has an adverse effect on you. He'll be okay. I swear. You need sustenance." She shook her head. "Philip will take good care of him. Come on. Let's

358

get something in you."

She didn't fight him, could hardly stand, and holding her up, they left the room. On the couch, his father was fast asleep with Alana's hand pressed to his heart. That everyone survived had him thanking God again. Those horrific "what-ifs" vaporized and drifted away. Alana's expression was a testament to their deep, true love. *May it always be so,* he prayed.

They took a slow walk into the kitchen. Luna leaned against the counter with her hands folded over her stomach. Lukas used a warm, wet kitchen towel to erase the blood tears, and then pulled a container from the fridge. "Drink it all. You have to. What happened tonight took loads of energy, and he'll need you strong and well-fed to care for him when he awakens."

Her eyes searched his. "*If* he awakens. Will he know me?"

"He'll know you."

"I… I can't change the dressings."

"One of us will do it for you. No worries, okay? I fully understand." Which he totally didn't, but she was such an anomaly that he had to take her word for it and just let it go. "You were something else back there with the vampire guards."

Her stance straightened, saying "They will bend to my wishes. Wait and see."

He studied her. "Wait for what?"

"I will rule the realm. They addressed me as my queen. It ensures peace, Lukas. I can locate blood slaves who want out of that forsaken realm and have Draven take them through the portal."

"The idea sounds good, but—"

"It's not an idea. It is a proposal. One that serves

humanity well."

She had a point. "I'll run it by the Georgian Council, if you like."

Her blink was slow, her eyes still red-rimmed. "It is appreciated, Lukas."

"Like I said. No worries. Ready to go back?"

She drank, and then placed the empty container in the sink. "Draven employs a chef."

"We don't want anyone in here who is not a Georgian, just in case, you know?"

"Michael has lost blood. Everyone needs sustenance. Mystical warriors included."

Walking her through the dining area, she suddenly pulled away. "I… I cannot see what is being done to him."

"Come sit with me, Luna," his mother offered in a soft voice. "Lu can pull a chair over and we can chat for a while if you don't mind my husband's snoring."

A soft "Thank you" accompanied the easing of her tense brow for the first time in hours.

"Besides, I like talking with you. Lu will give you a complete rundown of what's happening, won't you, sweetie?"

"Sure, Mom," he replied, setting a dining room chair close to the couch. She gave him a loving smile. He gave one back, an easy thing to do. Nothing about his parents was ordinary, not even the scope of their love for him. Seeing his mother holding her hand to his father's heart, he sent a text to Martine, asking her to hurry up and get here already.

****

Upon entering Draven's room, Lukas eyed four bags of blood on the dresser and another in Doc Baker's hand.

"Tap my vein now, John. His first transfusion should be my blood. I'm totally serious. Take a couple of pints."

"You aren't nicked or cut?" Baker asked.

"Nope. I'm good." After he unsnapped and shrugged off the tunic, he unbuttoned a cuff and rolled up his sleeve. "Where do you want me?"

"On the bed."

Although it felt good to stretch out, had anyone said that someday he'd be at rest next to a vampire and overly eager to share his mystical blood, well, he probably would have nixed the possibility with a few choice words.

Martine came in with two empty blood bags and medical paraphernalia that had to be for a transfusion. "Don't say a word. I was already in the club. This is the first time you're giving blood, so it may feel a little weird." He gave a mischievous grin and held out an arm. She placed a rubber tourniquet around his upper arm, really tight before slapping the crook of his arm. "Now close your eyes and when I tell you, flex your fist." He put his other arm under his head on the pillow very curious about the process. "I said close your eyes. And keep your other arm straight and relaxed at your side."

"Why," he asked, fully smitten by her nurse voice.

"Because I said so," she replied. The kiss to his lips was highly unprofessional, and after her sexy smile, Lukas complied. He felt the needle go into his vein and as soon as blood started to flow, he said, "What's your assessment, Baker?"

"I've realigned the bones in his nose and now I'm stitching where a stake went into his chest. It just missed his heart."

His jaw tightened, but Martine whispered, "Lu...

relaxed, okay?"

"Oh. Okay," he replied. But he was pissed off to Hell and back about what had been done to Draven. At least the sire's hideous screech before final death brought another reign of terror to its end.

"I mean it. Close down your mind and stay relaxed, but keep squeezing your hand," Martine whispered in his ear.

His eyelids grew heavy, his body did as well. "You put a spell on me."

A raised eyebrow and a crooked grin that graced her lovely face said he called it right. "Keep squeezing your fist and stay relaxed," she whispered again.

God, he loved her.

Chapter 42

Confrontations

A day later, Lukas sat at Draven's desk and continued taking first-hand accounts from all Guardians involved. Martine had brought over his laptop and his favorite chocolate cookies to munch on, something he truly appreciated.

He had slept for hours next to the vampire on that massive king-sized bed, showered in the ensuite, and had eaten a thick, juicy steak for breakfast and again for dinner. Finishing a second cup of coffee, he leaned back in the office chair and ticked off a few more boxes in his head. Eye-witness accounts about the destruction of vampire guards and six sires were ready for the Georgian Sovereign Council—even if they hadn't sanctioned the fight. Uri's statement had been in person because what the kid sent via text was indecipherable. He still had to add his own account about everything that happened both in this world and the Third Realm.

His friend Paige, now apparently pretty involved with Chris, had reported on the dark seer at St. Francis Hospital. Strings had been pulled for the Georgian nurse with administration. Just as the warlock said, the old lady woke up foggy, unsure about what had happened. A Guardian would keep an eye on her for a few weeks.

That they lost not one Guardian was a bonus. The

serious wounds would scar. This event left a lasting impression on everyone, including him. Another bonus: The other continents' Gatekeepers were now acutely aware of the power the Georgians maintained in the fight against evil. Any gatekeeper would be in deep shit should anything try to get out of the Third Realm.

Luna's request had been placed before the council. That email had been a bit tricky to compose, but Lukas vowed to be available for the in-person interview at any time, in any country.

The vault remained sealed. Until Draven proved to be completely sane, all communication with other realms were on hold. Whether or not the Second Realm sorcerers knew what happened to the seven sires, Lukas couldn't be sure, and really didn't care.

The office had been sanitized, along with every inch of the club. Furniture had been put back exactly as before, and Draven's pricey glass-topped desk looked none the worse for wear. Another perk? Donovan proved to be a team player, trusting Lukas's requests without question. But until further notice, *Destiny* stayed closed.

Taking over Draven's office allowed him to have eyes on the unconscious vampire. The power of their mystical blood worked like a miracle drug. Draven had little scarring. Exsanguination remained the variable. *If he wakes up bat shit crazy, I can't face what has to be.*

"Where do you want these," a Guardian said, pulling Lukas out of his thoughts. He eyed the nineteenth century wooden trunks. "Put them in the other bedroom so she has enough space to go through them," he replied. Then he leaned back in the office chair, swallowed a mouthful of coffee, and frowned at the scent of someone he didn't want to deal with.

"What are you doing back here?" Eyeing the too-tall kid scrunch his muscular frame into a leather armchair at the other side of the desk, Lukas's back was up before Uri even opened his mouth.

"I want to stay with you in New York."

"No way."

Not a hint of a smile crossed Uri's face. Those green eyes bore through him like laser beams. "I followed every order. That's not fair."

"You'll get over it. Cut the cord to Mum and Da and attend the Georgian Institute in England. Train with Nigel and Neeb until you turn seventeen."

"Those two can't teach me what you can."

"They trained me. Respect their abilities. Look. I totally appreciate what you did in this event."

"But it doesn't change your mind." Uri rolled his eyes. "I want to train with you."

"Too bad," he stated. The boy's whiny attitude could light anyone's fuse. "You'll study with Guardians your age, and then start university next September."

"Don't want to go to university. Just because you're a bookworm doesn't mean I have to be one."

He leaned forward. "You have to balance mystical skill with real-world knowledge, not to mention learn to write clear reports. Decide on a course of study that interests you."

"I don't like books."

"That's not an answer. At university, you'll learn about life, which happens to come with different types of nicks and bruises as well as some very awkward moments. Choose a subject area and excel in it."

"I have to read things over and over again. I'm not about to sit in a bloody lecture hall and listen to boring shit."

"Then how are you going to support yourself?"

"What," his cousin asked with a screw of his face.

"You know, make a living, pay for food and rent?"

"I kill demons, for fuck's sake!"

"You don't get paid for it, do you? Months, sometimes years go by between complicated events like this. I don't roam the countryside sniffing out vampires. If university isn't a good fit, then learn a trade and get a job."

"Why," Uri mumbled.

"Because we lead normal lives. Neeb is a first-rate mechanic like your da. Nigel teaches literature and he's a master at martial arts. Pet holds advanced degrees in technology and math. Philip is a monk. Are you getting this yet?"

"Getting what?"

He cleared his throat, thinking how to hit that one nerve. "Christ, you need to grow up."

Uri shot up with a blunt, "Fuck off."

Lukas stood, leaned over the desk. "Lose the attitude. At your age, I could take down a vampire with my eyes closed. But I didn't understand life."

"We aren't alike."

"No, we're not. I had huge emotional baggage and anger issues I wouldn't wish on any kid. Go to the Georgian Institute in England. Make a shit load of mistakes and get your ass kicked by Nigel time after time. And find a girlfriend."

His cousin's green eyes burned like an angry cat's. "What makes you think I don't have one already?"

"Trust me. I know you don't."

"That has nothing to do fighting vampires."

"It'll dawn on you soon enough. My answer is still no."

The thick-head yelled, "I want to train with you!"

"First follow orders. If I scent you in this city after today, you won't like how I deal with you."

His father walked in, saying, "You won't like how I deal with you, either."

Jerking back and catching himself before a tumble over the armchair, Uri said, "Uncle Michael, I was just telling, uh, just saying—"

"Oh, I know. I heard it all. Your parents said no. Lukas said no. Now I'm saying absolutely no."

Uri's face began to flush. "Okay, okay—"

"Okay what?" His father's signature stance was an intimidation in and of itself.

Uri crossed his arms and mumbled, "I go to England, Uncle Michael."

"Good. Your mother is beside herself with worry that you walked here without permission, I might add." *And here it comes...* "So before I get parental on your ass, you'd better run to the car waiting outside. Be sure to apologize to her, little boy, or you will painfully regret not following this particular order."

His cousin ran out, and Lukas chuckled. "I was handling it, Dad."

"Why speak paragraphs when a simple I-said-no works?" Glancing at the door behind them, his father asked, 'How's Draven?"

"Still unconscious."

"It's been long enough," his father said stepping through the door behind the desk.

Out of respect, Lukas shut down the ability to eavesdrop on a private conversation.

****

Michael entered the dimly lit bedroom. Luna stood up, her focus still on Draven. "Has he moved at all?"

"His eyelids flutter on and off, but they have not stayed open, and he hasn't spoken. I'm worried."

"I noticed trunks in the other room."

"From Iceland."

"Then go busy yourself."

"But he needs me."

He slowly shook his head. "There is no guarantee he'll be the same as before this happened. I gave him my blood, but I don't know how long he was bled out."

"I love him, Michael. I don't have to ask you to be gentle with him."

"No. But if he's not right, you know how this must go."

"You will not make a snap judgement! Give him a chance," she whispered in a desperate tone.

"Absolutely. I'll give him more than one."

At the door, she turned back. "Where is the stake?"

"At my back."

"Where it will stay," she said with her head high but not leaving.

The new Luna knows what she wants and isn't afraid to say it. You'd be proud of her, brother. "You and Lukas will be called in to witness if it comes to that."

"I'm not convinced you will not use it."

"I swear on my soul, Luna." As she closed the door, his worry surfaced.

Draven was on his stomach with his face turned to the side, his long black hair loose. Although bruised, his nose was once again perfectly straight. Michael pulled the quilt down far enough to notice little scarring on his back, no doubt because of their mystical blood. Only a slight discoloration could be seen where Draven's veins had been cruelly slashed. It was almost miraculous how all of Herodotus's handiwork had healed so quickly.

Placing a hand on a slightly scarred shoulder, Michael gave a careful shake. "Open your eyes, brother. It's time." He slid his hand to the back of the neck, ready to squeeze, to keep Draven prone with those long fangs far enough away should the beast-within surface first. He applied more pressure and waited. Shoving a stake through this unbeating heart wouldn't be easy. To destroy Draven, to be judge and jury sentencing him to final death made Michael extremely nauseous.

"Dear God, please don't let this go south. I will do what I must, but I beg You. Have a little mercy here."

Chapter 43

Second Chances

The scent of someone close enough to bite tugged like a coarse hemp rope tied to a drifting boat on a choppy sea. Growing pressure at the back of the neck. Whispered words in prayer. Raw emotion in a familiar voice ripe with sorrow.

The command to open his eyes started the pull within. But Draven existed in a fog of agony, perverse and purposeful, like his own private Hell. *Michael should not be here with me. He tamed his beast-within and has a second chance at life.*

Then it all came back. Thrown around the council chamber. The crunch of bones in his nose. The hole too close to his heart. His face against a marble wall. Hung up and stripped. Veins slashed. Tears in his flesh. Screams of agony... His eyes eased open, brimming with blood tears, his body heavy and weak. He slammed his lids shut and buried his sobs in the pillow.

"Thank God. Come on. Look at me. It is over. Look at me, I said."

His muffled, "I cannot," came out a shallow whisper, a shadow of his rich baritone voice. Once again, he felt broken, had no control over these feelings flooding his brain.

"Nonsense," Michael softly said as if he were

talking to a child. "Are you going to have me ask you again?"

When gently turned on his back, his arm shot across his eyes. Michael pulled it away, and blood tears raced down his temples. The quick sniffle through his nose hurt like hell and he let out a throaty "ugh!"

"What is your pain level?"

"On the scale of just a twinge to pure unadulterated misery… it is manageable."

"Good. Self-healing is in high-gear." Seconds slowly passed before Michael added, "And the beast-within?"

"What about it?"

"Do you sense it?"

"Of course I sense it," he answered all weepy again. "It didn't suddenly bleed out of me with that humiliating torture session." Swiftly pulled up and wrapped in a fierce hug, his chin rested on a broad shoulder. He swallowed another unexpected sob and held on as tight as he could. When Michael made no attempt to pull away, neither did he.

"You know the bastard is dust and bone. Along with six other sires."

"Your wife's plan was a success?"

"Absolutely. You did a hell of a job stringing them along and tricking them. First, dozens of guards turned into dust and bits of bone, then all six sires, dust and bits of bone as well. Then we came for you."

"Who, may I ask, sent Herodotus to Hell?"

"Lukas."

"Not you?"

"I bloody well pissed him off good, and then he flew at me."

"He had you pinned down, didn't he."

"Yes and no."

"You got a couple of choice digs into his ego, didn't you."

"Ah. You know I can't resist the urge."

"Too bad you didn't record it. I'd love to hear what you said to him."

"I mentioned his tiny balls and huge sadistic tendencies."

"How did Lukas take him out? Sword or stake."

"Stake. The look on the bastard's face was priceless."

He pulled off Michael's shoulder and palmed his eyes. "I drank from you."

"I didn't want you to wake up insane."

"No. Just fucking emotional again." He sniffled and let out a low, "Owww. The bastard broke my nose."

"Which Baker set immediately. It's barely bruised now. Seriously, though. How do you feel?"

Weak beyond belief, and still fucking weepy. "Not as bad as I thought I would," he lied.

"You have mystical blood in you. Everyone gave, except Chris and Petula."

"Your mystical blood. Is that why I'm so emotional?"

"I haven't a clue, brother."

Suddenly alarmed, he asked, "Chris and Petula, they survived, didn't they?"

"Everyone did, but they were both injured, not life-threatening."

"Good. And how is my Luna?"

"She is quite the warrior. More so than you know."

Michael's eyes narrowed. Draven knew the look,

what the man was thinking. "I promise you, I am not insane. I do not need a babysitter and I *will* be alone with her."

He went into the ensuite and came out with a wet washcloth. Taking it, Draven ran it over his face and then handed it back. "Hair tied back or loose and messy?" Draven held out a hand. The leather strip from the dresser landed in his lap. After threading his fingers through his hair, he tied it back. "Am I at least presentable?"

A typical dry grin appeared. "You're asking me? How the hell would I know. You are truly an arrogant pain in the ass. She's seen you much worse. You were a bloody fucking mess. I mean that literally. I'll send her in. But I won't be far, just in case."

That he still walked the earth had to be some kind of miracle. And when the love of his eternal existence embraced him, Draven felt as close to heaven as any man could possibly get.

****

Lukas's fingers sped across the keyboard documenting the description of Draven's awakening. He asked specific questions and his father, usually a man of few words, answered every one in detail. "So there's no need for Martine to come and transfuse him again?"

"He can take sustenance from a cup, the same way I did after the Mayhem in Manhattan all those years ago. Luna will keep him on schedule. Leave the lovebirds alone, but camp out here in the office until he's on his feet again."

"Sure. So are we back to taking shifts?"

"No. Have Guardians assist you. I want some down

time with Mom. You'll keep the blood donations coming?"

"Yeah. But what to do when he's physically able to hunt again is the real question."

"He's creative. He'll think of something and keep a low profile. Now we know what was always suspected. Crafty dark seers are everywhere. There's still too much evil in this city." They both stood. "You need some down time as well."

"I'm good. There's a lot to document. And I can't close out the file, until after I interview him." He paused. "About the sires, now we'll also be able to identify every vampire who ended up in the Third Realm. What about the sires still walking our world?"

"Speak with the Georgian Council after you finish your report. Let them decide where this goes next. It's not your goal in life to take out sires, Lukas. It's their mission."

"Their mission is usually my mission, Dad. I'll go if called."

"I disagree. Your life with Martine has just begun. Your focus should be on each other. By the way, Mom and I are looking forward to Sunday dinner tomorrow."

"Yeah, totally," he said with an easy smile. "It'll be the first time both of our families are together, well, except for my sisters."

"They will never set foot in New York."

"No? Not even when we get married?"

His father's eyebrows rose. "Are you already planning the wedding?"

"Not yet. But it will happen."

"Then plan the ceremony at the Georgian Estate if you want your sisters to attend."

Knowing that tone, he simply replied, "I hear you."

"Good. And don't text me unless it's necessary."

"You're worried his beast-within might surface."

"Or that he's yet to go out of his mind. Text me when you get home."

Lukas chuckled. "You just said don't text. Why? Are you worried?"

"About my children? Always, little boy. Don't ever think otherwise."

The endearing term warmed his heart as if he were still a troubled kid. When his father left, he stood and stretched, walked out to the dark club, and gave a respectful nod to the Guardians at the base of the stairs. The battle with the sires replayed in his head as he looked around before returning to Draven's desk. Minutes later, Luna called out to him, and he ran to the bedroom.

****

"Relax. I'm fine. You're suddenly as pale as one of us," Draven said with a frown. "Please leave us, my dear," he added, and waited until Luna closed the door. "Thank you for your mystical blood. It is very much appreciated."

"You're very welcome. What's wrong?"

"Congratulations for taking out the beady-eyed bastard. Perhaps someday you will give me the full play-by-play."

"Sure. What's wrong?"

"I would like to shower."

"Wait. What?"

"I believe I have had enough degradation in the past weeks to last the rest of my existence. I will not have Luna pick me up if I fall." He slowly turned his body around with his feet on the carpet while clutching the mattress. Lukas extended a hand, which he took.

"You have no grip, Draven."

He noted the look of concern. "I am... much too weak."

"That's all right. I've got you." Lukas's tight grip on his arm produced a hiss. "Sorry. I'll hold on below the welt."

"That's quite all right." Then he admitted, "I... I cannot push off the bed to stand."

Lukas bore most of his weight. Both legs spasmed as he put one foot in front of the other, walking like an infirmed ninety-year-old human into the ensuite. Lukas turned on the shower, and Draven stated, "I can hold onto the wall," as if thinking out loud. The tiled lip, just three inches to step over, had him already braced, locking his legs to remain upright.

"Forget about soap," Lukas said like a mother hen. "Just let the water wash over you for now."

He thrust his head back and the pulsating jets hit his face. With care, he shuffled closer to let tepid water run down his back, the god-awful sting pure agony—right up until the shower ended. Lukas patted down his shoulders, his chest and arms, then wrapped a dry towel around his waist. Still clinging to the tiles, he whispered, "This is not good. I am terribly weak."

"You'll get stronger in no time and continue to heal, but don't get any romantic notions with Luna right now."

"My love life is no concern of yours."

Another dry towel draped his shoulders, and a frown appeared on Lukas's face. "Yeah, right. Ready to brush your teeth all alone and walk back to bed without help?"

Of course, he didn't answer, holding on to the vanity while Lukas put toothpaste on the toothbrush. He took it without saying a word, accepted the cup of water to rinse out his mouth. He also had to accept the arm around his waist as his legs wobbled unsteady. When Draven sat on the bed, Lukas doubled the towel and placed it on his pillow. His hair was still dripping wet. The grunts and groans as both legs lifted to settle in bed were ignored. Every part of his body hurt like hell. He let out a long sigh as the thick quilt came up to his neck and whispered, "Thank you."

"Don't mention it. I'll bring sustenance in another hour. Take a nap."

"No more transfusions?"

"Nope. Now close your eyes," Lukas said as he left.

Strength and independence. That's what he needed. Plus, he had a business to run, investments to watch or shift around, and a white envelope with Michael's name on it to destroy.

A whispered conversation between Lukas and Luna could be heard, even though they weren't in the room. It should have angered him that Lukas kept telling her to unpack the trunks from Iceland—instead of coming into his bed. It should have, but it didn't.

He had been cared for. Soothed. Even fussed over. Yet he was exhausted. Simply exhausted.

Chapter 44

The Gala

Six days later, the woman who owned Lukas's heart looked stunning in a strapless ball gown, which hung on her curvy frame as if it had been made specifically for her. The color, a muted-purple, accented her long, raven-black hair, expertly piled high on her head, with tendrils framing her lovely face.

"Isn't it wonderful how everything went right back to normal again," Martine said as she straightened his bowtie. "You look totally hot in this morning coat."

"My what?"

"You know. The tails." She kissed his lips and then pulled away. "That dimpled smile of yours does it to me every time."

He kissed her again. "I feel like a monkey," he replied as she buttoned his vest.

"Well, you sure don't look like one," came with a little laugh.

She placed a necklace in his hand and turned around. The gemstones matched the color of her dress. Dark amethyst set in silver, her favorite metal with dangling earrings to match. Two days ago, when he saw the cloth bag hanging in the other bedroom's closet, nosiness got the better of him, so he took a look. A quick trip to the jewelers followed. The thrilled look on Martine's face when she opened the velvet box said he'd gotten it right. He kissed the back of her neck before springing the clasp shut.

"Honestly, Lu. Normal feels good. Except for tonight, I mean."

"Yeah. It does," he said, hearing a new type of excitement in her voice. Events usually ended with weeks of documentation. This one, however, would end with a gala extraordinaire in a ballroom at a prestigious five-star hotel.

"I can't remember the last time I attended one of Mare's charity balls. It has to be six or so years ago, at the very least. I went alone."

"But tonight I'll twirl you around that dance floor like there's no tomorrow. Which, of course, there will be, because the Third Realm is totally neutered."

"And Draven?"

"Back to his old, arrogant self. He healed exceptionally quick this time."

"I heard he reopened the club last night," she said as they left their bedroom.

He went down the stairs in front of her and took her hand as they walked into the small foyer. "I stopped by to check on him well after midnight. The place was packed."

"He was out and about, talking to his customers?"

"With Luna at his side." Lukas opened the front door, gave her his arm, and together they walked down the steps to a waiting black sedan. Once the partition went up, he whispered, "You look enchanting tonight, M." She tossed her head back with a smile. "We'll make an appearance and leave early." *So I can ravish you and drown in the feel of you loving me.*

"Hell no," she shot back. "You won't deny me the chance to show you off to everyone. I see the looks you get from women of all ages. You'll be eye candy tonight. Thank God your hair's tied back or else we'd have to pick them up off the floor." Her dramatic dark-brown eyes flecked with gold captured his. "Oooh… I see that familiar twinkle in those royal-blues, and I know what's running through your head. We dance every dance. We laugh with our friends and family—and stay till the end." She slipped a hand inside his vest and rubbed his chest.

"Don't get me started or I won't be able to walk into the hotel," he whispered.

She stopped, and as he cleared his throat, her mischievous cackle filled the car. "Just wait until I get you home," she whispered, placing both hands in her lap. He reached over and threaded his fingers with hers.

"Is that a threat or a promise," he replied studying her profile.

"If you know how to waltz, it's both."

"I'm pretty good on a dance floor." She squeezed his hand. Oh yeah, when he got her home, they'd dance in bed together as well.

****

Mary stood with Tristan and Freya at the entrance to the hotel's ballroom, greeting influential guests with light conversation and a perfectly placed smile. The gala had already soared well past last year's goal with hefty checks with lots of zeroes. Art programs for the underprivileged youth and aid to survivors of loss would be fully funded. Patrons of the arts, millionaires, business professionals and everyday hard-working people knew that the Kendrick Art Gallery sponsorship programs made a difference to hundreds in the city and beyond.

She took in the dance floor and all the gorgeous ball gowns, men in tails and various styles of tuxes. Her senses tingled and she quickly turned. One would never know she stared at two vampires. Draven looked as handsome as ever in tails, and Luna utterly gorgeous in a strapless gown that matched the shade of her light-blue eyes. It had been Michael's idea to invite them, which didn't make her as uncomfortable as she thought she'd feel being near him again.

Celia's mind-vision had shown Mary what Draven had endured. Appalling and degrading didn't even begin to describe it. Yet he appeared completely healed, not to mention perfectly at home entering a ballroom. The way he wore tails, with the jacket perfectly cut at the waist, only embellished his good looks. Luna and Freya were engaged in conversation, and he approached her, saying, "You look ravishing this evening, Mary Kendrick. Perhaps you will grace me with a dance later this the evening."

She gave a genuine smile and a soft, "Thanks, but I'll have to pass. I've a lot riding on the gala's success and I prefer to remain a wallflower."

"As you wish. I am, however, forever in your debt for all you have done. Indeed, my Luna is as well. Given our history—"

Mary cut him off saying, "That was a very long time ago. I'm glad you're okay. And thank you very much for the incredibly generous anonymous donation."

He gave a charming grin. "You knew it was mine."

"Does a bat have wings," she replied with a wry smile.

One eyebrow raised, as if amused. "Consider it a

yearly contribution. Should you have extra funds, perhaps include a music component to your arts education program."

"That a fantastic suggestion. I'll look into it," she answered.

Luna came back to his side, took his arm. "Thank you for inviting us, Mary. Thank you for all you've done."

Funny. She was as easy to read as a living, breathing woman. Genuinely thoughtful, bringing to mind a soft, spring breeze. Mary gave a knowing smile. "You're not returning to Iceland."

"No. My place is at Draven's side. We have pledged ourselves to each other," she whispered as she leaned in.

With a quick glance, she noted a simple gold band on Luna's ring finger. To her surprise, Draven wore one as well. Her senses tingled and her eyes narrowed. "But there's more you are not saying." As the words *my queen* came to her, her brow eased. "Oh my. The Third Realm?"

"I'll bring peace. No war will be tolerated. Realm inhabitants will be weaned off human blood. If it does not satisfy them, they may stake themselves for all I care."

"Wow, and Draven's okay with you doing this?"

"He sees my logic. The human world will be safer this way."

"By leaps and bounds. Please enjoy the evening." Both love and devotion were sensed in them.

Luna looked at Draven. "I am so looking forward to dancing with you, my love," she whispered. His response was a kiss to her cheek, both charming and captivating. Then they approached Michael and Alana. Within seconds, the conversation included Lukas and Martine as well.

"I will miss her, but I'm very happy for them," Freya said, standing at her side.

Mary turned to the good witch. "Makes you wonder what this world is coming to. I never thought I'd see him tamed like that."

"True love is always powerful," Freya replied.

A new melody filled the air. Lukas and her daughter walked over to Chris and Paige. But on the dance floor, Draven's form was meticulous as they began to waltz, his movements fluid and schooled. When Michael joined in with Alana, it looked like the ballroom belonged to them. The way coattails lifted and the woosh of their ball gowns became a cinematic fantasy from days long gone. Sensual, in a way.

Michael glanced at Draven, and in a sweeping move, they switched partners. The sound of a collective "Ooooh" came from all sides of the ballroom as the waltz continued. *Just breathtaking. A planned move, giving a glimpse into the past when two arrogant vampires never missed a beat in a gutsy switch so gracefully executed. Something younger generations at tonight's event most probably never see.* Many couples sipped champagne; tried to disguise stares and whispers of admiration, as if it were a planned demonstration put on by hired professionals.

Another collective sigh came from the crowd when Alana and Luna returned to their lovers' arms. Suddenly swept back in time, Mary caught a glimpse of what it had been like when Johann Strauss wrote the waltz. Michael and Draven dancing to famous melodies while the composer himself conducted the orchestra. She sensed

Luna taken back to the late 1800s, twirling across a Parisian dance floor in her Henri's arms.

Lukas and Martine joined in the waltz. Now three stunning couples claimed the dance floor as their own. More ooohs and aaahs sounded. A quick sweep of minds told Mary just how mesmerized everyone was. Both men and women had their pick of fantasies. The three couples, elegantly dancing, would be the talk of the town tomorrow. But seeing her daughter and Lukas, so very much in love and in each other's arms, gave her a special thrill. To find each other again had been a blessing in disguise. To find the courage to open your heart after devastating loss filled her with joy for Martine.

Mary shook her head, noticed Martine's co-worker off to the side in conversation with Doctor Baker. Dottie's animation was as visible as his attentive smile. "Now that's an interesting couple. Oh boy. That one, too," she whispered, spotting Chris Forbes, who held Paige's hand in the far corner of the ballroom. "I'm sure they're not talking about that water-color painting."

She leaned against the doorway. Hard work had paid off. The gala looked to be a success in more ways than one. She took a flute glass filled with expensive champagne off a waiter's tray and raised it. "Here's to an outstanding night full of great music, generous guests, loving family and friends. As it is, so shall it be," she whispered, "And blessed be."

****

Draven held Luna close, swaying to the slow tempo of a love song from the 1940s. The gasps and sighs when he and Michael switched partners had been expected. The well-rehearsed move had gotten the same reaction long ago, in the dancehalls of Vienna, Paris, and Berne.

In his arms, Alana had been as light on her feet as a ballerina. Of course, like Michael, he towered over the petite woman, the perfect blend of sensual and strong, possessing both grace and spirit, someone to be admired. He now understood how Michael had become obsessed the first time he saw her. But having Luna in his arms, so striking and statuesque as they waltzed, brought back memories of those long-ago, passionate nights. Dancing with her again felt as if no time had passed at all. Yet now, so much had changed in his existence. In hers as well.

During quick conversations with certain guests, he kept Luna close, kept his replies minimal to nosy patrons of the arts. No doubt, Mary Kendrick would have a slew of questions as to who they were and why they had not been seen before. Perhaps their flair on the dance floor would make anonymity impossible. Instinct, however, told him she'd be discreet.

With lovely Luna in his arms, he felt comfortable in every emotion that swelled within, as if he were one in a million, a mortal man dancing with the love of his life. And like a mortal man, he had placed a band of gold on her finger with a solemn pledge. She took the other ring he had made and slipped it on his finger with a solemn pledge of her own. No more courtesans. No secrets between them. She was truly his.

"Where are you, my love," Luna whispered in his ear.

"Did you enjoy yourself tonight," he asked instead of answering her question.

"Very much so. Will we be able to do something like this again?"

"There are clubs in the city we might visit once in a

while. None of them have orchestras like this, that play waltzes from a time gone by. But we can take in shows on Broadway, attend operas at the Met and concerts at Carnegie Hall. You will experience it all."

"I'd like that."

He pulled her closer and when their lips met as they danced, he wanted her more than ever before. Perhaps it was because of the way they were dressed, or the excellent orchestra playing familiar music, that had him recall Strauss. For years before Luna was sired, he and Michael made quite the pair on and off the dance floor. Afterward, they had dozens of unsuspecting women to choose from for sexual pleasure and release. *And there is the difference,* he thought as he kissed Luna's full lips again. It wasn't his reality anymore.

If, in the 1880s, a psychic had read his palm and foretold the future change in him, the change in his brother in blood, Draven would have laughed in her face, surely allowing a glimpse of the deadly fangs in his mouth. *Yet here I am, in a ballroom full of humans, fully able to control my beast-within.* And deeply in love with the beautiful vampire in his arms. She was all he needed. All he wanted.

"When the song ends we will bid all a good night," he whispered.

"So soon," Luna sighed.

"I didn't say the night is over, my dear. Our bed awaits."

"And what will happen in our bed," she asked with a tease in her tone.

"I prefer to keep you guessing," he whispered as he kissed her neck. He could scent her arousal, certain that she could scent his as well.

Chapter 45

Hard Good-Byes

Luna held Draven's hand as they approached their table. Michael and Alana, as well as Lukas and Martine, were in conversation. She had been introduced to Doctor Baker's date, a sweet co-worker of Martine's who was talking with Chris and a lovely, dark-haired woman. According to Draven, the petite nurse had met Chris during the previous event. Never in her undead existence had Luna felt this type of friendship with so many.

"We will be leaving," Draven said to Michael.

"Like hell," Michael replied, which made her smile. "Sit down and enjoy a brandy with us."

She felt connected to everyone at this table. Funny how after decades of seclusion, she now enjoyed conversations, different opinions, simply their company. She didn't fear Alana's mystical warrior skills. She had enjoyed Petula's personality-plus, the warrior's witty way had put her at ease during the breaks between staking realm guards. Mary and Martine's warmness and the good witches' had easily accepted her. Lukas was sensitive, such a sweet, honest man. And Michael— compassion, consideration, and commanding all rolled into one handsome package. When Draven held out a chair, Luna chose to sit next to Alana and studied her new friends again.

"You had fun tonight, and you dance beautifully," Alana leaned in to whisper.

She noticed the doctor and his date excuse themselves and return to the dance floor. Luna wondered if Dottie knew what she and Draven were.

"She doesn't," Martine suddenly said. Lukas's true love, the gorgeous woman with raven-black hair, sat at her other side. "Sorry. It's very easy to read your thoughts. Almost as if you were, uh, well, you know."

"Does Dottie suspect your powers?"

"I think she does, and I sense that the conversation about who we are and what we do will be important if she continues to see John. But we'll cross that bridge when we come to it."

"Our world is very different," Alana said.

With a slight nod, Luna replied, "Yes. It is."

"Our men are certainly very different. I'm happy to have gotten to know a little piece of you, Luna."

"So am I, Alana. I know you're leaving to go back to your home soon."

Michael's wife gave a loose shrug. "Tomorrow."

"We'll miss you," Martine said. "I think Lu will miss you more than anything."

Alana's radiant smile appeared. "You'll have to visit us really soon. Hopefully, there won't be any more threats to humanity for a while. Michael needs some down time."

"So does Lu." Martine leaned in closer. "What about you and Draven? All settled in?" Her dark eyes slid down to the gold ring. "Oh my."

"We both wear one and made vows to each other before we came here tonight. I belong at his side."

"He's your eternal love. I know something about

that," Alana said. "And your new position in the Third Realm?"

"There is much to do."

"What about the blood slaves?" Martine asked as she set her martini glass down.

"Doctor Baker will have his work cut out for him with those who want to return. I would like him to personally evaluate each one and decide if he or she can be reoriented to the human world."

A serious expression settled on Martine's face. "I'd like to help with that."

"Your sixth sense will be very useful," Luna replied with a smile. "It's my hope that many will want to depart."

"It's the only life they've known for well over a decade," Alana said. "You may find some resistance. It's like an addiction to a human, be it man or woman," Alana said with a nod. "Once bitten, always craved. You have loads of important work ahead of you."

Michael stood behind his wife, kissed her cheek. "Stop talking shop."

"I believe it is time, my dear," Draven said as he came around the table.

Alana leaned in with the whisper, "Keep in touch with Martine and Lu. And I'm only a phone call away if you need my support."

"Thank you for everything," she quickly replied. When Alana took her hands, Luna felt close to overwhelmed. "Without Michael and Lukas, none of this would have been possible. I might have been lost to him forever."

Alana's grip tightened. "This is where you belong. Don't forget. Just a phone call away."

Luna stood, slipped her hand into Draven's. Pleasantries were expressed by all, and when they left the table, his arm came around her waist. It had been a wonderful evening full of many pleasant moments. So much had changed in one short week, a mere drop in the bucket of time. Compared to that long, lonely existence in Husavik, what lay ahead appeared a monumental task. She felt ready to face it.

Chapter 46

Eternal Love

Draven took his sustenance before entering their bedroom. It was just past two in the morning, which was the middle of his day. The club had been crowded when they walked down the stairs. Under his employees' watchful eyes, everything would continue to run smoothly tonight.

Closing the bedroom door, he leaned against it. Over the course of many years, he had watched hundreds of courtesans undress themselves for heady sex, but never in this room. Their hands had never been permitted to roam freely over his body. He had taken his pleasure with them in a variety of ways in his office or in the other bedroom, but never face to face. No kiss. No embrace. No love. Only sex. It was suddenly very easy to let go of his past.

With Luna, he desired her kisses, felt at ease with her embraces. He loved watching her reach the peak of bliss, knowing he alone brought her to the precipice of passion. He walked over, unzipped her dress, peeling it down, loving the way her head craned back and her lips fell apart. He took off his tails and vest.

Her hands slid up his chest, untied his bowtie. As he popped the cufflinks, Luna unbuttoned his shirt and palmed his chest. The shirt slid off as well. Stepping out

391

of her heels, he watched her carefully drape her dress over the chair. He made quick work of sitting on the bed's edge to remove his shoes and socks, and then went to her again. As she opened his trousers, he took them off. His kiss to her lips turned sensual. Her hand on his erection was just as greedy as his kiss when she led him to their bed.

Never had Draven desired her more. Tasting her produced a whimper. "I am hungry for you tonight," he said with a growl. She squirmed as if searching for his tongue. He kept it slow and sexy as she fumbled with the leather tie at the nape of his neck. And when his hair fell loose, she fisted it. As he pleasured her, he grabbed her bottom and she let out a high-pitched shriek. She was wet and throbbing when he loomed over her with his weight on his elbows. The feel of her legs against his hips had him on the verge of release. And when he guided himself into her with a slow thrust, she gasped. The rhythm built, one body in sync with the other. Every kiss, every touch, every thrust said how much he loved her.

When his fangs sank into her neck, they orgasmed together.

****

Making love with Draven was a new, erotic experience every time. Tonight had been no different. The feel of him, every thick inch of him, the weight of him on top of her only made her want more. How she had been starved for his affection through the decades. How she had touched herself in every fantasy, wanting it to be him bringing her release.

Lying here tight in his arms, Luna recalled each Hunter's Moon. Standing on the dock, searching the horizon and lost in memories of her Henri. Every time, she'd sink into a lover's grief so intense that it flooded her skin and rattled through her veins.

Though they'd been together for half a century, nothing equaled what she now felt. Arrogance and power suited Draven. The reinvention of himself had been an arduous journey. Yet the differences in him now were, perhaps, always waiting to surface, to take over. For his survival. For hers. They had sustained him, taught him, groomed him for her return. None of this would have happened had it not been for a simple conversation during the last Hunter's Moon. Bumping into the good witch as she walked off the dock. An invitation to have a glass of wine and her friend sensing distress while she, a vampire, told the secret story of a lost love. That chance encounter led her back to his arms.

Spooned together in the massive bed, Draven sighed and pulled her closer. She loved the feel of him behind her, the sexy way he possessed her, the safety of his nearness. Shedding her quiet demeanor blossomed into who she was today. They were equals now. His input would be invaluable, with her own moral code feeding off his. The human world was precious. While she no longer needed protection, the innocents who lived in it did.

She may not need breath to exist. She may not have a heartbeat or have the ability to grow old or to give him a child. Yet they would exist as if they were full of life, a typical man and woman. They would love as if they had spoken vows to each other in a chapel before God. In the truest sense of the word, they would forge a unique path.

When the next Hunter's Moon appeared in the night sky, together they would admire the bright orange orb in the high heavens. Once again in each other's arms. For all of eternity.

A word about the author…

M. Flagg's imaginative world is full of mystical warriors, witches, the not-so-normal vampires, and now, teenage ghosts. With six novels in the paranormal genre, spinning tales about the paradox of love is a passion, and there is always a twist of fate involved. Mickey is a contributor in a book on urban music education and has been published in Still Standing, a web-magazine about loss and healing. She is a life-long New Jersey resident, a member of Liberty States Fiction Writers, NJ Author Network, and NJRW. Learn more about her at www.mflagg-author.com

Thank you for purchasing
this publication of The Wild Rose Press, Inc.

For questions or more information
contact us at
info@thewildrosepress.com.

The Wild Rose Press, Inc.
www.thewildrosepress.com